TRAVELING INTO CHAOS

Author, Richard Jan

Library of Congress, TXu 1-937-134

Copyright: May 7, 2014: Richard Jan Hoekstra, Grand Rapids, Michigan

Published by Richard Jan Hoekstra

Edited, 03/01/2024

ISBN:

Hardcover: 978-1-970399-34-9

Paperback: 978-1-970399-33-2

Dedicated to my sister, Christine Ann Lamberts, who was killed at the age of 40 in an act of violence towards women. You were a beautiful woman, and I miss you.

Series: DYING TO SUCCEED

This book titled: TRAVELING TO CHAOS, is the eleventh book in the series, written foremost for your entertainment. God willing, more books may be available in the future.

Other books in the series include:

Book 1, Winds of Success
Book 1, Living with Death
Book 3, Pretending to be Alive
Book 4, Presumption of Sanity
Book 5, Running from Regret
Book 6, Longing to go Home
Book 7, Afraid to Hope
Book 8, Waiting in Infinity
Book 9, Chasing after Time
Book 10, Casualties of Words
Book 12, Snows of Fear

Although I have edited these books more times than I can remember, I still find errors, missing words, misspelled words, etc. For these, I apologize. I would not ask, but if you are inclined to inform me of any error, please send your corrections or comments to my email,
rhoekstra@sbcglobal.net

The spirit gives birth to the spirit…
Like the wind, it blows wherever it pleases.
You may hear its sound,
But you do not know where it came from.
Or where it is going.

Should you have comments and questions, please feel free to email me at rhoekstra@sbcglobal.net

FOREWORD

My books do not have traditional chapters. Instead, they have, what I call episodes which read like a journal entry identified by place, date, time, and person. When only the time has changed from a previous episode, the date and place may not be repeated, but the point of view is always identified. Please forgive me if this is initially confusing. Hopefully, it will become easier once you have read a few pages.

Background: I kept a personal journal for many years. When I began to write, it seemed a natural format. Initially, I expected to write only from the first-person point of view, again following my previous experience in keeping a journal. But as I wrote, I began to think that adding additional characters' observations would enhance the depth of the story.

And may I also ask your indulgence in regard to the descriptive sentences which may initially seem to be an unnecessary extravagance, but are in fact an important element, much like painter who fills his canvases with shades of colorful imagery influencing our perception of the focal point of a painting.

And finally, I would like to suggest that you listen to music when you read my books. As I write, I often play music in the background to influence my writing to flow much like a musical composition; using the sounds, size of the words, as well as the length of the sentences and the episodes to flow much like a musical composition, adding another layer of expression to the story.

Because it is my belief that music may best exemplify the internal workings of the mind. Not logic as is commonly thought. If logic ruled the world, we would live in a different world. Perhaps our problem is that we believe we live by logic when in fact our minds are governed by an operating system which is far more complex and elusive.

Richard Jan

ABOUT THE AUTHOR

As I looked out the window of my office, it occurred to me that perhaps there is no more perfect metaphor for the work of a writer than how warm rays of sunshine highlight the dying, golden leaves of a forest on a fall day. To succeed as a writer is to shine a light on the death watch that we call life, while at the same time seeing life in all its golden glory even when we know that the end is coming… to somehow attempt to understand how these two contrasting truths can exist side by side without negating the absolute reality of both of them,

Richard Jan Hoekstra

Contents

GRAND HAVEN, MICHIGAN, USA, FRIDAY, SEPTEMBER 30, 2011, 7:45 PM, JOHN

When a traumatic event occurs and it is your unfortunate fate to have witnessed pain and death in real time, a din of subconscious noise may begin to forcibly occupy your brain against your will; a relentless, irritatingly dreary, disturbing reminder that death and sorrow follow us all, never far behind.

Rachel and I had regrettably witnessed the violent death of two young men who never should have died. And although I wasn't sure the boisterous scourge in my brain caused by seeing their dead bodies was as loud in Rachel's head as it was in mine, I sensed a souring anger in her whenever we were together. She had been acting distant since witnessing the boys' death. I assumed this was because she was hearing the same noise I was hearing. The same discordant notes were playing in her brain as mine, a disruptive dirge that was a new constant. Against our will, we had been unceremoniously forced to become aware that life could be instantly thrown into a state of tears with no warning.

That evening, while Rachel and I were having dinner, my cell phone rang. I got up and excused myself to take the call in another room, even though she didn't look too happy with the interruption.

'My name is Kamyar,' a voice stated in a foreign accent I did not immediately recognize. 'I am phoning you because I wish to sell to your company my many emeralds. I have been told your company wants to buy these gemstones. Is this not true?'

'It's true,' I answered. The call was unexpected. Although in my business, no call is ever completely unexpected.

'I am presently traveling in your Michigan,' Kamyar continued. 'Now, staying not far from you. I was hoping to come see you so we may do business. Please excuse my calling you at this late hour, but I do not have many days in your country. I am hoping I can meet with you.'

'May I ask how you got my name?' I enquired when he finally took a breath. I prefer doing business with people I know, and I had no idea who this guy was. He spoke English reasonably well, but with an obvious accent, perhaps from somewhere in the Middle East.

'My brother lives in your country, near the city you call Detroit,' Kamyar continued without answering my question. 'He found your website on his computer. He says your company buys rough gemstones.'

'That's true,' I replied. 'But I don't run the company anymore. Another man has taken my place. I can give you his name and number.'

'You are Mr. John Van Lan?'

'Yes,' I answered, hoping to put a quick end to this conversation. My dinner was getting cold.

'The information on your website states you are the Chairman of the Board of this company. Is this not true?'

'It is.'

'And this is the most important job in your company.'

'Yes, I guess you could say that.'

'Mr. Van Laan, I am the chief of many people in my country, Afghanistan,' he continued. 'You hold the position of power in your company. I want to speak with you, no one else. I have millions of dollars' worth of beautiful emeralds to sell. This can be very good for your company, but only if you agree to meet with me. Tell me quickly. I am a busy man with many duties and very little time. Do you wish to do business with me or should I find another company to sell my stones?'

I had no choice. I could not turn him down. One of the future goals of my company was to gain a prominent share of the international market in emeralds. If what he said was true, he could help us achieve that goal.

'Of course,' I replied. 'I would be happy to meet with you.'

'Good, I am staying with my brother in Detroit. I can travel to your city of Grand Haven tomorrow so we can do business.'

'Tomorrow is Saturday and I have plans,' I tried to object. 'Could we meet on Monday?' Rachel and I had planned to go to Chicago, fly in the morning and spend the weekend in the windy city.

'I will be on an airplane to go home on Monday,' Kamyar explained. 'And I have a meeting in another city on Sunday. If we are to meet, it must be tomorrow.'

Now I was in trouble. Rachel had been looking forward to the weekend trip and so had I.

'Okay, may I ask you your full name?' I requested politely. If I was going to meet with him, I wanted to do some due diligence before he arrived. On the surface, he sounded innocent enough, but nothing and no one is ever completely innocent. I had learned this the hard way. When he mentioned Afghanistan, my shit detector had gone off immediately, not real loud; but low enough that I couldn't ignore it. Afghanistan was a troubled area. I began to wonder if perhaps meeting with him was a good idea after all. Perhaps I should just say no and make Rachel happy instead. But then, didn't he say he had millions of dollars worth of gems to sell? As the Chairman of the Board of my company, I had an obligation I couldn't ignore.

'I will tell you all you need to know tomorrow when we meet,' Kamyar answered to my displeasure. 'Please give me your address so I can find you.'

I gave him the address of my cottage because I had no business address in town.

'Thank you, I will see you at ten o'clock,' he replied.

My cell phone went dead before I could say another word.

He didn't even give me the courtesy of choosing the time for our meeting.

7:55 PM, JOHN

Rachel continued to eat her meal without looking up at me when I returned.

We were having dinner at her place, a condo overlooking the channel in Grand Haven, Michigan. Chinese takeout was our meal, not because this was my choice. It was hers. I had suggested a restaurant of her choosing. But she said no. Said she was tired. It had been a long week of seeing patients at her work. I understood. She was a doctor of oncology. Her work took her close to death's door. She treated extreme cases. Some had no hope. Each case was personal. But nothing seemed to affect her as deeply as the death of two young men in a park in Washington DC, not long ago. I knew because she often brought up their deaths when we were together, like that night.

She kept asking me to explain to her why they needed to die.

Unfortunately, I had very few answers for her except to say sometimes life leads us to the wrong place at the wrong time, like an automobile accident. If the occupants of the car had been a few seconds distant from the place of their death, they would still be alive today. But life doesn't offer second chances. We don't have a choice even when our fate is death.

However, my good doctor friend was not ready to accept my explanation. Rachel said these boys didn't need to die. The FBI didn't need to kill them.

Truth was, I agreed with her.

But in the FBI's defense, the agents didn't know what they were facing. The boys had been running from them, driving their car through traffic at speeds out of control. They were not acting rationally. No one knew what their true intentions were. An alert had gone out. The suspects were considered armed and dangerous, on a terror watch list. They could have been wearing suicide vests filled with explosives, guns and bombs. The FBI agents were required to stop them. They did, using lethal force. In retrospect, it was unfortunate and unnecessary, but it happened.

Not good enough. Not according to Rachel.

Their deaths were still bothering her and she wanted a resolution. She continued to argue. Said she was a doctor and she worked tirelessly to keep her patients alive, sometimes twenty-four/seven, when the situation demanded. She tried to extend her patients' lives, even those who eventually died despite her efforts. So, if she chose not to accept the needless deaths of these two promising, healthy young men because some idiot had decided in the heat of the moment to use a gun instead of his brain, she felt justified in her opinion.

The FBI did not need to kill those boys.

Okay, I was losing the argument badly and thankfully, the call on my cell phone had offered a welcome reprieve from her drubbing me. My cellphone had been in my coat, lying on a couch in her living room. I was in no hurry to return to the dinner table, no longer hungry at the time. Discussing the deaths of these two boys had ruined my appetite. The truth was, I didn't disagree with her in principle. But more importantly, I didn't want to argue with her anymore, mostly because I was failing miserably.

All of which was very frustrating because none of this was my fault.

If my friend Charlie, a CIA agent, had not asked me to get involved in a certain situation, I would never have been anywhere near those boys. But Charlie could be very persuasive when he chose to be. He asked me to help him look into a matter that had come onto the radar screen of the CIA. He said I owed him a favor for all the times he had saved my ass, all of which was true. I did owe him. He said my mission wouldn't be dangerous. It was minor field work, a job I was uniquely qualified to accomplish because of my business connections. He finished by suggesting it was my turn to do something for my country. As I said before, Charlie could be very persuasive when he chose to be.

Anyway, this was why Rachel and I happened to witness the two dead bodies. We had been unassuming participants in the events that caused their deaths. Rachel was less than me. She was only at the scene because she was with me. And that's why I felt bad for her and I was trying to find some way to help her cope with the pain of seeing those young boys lying dead on the green grass of a park, their blood seeping into the cool afternoon soil. However, none of my rationalizing was working and the ringing of my cell phone in the other room offered me a welcome reprieve from a situation that held little promise of anything good.

However, the call only made everything worse.

SATURDAY, OCTOBER 1, 9:50 AM, JOHN

Rachel was not pleased that our trip to Chicago had to be delayed even after I had patiently explained why I couldn't say no to the man on the phone.

After dinner, she hastily suggested that she was tired and wanted to turn in early. And to make matters worse, she asked me if I wouldn't mind returning to my cottage that evening to sleep. She hoped I understood.

Now this was unwelcome news to me for so many reasons, first, because I had been looking forward to sleeping with her lovely body. And second, because our planned weekend trip had been highlighted on my calendar for several weeks. I wanted to go as much as she did. In my opinion, she was not being fair,.

However, I tried to be understanding. She was a busy doctor who needed her rest.

Rachael's practice of medicine, performing the duties of an oncologist, included handling emergencies at all hours of the day and night. It was a strenuous practice. She was good at her work, excellent in fact. I hoped returning to her former routine would help her deal with the dramatic events we had witnessed, give her something to think about, something to occupy her time, something she was trained to accomplish. I encouraged her in this, even though I would have preferred to have her available more often than occasionally on weekends and evenings when she wasn't too tired.

The delay of our Chicago trip was, as I said, equally disappointing for me as it was for her, but I couldn't help it. I had a responsibility to my company. As long as I was the Chairman of the Board, I had to take the goals of the company seriously. A meeting with a potential new supplier was not something I could ignore.

I spent the early Saturday morning cleaning my cottage in preparation for the arrival of my guest. I did as well as I was able, using my tried and true method of picking up loose items:

magazines clothes, dishes, beer bottles, etc. spread around the cottage in a random fashion and putting the errant objects in drawers and closets wherever they wouldn't be noticed, along with hiding dirty dishes in the dishwasher.

Fortunately, the place wasn't in bad shape. A cleaning lady came once a week. She did a thorough job of housework, far better than I was capable. Rachel had found her for me. She was the same woman Rachel used to maintain her condo. Apparently not satisfied with my sanitary habits, Rachel had frequently mentioned I could use some help in this department, and she offered a solution. I didn't object. Actually, I began to look forward to this lady's visits. Her name was Catherine Mulder, an older Dutch woman who lived in the city, a widow in her sixties. We established a reasonable relationship after an awkward start. She wisely upped her monthly fee after a quick assessment of my cottage, explaining my house required more work than she had initially anticipated. According to my new Dutch friend Catherine, my cottage was a mess when she first arrived, with dust everywhere. However, she said not to worry, she would take care of everything if I promised to stay out of her way one afternoon a week on Thursdays. I did what I was told.

A knock on my door came before I was completely prepared for Kamyar. He arrived ten minutes early. Coffee was brewing, but the rolls I picked up at the grocery store on the way home last night were still in my fridge. I had planned to warm them, place them on a serving plate, along with cups and saucers, dishes etc, in preparation for my guest's visit. None of this was accomplished. I was still cleaning my living room when I heard him at the back door.

I grabbed a few magazines off the floor, tossing them on a table before going to open the door.

He smiled politely and offered his hand in a western-style greeting. 'My name is Kamyar Abdul. I called you yesterday,' he stated.

'Yes, please come in.'

'This is Abbas,' Kamyar introduced a companion standing behind him. 'He is my assistant. May he also join us?'

Kamyar was tall, a handsome man with thick black hair, neatly combed. He had a closely trimmed beard with a tint of gray, intense black eyes and a pleasant smile. His eyes were not deeply set and yet, I read a quiet warning in those eyes. It was hard to look away from him. His eyes were so intense, almost as if he could see right into my soul. His smile, on the other hand, was captivating, a broad and kindly smile which was disarming. And the contrast between his eyes and his smile was difficult to assimilate immediately. It was as if I was looking at two different men. His eyes told me I did not want this man as an enemy, but his smile seemed to be welcoming me to be a friend.

The weather that morning was mild with a late summer, warm breeze off Lake Michigan, accompanied by blue skies. It promised to be a great day, a day I should have been spending with Rachel in Chicago. Last night, before leaving her condo, I asked if she would still like to go to Chicago, just leave a little later than we planned, head for the airport as soon as my meeting was over.

She thought about my suggestion, but only briefly... too briefly, before quickly saying no.

'You don't know how long this meeting will take, do you?' she noted from previous experience of my business dealings.

'I don't know,' I admitted.

'Let's just stay in town. I have some work I can do in the morning.'

'Why don't I call you as soon as I'm done?' I hopefully suggested

'Okay,' she answered, promising nothing.

'We could go somewhere pleasant in the afternoon.'

'Let's talk about it tomorrow.'

Abbas, Kamyar's companion, was not as tall as his boss. Well-built with a thick chest and broad, powerful shoulders, he did not smile and offered no hand in greeting. I deferred to his absence of a friendly gesture by simply nodding yes to Kamyar's request that he join us.

They were both dressed in loose-fitting linen shirts with high collars, which were the style of their country. Western-style pleated trousers and leather shoes were their only concession to our culture. A gray colored traditional hat covered his head. His beard was long and unkempt.

I led the men down a hall to the main room in my cottage. A fieldstone fireplace rising to the peak of the roof was the architectural centerpiece of the room. Two sets of sliding glass doors on either side of the fireplace opened to an expanded view of Lake Michigan spreading north and south across a vast horizon, which bent with the curvature of the earth. The lake was relatively placid that day, with low, gentle curling waves washing on a sunlit, sandy beach. A few boats could be seen near the horizon, occupied by early morning fishermen.

Kamyar's assistant didn't strike me as an especially friendly individual. I briefly considered asking Kamyar to have the man wait in his car, but I feared this would create an atmosphere of distrust.

The room where we sat was furnished with cushioned armchairs and couches surrounding low glass-topped tables. A few of the tables had bases made from rescued driftwood taken from the shore. Abstract modern artwork adorned otherwise stark white walls.

'I have coffee brewing,' I offered. 'May I bring you a cup?'

'We are early, I apologize,' Kamyar stated. 'We did not know how long it would take to drive here and we did not want to be late.'

'Not a problem,' I smiled. 'I have some nice rolls in the refrigerator. It will take me only a minute to warm them up.'

'No, please, do not make any work. We are here to do business.'

'You sure you don't want some coffee?'

'Yes, coffee is good.' Kamyar acknowledged.

His companion said nothing. I began to wonder if he spoke English.

'Abbas also likes coffee. He does not speak English well,' Kamyar confirmed my suspicions.

'Please have a seat. I will be right back.'

I went to the kitchen for coffee. When I returned, Abbas was spreading a mound of glittering green crystals across my glass table in the middle of the room. I couldn't calculate how many carats of stones were in the pile, but it was considerable. After placing a cup of coffee in front of each of these men, I was drawn by the intense green color of the stones. They varied in size from small two and three-carat stones, although some were much larger, ten to fifteen carats.

'May I?' I asked Kamyar.'

'Of course.'

A large stone in the pile captured my attention. Taking it to the window, the early morning sunlight enhanced its deep green color, tinted with a hint of blue. The stone exhibited unusual clarity for emerald. It was almost eye clean with a few visible fissures on the edges. But that was acceptable for an emerald. They are not normally eye-clean, unlike diamonds or sapphires. Their crystal formation is more problematic, causing fissures. And as a result, they are not nearly as hard as a diamond and are prone to cracking. However, it is their color that endears them to customers. The color takes over your soul with its effervescent, brilliant green. The emerald gemstones in the pile were unusual in this respect. Their color was deeper and clearer than most examples from the Middle East I had previously seen. I was very impressed.

I turned to see my guest smiling.

'Do you like?' Kamyar asked.

'What's not to like?' I replied. 'These stones are beautiful.'

'Please accept the stone you have in your hand as a gift.'

'No, I cannot.'

'Please, I have many more like it. Accept it as a good-faith token of my desire to do business with you.'

The stone was a rough crystal taken directly from the earth. I knew once it was properly cut, it would make a brilliant gemstone.

'I can't,' I reiterated. 'It wouldn't be right.'

'Mr. Van Laan, this is the way we do business in my country. If you do not accept my gift, we cannot continue.'

'Okay.' I placed the gemstone on the table next to my coffee cup, knowing customs are different from country to country. In my country, the gift could be deemed a bribe. In his country, it was a symbol inferring he wished to establish a friendly relationship.

'You have a good eye,' Kamyar commented. 'It is an exceptional stone.'

'Yes, it is.'

When cut, I guessed the stone would make a magnificent gemstone worth thousands of dollars.

AKRON, OHIO, 10:30 AM, FRED SMITH

The windows in his office displayed a bright sunny warm day, green manicured lawns amid cultivated gardens, all arranged to enhance the entrance to his company's corporate headquarters.

Mr. Fred Smith wasn't in his office on that Saturday because he wanted to be there. He badly wanted to be somewhere else, like playing golf with his buddies at his club, his customary occupation on Saturday mornings, especially on a nice Saturday such as this.

However, the charts on his desk explained why he was working this Saturday. They were the reason he wasn't playing golf. Sales were down twenty-five percent and falling. Worse yet were profits. They were non-existent. His company was in the red, losing money fast. It wasn't a disaster yet. Profits from previous years had been stockpiled. The company could withstand a one or two-year fallback. But anything beyond this would lead to bankruptcy and this was not a prospect Mr. Fred Smith could envision.

His hopes for a turnaround were based on a change in the political landscape. His world would be right again as soon as the Democrats lost the White House in 2012, meaning the hated President Obama was gone. If this happened, Fred felt assured he could quickly turn things around and he was counting on it. Fox News pundits forecast a Republican victory. Romney was their man, their candidate. They were confident he would be President in the next term. In the meantime, Fred needed to do everything he could to keep his company afloat.

His current problems were the direct result of a presidential order which had been unofficially floated from Pennsylvania Avenue to the Pentagon. The Leader of the Free World had designated Mr. Fred Smith as a person of ill repute. His company was put on a 'no military contract' list. Of course, Fred knew why this happened and he knew who was responsible. He was responsible. He had been complicit in an ill-advised attempt to take down the president of the United States by rumor and insinuation. The ill-fated attempt had failed miserably, his scheme discredited. Worse yet, President Obama had discovered the names of the men who were responsible. And Fred Smith's name was at the top of his list.

This should never have happened. And it was due to one man. The responsible person was one despicable scoundrel. His name was Mr. John Van Laan.

Fred promised himself he would deal with Mr. Van Laan when he had an opportunity. But for now, his hands were tied. An agent from the CIA had paid him a visit. Agent Charles Stewart had come to his office personally to inform him in no uncertain terms that if anything which even smelled of foul play happened to John Van Laan; agent Stewart promised he would personally deliver Fred Smith to an interrogation room located somewhere in a dark place, deep in a third world country where no one would ever find him. Mr. Stewart suggested it could be a very unpleasant experience for Fred.

The visit from the CIA officer only made Fred even madder than before, if that was possible. But for now, there was nothing he could do. Even though he had the means and money to pay back John Van Laan by hiring someone trained to deal with the traitor, Fred did not think this wise. He did not want to incur the wrath of the CIA. He needed to concentrate on his business problems instead.

Not all of his business had dried up. Using backdoor contracts from friends, he produced goods for companies that sold them to the Pentagon. However, these contracts were not nearly as lucrative as the open-ended military contracts, which had made him a very wealthy man. His buddies took a healthy cut off the top, which greatly cut into his bottom line. But Fred had no choice. He needed the business.

In previous years, his company's profit margins had been envied. This made his current situation a particularly difficult pill to swallow, forcing him to beg his buddies for work from the Pentagon, which should have been his in the first place.

Fred sat in his oversized, executive, leather-covered armchair and took a breath while reviewing his options. He was a large man, heavy set and muscular from years of physical discipline learned originally in the military. His brown hair was cut short, army style. He always sat upright, stared straight ahead and never wavered after making a decision. Although older now, he felt strong and secure in the knowledge that he was a man who was born to command other men. He was a leader, not a follower. He set the tone for his company. Always move ahead was his motto. Never look back, never retreat from a decision, and never dwell on the possibility that a mistake has been made. The past is the past. The present is never the time to look backwards. Now was the time to review his options and move forward like a good general.

Although he had never actually achieved the rank of general, he always assumed this was the result of jealousy in the ranks. He had been a colonel who should have made general, but his military career had been stymied by others. When he failed to reach his full potential, he resigned from the army and started a very successful company.

Fortunately for Fred, a portion of his current business, making tires, was not related to military spending. A safe and secure subsidiary was growing thanks to an aggressive VP who had been hired not too long ago. The man previously worked for a competitor before Fred hired him by offering to pay the man more money. That part of his business was secure and growing. It was the military aspect of his business that was struggling, leaking red ink and it would continue to struggle until after two thousand twelve, when hopefully a Republican president would rescind the order excluding him from dealing directly with the military. In the meantime, Fred would be forced to cut costs to right the ship. A few heads would have to roll. And although this was somewhat problematic, firing employees was a necessary step. He couldn't continue to operate in the red.

Fred took out a personnel chart showing the number of employees in each department. He began to make cuts affecting the lives of families. Not Mr. Fred Smith's life, of course. He would survive very nicely. He would make sure his life style did not require change.

Regardless, his situation made him mad. And if an opportunity ever presented itself, if he could find a way, a method the CIA could not question, he would deal with the man who had caused him all this grief.

That was for darned sure.

GRAND HAVEN, MICHIGAN, 6:35 PM, JOHN

'I'll clean that,' Rachel said with authority, referring to a few errant potato chips lying scattered over her otherwise pristine kitchen counter.

I, John Van Laan, the person guilty of disturbing the natural order of things, had been carelessly munching chips while sitting at her kitchen counter, waiting for dinner. Knowing how fastidious she was about keeping things clean and in an attempt to remain in her good graces, I was in the process of wiping the offending items from the surface into my hand, thinking I would deposit them in a wastebasket under her sink; thus eliminating this unsightly problem. But the good doctor would have none of this. With one deft swipe of her dishcloth, Dr. Rachel gathered the disgraceful crumbs and rinsed her cloth in the sink.

'Thanks,' I said. 'Sorry about my mess.'

Her silence was a clear indication of how she felt about my messy behavior. Drinking a beer and munching chips while she was cooking was apparently not good form in her eyes. In my defense, I had been trying to stay out of her way. And it had been great watching her work, preparing our dinner, pans sizzling, shrimp in pasta with a sauce. A salad was previously prepared in bowls, waiting on her counter. The smell of cooking shrimp and pasta was wonderful. I could already taste the delicate flavor of the aroma.

Rachel looked absolutely irresistible that evening, dressed simply in khaki shorts and a loosely fitted white tee shirt with sandals on her bare feet. Her long brown hair was tied loosely in a ponytail, flowing over her shoulders as she worked. Earlier, we had gone for a walk on a pier which jutted into Lake Michigan, taking our time while getting some fresh air, exercise. A short stroll along the beach added to our enjoyment and sense of physical well-being. The beach was busy for an October afternoon. The warm weather that Saturday brought out the local residents.

Anyway, as I said, she looked good. Or perhaps I was just horny and being in close proximity to the object of my affection prejudiced my opinion in favor of her physical attraction. But I didn't think I was wrong. The lady was gorgeous, no matter what she was wearing. A tall woman, she worked out in her spare time. Her body was lean with softly flowing feminine lines. Her posture was erect, even as she worked. Her back was perfectly arched in harmony with her tasks.

'What are you doing?' She turned for no apparent reason and confronted me abruptly for what she assumed was my errant behavior.

'Nothing, why do you ask?'

'You are too. You are staring at me.'

'Is it wrong to stare at a creature as beautiful as you?'

'But you aren't just staring, are you?'

'Okay, what am I doing?' I took a long draw from the beer in my glass and waited. Obviously, I was guilty of something and it was only a matter of time before she made me aware of what it was that needed correcting.

'You are lusting?'

'Okay, tell me, what's the difference between lusting and admiring?'

'Lusting is evil.'

'Really, where did you get that idea?' I asked. 'Out of a catechism book from your church.'

'You know what I mean,' she retorted.

I sighed. 'Yea, I guess I do. And yes, of course I am guilty,' I admitted with a smile.

'Just keep all those wicked thoughts to yourself.'

'Sorry, I was kind of hoping we could work on my problem tonight.'

'We'll see. Right now, the sun is setting and I want to turn down the stove and grab a glass of wine. Want to join me on my deck?'

I sighed, grabbed my beer glass, and followed her outside.

6:55 PM, JOHN

The sun had disappeared over Lake Michigan beyond a far-reaching pier as we sat on her deck along the channel.

My mind was again occupied with thoughts of Kamyar. He was a very interesting individual. I sensed I had only begun to scratch the surface in understanding this complicated man. The conversation we shared in the morning had been very brief. He suggested we could talk more if I agreed to buy his stones. If not, what was there to discuss?

He told me I could show his stones to anyone I chose, check them out, do whatever I needed to do to decide if I wished to buy them. But he specifically asked me not to mention his name to anyone. Even more importantly, I was asked not to tell anyone where the stones came from. This was the one absolute condition he placed on my keeping the stones for examination. He said if I betrayed him, he would immediately cease doing business with me. But if I agreed to his terms, which he promised would be reasonable given the obvious quality of the stones, he would sell my company his gemstones exclusively. And what he had brought with him was just the beginning. Millions more valuable gemstones could be made available, but only if I agreed to his conditions.

As soon as I said the word, yes, I instantly began to regret it. I had the feeling that if I betrayed him, he might do far more than simply withdraw from doing business with me. It was possible I was putting my life in danger. But I said yes anyway because the stones were beautiful. Now perhaps this may not seem like a rational answer and it probably was not, but the truth was, the stones drew me in. As light flowed through them and into my eye, I was drawn to the stones as I have always been drawn to the beauty of natural gemstones. These emeralds were sensational. I had to have them. I wanted to discover their inner soul.

I'm not a gemologist by profession, just a simple businessman. I don't know the science of gemstones, not in depth, not more than a rudimentary knowledge of their formation. But it is not the science of the stones which intrigues me; it is their color and how the color in light plays with my mind. This is what intrigues me.

From a business point of view, I had other goals. First, I wanted to know if these stones were real. My gemologist could do that, verify if they were real and not synthetic stones. I couldn't do this without keeping the samples. That's why I agreed to what he asked. But at the same time, I wondered if this was wise. Something about the deal bothered me. Something that would take time to discover.

Not now.

Now was the time to solve another puzzle of the feminine variety. As the evening sky evolved to shades of orange, I turned to her, to Rachel. She had been unusually quiet that evening, almost brooding. She had asked nothing about my meeting, even though she knew about it. It was the reason our travel plans had been interrupted. But she had not bothered to ask me about it.

'Don't you want to know how my meeting went?' I finally introduced the subject.

'Not really,' Rachel replied.

'Why not?'

'That's your business, John. I have my own business to worry about.'

'That doesn't sound very friendly,' I smiled, hoping some humor might change the mood.

'What's not friendly? I'm making you dinner, and I know what you want tonight. What are you contributing to our evening?'

'I'm here. I could be somewhere else.'

'I think you are somewhere else.'

'What are you talking about?'

'Nothing, just tell me about your meeting. Apparently, you want to talk about it.'

I took the large, rough emerald Kamyar had given me from my pocket. I had brought it with me to show her. Even in the diminishing light of the evening sunset, the jewel sparkled with an iridescent green glowing from its inner core and her demeanor softened immediately when I handed her the stone.

'It's beautiful, John,' she held it up to the light.

'Would you like it?' I made an instant decision. 'I know a cutter in New York who will turn it into a beautiful gemstone.'

'No, it's much too large. What would I do with a stone like this?'

'Make a pendant out of it. Surround it with diamonds.'

'Too fancy for me.'

'Okay, we'll keep it simple. I'll let you choose the design.'

Rachel held the stone in her hand, obviously entranced with its natural beauty. Even though it was currently in its natural crystalline form, it was beautiful. Once cut, it would be even more spectacular.

'He gave it to me as a gift,' I said. 'It cost me nothing. I would like to give it to you.'

'Okay, but only if you let me pay for the pendant.'

'We'll see. First, we need to have the stone cut and polished. Then we can determine what to do about a setting.'

11:35 PM, JOHN

As hoped, the mood that evening changed considerably after I showed her the emerald gemstone. Her face brightened and she smiled often.

What remained of our time together was concluded in pleasant conversation. Dinner was good, great in fact, a shrimp pasta worth the wait. A bottle of wine complemented the meal, relaxing and fulfilling. After eating, she suggested we go for another walk.

The evening was warm. This time we headed downtown, had a drink at a local bar on Washington Street, listened to a jazz band for a while before meandering back to her condo along the channel in no hurry. Her hand found my hand as we walked.

Without saying a word, she went straight to her bedroom after arriving at her condo, turning back the bedspread and beginning to remove her clothes.

'Would you like some help?' I suggested.

'John, I can undress myself. I'm a big girl.'

'I know you are a big girl. That's what makes it fun to help you.'

'You want to undress me?' she questioned my mental stability.

'It would be my pleasure.'

'I see,' she replied. 'Well, in that case.' She sat down on the bed, her arms at her side and stared at me.

'Lie back,' I suggested.

She did as I asked. laying on the bed with her legs dangling over the side. After untying her shoes and removing them along with her socks, I gently pulled down her shorts, sliding them along with her panties down her long legs.

'You can sit up now,' I instructed. When she complied with my wish, I gently kissed her on the mouth.

'You are way too slow,' she grumbled. Grabbing my shirt, she pulled me onto the bed, forcing me to lie down while she undid my belt, pulled down the zipper and removed the unnecessary items before pouncing on me with her knees on both sides.

'What are you waiting for, big boy?' she asked.

'Well, I was going to get rid of your shirt first.'

She quickly pulled the shirt over her head, tossing it in a corner of the bedroom.

'Okay, now what?' she asked with a smile.

'You know what,' I laughed.

The dark night sky outside her bedroom windows slowly changed as we made love, the stars moving almost imperceptibly through vast canyons in the sky, light-years away, gliding through my imagination with songs sung silently. I could hear these songs in my head. The bright orbs in the sky were calling to me from places I could not understand. They spoke from times long forgotten in a language which I did not know but somehow understood, whispering to me with strange words which twisted in my soul, causing me to want to cry out.

I said nothing in return.

I simply existed in the soft curves of her body, her thighs, her hips, in the voluptuous breasts of a beautiful woman, which can cause a man to yearn for something as far away as the stars, something he can never, ever fully have.

WEDNESDAY, OCTOBER 5, 10:35 AM, JOHN

The report lay on my desk.

Helen had faxed it over from Charlottesville as soon as it was done, but I already knew what was in it. I had been talking to my guy in the lab.

Soon after the sample package of emeralds arrived at my company's headquarters in Virginia, our head gemologist called and verified what I suspected. The stones were genuine, natural emeralds of the highest quality. He was amazed at the clarity and color. In his opinion, the rough stones clearly rivaled any emerald he had examined from Colombia or Southeast Asia. However, like all good scientists, he wished to be thorough and requested more time to completely examine the entire sample. It could contain some fakes. This is not an uncommon occurrence. The purpose is to increase the overall carat weight. Therefore, to thoroughly do his job, he would need to examine each and every stone. He warned me this would take time and he promised to report to me as soon as he was finished.

It was Wednesday when he completed his work. He called before I received his written report. He sounded very excited, wanted to give me the good news himself. Every stone was genuine. He placed the value of the parcel in the seven figure range. Said it could be more depending on a final stone by stone evaluation. He asked to know where the rough stones came from. When I told him Afghanistan, he wanted to know what part of Afghanistan, was it the Panjshir Valley, which was a known source of emeralds in the country.

I said I did not know exactly.

He asked who gave me the stones.

I said I was not at liberty to tell him.

This news disappointed him and I understood why. The stones could be from a new and exciting source of emeralds. It was the kind of event gemologists live for: a new discovery. I'm sure he wanted to reveal the news to his buddies in the profession.

However, when I told him it was extremely important to keep this information confidential, he said he understood and didn't press me for more information.

It was after ten in the morning when I received the faxed report. I calculated it was close to eight in the evening in Afghanistan. If I wanted to call Kamyar today, I had to do it soon.

I dialed his long international number. It took a few seconds before it rang. Kamyar had previously explained to me that I would be dialing a satellite phone. These communication instruments are far more reliable than any local telephone system where he lived. I had no idea where he was, just assumed he was in his home country.

He answered with an expected Arabic greeting, words from his religion which I did not understand.

'This is John Van Laan calling from the United States,' I said in English, thinking I needed to learn more of his customs if we were to have a long-term relationship. I felt guilty for not being better prepared.

'Yes, Mr. Van Laan. Do you like my stones?' Kamyar Abdul replied quickly.

'Yes, I like them very much.'

'So, we can do business now?'

'Yes, it would be my pleasure to do business.'

5:10 PM, JOHN

My day had been busy, busier than most days.

It was a good day in a way, went fast, many telephone calls, almost like when I was the CEO, working sixty to seventy hours a week. Lunch was eaten on the fly with a phone to my ear. Jason, the current CEO of the company, the man who replaced me when I decided to step down, was at the top of my call list. He sounded very excited when I told him the news of a new source for emeralds. He knew what this meant for our company: an opportunity to increase our dominance in the colored gemstone business.

He thanked me.

I said I did what needed to be done, nothing more.

He asked if I would like him to take over now that the contact was established.

I said, no. I knew Kamyar preferred to work with a person who held the highest position in the company. I didn't tell this to Jason, didn't want to offend him, just said I had initially established the relationship. Until it was well entrenched, I thought I should continue to be the main contact.

Jason didn't argue, seemed almost relieved this was one task he would not have to add to his already busy schedule of duties. I asked him to prepare a seven-figure wire transfer; send the money to a Swiss bank account as an initial payment for the emeralds. I gave Jason the wire transfer numbers for Kamyar's bank account and asked him to expedite the payment immediately as a good-faith gesture.

Kamyar had been promised the preliminary payment by the end of the week, offered with the hope it would ensure he continued to do business with us. Exclusive rights to purchase his stones were part of our discussion. This was important to me. He had answered cautiously when I proposed the idea, saying he would agree as long as I fulfilled my end of the deal. He reminded me again of the conditions for our continued relationship. I could tell no one his name or where the stones came from, other than to say they were Afghan.

I agreed.

As soon as I had a full report on all the stones, I promised to make a final payment based on the price per carat we negotiated. I assumed I would owe him additional funds. He said he understood. He had a complete accounting of the stones in the parcel. He would compare his numbers to mine, although he did not doubt the two reports would match. He knew I had nothing to gain by trying to cheat him. We were only in the first phase of doing business. There was no reason to risk a long-term relationship that potentially could be worth millions by cheating now?

He then asked when I would like to receive the next shipment.

The question floored me.

I did not expect another shipment for months, but he assured me mining had been ongoing throughout the summer months in his country. He had many stones to sell. Our business would be restricted only by my ability to pay him.

Fortunately, my company had been very profitable in the past, with cash reserves far in excess of most companies. Because we were a private company, we could hold as much money as we wished. Distributions to stockholders were at the discretion of the Board of Directors. And by mutual agreement, a large cash reserve was established for contingencies. However, we were not a bank. A large portion of his gems would have to be sold first before we could take in too much more. However, I was confident after seeing the quality of his stones that we would have no trouble moving his emeralds.

All this was good because I had the distinct feeling that the company's considerable financial resources and an excellent marketing and distribution network would be severely tested by Mr. Kamyar Abdul.

Finally, I asked him if I should prepare a written contract to finalize our new business relationship. I explained that contracts were good because they solidified verbal agreements. He stopped me, saying no, and said we would work off a handshake. He had checked me out. My reputation was one of honesty. If I did not violate our agreement, I could expect to do business for many years. However, if I violated his trust in any way, he would simply cease doing business. He assumed this was reason enough to maintain his trust.

I agreed.

My Charlottesville office was informed. A new shipment would be delivered personally by one of his men. Kamyar said we should expect it the following week. It would be larger than the first parcel, which was a sample parcel. The next shipment would be more representative of what we could expect in the future.

I asked how he was expected to bring the stones into the country. I assumed Customs would need to be informed. I suggested my company might help him with the paperwork.

He stated this was not my concern. He would handle shipping.

My work was done.

It was after five.

It felt good to have accomplished something, almost triumphant. My company had gained access to a new line of gemstones and I had been the person responsible. But in another way, it was a letdown when all the activity ceased. I was alone at my cottage at the time with no one to share my news.

The lake outside my windows reached out to me. Called me to come for a walk. The water beckoned. Let your eyes flow over my gently, glassy spirit and carry you away to places beyond the horizon.

It was a warm day, sunshine and clear skies with a hint of fall in the air. Not exactly a swimsuit day, but a walk on the beach would be pleasant. Normally, I would have done exactly that, gone for a walk. But I was alone and the prospect of walking by myself held no interest. I needed someone to share my triumph. Rachel was the only person who immediately came to mind.

'Hey you,' I got her on the phone.

'Can I call you back?' she asked, sounding exasperated, lacking time. 'I'm expecting a call from a patient. He's not doing well.'

'Sure,' I answered, even though I didn't want to wait.

Then I remembered, Sandy, my former girlfriend, how she had been during the last few months of her life, how much she relied on Dr. Rachel Harren. How much it meant for her to talk to her doctor. I let it go.

'Call me when you get a chance,' I said.

'I will.'

The phone clicked off.

9:15 PM, JOHN

Dinner was a few leftovers, handpicked from the refrigerator, one at a time, eaten from plastic containers. No plates, nothing heated up, just random grazing, finger food, whatever I could find as an interim snack until I could ask her if she would like to go to dinner somewhere. But she didn't call back until late, after nine o'clock. By that time, I wasn't hungry anymore.

'John, sorry, I've been tied up all evening with a patient.'

'No problem,' I tried not to sound as disappointed as I actually felt.

'I'm in my car on the way home. It's been an exhausting day,' she explained. 'Can't wait to go home to bed.'

'Have you had anything to eat?' I asked.

'No, no time.'

'Can I bring you anything, Chinese, pizza?'

'That's kind of you to offer, but no, I'm not really hungry, just tired.'

'Want me to tuck you in bed?'

'If I could depend on you to do no more than tuck me in, I would say yes. But that's not what you are offering, is it?'

I didn't reply.

'How was your day?' she asked.

'Oh, you know… nothing special, a few phone calls.' I didn't have the heart to tell her what happened. It would have taken too long and I didn't think she really wanted to hear it anyway.

'I'll see you Friday,' she said cheerfully.

'Sure, Friday.'

'Do you have anything special planned for me?'

'I'll think of something.'

'Okay, Friday then.'

'Yes, Friday.'

'Love you, John,' she said as if it was an afterthought.

'Love you too,' I replied, but she was already gone, the phone line silent.

WEDNESDAY, OCTOBER 19, 4:10 PM, JOHN

Allen called.

He is our company's head gemologist. His main focus in the last few weeks had been Kamyar's emeralds. He called to ask a question. Actually, he did more than ask. He made an unsettling suggestion which I had not anticipated.

It was late in the day when my phone rang.

I played golf in the morning. Not a spectacular round, but it was good to be outside enjoying the fresh air. Lunch was afterwards at the club with my golfing buddies. Wuskowhan Players Club was not far from my cottage. The day had been enjoyable with light breezes and clear sunny skies. Rain was forecast for the evening. Already, the horizon over the lake was cloudy, destroying any possibility of a sunset. The sky seemed to be closing in, deflating the view to one which was darker, smaller and more confined. It is a different world when clouds dominate the sky, a world reduced in size, lacking the expansive view that can range forever over the lake to the stars.

It was Wednesday, the middle day of the work week. I normally don't bother Rachel on working days. Even so, I was thinking about calling her, wondering if I could buy her dinner. No sex required, just like to have her company for a few hours in the evening. I wasn't looking forward to another evening of being alone.

She was what was on my mind when my phone rang.

I thought it might be her calling.

'John, I'm glad you are home,' Allen said when I answered.

'What can I do for you?' I answered, attempting not to sound disappointed.

'I have a question which has been bothering me.'

'What is it?'

'It's actually more than a question.'

'Okay, what's on your mind?'

'You remember I asked you where the emeralds came from.'

'Yes.'

'And you said you couldn't tell me.'

'Yes.'

'Is that because you don't know?'

'I know they are from Afghanistan.'

'Yes, but where in Afghanistan?'

'I'm not sure.'

'So, you don't really know?'

'Yes, that's correct.'

'I have been researching these stones,' Allen continued. 'And I can tell you for certain they are not from the Panjhir Mountains in Afghanistan, which is the only known area in the country that produces emeralds.'

Allen could make this statement because every natural gemstone has distinctive qualities, markers that tell where they are from. Geologists know these markers and are able to quickly determine the source of a stone.

'I understand, but this doesn't mean they couldn't have come from another area, a new source for emeralds which has not been previously discovered.'

'Yes, that's true,' Allen conceded. 'But there's one other possibility.'

'And what is that?'

'They could be stolen. We could be dealing in stolen goods.'

This was not a possibility I had considered. It sent a shockwave up my spine. I certainly did not want to be party to a crime. Apart from the fact that it could cause my company serious legal problems, it was not good business practice. The gem business depends to a great degree on the honesty of the people involved, especially the larger dealers such as my company.

'Do the stones resemble emeralds from any mine you know?' I asked, almost holding my breath, waiting for his answer. For the last two weeks, I had relished the idea that this new discovery might help my company take a giant step forward in controlling the international market in emeralds. If what Kamyar was telling me was true, if he had a large quantity of emeralds to sell, this could quickly allow us to assume a predominant position in the market. This was great news and I didn't want anything to interfere with it.

'No,' Allen answered. 'But they are similar in many ways to Colombian emeralds.'

'But they are not the same.'

'No, they are not the same, but they could come from somewhere near the mines in this country.'

I paused before asking the next question. 'But you don't know for sure.'

'No, I don't. However, until we verify where these stones come from, we are in the dark.'

'And this means we can't be sure they are not stolen.'

'And that's a problem?' I finished his line of thought.

'Yes.' Allen answered.

'Okay, thanks. I'll let you know what I decide.'

'I'm sorry,' Allen said. 'I don't mean to cause you trouble. But I thought you should know.'

'You did the right thing, Allen. Now go home. I'll handle this.'

'Thanks, Mr. Van Laan.'

5:35 PM, JOHN

Allen's call did nothing to improve my mood.

And it was too late to call Kamyar to get any answers. The time difference between where I lived in the eastern part of the United States and Afghanistan was nine and a half hours, meaning it was the middle of the night in his country. I would have to wait until morning to clear up Allen's question.

Allen was right to call.

I had come to a conclusion too quickly, assuming the emeralds Kamyar gave me were genuine, from his country, from a mine he controlled. I did this because I wanted to believe him. I wanted the business. I wanted the profits his stones would offer. I didn't want anything to go wrong. But assuming anything in business is usually a bad idea. It can quickly lead to disaster. Allen was right. We needed to know for certain that the emeralds had a clean line of ownership. Nothing else was acceptable. If we couldn't prove the authenticity of the stones, then I would have no choice but to back away from the deal.

Obviously, it was very important that I get this matter cleared up immediately. However, I had to wait until morning, and waiting has never been something I enjoy. All of which made it even more important I find a diversion for my evening. Rachel was the clear choice.

I dialed her number, hoping she would agree to see me. As I listened to the ominous ringing of her phone, rain began to pelt my windows further distorting my view, closing in on my world, reducing it to simply the room where I waited, listening to the hollow sound of her phone ringing; finally concluding I should just hang up before her voice mail answered. I didn't want to talk to voicemail. I was convinced I would sound too needy. It is difficult to ask for a favor when talking to a real person. It is almost impossible to get it right when talking to a machine.

'John,' she answered.

'Hey, I just about gave up on you.'

'Well, I'm here now. What do you need?'

'What makes you think I need anything?'

'Because you don't normally call me in the middle of the week unless you need something.'

'That doesn't make me sound very attractive.'

'Am I wrong?' she inquired innocently.

'No, you're not wrong. The fact is, you're almost never wrong. You are just too darned smart.'

'What do you want, John?' she said impatiently. 'I was getting ready to go to the gym.'

'How about meeting me afterwards for dinner?'

'I'll be all hot and sweaty.'

'Sounds great. I like hot and sweaty.'

'John, do you want dinner or sex?'

'Again, way too analytical.'

'Again, am I wrong?'

'Just dinner. I could use some company.'

'Feeling lonely, John?'

'Yes, if you must know.'

'Okay, I'll skip the gym. Pick me up in an hour.'

'Thanks Rachel.'

'You're welcome. Just remember your promise.'

'What promise?'

'No sex.'

'Oh yea, that.'

THURSDAY, OCTOBER 20, 4:20 AM, JOHN

I couldn't sleep.

And with no reason to stay in bed, I finally got up early.

Allen's question was on my mind. It kept me awake for most of the night. I needed to make a call.

I had been a good boy last night, took Rachel to dinner and even though she offered to have me up to her condo for an after dinner drink; I resisted, saying I was fulfilling my end of the deal as promised: dinner only, no sex required. She countered by saying she was simply asking me for a drink. She wasn't offering anything more.

I said sure. She would get a couple of drinks in me, then lure me into her bedroom to take advantage of me. The only way I could be certain to maintain my integrity was to kiss her goodnight in the car and head home before my willpower gave in.

The lights along the channel reflected off my windshield in the rain as I leaned over to kiss her shadowed lips. The damp, dark night outside was not a pleasant sight, cold and rainy. The truth was I wanted nothing more than to curl up in her bed and listen to the rain gently fall against the windows, knowing I was safe and secure next to her warm, luscious body. I was having a very hard time not accepting her offer, but I did it anyway, drove away as soon as she was out of the car door.

I went home and waited to make my call.

He answered after I identified myself, 'Mr. Van Laan, you are up early,' he said. 'What can I do for you?'

'First, please call me John.'

'And you may please call me, Kamyar.'

'Thank you. Kamyar, I have a problem. I need to verify where your stones are from. I can't sell them without establishing a clear line of ownership.'

A pause followed.

'John,' he finally came back on the line. 'This is a subject we need to discuss in person.'

'It's very important, Kamyar.'

'I understand its importance and I will have answers for you soon. But I do not wish to discuss this on the phone. I will be in your country next week. We can discuss it then.'

'I was hoping we could deal with the issue today.' I pressed him, not wishing for a delay.

'John, I will talk to you soon.'

The phone line went silent.

SUNDAY, OCTOBER 23, 4:55 PM, JOHN

A golf tournament was on TV.

I wasn't paying much attention at the time. The leader was five shots ahead of the second-place competitor. There wasn't much drama involved, only a few finishing holes with one question yet to be answered. Could the leader hold up under pressure without a major screw up. I assumed he could.

We had flown back early from Chicago in the afternoon. Rachel and I concluded our delayed trip, had a fine time dining and shopping and generally enjoying the Windy City. She was in a good mood, doing something in my kitchen. I presumed getting ready for cocktail time, preparing some snacks she had promised. I could smell the food cooking in the oven. I was getting hungry.

I turned off the TV, deciding it was almost five o'clock, time to get a beer from the fridge.

'Food is almost done,' Rachel said as I entered my kitchen.

'Smells good.'

'I think I'll be running along,' she announced. 'Just take it out of the oven when the buzzer goes off. Think you can do that?'

'Aren't you staying for cocktails? Looks like it will be a great sunset.'

A few clouds marred an otherwise blue sky, hanging low over the horizon, perfectly positioned to reflect the deepening rays of the retreating golden orb as it slid below the horizon and intensified under the influence of the gravitational pull of the Earth.

'No, I think I'll head for the gym. If you remember, you interrupted my Wednesday workout. And with all the good food we ate over the weekend, I'm sure I put on a pound or two.'

'Your body can handle a couple of pounds and still look great,' I observed.

'You're either prejudiced or you're trying to get in my pants again.'

'I'm both,' I laughed.

'Yes, I believe you are. Now give me a kiss so I can run along.'

'But I don't want you to leave.'

'Well, I'm leaving anyway.'

I didn't know what to say and it occurred to me that making any suggestion now might not be wise, might not be the right time. But I had been thinking about something for a few weeks and I wanted to ask her. I wanted to ask her when she would say yes and now was probably not the right time, but I was impatient and I said it anyway.'

'Why not just stay here all the time, move in with me. I have plenty of room. You don't need a condo.'

'But I like my place.'

'I like it too, but I like you better here.'

She said nothing in reply and I should have taken this as a clue to keep my mouth shut. But, you know, I'm not that smart.

'Oh, come on, Rachel,' I argued. 'My place is larger. It's on the lake. It's a lot better than your condo.'

'Really,' she said. 'You don't like my place?'

'Of course, I like it. I just happen to think this would be better for us.'

'Well, good! Now that I know what you think, I think it's time for me to leave.'

'What does that mean?'

'It means I'm going to the gym.'

And she did, walking out without saying another word. This woman could be so exasperating at times.

The telephone rang before I heard the door slam shut. I picked it up while watching her walk down my driveway to her car.

'Hello,'

'It's me, old buddy,' he said.

'Charlie?'

'Yes, got a minute?'

8:45 PM, JOHN

The last rays of sunlight cast an orange halo over the length of the lake as I sat in a lounge chair on my deck.

The vivid color glowed for long minutes before finally extinguishing in shades of gray, leaving behind a dark scene devoid of color. The day was done, another day, a day which had begun well but finished poorly.

In the morning, Rachel and I made love in our Chicago hotel room with a window overlooking a skyscraper sky to the vast flat panorama of glassy Lake Michigan in the distance. It was a beautiful room, modern in décor with soft colors and wood-grained furniture. I felt comfortable in this room and great in her arms, in the expression and exercise of making love to a beautiful woman. Her naked body was long and trim. Her breasts were full and young. Her mind was eager and willing to give me as much as I could give her. We cared for each other, took our time. We existed for long, lovely moments on luxurious hotel sheets. Breakfast was ordered in, croissants and eggs sunny side up with coffee and yogurt for her. A walk through the quiet city streets on a Sunday morning was followed by lunch at a downtown restaurant before boarding our private jet to return home.

This was how my day began. This was good. This was fun. But what happened in the evening was completely different.

That did not end well.

Late afternoon, she left my cottage in a hurry, in the middle of an argument, or should I say a mild disagreement. I had asked her to move in with me, asked with a smile as if it was a joke. It wasn't a joke and I hadn't planned to ask her until the time was right. It just came out when she was getting ready to leave. This was not good timing, but it was something I obviously wanted. It came from somewhere inside me. I didn't want her to go. I wanted to be with her for more than a few nights each week. I wanted more, but apparently, she did not share my feelings. She was more eager to leave than to stay. This was not how I wished my day to end.

Then Charlie called and he turned a deteriorating evening into a complete disaster.

The whiskey in my glass warmed my soul, but offered only meager solace for the sour events of the evening, not enough to make up for what happened. I was brooding, pissed, irritated, and slipping slowly into an angry state of discontent.

I knew I needed to move on. I badly needed to move on. Everything was not lost. Rachel and I could resolve our relationship. I simply had to be patient. I had to give her time. Then… well… perhaps we could discuss it in a more rational manner. That was my hope anyway.

Zipping my jacket against a cool breeze off the lake, I was reluctant to go inside even though it was getting cold. Evenings in the summer were spent on my deck, the sun high in the sky for long hours into the night. When fall arrives, everything changes, not for the better. The sun sets much earlier, around seven. And as soon as the golden orb disappears below the horizon, the air cools quickly. However, putting on a winter jacket and hat makes it possible to stay outside for a few more weeks, but I knew time was short. Winter would soon make this impossible. Winds off the lake would blow hard and cold, the air clammy and frigid. Snow would dominate the land, covering the deck, making life outside wretched. Only a few good weeks remained to enjoy.

To make things worse, Charlie informed me he was coming whether I wanted him or not. My buddy Charlie was an agent for the CIA. He informed me he wanted to talk. And that had me concerned because in the past, his interference in my life did not always lead to something good. I needed to mentally prepare for him. The man was always a challenge and often a problem.

Whatever he wanted to discuss, we could discuss on the phone. That was my opinion and I told him so. But not according to Charlie. He said we needed to do it in person. This was not a good sign. This normally meant trouble. He informed me his plane was scheduled to arrive in Grand Rapids in the morning. Could I pick him up at the airport around nine thirty?

Sure, but what's this all about? Could he at least give me a clue?

He told me it involved an Afghan. He asked if I knew who he was talking about.

I had to be truthful. Charlie was CIA after all and the CIA knows everything. I said, I did.

He then asked if I was doing business with this man, assuming again, that I knew who he was talking about, which of course, I did.

I said I was.

'Okay,' he replied. 'Then we need to talk.'

'Can it wait?' I asked.

'No.'

MONDAY, OCTOBER 24, 11:35 AM, JOHN

A warm fall sun felt good in a cool, brisk breeze blowing in off the lake under a clear blue sky when I had stepped outside the cottage early in the morning with a cup of coffee before heading for the airport

My drive was uneventful. Charlie's plane was on time. He didn't have too much to say during our trip from Grand Rapids to Grand Haven. I had the distinct feeling he was holding back and I didn't push him even though I was anxious to know what was on his mind. Anything to do with Kamyar and his emeralds was important to me. I didn't want anything to interfere with our business arrangement.

'Want some lunch?' I asked Charlie after we arrived at my cottage. 'I assume you got up early this morning to make your flight.'

'I think we should talk first,' Charlie replied. 'Got any coffee?'

'I'll make some.'

'Thanks, usual accommodations?' he inquired, holding his suitcase.

'Yes.'

Charlie had been at my cottage many times in the past. He knew the layout. A small apartment had been built in the back a few years ago for a special friend who had since died. Now it was used primarily for houseguests. Charlie headed down the hall for his usual room. Soon the coffee maker was perking. I found two mugs and set some rolls on a dish. He returned, dressed in jeans and a sweater after arriving at the airport in a suit and tie, his normal CIA uniform.

'You look more comfortable,' I commented.

My African American, CIA buddy only wore casual clothes when off duty. Handsome, Charlie was a tall man with a lean, hard body and a ready smile. His dark black hair was cut short, close to his head. His eyes were alert, always on the go. I seldom saw him when he was totally relaxed. The man seemed to be in a perpetual state of anxious activity. I assumed this was one reason he moved so quickly up the ladder of success at the agency.

'When in Rome,' he replied.

The coffee pot peeped twice, indicating it was done.

'Grab a cup and a roll,' I suggested. 'Let's go into the living room.'

'Thanks.' He followed my lead.

Whitecaps could be seen on the water through the sliders in the living room, driving relentlessly across the lake towards shore, waves washing high on a sandy beach before retreating back into the water.

'Now, what brings you to my humble abode?' I asked, impatient to discover what was so important that he felt the need to fly in and tell me in person.

'You recently met a man by the name of Kamyar Abdul,' he answered as I feared.

'Yes, apparently you know I have. May I ask how you know?'

'We have been watching him for some time.'

'When you say watching, what you mean is that you are spying on him.'

'John,' Charlie said. 'He is an important man in Afghanistan. Some say he may hold the balance of power between the insurgents and those friendly to us.'

I thought about this for a moment before asking because I couldn't help it. 'Is anyone in that god forsaken country actually friendly to us, anyone who isn't on your payroll?'

'Look, John, I didn't come here to talk politics.'

'Sorry.'

'Right, now can we please talk about what I need from you?' he asked impatiently.

Charlie was always straightforward in his view of the world. Good guys and bad guys. Nothing important existed in his world except in his black and white perspective. This worked well for him. It served him in his job. To get caught up in the gray areas of life would make his work much more difficult. It was already a difficult job, trying to defend our country against many determined foes. He needed to stay focused. I understood. But I also enjoyed pricking his conscience from time to time.

'Yes.'

WEDNESDAY, OCTOBER 26, 2:55 PM, JOHN

A knock on my back door temporarily startled me.

A report I was writing for the board of directors was only half done. I was deep into the work at the time. It was important. The board needed to understand the potential that my new relationship with Kamyar meant for the company. They had to be on my side. I needed the resources of the company to back me up. If what Kamyar was promising came true, the company had to be ready and willing to take on what could be a major new source of business. And like any new business opportunity, this one would require an investment of both money and people to make it happen. And it was becoming increasingly apparent that it would undoubtedly take more than the normal financial resources of the company.

I reluctantly got up from my desk, thinking it was probably someone soliciting something. I was determined to get rid of the person quickly to return to my report, get the report done before the end of the day, and send it off to Helen in Charlottesville at the home office for her to fax to the board members.

'Mr. Van Laan,' Kamyar said when I opened the door. 'I hope you are not unhappy I came unannounced.'

His arrival caught me completely off guard, but I quickly recovered. 'No, come in, please.'

He shook the rain off his coat.

'May I take your coat,' I offered.

He looked at me strangely as if asking why I would want his coat.

'I'll hang it up to dry,' I explained.

He handed me his coat. It was soaked from a short walk up the driveway from his car. The rain was pouring hard at that time. It was a wet, cool, and windy day. Through the open door, I noticed his manservant sitting in his car.

'Would your assistant like to come in?' I asked.

'No, he's fine where he is.'

'It's going to get cold in the car,' I suggested.

'He's used to the cold,' Kamyar said without emotion.

'May I get you some hot coffee?' I asked before remembering the coffee in the pot had been ignored while I was working. It had been on for several hours,

'That would be very good of you,' he responded.

'I'll start a new pot.' I headed for the kitchen. 'The coffee in the pot is old.'

He followed me. 'Please, do not make any fuss. This old coffee will be good. I am used to old coffee.'

'As you wish.' I poured coffee into two mugs and handed him one.

'Can I get you something to eat?'

'No, thank you for your offer of hospitality, but I am not hungry.'

The conversation that followed was not one I could have ever anticipated. It began with him apologizing again for showing up unannounced.

I said it was no problem and then I listened, just let him talk. And as I listened, I could hear Charlie talking to me in my mind. Everything Charlie had warned me about was coming true. Apparently, there was much more to Mr. Kamyar Abdul than I originally considered. He was far more than simply a dealer in rough gemstones, a miner from the mountains of his native country. He was a man of considerable influence and importance in his home country. He made this very clear. He said if we were to continue to do business, I must respect his situation.

'Mr. John Van Laan,' he interjected. 'It is very important our conversations are not overheard by anyone, including electronic devices. Do you understand what I am telling you?'

'Yes, I understand.'

'Good,' he said quickly.

I interrupted him before he could continue, 'Please call me John.'

'Thank you, yes, I remember now, you wish to be called John. And you may call me Kamyar.' He paused. 'I am sorry I forgot to call you John. It is just that I have much on my mind and it is important you understand what I am telling you, John.'

'I think I do.'

'Good. And it is important you do not mention my name to many of your associates. I do not wish for many people to know we are doing good business.'

'Okay,' I answered, thinking about my conversation with Charlie. Wondering if I should tell him about my connection to the CIA. I decided to wait.

'This is very important to me,' he repeated for emphasis.

'I understand.'

'Thank you. Finally, please do not attempt to call me in the future. I will call you. Or I will send someone to talk to you if I am unable to call. I came myself today because I did not trust anyone to tell you what I had to say.'

'I understand, but what if I have a question?'

'I will give you a number to call in Mumbai, India. Please leave a message with the person who answers the phone. I will return your call when I am able.'

'Okay,' I agreed.

'Now, you wanted to talk to me about something when you called me last week?' he asked.

'Yes, it is important I verify the origin of your stones.'

'Where are they mined?' he asked.

'Yes.'

'Why is this important?'

'Please do not be offended by what I am going to tell you.'

'I will not,' he looked at me directly.

'Okay, I need to know for certain where the gemstones are mined in order to dismiss the possibility that they are stolen. This is simply a matter of due diligence on my part, something I must do as a respected seller of gemstones.'

Kamyar considered this for a minute before answering. 'I understand. Trust is very important and some things cannot be trusted. Am I right?'

'Yes, some things need to be verified.'

'Then you should see with your own eyes what I am telling you is true.'

'How can I do that?'

'You must come to Afghanistan with me.'

'Can I send someone in my place?' I asked quickly because I wasn't sure I wanted to go to this troubled region of the world.

He paused again, considering perhaps he had made a mistake in trusting me. 'No John, as I have told you. My business is with you only. It is you who must come.'

FRIDAY, OCTOBER 28, 9:50 PM, JOHN

'When are you leaving?' Rachel asked.

I had called her earlier in the day to ask what she would like to do this evening. Dinner, movie, said I was open to anything which would make her happy, Rachel replied she was tired after a long week of work. Could we eat in? Takeout was her suggestion, Chinese or pizza, eat at her condo, maybe watch a DVD movie on her TV afterwards?

The subject of my staying overnight was not mentioned by my sweet lady, but I went along with her program anyway, trying to be optimistic. The last thing I wanted was another disgusting discussion similar to what happened last week when we argued after I unwisely asked her to move in with me. I was determined not to bring up this subject again, and I didn't. But as it turned out, we had more than enough acrimonious issues to discuss.

'I'm leaving on Tuesday, early in the morning, going to Langley, Virginia, first to meet with Charlie. He has a few things he wants to go over with me before I go.'

This was his suggestion, not mine and it is more than simply a suggestion. Fact was he insisted I come.

'I don't think you should go to Afghanistan,' she announced.

'Why not?' I asked. 'I told you how important it is.'

'Because I don't think you have thought it through. For example, how well do you know this man? He comes from a different part of the world, John. He doesn't think like you do. The people in his country have been fighting for years. Life is cheap where he comes from.'

From her answer, it was obvious she had thought it through. 'I understand,' I countered. 'And that's all the more reason to go. I have to know who I'm dealing with.'

'No, you don't.'

'Rachel, I can't do business with this man if I don't go.

'Good, then stop doing business. You have more than enough business now. You are rich. You don't need the money. Why take the risk?'

She was right of course. I didn't need the money or the hassle. But a new source of product would help my company grow and the deal with Kamyar was more than simply a new source; it was a considerably large source of product, one which could not be ignored. I had spent years building the company in the past. In the beginning years, I would never have thought for a second about not going. It was just business. It had to be done. Jobs depended on it. A company that stops growing is prone to fail. It would be the same for my company. As an employee of the company, I was obligated to follow our mission. If not, things could begin to slip. I had seen it before in other companies. Limiting growth was a strategy for failure.

'The company needs this business,' I tried to explain.

She paused before asking, 'What does Charlie think?'

Now this was a question which I had hoped would not come up. I knew the answer, but I didn't want to tell her.

'It's not important what Charlie thinks. This is my decision,' I replied.

Our dinner was in her small dining room with windows overlooking the channel. She was dressed casually jeans and a sweater open at the top. Her lovely, clear skin was still tan from the summer sun. Her long naturally brown hair was down, the way I liked it, released from the pins which normally held her tightly confined lovely curls to her head as she worked during the day. The only remnant of her professional appearance was her white metal, doctor glasses covering her big, gorgeous brown eyes. She looked sensational, tempting, alluring in a way that natural beauty draws in a man. It can't be explained. It just is. When a woman has it, it is undeniable and Rachel had it all, an engagingly intelligent mind combined with a body which had the strength of an athlete and the stature of a model.

A restaurant in Grand Haven, not far from her condo, had prepared our meal. I ate there often in the past because I liked the view down the channel to the big lake. In the evening, when the conditions were right, sunsets from their deck could be spectacular, a ball of fire settling in the west, shadowed by low dunes.

The hostess at the restaurant knew me well. She was kind, asked the chef to prepare two great seafood dinners, scallops for Rachel on a bed of noodles and a lightly breaded perch dinner for me, along with a couple of salads. I contributed a bottle of wine and bread from a local bakery, all in effort to make Dr. Rachel happy. But nothing was working. The good doctor Rachel was not in a good mood. Dinner conversation was the reason, not the food. I was beginning to fear her choice of a topic for the evening was not conducive to setting the right tone for my romantic intentions and I was failing fast in a vain attempt to change the subject.

It all started when she suggested we go to Grand Rapids to see a play next week. That's when I had to tell her. I couldn't go because I would be out of town on business. Unfortunately, this wasn't enough information for my female friend. She wanted the details. Like any good doctor, it wasn't enough to know the name of the disease. She needed to know everything there was to know about how it functioned before she was satisfied.

Her question about what Charlie thought only made things worse. I should never have told her about him and I don't remember when or exactly how it slipped out. Somewhere in one of our previous conversations, I must have mentioned that Charlie came to visit me on Monday. Well, she wanted to know all about this as well. I said I would tell her, but first I had to swear her to secrecy. You can tell no one, I instructed her, said it was CIA business. She agreed, so I told her about Kamyar, said the CIA was interested in him. They didn't know whose side he was on, ours or the Taliban, and this was important because he was an influential man in his country, the leader of a large tribe which dominated a region north and west of Kabul. It was thought the tribe was attempting to maintain its neutrality in the conflict between the Americans and the Talib, but the CIA wasn't sure this was true. Neutrality is not something that is easy to preserve during times of war.

Naturally, the CIA is suspicious of anyone who does not swear allegiance to them. They were concerned that some of Kamyar's tribe might be secretly supporting the Taliban. And when they discovered I was talking to Kamyar, they became very interested. Charlie asked me to help him discover the true allegiance of this man. I agreed, but said I would do it only if I could do it my way without his interference. He reluctantly agreed, although I wasn't sure he was telling the truth. In the past, Charlie always found a way to accomplish what he needed, regardless of what I asked. I assumed this time would be no different.

'Not good enough, John. I want you to tell me what Charlie thinks of your trip?' Rachel demanded again as I mulled several options to avoid her question.

'He doesn't think I should go,' I finally admitted because I couldn't think of anything else to say that didn't include a lie.

The truth was that Charlie was interested in what I could find out about Kamyar, but he was also not interested in putting me into harm's way. He was adamant when telling me I should not go to Afghanistan. The country was dangerous, he said. In my defense, I told him my going on this trip was no more risky than what he required of his agents. He replied that I was not one of his agents. I was not trained for field work. Therefore, he could not in good conscience let me go. I said it wasn't up to him. He said, in a way, it was. He informed me he could put me on a no-fly list, in which case I would have to stay home.

'You can't do that, can you?' I pushed him.

'I can,' Charlie answered.

'But you won't.'

'No,' he said. 'I won't. But I also want you to understand how strongly I suggest you not go.'

That's how we left it. He knew I was going.

'Why not?' Rachel asked.

'Too many variables, Charlie says he can't protect me in this part of the world.'

'Okay, good, then you aren't going, right?'

'No, I'm going.'

'John,' she looked exasperated.

'Rachel, I told you why I need to go. I have to prove that the stones are genuine. I can't sell them in good faith if I don't know where they come from.'

'Let someone else go. You're the Chairman of the Board. It's not your job to fly around the globe for your company.'

'That true, but Kamyar won't deal with anyone but me. If I say no to him, the deal is off.'

'You don't know this for a fact.'

'Yes, I do. I already asked and he said no.' I didn't want to argue with her, but she gave me no choice.

She looked at me before turning and staring over the channel, took her time before finally saying, 'John, I'm sorry.'

'Sorry for what? What are you talking about?'

'I'm sorry because I need to tell you something. And I'm sorry because this probably is not the right time to tell you, not before you leave on your trip.'

I waited, didn't say a word, just sat, feeling a knot form in my gut.

'There's probably no good time to tell you,' she continued.

'Tell me what.' I asked in frustration.

She sat silently.

'I'm waiting.'

'This isn't working.'

'What isn't working?' I asked, even though I knew instantly in my gut what she was going to say.

'Just be quiet for a minute, will you?'

I shut up.

'You remember, a week ago when you asked me to move in with you.'

'Yes, what has that got to do with anything?'

She stared at me again, waiting for me to be quiet. When I said nothing more, she continued, 'Okay, and then tonight you inform me you are traveling to some scary place and you won't listen to me when I tell you I don't want you to go.'

'Oh, come on Rachel. It's not like I'm on the road all the time. This is one trip. It will be over soon.'

'John please, I asked you to let me talk without interrupting.'

'Sorry.'

She again looked out her windows before continuing, 'I don't know, John. Maybe your trip is what is needed. Perhaps it would be good for us to spend some time apart.'

'What does that mean?' I asked, now really concerned.

'It means we have some really difficult problems to work out. Perhaps it means we aren't meant to be together. We don't have the same goals.'

'You have been thinking about this, haven't you? I mean, this isn't something which popped into your head tonight.'

Again, she turned to look outside for direction. The harbor lights on the pier glowed in the darkness. It was a grand sight, the water calm with gentle rolling swells moving up a glassy channel.

'Yes, that's true,' she replied. 'Ever since you asked me to move in with you, I have been thinking about what to do. I thought I knew the answer, but now I'm not sure. Now I think we are not meant to be together.'

'I'm sorry,' I said. 'I'm sorry I ever brought up the subject of your moving in. Can we just forget about it?'

'No, I don't think we can. It's obvious it was something you want, but I'm not sure it's something I can give you. I have a job for one thing which takes most of my time, and it appears you do too. Right now, our jobs seem to be a problem with no solution. Perhaps our relationship was a bad idea from the beginning.'

'You don't really mean that.'

'I do,' she said simply.

An anxious silence followed, a nervous, worried silence which smelled of endings and not beginnings; a poignant, heart-beating silence lacking joy.

'This doesn't have anything to do with those boys who died in DC, does it?' I asked because there had to be more to her sudden, drastic change of heart, more than she was expressing.

'In a way it does,' she confessed after a pause.

'You don't blame me, do you?'

'No, you didn't pull the trigger to kill those boys,' she paused. 'But you also did nothing to stop the cops from killing them.'

'What could I have done?' I asked, knowing I was right about asking her about the boys. And I was glad she was finally being honest with me. For some time now, I had the feeling that this incident, more than anything else, was the cause for all her uncertainty. Everything changed the day they died.

'You could have talked to Charlie.'

'Told him what?'

'Told him these boys were innocents caught up in something they knew nothing about. Got them taken off a terror watch list.'

'Do you really think Charlie and I had the clout to take on the CIA and the President of the United States?'

'You should have done something,' she added quickly, anger coming from deep inside.

'The stakes were high,' I argued. 'A president's future was in jeopardy. There was nothing I could do.' Despite my trying to be calm, my voice rose in volume, not exactly shouting, but words spoken in frustration.

'I think you should go now, John,' she looked away. 'I'm tired and I don't think it will do either of us any good to continue this discussion tonight.'

'Rachel, please.'

'No, enough. Just go,' she said, sounding very determined.

'Can I see you tomorrow?' I pleaded.

'I don't know.'

'Can I call you?'

'Sure, give me a call,' she said the words, but it didn't sound like she really meant them, just said the words to get me to leave.

I reluctantly got up from the table with my dinner half eaten, found my coat, and headed for the door.

GRAND RAPIDS AIRPORT, TUESDAY, NOVEMBER 1, 1:40 PM, JOHN

Two large commercial jets were ahead of my plane.

We were stationary on the runway, waiting in line to take off.

I was tempted to tell the pilot to turn around, go back to the gate. I had something I needed to do. I needed to see a lady and beg her forgiveness. I needed to give up the idea of going to Afghanistan. I needed to stay home because that was what she had asked me to do.

She said 'no' when I called her Saturday morning and asked if I could come over. She said she needed time to think.

I told her I was leaving on Tuesday. I wasn't sure when I would be home again. I really wanted to see her before I left.

'No, don't come,' Rachel replied. 'Perhaps it is good that you are going away for a while. The trip will give us both some time to think about what we want in life. We can talk again when you get home, whenever that is… That is if you make it,' she added for emphasis, obviously unhappy with my decision to travel.

I begged her, said I really wanted to see her.

She hesitated, the phone line momentarily silent before finally saying, okay; I could come over. But I couldn't stay long.'

Now, I asked. 'Would now be a good time?'

Now would be as good a time as any, she had replied. If I wanted to see her, I should come now, not later.

The drive to her place was filled with anxiety, rehearsing a hundred speeches, a hundred ways to plead with her. But when pulling into the parking lot next to her condo, I really didn't have a clue what to say, just prayed I would find the right words. And as it turned out, shouldn't have wasted my time.

She controlled the conversation from the beginning to the end. Dressed in a cut-off sweatshirt and running pants, with very little makeup, her dark brown hair tied up in a bun. Her only sacrifice to looking good was the absence of her metal rimmed doctor glasses. She had contacts in her beautiful eyes. I assumed she was headed to the gym as soon as I walked out the door

'Sit down, John,' she demanded. 'I'm glad you came. I think we should settle this now, not later.'

I did as instructed; I sat in a chair at her dining room table across from her without saying a word.

'John,' I'm sorry, she began. 'But I don't think we can continue.'

When I opened my mouth to object, she raised her hand. 'Just listen, John. You can talk when I'm finished.'

I shut up.

'I want more from life than you can give me.'

I listened silently as she pronounced my sentence. I didn't object because I had the distinct feeling that anything I said would be a waste of time. I was not in control. She was.

'You have helped me, John,' she smiled. 'You know you have helped me when I needed help, taught me I could love again. You have stirred my soul, brought me back to life. I will love you for this forever, John. I will love you for as long as I live. But I'm not sure I can live with you because something in you will always take you away from me. Someone will call. Some ill wind will take you away from me. Some irresistible urge will cause you to go where I cannot go, where I do not want to go, where you and I cannot be together.'

'I don't know what you are talking about,' I tried to object.

'I think you do,' she continued. 'John, if I move in with you, I will spend my life waiting for you and worrying about you… I don't want to spend my life worrying about you when you are gone. I don't want that, John. I want a man who is devoted to me and no one else. Not every second of every day, but most days, and most weeks. I want my man with me. My work is hard and my life is not easy… I want… no, I need the comfort and joy a family will bring, kids and grandkids. I want that life, John. And although you may say you want these things too, I know you will agree only to keep me. But you will not really mean it, not in the place in your soul which really counts, the place which makes you who you are. Because when you get a call, and you will always get a call, that call will take you away from me. You will fly away in search of what you may never find. And I will be home, John… waiting and worrying and alone. I don't want that, John. I can't have that in my life.'

'Rachel,' I pleaded.

'No, listen to me, John. You are not ready to settle down, and you may never be ready to settle down… I don't want to wait for you. I'm not going to wait for you to understand you have everything you need right here with me, now.'

'You're wrong,' I argued.

'No, I'm right. You know I'm right.'

'You don't know me. I can…' I tried to counter.

'I do know you. Don't tell me I don't know you.' She was adamant.

I looked at her, attempting to measure her will.

'You sure you want to do this?' I asked.

She answered by handing me the emerald I had given her only a few days before. 'This belongs to you,'

'No, you keep it.'

'No, I don't want it.'

I took the stone from her. I didn't know what else to do or say. The woman so exasperated me I couldn't think of one word to change her mind. She put me in a box, a box with two doors. Door one, stay here with her and do as I was told. Door two, go to Afghanistan.

I chose to go. It was my job to go. I had spent years creating a company. It was my duty to continue what I had started. She didn't understand. She didn't know what I had invested in time and energy and blood. She would never understand the sacrifice it took to build this company from scratch. Although it was no longer my day job, it was still very important to me.

'I'm sorry,' she said.

'And I'm sorry I have to go to Afghanistan.' I kissed her on the cheek, held her for a long minute until she pushed me away with a tear in her eye before turning her back to me.

I had hoped for something different. I fervently hoped we could work it out. It did not happen. She had made up her mind. I couldn't change her mind, not before I had to leave. Maybe when I got back, but it did not seem promising, not after what she said. If I had to guess, I didn't think she would take me back.

I had debated whether to stay or go ever since we talked. Even while I packed my suitcase in the morning, even as I sat on the runway in the plane, she was on my mind. Even then, I didn't know if what I was doing was what I should be doing.

As I continued to debate my sorry situation in my head, the plane turned onto the runway, its jet engines revving, screaming power while still stationary until the Captain released the brake. Pushed into the seat by acceleration, the man made contraption rumbled clumsily down the concrete runway until its wheels lifted off the ground and the shining silver, mechanical bird assumed its desired place in the universe, climbing high on stationary wings made of aluminum, bent into shapes that could ride the wind.

It was done. Decision made. I couldn't go back.

It was time to move on.

JFK INTERNATIONAL AIRPORT, 5:05 PM, JOHN

I searched for a map of the airport once inside the busy terminal building.

Normally, I don't spend much time in big airports, not any more than I have to. The confusion, long hallways, trams, elevators, signs, numbers, flights, arrivals, departures, on time, delayed; airports are a maze not easily navigated. Travel by private plane is far less complicated. But for international travel, private travel is not practical. Even though I could afford to travel by private jet, my small town, Midwestern heritage does not allow me the luxury of flying long distances in a private plane. It is just too expensive.

Charlie had promised to meet me at a restaurant at the terminal. He said he would fly in from DC because he wanted to talk to me. I had asked why he couldn't just tell me whatever the hell he wanted to say on the phone. I wasn't sure how much time I wanted to spend with him. I wasn't in the mood, not after what happened with Rachel. Plus, I assumed he was coming to talk me out of my trip, but he had insisted.

After navigating through a maze of hallways and elevators, I found Charlie sitting in a previously designated restaurant of his choice, having a beer, looking far more content than I felt.

'Hey buddy,' I pulled my suitcase next to the table and sat down.

'Hi John,' he said, dressed in his usual CIA dress uniform: white shirt, tie, and suit. He looked good, fit, and smiling. His tie hung loose around his neck, indicating, I suppose, that his day was almost over.

A waitress immediately brought me a beer after he signaled her with a wave.

'I'm not sure I want a beer,' I said.

'My treat.'

'What do you want, Charlie? I have a plane to catch. Out with it.'

'Who says I want anything?'

'You don't normally buy me a beer. I assume that means you want something.'

'You are way too suspicious, John. You would make a good agent.'

'Flattery will get you nowhere.' I smiled.

'Have a relaxing flight to New York?'

'Yes.'

'Good, because now it will get harder.'

'You aren't going to try to talk me out of going, are you?'

'No. I'm not going to waste my time trying to bore into that thick skull of yours.'

'Good.'

Charlie proceeded to hand me a small black satellite phone with instructions to call him every day and give him a report on my progress. He said I was his field agent now, which meant I needed to follow a protocol set up by him requiring one call per day. He explained the phone was a special CIA issue, encrypted so no one except high-level security personnel could hear our conversations.

I asked him if this meant I was now on the government payroll.

He said he was happy to inform me that this unadvised exercise of mine was another opportunity to serve my country, pro bono.

Thanks a lot.

Then he got serious. He told me that where I was going could be very dangerous. He said he could get me out of Afghanistan in an emergency, but only if he knew my exact location at all times. And that was why it was important for me to stay in touch daily. He asked me if I understood.

'I do.'

'No, I don't think you do, John. I don't think you have any idea.' He paused. 'Good luck, John. And remember, call me every day. I want to hear from you every day.' He got up and walked away without finishing his beer.

My plane was scheduled to depart at six-twenty pm. I took one final swig of beer and headed for the Swiss Air gate. It would be a long flight with one stopover in Europe before heading for India.

Charlie's discouraging words of warning echoed through my head as I walked the long, endless halls of the airport with all the other worried travelers.

MUMBAI, INDIA, SATURDAY, NOVEMBER 5, 4:55 PM, JOHN

Jet lag weighed heavy on my body.

It was a drag I couldn't quantify, but which I knew was real; a dulling obstruction to my mental and physical ability from which I was recovering slowly after taking several naps during the day.

One of Kamyar's men met me at the airport in Mumbai, drove me through the crowded streets of the city. A stench, smelling of open sewers, heated, humid air, and human sweat, penetrated the air-conditioned interior of the luxury Mercedes sedan as we drove slowly through the city. It seemed that nowhere was immune from utter confusion and pressing human flesh, which was in evidence everywhere I looked outside the sheltering windows of the automobile. Progress was slow, and my driver was patient with the crush of people and traffic. My host seldom spoke in broken English; he was taking me to my hotel. A room had been reserved for me. After a long eighteen-hour flight from New York with one stopover in Lucerne, he said I should rest. Someone would contact me in a couple of days.

The hotel was pleasant. The Grand Hyatt, Mumbai, was stylish to the point of excess with granite floors and furniture the color of soft earth. The lobby was defined by oversized sculptures made of polished metal, grand sloping shapes representing nothing, simply abstract forms which had no function except to occupy space and offer contrast to the high ceilings and sharp corners of the expanse. Glass partitions added ambiance in this expensive oasis in a city known for abject poverty evidenced by slums filled with people sleeping on the streets. The extreme luxury of the hotel appeared almost surreal in contrast; a virtual escape from the merciless, confusing life which existed on the other side of its doors.

The relentless activity in the city made it an exceptionally easy place to drop out of existence, to disappear from sight, to fall in with the throngs of people who occupied its streets, cursing, laughing, both courteous beyond reproach and hostile to the point of fear. It was hard to describe the city. I had never been to a place where the poor from the agricultural countryside came to find hope and a better future. They came in large numbers, too large to understand, came in a constant throng, too many for the city to deliver all of them from their despair. And yet I witnessed more smiles in this city by the sea than I could remember seeing on the streets of New York. I wondered how this could be, but I didn't have time to find out. I would be leaving soon. I had come here to disappear into the rush of this city. That's why I was in Mumbai. I had come for the same reason as most of its inhabitants.

When I met with Kamyar in Grand Haven, he explained the reason for my flying to India first. He said, I needed to disappear into the city. He didn't want anyone following me on my journey. That was as much as he would tell him, except to say, I need not worry. He would handle everything. Again, he demanded I tell no one his name or the source of his gemstones. He said if anyone discovered this information, he would have great trouble with his government, which he characterized as corrupt to the core. He said men in his country would demand what he found. A war could ensue for control of the millions of dollars of valuable gemstones, the people in his tribe had discovered. It was important that he avoid this war at all costs. He assured me the money received from the stones was for the benefit of his people.

That's what he said.

I wasn't sure I totally believed him, not the part about improving the plight of his people. I assumed he would use the funds to enrich his pockets, but this was not my business. My business was to buy and sell natural gemstones. He was my client. Unless he used the money for something illegal, it was none of my business.

His bank, the place where I wired the first payment, was in Switzerland. That was not unusual. The Swiss banking system was known for being discreet. His identity and his money would be a secret. Again, this was not my concern. As long as I could establish the gemstones were not stolen, I could deal with him. This was the reason for my trip. I had a fiduciary responsibility to my company. I was obligated to report to the board of directors concerning this new client. I needed to know that what he was telling me was true.

Locking the door to my hotel room, I headed for an elevator down to a bar in the lobby. It was time for a cocktail and perhaps a short walk in the city. The man who delivered me to the hotel had warned me not to stray too far. He said the city could be very confusing for a traveler. I didn't doubt him. I decided to skip the walk, have a drink and dinner in the hotel before another good night's sleep. Tomorrow, my journey will continue. Kamyar's man had called to say he was meeting me after lunch with the car.

He said I needed to be packed and ready to go.

SUNDAY, NOVEMBER 4:05 PM, JOHN

The chauffeur handed me a first-class train ticket as soon as I settled into the back seat of his Mercedes. The name on the ticket said, 'Steve Johnson'.

Prior to his arrival, I knew nothing of my travel plans except to be ready when Kamyar's black, four-door Mercedes sedan arrived at the hotel. The drive to the train station was conducted in apprehensive silence. The chauffeur drove through the dense afternoon traffic, deftly avoiding countless accidents; pedestrians darting into the streets, motorbikes everywhere, weaving in and around, trucks motoring with assumed invulnerability based on their immense size, obstacles everywhere. He got me to the train station on time.

'That's not my name,' I leaned over the front seat and pointed to the ticket after our car came to a stop.

He turned and handed me a passport. 'Your name is now Steve Johnson.'

My picture was on the inside of the passport. I remembered him using a camera when I was sitting in his automobile at the airport. He must have taken it for use in this new passport. According to an information sheet he handed me along with the passport, Mr. Steve Johnson was a Canadian businessman who lived in Toronto.

Kamyar's chauffeur was a man of few words, offering no explanation except to say someone would meet me on the train to help with my travel. It was time for me to get on board, he advised. Once I was outside the car, he handed me my suitcase and drove away before I could thank him.

The ticket in my hand indicated that my train was leaving at four forty pm, arriving in New Delhi at eight thirty am the next day.

4:15 PM, JOHN

A porter led me through a narrow, gray-walled hall inside the train to a reserved compartment where I would be staying for the night.

I was told dinner would be served in the dining car. He said I should have no trouble knowing it when I saw it. It was located several cars back. The food was excellent, he smiled. I should have an excellent journey on this very fine, fast train. If I needed any little thing, please push the button on the wall and he would come to my service immediately. He asked if I required anything at this time.

'Some water would be appreciated, otherwise I'm good,' I answered.

He returned very quickly with a bottle of water nestled in a bowl of ice.

I thanked him with a tip in rupees, which I had purchased before leaving the hotel, a couple of dollars' worth by my calculations.

'Thank you so very much.' The man smiled a big, broad, appreciable smile. 'Please, sir, if you are in need of anything more, I am too happy to be at your service.' He closed the door.

The compartment was clean and looked to be very comfortable with black cloth seats and a large window to the outside world. As I was stowing my suitcase under the seat in preparation for the journey, she walked in.

'Hi, my name is Amanda Johnson.' She smiled and offered her hand. 'You may call me Mandy.'

She was very pretty, not too tall, medium height, trim with straight light brown hair curling near her shoulders. Oddly, she spoke with no accent, like she was an authentic American. There was a melody in the way she said her words and a gentle, lovely rhythm to her actions. It was hard to define, simply the way she moved, with grace and confidence, almost as if she were a dancer and everything in her life was done to a song. She smiled easily as she stowed her luggage.

Wait… what did she say was her last name, Johnson, same as the last name on my passport? Before I could ask her, she sat down across from me and explained, 'I'm your tour guide for this trip. A couple traveling together raises few red flags.'

'I see,' I smiled.

'I'm an excellent guide,' she continued. 'I have lived in India for almost ten years.'

'Where are we going?' I asked.'

'First to New Delhi.'

'And then.'

'You will see.'

'So, don't ask?'

'Right, don't ask because you don't need to know.'

'Did you say that your last name was Johnson?'

'Yes, same as yours.'

'But that's not your real name, is it?'

'Is it yours?' she smiled.

'No.'

'Well then, I guess you can assume it's not mine either.'

'What's your real name?'

She looked at me. 'You don't need to know.'

'Okay.'

'Any other questions?'

'Just one. Are you my wife for this trip?' I grinned.

'In name only. Don't get any ideas, Mr. Johnson.' She smiled. 'I've been hired to assist you in your travel, not to be your prostitute. Apparently, you are a very important person to my employer… but not that important.'

'Who hired you?'

'Actually, I don't know.'

'You don't know,' I probed. 'Or you have been instructed to say you don't know?'

She looked at me. 'Either way, my answer is the same.'

'It would seem.' I smiled. 'Okay, I guess I understand the ground rules, Mrs. Johnson. It's very nice to meet you.'

'Thank you. It's nice to meet you too, Mr. Johnson.'

6:20 PM, JOHN

'Are you married?' Mandy asked with a smile. 'I mean, to someone other than me?'

The dining car wheels clicked in a constant rhythm over the railroad tracks, a repetitive beat which filled the passing minutes leisurely as I sampled the food provided on the Great Rajdhani Express Train. According to my tour guide/wife, this was a very famous train in India, well known for its lavish accommodations and speedy service. The train made very few stops along the way. It was a priority train with first-class accommodations for the very rich.

The view out our window was nothing special that evening. A gray haze in the air followed us beyond the city of Mumbai for miles into the countryside, coloring everything in muted dusty hues, colors lacking vitality. Trash was everywhere along the tracks. The population sprawl seemed to have no end in sight, extending for miles outside the city. I assumed this was a natural product of the railroad, a dense pack of civilization which developed along the tracks. Public transportation for the poor masses was an important ingredient for life in India, a function that the railroad served well. However, the railroad also attracted the ill-gotten consequences of human activity. The view through the window was not a pretty sight.

I looked away when she asked her question.

The hurt I felt from Rachel's abrupt decision to move on in her life without me, this hurt sat like a rock in my gut, still burdened by the heavy loss of Sandy's death. I briefly wondered if I should have gone out with Rachel in the first place. Perhaps I had moved on too quickly after Sandy's death, too quickly on the rebound? Was I now paying for my indiscretion? Was I guilty of not honoring Sandy by refraining from feminine contact for a more reasonable time of mourning? I didn't know. I only knew that guilt had a part to play in the equation, a part of the dead feeling that was lying on my soul.

The muted note of the locomotive's horn sounded forlornly at an intersection as my mind raced over the recent events in my life with no answer to her question in sight. The train was an express, meaning it did not stop in most of the towns along its route, passing through quickly, blowing its horn, a signal to get out of the way. The common people waited on platforms for slower trains as we passed at speed. This train was not meant for them. It was only for the elite.

A mild curry rice and meat dish was the main course, served after a soup I couldn't identify, but tasted very good. Mandy smiled occasionally as we ate, didn't say much, seemingly content to enjoy her meal in silence. I didn't push her to talk, assuming we would not be together for long.

When she asked me her question, I gave her an honest answer. 'No, I'm not married.'

'Are you telling me the truth, Mr. Johnson?' she smiled.

'I am.'

'Scout's honor.'

'Yes, scout's honor.'

'I haven't met many honorable boy scouts,' she said. 'Are you one, Mr. Johnson?'

'I am.'

'How about girlfriends, got any of those back in the states?'

I smiled. 'Oh, yes, too many to count. They recently formed a fan club to keep tabs on me.'

'Seriously?'

'Yup.'

'Now I know you're lying.'

'Really, how do you know?'

She didn't respond immediately when it became obvious that I wasn't going to give her a straight answer. 'Sorry,' she finally said, 'I was just trying to learn how to treat you.'

'Treat me like any other husband,' I replied.

'What does that mean?'

'I don't know. I've never been married.'

'Really, you don't look like the single type.'

'And what type is that?'

'Independent type.'

'Are you saying I look like the dependent type?' I laughed.

'A little,' she smiled.

'Okay, but don't all men look a little needy and dependent?'

'Are they?' she answered my question with a question.

I smiled and didn't answer, took a bite of the curry instead. I was happy the food was not too spicy. Only enough to add some flavor to the lamb.

When we returned to our compartment, the beds were made. Two single beds, one on top of the other, like in a dormitory. The constant undercurrent of clicking wheels over tracks added a measured contentment to our journey. The sound indicated steady progress to our destination. We had only to relax and enjoy our time of travel.

I asked her where she was from.

'Do you really want to know?' she answered curtly.

I looked at her and smiled. 'Look, we don't have to talk if you don't want to.'

'I don't mind,' she smiled.

She was very pretty when she smiled, which was not often. Most of the time, she was quiet — pensive, as if she had a hidden secret she didn't want to share. Something which seemed to weigh on her. Something that kept her from fully enjoying life.

'I'm from Madison, Wisconsin.'

'Why are you in India?'

'I needed to get away.'

'From what?'

'Now you are getting too personal.'

'Sorry.'

'There's a small bar in this compartment. Want a drink?'

'Sure.'

She took two bottles of wine from an enclosed cabinet and poured the contents into glasses as I watched her. Dressed in long black flowing pants and a white linen shirt open at the neck, she moved with careful precision in the rocking train car, maintaining her balance and composure as if she had done this many times in the past.

'Is this how you make your living?' I asked after she had passed me a glass of wine.

'You mean as a female escort?'

'Yes, I guess.'

'No, I'm not a professional escort if that's what you are asking.'

'So why are you doing this?'

'Because Kamyar asked me.'

'I thought you said you didn't know who hired you?'

'Did I?'

'Yes.'

'I lied.'

I let it pass, paused before asking her, 'Do you know him well?'

'I work for him. He has an office in Mumbai.'

'What business is he in?'

'I'm not at liberty to answer your question.'

The train's air horn blew, sounding in the night like a foghorn off the coast.

'Want to tell me what it's like to live in India?' I asked.

'Not really.'

'Okay, will you tell me if you are married or if you are in love?' I asked.

She had asked me. I thought it was only fair to ask her the same question.

'I'll tell you if you tell me first,' she replied. 'Remember you didn't answer when I asked you that question.'

I wasn't sure I wanted to answer her question, mostly because I didn't know the answer. I took a moment to look out the window, trying to decide what to say. Lights from windows of houses along the railroad track flashed for brief seconds in my eye, extinguished by dark blotches of passing tree shadows. Another world existed outside this train, passing quickly in the night, a world I would never know.

'I thought I was in love... Now I don't know,' I finally answered her.

Mandy took a sip of wine. 'Why is that?'

'My girlfriend and I had an argument before I left. I guess you could say we broke up.'

'Why did she do that?' Mandy asked.

'It's complicated.'

'Is it salvageable?'

'I don't think so.'

'What's she like?'

'She's a doctor if you really want to know.'

'Is she pretty?'

'Yes, she is very pretty.'

'Do you love her?'

'That's personal.'

MONDAY, NOVEMBER 7, 7:05 AM, JOHN

The gray light of a new morning peeked around the window curtains into our train compartment.

I was awake. The truth was, I had been awake for some time, unable to sleep. Dozing off and on during the night, trying to rest. Mandy was the problem. She was on my mind. I wondered if I would have enough time on this trip to unlock the mystery which was this woman. I assumed she would leave as soon as we arrived in New Delhi, when her job of escorting me was done. Someone else would take over. She told me I would be traveling by car for most of the journey. Other than this, she had not offered much in the way of information, saying only I would be told more details when the time came. I asked her if Kamyar would join me during the trip. She said no. He would meet me once I arrived in Afghanistan.

The train's horn blew. By this time, I was accustomed to its plaintive cry. It blew every minute or so at every intersection. It was the other reason I had received almost no sleep. I closed my eyes again, trying to rest. Only silence emanated from the bunk below me. Mandy was apparently a good sleeper, better than I. I was anxious to get up, but I decided to stay in bed so as not to disturb her when climbing down.

She was a very pretty lady, but it wasn't only her physical beauty that was attractive. There was a sense of mystery that seemed to surround her, some sort of melancholy coming from somewhere deep in her soul. Not that she was overly moody. She was cheerful, but in a guarded way. Almost as if she couldn't laugh. Smiles needed to be pulled from her, pulled from somewhere deep inside where laughter had been forcefully hidden for years. When she finally did laugh, her smile was engaging. However, that did not happen often, only once in a while, when she let her guard down. Her big blue eyes would crinkle at the corners, and she would actually grin; not for long, for only a few careless moments of delight which seemed to slip away too quickly. Then she would again settle into a somber musing posture, observing the world, but not really seeming to want to test the waters. Unwilling to engage in life. More content to languish around the edges without getting involved any more than necessary.

One example of her outlook on life was the way she answered my question about love.

'I'm not sure what love is,' she had replied while looking at me closely. 'Do you know what love is, Steve?'

We decided to use the names on our new passports in conversation to become accustomed to them and not slip up at the wrong time.

'I thought I did at one time,' I answered, honestly. 'Now, I'm not so sure.'

'I don't know,' she paused. 'Which means, I guess, I'm not in love.'

As I lay in bed thinking about her, thinking about her answer, thinking it was a small clue to the mystery that was this woman.

I heard her stir quietly below me.

Good, I was ready to get out of bed.

New Delhi, India, 9:05 AM, JOHN

The hustle of humanity created a crushing confusion, tightening its grip around us as we attempted to find a path through the crowd at the train station.

'Follow me,' she directed. I did, as well as I was able, having trouble keeping up with her as she expertly weaved through the crowd heading for an exit with her cell phone in her hand, planted against her ear. She was talking to someone; I didn't know who. I soon discovered it was our driver. When we arrived at a street outside the train station, a Land Rover was waiting for us. I threw my suitcase in the back, expecting to say goodbye to Mandy, but the lady got into the front seat. I sat in the back. Without saying a word, our driver put the car into gear and turned onto the street. We were on our way.

Mandy turned to me. 'Give me your passport.'

I took the book from my pocket, handed it to her as requested. She, in turn, handed me a new one, similar to the first one, except this one said my name was Steve Taylor.

'Why do I need a new passport?' I asked her.

'Steve Johnson is staying in this city. He will check into a local hotel. Steve Taylor is traveling with us. We need to be sure no one is following you. Do you understand?' she asked in a condescending voice, wondering I guess, why she was required to explain these things to me.

'Say,' I asked, because I hadn't thought about it before, '… do you have my real passport? I don't remember getting it back.'

'No, your passport is in Hong Kong, where you are. You took a flight there late last night from Mumbai, continuing your business travels.'

'So, no one knows where I am,' I said, remembering for the first time since landing in Mumbai. I owed Charlie a call. He had given me a phone with explicit instructions to call him every day. The phone was in my suitcase.

'That's right,' Mandy said without further explanation.

'Are you traveling with me?'

'Yes. Is this okay with you?' she smiled briefly.

'Of course.'

'It's my job to deliver you safely to Kamyar in Afghanistan.'

I didn't say anything; didn't tell her I was pleased. She would make my trip more enjoyable. I think she knew.

'You're now a professor from the University of Toronto, Trinity College, which has a divinity school,' Mandy explained. 'You are a professor of ancient religions. Do you think you can manage that?'

'I'll do my best.'

'Good.'

The driver said nothing during this exchange. I had no idea if he could speak English. Mandy read my mind.

'This is Ahmed,' she said. 'He will be coming with us from now on.'

This driver said nothing during this exchange, eyes straight ahead, expertly dodging traffic.

'Does he speak English?' I asked Mandy.

'Yes, you may ask him anything. He is trusted by Kamyar.'

'Okay, one more question for you.'

'What's that?'

'Are you still my wife?'

'I am,' Mandy said without smiling. 'Does this please you?'

'Yes.'

She turned towards the windshield with her back to me.

Slowly, but not without effort, our Land Rover traveled through a never-ending city filled with bumpy roads, people everywhere, buildings that were mostly nondescript, one and two-story structures, old-looking and tired, interspersed with a few new examples of modern architecture, which were exceptions to the rule. I knew I was passing by many archaeological wonders. I had read of these marvels of human imagination before flying to India.

'I don't suppose we could stop and see some temples?' I asked, making casual conversation. Our trip had already been long and boring, and we were still in New Delhi.

'You already saw them,' Mandy answered. 'Now you are on your way to Pakistan to see more.'

'How long will this trip last?'

'Two, maybe three days, depending on weather and traffic.'

She was right about the traffic in the city. It was demanding, stop and go for the most part, making little or no progress. I already wanted it to be over.

'Why don't we just fly? Wouldn't that be faster?' I suggested.

'Yes, but flying could attract attention. The sort of attention we don't need. Airport security in Afghanistan is very thorough due to the US military. Hopefully, we can slip into the country by car without anyone taking notice.'

I didn't comment, trying to adjust to the idea of a three-day car trip mentally.

'What are we supposed to be visiting?'

'Thank you for asking. I almost forgot.' She dug in her purse, handing me a list of religious sites for each country. 'Please try to memorize these in case you are asked at the border.'

I looked over the sheet. She had prepared one list for Pakistan and one for Afghanistan, mostly temples, religious sites —places an academic might be interested in visiting. I didn't think I could memorize all the foreign-sounding names on the paper. I read the first couple of sites from the Pakistan list over and over, trying to memorize them before putting the list in my pocket for future reference, hoping no one would ever ask me to pronounce names I couldn't say.

'Are we stopping along the way?' I asked.

'Yes, of course,' she turned to me. 'We need to eat.'

'How about at night?'

'We'll find a hotel. It isn't wise to travel at night in these countries.'

I didn't say anything. My physical well-being had begun to take a beating, my stomach queasy. I fervently hoped the feeling would pass quickly, thinking it was from sitting in a car for hours in the back seat. I never liked being a passenger, much less being a back-seat passenger.

The crush of New Delhi civilization eventually thinned. Cultivated fields appeared. Occasionally, a town would slow us down, some rather large, taking as long as an hour to navigate. Others were small, a few buildings at a crossroads, looking mostly the same, old buildings, brick and stone. People on the side of the road often turned to watch our car travel a highway shared with cows.

Ahmed drove mostly in silence. Occasionally, he talked softly to Mandy in the front seat, speaking in a language I did not understand.

LAHORE, PAKISTAN, 8:05 PM, JOHN

Our devoted driver and vehicle disappeared into evening traffic after dropping us at the front door of our hotel.

Bone tired from a day of travel over bumpy roads in various stages of disrepair, the king-size bed in the hotel suite looked especially inviting; big white covers, pillows fluffy and soft. The couch, in contrast, looked far less inviting, small with hard cushions. Unfortunately, it was where I assumed I would be sleeping.

Stained dark wood floors, matching cabinets, everything in our small suite reeked of luxury, not the kind of modern luxury I had experienced in my New Delhi hotel, which was more refined and traditional. However, the Heritage Luxury Suites in the town of Lahore, Pakistan, were more than adequate. Ruffled curtains were drawn over the windows.

I handed the valet a tip. He insisted on taking our luggage from us at the desk, directing us to the elevator, and opening the door to our room.

'Anything more I may do for you, sir?' he asked politely, dressed in a black and white uniform.

'No,' Mandy replied for me. 'Thank you.'

'Please be so kind as to ask for me if you are in need of anything.'

She smiled.

The exterior of the hotel was Moorish in architecture, white stucco and brick accented with gray window casings formed into pointed peaks emblematic of this style of building. Inside was no less impressive, a high-ceiling lobby in ornate reliefs of intricate design, which must have taken months, if not years, of work to build. Everything was exquisite in detail; everywhere I looked was special. But as I said, the bed was what appealed to me most. However, I did not think I would be sleeping in a bed. I was resigned to accepting poorer accommodations. Mandy would have the bed.

The border crossing into Pakistan had been accomplished without trouble. After handing the guard my passport, he asked about my business. I said I was a professor on sabbatical from Canada, traveling to fulfill obligations for my studies. He looked at me, but only briefly, before handing the passport back.

Before we stopped for the night, Mandy mentioned we were making good time. I wondered what she meant. We had been impatiently delayed numerous times along the road. I was accustomed to traveling in the US, where highways were dedicated to speed. This was not the case in India. Travel was a luxury afforded by few. The roads were for the locals, for their use, crowded by the slow flow of commerce.

As soon as we were in our hotel room, Mandy used the phone to order dinner. Although I noticed our suite contained a small kitchen, apparently, my travel guide was not in the mood to cook.

'I hope it's okay with you to eat in tonight?' she asked as an afterthought. 'I ordered dinner for us. I hope you like the food.'

'Sure, no problem. Fact is, I'm not very hungry.'

We had stopped only once after the train, a short stop along the road. Ahmed bought cheese and water at a store in the small town. Mandy mentioned it was best to maintain a low profile, never stop long in one place, always keep moving. Despite the fact that I hadn't eaten much all day, I wasn't very hungry, my stomach slightly upset from long hours of travel. My first obligation after entering the hotel was to find a bathroom. My lower intestine needed relief. I really didn't care what the hotel prepared for us to eat, just hoped the food wasn't too spicy.

She took a shower without asking, simply disappeared into the bathroom and came out after twenty minutes, dressed in a white terrycloth bathrobe, her hair tied up in a towel.

'If you wish, you can take a shower before dinner,' Mandy offered. 'I'll sign the bill when the food arrives.'

The hot water running over my tired, aching body felt great. We had been traveling now for almost two days. It was wonderful to feel clean again. A fresh pair of jeans was laid out on a table in the bathroom along with an unfolded white shirt. My carry-on suitcase didn't hold more than a few days of clean clothes. I hadn't planned to stay long, and I certainly never considered I would be traveling with a woman.

Decorum dictated that laundry service would be required soon.

10:50 PM, JOHN

Pulling the soft, white comforter up to my chin, I turned over on my side and rested under the luxurious sheets of the bed, content in a dark night while mulling over the unanticipated events of the day and evening.

Nothing had prepared me for this trip. For one thing, its duration was longer than I anticipated. I thought it might take a week at most. Now it appeared I might be gone two weeks, maybe more. I guessed I should have asked more questions before leaving. But Kamyar had been very convincing, assuring me he would take care of everything, nothing to worry about. 'Just fly to Mumbai,' he said. 'Someone will meet you there.'

It wasn't as if he had not lived up to his end of the deal. He did, but not in the way I anticipated. I assumed we would be flying together from India to Afghanistan. A physical inspection of his mine might take a day or two, no more. Then I would be flying out. That's what I thought would happen. A short trip, work done, I could return home to deal with Rachel and her accusations based on nothing but consternation.

The truth was I hadn't spent much time thinking about Rachel during the trip. Too much was ongoing, too much to see and do. Now, as I lay in close proximity to Mandy's enticing body, I felt guilty. Thoughts of Rachel roamed through my stressed brain, her smiling face, her slim body. I longed for her, wanted her, wanted to wrap my arms around her, but she was thousands of miles away. Worse yet… we had quarreled and I wasn't sure how much damage it had done to our relationship. I didn't know, and not knowing was a problem. Could our relationship be saved? Possibly, but maybe not. What she said didn't sound too positive. Not that I blamed her. I didn't blame her. Too much of what she said was true, especially the stuff she said about me. We didn't share the same goals. Maybe she was right. Maybe I wasn't right for her. Our discussion had sounded more like the end of a relationship than a continuation.

Mandy stirred under the covers. As much as I wanted to sleep, I couldn't. I lay awake wondering what tomorrow would bring. Perhaps it was the closeness of her body, the sexual tension between the two of us. It was hard not to think about Mandy when she was so physically attainable, but mentally unavailable.

Dinner with her had been uneventful, under a spell of long, quiet minutes of anxious silence. The lady made no effort to communicate, and I felt obligated to follow her lead. Which, in a way, was a relief. I really didn't have the energy.

The meal was good, nothing exceptional. I wasn't very hungry, picked at my food, eating only as much as my nervous stomach would allow.

She, in contrast, ate everything on her plate, seemingly content to consume her dinner in silence.

'You okay?' she asked.

'Yes, fine… just not very hungry.'

'Can I get you anything?'

'No, just tired.'

I slipped outside after dinner for fresh air after putting Charlie's satellite phone in my pocket when she wasn't looking. The night was cool and calm as I strolled through a dimly lit courtyard attached to the hotel, dialing his number.

'Charlie.'

'I'm here, John,' he sounded sleepy. 'Do you know what time it is?'

'No, but thanks for asking. That's why I called. I need to reset my watch, and I have no idea what time it is,' I replied sarcastically.

'Glad to be of service. It's past five thirty in the morning.'

'Thanks, but I'm more interested in what time it is here, where I am.'

'I can't tell you that, because I don't know where you are, because you haven't told me where you are, and may I add, you haven't called for several days like I asked.'

'Yes, well, I'm calling now.'

'Great, it's about time.'

'You're welcome. Anything else I can do for you?'

'Tell me where you are.'

'Lahore, Pakistan.'

'Okay, good. Now can I go back to sleep?'

'What's the problem? Is it too early for you?'

'Yes. Would you mind calling a little later in the morning next time?'

'Sure, what time would you like me to call? I'll set my watch as soon as you tell me what time it is here.'

'Enough humor, John. What's going on with you?'

I gave him a brief rendition of the last few days of my journey. He was most interested in the fact that I was traveling under a fake passport.

'Look, John, you need to stay in contact. I don't like the sound of this.'

'Why?' I asked.

'Don't know, just doesn't add up.'

Charlie always wanted to understand everything in terms of the simplest possible explanation. He didn't like gray areas. He didn't like complications. He didn't like anything he didn't understand.

He asked, 'Are you okay? Or should I get you out of there?'

'I'm okay, Charlie. Let's see how things go. If I need help, I'll give you a call.'

'John.'

'Yes?'

'Call me every day. It's important.'

When I returned to the room, I began to look through the cabinets for a blanket and a pillow for the couch. When she saw what I was doing, she said I could sleep in the bed with her.

'It's a big bed.' She smiled. 'You won't disturb me.'

'You sure?' I asked. 'Because I'm happy to sleep on the couch.'

She took her time answering. 'I'm sure,' she finally replied.

After preparing for bed in the bathroom, she returned to the room, said she wanted to sleep, and asked if I could turn down the lights. I nodded in approval. The room became dark. She took off her bathrobe. Dressed in a T-shirt and panties, she slipped effortlessly under the covers, turning her back to me.

It was my turn in the bathroom.

The night was long, my dreams anxious, my stomach not cooperating.

Sleep was a luxury that came finally, but only after time lost in worried thoughts.

TUESDAY, NOVEMBER 8, 8:10 AM, JOHN

Ahmed appeared at the appointed time.

Our Land Rover drove up to the entrance of our hotel, followed by a cloud of dust desecrating the clear morning air. Fueled and ready for another long day of travel, our driver looked implacable as ever; a picture of disdain. I began to wonder if the big Afghan did not like me.

Personally, I was not looking forward to another long day of travel with him any more than he seemed to be disgruntled with me. Regardless, I dragged the dead weight of my carry-on suitcase behind me out of the door to the hotel and loaded it in the back of our Land Rover. Mandy transported her brown leather bag over her shoulder like a backpack. Dressed in jeans and a sweater, she looked far more comfortable than I felt at the moment. Breakfast had been uneventful, not much in the way of small talk to pass the time. Coffee and some toast were all I could stomach. My gastrointestinal system was still upset. It could be something I ate on the train or in Mumbai. I had felt sick ever since getting off the train, an uncomfortable feeling in my gut which indicated I might require more than one bathroom break during the day, but apparently this was not a priority for my traveling companions. Mandy said our trip today would be long without many stops. It would take twelve hours if everything went well. If not, it could take longer. We needed to get on the road.

I dutifully took my designated place in the back seat, which was where I had been relegated the previous day. I would have preferred being up front with a better view of the road. It was possible I was merely car sick, but apparently, I wouldn't be allowed to test my theory. Mandy had already planted her sweet little butt up there. I didn't argue.

Before leaving the hotel room, I slipped Charlie's satellite phone into a hidden inner pocket in my jacket where I could get to it if I needed it. Something about what Charlie said to me on the phone last night made me cautious. We would be crossing the Afghan border during the day.

The first part of the journey through Pakistan was boring with the exception of a few hair-raising incidents when our impatient driver, Ahmed, forced our Land Rover through dense crowds of local traffic. I swear he missed several pedestrians by mere millimeters. Seemingly unconcerned with their wellbeing, he honked his horn annoyingly, barely slowed, braked only when absolutely necessary to avoid a collision. Apart from these adrenaline-generating incidents, the trip progressed as planned. Long distances were covered at speed. The road was generally good, running through flat cultivated farmland. After crossing the delta of a large river basin, we skirted a mountain ridge for miles before turning into the hills. The terrain here was more interesting than the flatlands. That was good because it was boring sitting in the backseat with nothing to see. Conversation was nonexistent except for a few words from Mandy to Ahmed, words I did not understand, even if I could hear them clearly, which I could not from the backseat. Eventually, the road exited the mountains and followed a river valley through cultivated farmland. I tried to rest, closing my eyes while ignoring my queasy stomach. Riding in the back seat of the Land Rover over bumpy roads for long hours with nothing to do was not a prescription for calming my overstressed gastrointestinal system.

Eventually, I dozed off.

'Steve.' Mandy turned in her seat. 'We're stopping. Do you need to use the facilities?'

'Ya, sure,' I replied, not fully awake.

The Land Rover needed gas. I needed a bathroom. After using the facilities, I tried to stretch my legs and clear my head. The air was cool. We were in the mountains again. I didn't feel that great, but I was getting by.

'The border to Afghanistan is not far.' She came up beside me.

'Okay.'

'You ready?' Mandy asked.

'For what?'

'The Border Patrol will ask questions. You need to be ready.'

'I'm ready.'

'Remember, I'm your wife,' she smiled.

'How could I forget?'

When it was time to get back on the road, she sat in the back seat next to me without explanation. I guess to indicate that she was my wife to the border patrol, not just my tour guide, which was what she was in reality.

AFGHANISTAN, 2:35 PM, JOHN

Gray rolling hills passed in repetitious monotony as we drove.

The scenery was treeless for the most part, consisting of rocks and dirt, with little to look at. I didn't mind. After the agonizing tension of waiting at the border crossing, the hills were a comfort even if they lacked interest. However, nothing I saw completely distracted me from a growing sensation that I had got myself into something far more complicated than I anticipated.

I wondered if my stomach was causing my anxiety or if my anxiety was causing my upset stomach. Either way, I still didn't feel very good; upset and queasy. Not to the point of wanting to throw up… not yet. I suspected I had a mild case of dysentery. That is… if there is such a thing as a mild case of this malady.

I said nothing to Mandy about my problem, simply soldiered on without complaining, hoping that my lower intestines would give me a break soon.

The border crossing guards had been agonizingly thorough. Dressed in army uniforms, our interrogators expertly searched our luggage with military precision. Every item was taken out, examined, and scrutinized before being thrown into a heap. The inside of our Land Rover did not escape their meticulous attention. They took their sweet time, checking everything. Fortunately, my passport passed muster, as did my story. Although I think they wondered why a traveling professor and his wife were entering their country by car. I was happy they asked only a few questions. I gathered my scattered personal belongings after inspection and repacked quickly so we could hit the road as soon as they nodded their contemptuous approval. It was a relief to return to the road.

'You did fine.' Mandy said while again sitting in the back seat.

'Thanks,' I replied as the hills passed into the distance. 'I didn't know it was a test.'

She looked at me. 'You okay?'

'Yes, sure. Why do you ask?'

'You seem a little edgy.'

'I'm always like this.' I smiled.

She bent down, lifted the carpet from the floor in front of her seat, and tore a Velcro-secured plastic cover off the top of a hidden compartment. Taking three handguns from the space, she gave one to Ahmed, who placed the weapon on the console next to his seat.

'Know how to use one of these?' She offered me a gun.

'Unfortunately, I do,' I replied, remembering the last time I held a gun in my hand, the night I killed a man. 'Is this really necessary?' I asked, reluctant to take the gun. After my last dreadful experience with a handgun, I had vowed to never hold a weapon again for as long as I lived.

'Yes,' she answered. 'Very necessary. These roads are dangerous. Bandits, kidnappers are not uncommon. The border patrol can be bribed. They may have alerted friends, told them easy marks were coming down the road.'

I looked out the window, searching the dusty hills for signs of life, seeing nothing. However, this did not mean the bad guys weren't there. The gun felt heavy in my hand. I immediately put it on the floor.

'You don't have to take it,' she said. 'Ahmed and I will do our best to protect you.'

'No, it's okay. I just don't like guns.'

'Why?' she asked.

'I killed a man with a gun. I don't want to ever do that again.'

She said nothing for a moment. 'It may be necessary in this country. Life is cheap.'

'I understand. I'll do my best.' I turned to the window.

Our conversation did nothing to ease my queasy stomach.

KABUL, 11:05 PM, JOHN

Convoys of trucks slowed our progress, long lines of army vehicles on the road, which were in no mood to make our lives easy.

Ahmed had a difficult time passing the trucks, especially in the hills where the roads were winding and treacherous. He did his best, avoiding potholes and fallen rocks. Looking for speed, he accelerated at every opportunity he could, but it was slow going. I was pleased when the first signs of Kabul finally came into view, but we were still a long way from our hotel. The road led down into a valley, passing through miles of rural farmland before reaching city streets filled with locals in no hurry to get out of our way. Once we were near the center of the city, the traffic became dense, making progress exasperating.

We had been delayed at the border, and roads in Afghanistan were not as good as Pakistan. All of this meant we did not arrive in Kabul until late. It was dark, but our hotel looked inviting under street lights; an elegance old building in a classic tradition of Arab architecture. However, I was primarily interested in finding a bathroom. My slightly upset and queasy intestines required immediate relief.

Entering the lobby of the hotel, I tried not to look sick, but the truth was I felt very weak.

Mandy approached the desk for the two of us. I think she sensed I was not well and took the lead. A room had been reserved for us. She accepted the key from the clerk who checked us in. A bellhop grabbed our bags and headed for the elevator. I followed, dragging my depleted body like an old, weathered suitcase. I had eaten almost nothing during the day except for a light lunch. Before crossing the border, we made a stop on the road in a small town where I had a bowl of soup, nothing more; some warm liquid. Mandy watched me carefully during the meal, finally asking how I was doing. I said okay, but I think she knew.

Ahmed seemed unconcerned. His job was to deliver us to our destination in one piece. It was a job he took seriously. His gun lay on the console of the SUV within easy reach during the trip. My health was not his worry.

Mandy warned me that once we were in Afghanistan, we would not stop for anything except gas. This was to avoid attention as much as possible. Foreigners were targets. At one point, I badly needed a bathroom break while driving in the mountains. I told Mandy it couldn't wait. Ahmed stopped the car and motioned impatiently for me to go behind some rocks. He looked nervous the whole time, standing guard by the car with his hand was on his gun, which was in his belt behind his back. He spent the whole time searching the nearby hillsides for signs of trouble in the rocks.

'Why don't you use the bathroom first to get ready for bed?' Mandy suggested as soon as the bellhop closed the door to our room.

'Do I look that bad?'

'You don't look too good.'

I normally would have insisted she go first, but I was too tired to care. Gentility was not a premium. Heading for the bathroom after a quick look around the room, this was obviously a first-class hotel. The room was large and well decorated with wood floors immaculately clean, covered by expensive throw rugs, and furnished with dark red furniture. However, it was the bed that first caught my eye, large with many fluffy pillows. Quickly washing, I changed into pajamas. Mandy had dimmed the lights by the time I exited the bathroom. The covers on the bed were turned back. Soft white sheets beckoned.

'Thanks,' I said.

'You're welcome.'

'Please feel free to sleep with me,' I offered.

'I'm your wife. Why wouldn't I sleep with you?'

I nodded, too tired to acknowledge her humor.

'You aren't contagious, are you?' she asked after watching me drag my dead-tired body into bed.

'I don't think so. Probably just something I ate.' I closed my eyes after pulling up the blankets, happy to finally be in bed after a long day on the road.

'You going to be okay?' She looked at me inquisitively.

'Hopefully, just need some sleep.' I smiled at her grimly.

I don't know when she came to bed or even if she did. I didn't remember anything after my head hit the pillow. Sometime in the night, I felt her move beside me, but I wasn't sure.

It could have been a dream.

WEDNESDAY, NOVEMBER 9, 10:25 AM, JOHN

The room was dimly lit.

It was mid-morning before I woke up. The curtains were drawn. A few shafts of light crept past the folds of the curtains, reflecting off polished wood floors and casting dark shadows over rugs beside my bed. After almost ten hours of sleep, I felt better. A quick inventory of my internal organs seemed to indicate all were up and functioning normally again, especially my stomach. Although it didn't feel completely comfortable, I felt far better than last night. Mandy was sitting in a chair by the window, reading a book. She had parted the curtain behind her, allowing enough light to enter the room, enough read the words on the pages of her book.

I sat up to take a better account of my wellbeing.

She must have heard me because she asked, 'How you doing?'

'Better, I think.'

'Good, you hungry?'

'A little,' I answered timidly, not really sure I wanted to push my gastrological system too hard, too soon.

'I'll order something,' she offered.

'Some toast and jam, please. Coffee would be great.'

We spent our day in the hotel. I never ventured outside the room, rested and ate sparingly. Mandy called Kamyar and explained the situation. She said we would be delayed a day or two. I needed to rest.

She explained to me that the journey would be harder from this point on. Hiking up mountain trails was required. I needed my strength before we could continue.

I didn't argue. Even though I felt better, I was still weak, very weak.

She left the room once for a walk in the afternoon. I told her I was fine. She could go, get some fresh air. When she was gone, I took the opportunity to step outside on the balcony and call Charlie on the satellite phone. Calling outside was a precaution. The room could be bugged.

Gray mountains loomed in the distance as I dialed his number, mountains I would soon visit. I wondered what I would find.

'Kabul?' he questioned after exchanging greetings. 'How do you like the city?'

'I don't know, Charlie,' I replied. 'I've not seen much of it except the interior of my luxury hotel room.'

'Tough duty. Remind me to give you a harder assignment next time.'

'Yea, thanks, Charlie. I'm not sure I want a next time.'

'Aren't you having fun?'

'Yes, loads of fun. Ever had dysentery?'

'No.'

'Believe me, you don't want it.'

'I have a friend in the army, a general.' Charlie abruptly changed the subject. 'We went to law school together at the University of Virginia. I think he's stationed somewhere near you. I'm going to call and ask him to keep an eye on you,' Charlie remarked, thinking out loud.

'Please, Charlie, tell him to stay in the background. Kamyar doesn't like having anyone looking over his shoulder.'

'My friend will be discreet, I promise.'

'Good.'

8:10 PM, JOHN

Golden amber distilled for the sole purpose of quieting a mind. The liquid medication gladly inhabited my glass.

I took another smooth sip, allowing the alcohol to warm my throat, settle in my stomach, and relax my anxious mind for what seemed like the first time since landing in New Delhi.

Our suite in the hotel had all the comforts of a luxury hotel, including a small sitting room and a mini bar which provided my drink. Mandy was curled up in a chair surrounded by pillows. She looked good, dressed in baggy pants and a sweater. A book was in her lap, a novel she had been reading.

I had taken several naps during the day, each nap followed by a session on the toilet in the bathroom. In total, I calculated I must have fully emptied my intestines of all remaining remnants of dreaded dysentery. By evening, I was actually hungry. Mandy ordered a steak dinner, which was mediocre by Western standards, but more than adequate for my needs. I could feel my strength returning, and this was great because I badly wanted to see Kamyar's mine so I could go home. The only exception to my desire for a quick exit from Afghanistan was Mandy. I was intrigued by the lady. She had been very kind to me, looking after my every need, something she explained was a requirement of her job. I said it was what any self-respecting wife would do for their sickly husband. A sly smile was her only tacit acknowledgment of my comment, nothing to indicate her attention to my well-being was anything more than work. The woman was a cool customer, difficult to read. I couldn't help but wonder what was really going on inside her beautiful brain. She was a mystery I wished to unlock. But I also knew it was highly doubtful I would have the time or opportunity to solve this puzzle.

I took another sip of Scotch, rested for a moment, allowing recent events to slowly drift through my thoughts. By now, it was more than obvious Kamyar had gone to a lot of trouble to disguise my identity and itinerary from anyone who might be looking. Clearly indicating that keeping the location of his mine secret was a top priority for him, and I didn't doubt its importance. His country was politically unstable, having been torn apart by various warring factions for years, including the recent involvement of the US military. Still uncertain was any semblance of peace. No one political entity had a stranglehold on power. The US military was probably in the strongest position, but they were constantly being challenged by a number of factions.

I hoped to learn more from Kamyar when we met. I didn't want my company to become a pawn in the fight for control of his country. Everything I had previously read indicated the region had not been secure for a long time, and this might not change anytime soon. It seemed war was a way of life for the people of this area, a cultural heritage which would be difficult to change.

I wondered if the generals who had counseled our previous president to invade the country, I wondered if they had advised him of this situation before the United States got involved in this tangled affair.

But that was none of my business. My business was gem sales. I had a client I needed to evaluate. That was why I was here, nothing more. Now that I was feeling better, I was anxious to get on with the job.

'Are we leaving in the morning?' I quizzed Mandy.

She put down her book. 'Do you feel well enough to travel?'

'I do.'

'You sure, because you will be climbing mountain trails in the next few days?'

'I'm good.'

'Okay, I'll make the arrangements.' She returned to reading her book, signaling our conversation was over.

'Are you going with me?' I asked for no other reason than to keep her attention.

She looked up. 'Do you want me to go?' she challenged.

'Should I?'

'Should you what?'

'Should I want you to come?' I asked.

'Well, I guess that depends.'

'Depends on what?'

'Depends on if you want me to come.'

'Do I?'

She sighed. 'You know we could do this all night.'

'I guess. Want to keep going?'

'No,' she answered.

'Okay. How do we stop?'

'You tell me if you want me to come.'

'I do.'

AKRON, OHIO, USA 11:05 AM, FRED

Fred Smith put down his phone with a big, broad smile.

He had not felt this happy in months, and to reward his newfound joy, he decided to lunch at his club.

His uppity, snobbish establishment of social egotism had not been visited by him for weeks. He didn't have the heart for going lately. Recent business problems were public knowledge, and he wasn't in the mood to mingle with the disparaging examples of human behavior he knew were gossiping behind his back. His buddies were aware that he was struggling. It was common knowledge that his business wasn't producing the boastful, gross income profits he had previously enjoyed; profits which generated annual bonuses worth millions of dollars. Recently, he had been forced to live off his salary alone. Not that his earnings were meager by common standards. He still made a seven-figure salary. But several previous spending habits had to be curtailed. A new budget limited the use of the company jet; no more pleasure trips on a whim as in the past. Now his flights were based only on business objectives. In addition, several personal residences had been sold. Their enormous mortgage payments could not be afforded. Worst of all, he didn't have a couple of million spare dollars to lavish on political causes. He was no longer a big-time, mucky muck in the Republican Party.

Life for Fred Smith had become a real downer.

But all that was about to change. Fred felt certain everything would change now. Even though the information he received would not immediately boost his business prospects, it made him happy. It was symbolic if nothing else; a sign he was destined to once again enjoy his previous stature in the community.

An army colonel had called; a man Fred had previously wined and dined to gain military contracts. This officer gave Fred some good news. He explained that being in the upper level of a general's staff paid dividends. One such dividend was being privy to classified information. Colonel Jack Raymond discovered an

American by the name of John Van Laan was in the country traveling under a false passport.

It took the colonel time to place the name. He knew he had heard it before; he just wasn't sure in what context. After doing some research, he found his answer. Mr. John Van Laan had been involved in a delicate situation which had produced dire consequences for his friend, Mr. Fred Smith.

He offered to assist Mr. Smith with his problem. Afghanistan provided opportunities not available on USA soil. Problems here could be solved quickly.

Force could be applied to undesirable individuals in lethal quantities without fear of reprisal.

KABUL, THURSDAY, NOVEMBER 10, 4:25 AM, JOHN

Sleeping occasionally during the night, I existed for long moments in worlds lost somewhere between wishful dreams and worried reality, in between periods of resting quietly in bed, waiting for morning.

The lingering light touch of her hand on my shoulder did not immediately register in my brain. As I slept with whimsical visions from the past, times when I had been touched in the night by lovers, I stirred instinctively to the feel of her hand, allowing the sensation to slowly evolve into something potentially real, while having difficulty accepting it as anything more than a pleasant dream.

She kissed me gently on the cheek and ran her hand lazily through my hair. Hesitating for a moment, perhaps wondering if she should continue... she rose up on one elbow in bed and leaned over to kiss me again; a kiss I returned while still living in a world bordering on whimsical and enchanting, a world I believed could not exist except in my imagination.

I smiled at her in the dim light coming in through our hotel windows from street lamps in the night. My mouth opened to ask a question, buried in hesitation to accept what I could not believe was real. She put her finger on my lips, disallowing my impudence. Sitting up in bed, she removed her top pajama, revealing her wonderous breasts… as if to say… is this the answer your impertinent question was wishing, an answer manifested in a shadowed image of her lovely body. I touched her nipples gently with my fingers to determine if they were real. Sitting up, I kissed her again, this time on the lips with more intensity, holding her around the waist, drawing her to me. She pushed back, withdrew slowly from my embrace, not wanting to be forced. Lying down to look up at me, she made me wait… tacitly telling me this was her decision, not mine. Wavering perhaps for a moment before deciding, she slid her panties down her long legs and lay naked on our bed, smiling as she watched me remove my bed clothing.

Kissing the soft hollow circle of her belly button, I touched her between her legs, felt her become wet and hard and irresistible to my desires. We made love slowly. The mystery which was this woman seemed content to languish for the long moments in our pleasure, to fully enjoy our time together… She made it last as if loving me was something which might never be repeated. It might be just this one time; something to be remembered when times were different, more difficult, closer to death.

We took our time.

The dawn of a new morning would arrive soon enough and with it, a difficult journey into the mountains would begin.

4:10 PM, JOHN

An early morning dream, which had existed in a luxury hotel room in Kabul, was only a pleasant memory by afternoon.

A long day of travel in a Land Rover through lush green valleys surrounded by distant mountain scenery was our duty that day. Once outside the city, the road took us through mostly identical, pathetically poor hamlets of civilization surrounded by acres of farmland. Travel became even more dismal the farther we drove from the city, pitted and bumpy roads, making our journey difficult.

As usual, Mandy sat up front with Ahmed, and I was once again relegated to the dismal back seat, alone. After our early morning liaison, I had hoped my relationship with Mandy would be different, improved, more cordial. But she acted as if it never happened. When I attempted to bring up the subject at breakfast, she simply smiled and mentioned that Ahmed would be coming soon. We needed to be ready, which was exactly what she did. She got up from the table and went to our room to methodically pack her bag for travel in silence, expecting me to do the same.

At one point during the trip, I asked her the name of the town we were passing. She said it was not important. Adding, it was probably better if I didn't know.

'Why?'

'Because then you won't be able to answer if you are asked where you traveled.'

This was her reply, brief and to the point. She didn't offer a more detailed explanation, and I didn't ask because I assumed I probably wouldn't want to know under what circumstances I might be asked a question I didn't want to answer, like perhaps when I was being tortured for the location of Kamyar's mine? But she didn't say this was the reason. I only assumed it to be true.

We ate cheese and bread in the car, didn't stop for lunch. Ahmed brought water containers for the trip, stopping only for gas and welcome bathroom breaks. Sometime in the afternoon, the flat grasslands disappeared and the road took us up into the mountains.

I had the distinct impression we were headed north. Judging by the position of the sun in the sky, I thought we were traveling northwest towards the Pakistan border, but that was a guess.

Rocky gray mountains rose high in the distance; some covered with snow on their peaks. A few of the mountains were ringed with clouds, their summits invisible to the eye. Occasionally, we encountered military vehicles. Ahmed had given me a round cloth hat, the kind used by locals, which Mandy suggested I wear while we were on the road. A traditional black-and-white patterned scarf covered her head and shoulders. She also wore a loose-fitting, non-descript tan jacket I had seen on some women in the area. I assumed my guide hoped the American soldiers who traveled the road saw us, they would take us for locals and not bother us.

After what seemed to be an interminably long journey, the road climbed up through a pass between two mountains which eventually opened into a lush green valley. A stream of clear blue water ran through the area, wide at one point, forming a small lake. A village stood beside the lake. The houses were made of gray-brown brick in various sizes and shapes, with flat roofs. Trees grew along the stream, some in autumn colors, with yellows, ambers, and golds. It was a beautiful valley, cut off from the world, shielded by mountains forming a natural walled fortress around this lost land. A few children ran beside our SUV, smiling and waving as we entered the village. Although the weather was cool, they appeared to be happy to be outside, free to run and play along the stream.

'We will be staying in this area tonight,' Mandy informed me from the front seat as

Ahmed turned up a side street between houses onto a dirt road which climbed a hill for about a mile, leaving the village behind. Two similar-looking SUVs to ours, had joined us, following for the last several miles of our trip. Ahmed didn't seem to be concerned about them.

Our convoy approached a gate near the top of the hill, which automatically opened slowly as we waited. A black wrought iron fence extended from the gate, circling around the perimeter of the property, which included several acres of land. All three vehicles drove through the gate to a brick driveway several hundred yards long, which led to a large brown, stucco home at the top of the hill. Trees dotted the grounds. Cultivated gardens near the house were filled with colorful autumn flowers.

Our Land Rover stopped at a stone walkway leading to the front door of the house. Mandy and Ahmed opened their car doors without comment. I followed their lead. Several men exited the two vehicles behind us, standing silently at a distance of several yards. Dressed in army uniforms, two of them carried automatic rifles. The others had pistols in their belts. Neither Ahmed nor Mandy paid any attention to them, and I didn't ask, assuming they were security guards.

Two large varnished wood doors gave entry into the interior of the house. A man greeted us inside the entrance, taking Mandy's bag from Ahmed, who silently returned to our vehicle and drove away as we were entering the house.

After a brief conversation with Mandy in a language I did not understand, the doorman led us down a front hall. The floor was wonderfully polished stone, and the walls held artwork of local drawings and sculptures. We passed a large room at the end of the hall, furnished with cloth-cushioned furniture and wooden tables surrounding a large stone fireplace; following our guide without stopping, down another hall filled with closed doors until we came to an open door at the end where Mandy thanked the doorman in his native tongue. He bowed and closed the door after we entered the room.

Unlike the hotel room we had left in the morning, our accommodations in this house were a suite of several rooms, including a small sitting area with a couch, a desk, and chairs. The curtains over the windows were open to an expansive view shared by the main room of the house, filled with pastures and orchards. Throw rugs covered the stone floor, just like what I had seen in the lobby.

'Do you need to use the bathroom?' Mandy asked.

'You first,' I responded.

'Thanks.'

6:10 PM, JOHN

I didn't know what I was drinking, but the reddish liquid in my glass tasted very good, smooth and warming my soul.

I assumed it was a local wine. Mandy told me the name, but I forgot it as soon as I took one drink, immediately aware this pleasurable brew was loaded with high potency. I sipped the liquid sparingly while sampling a plate of sweet breads which had been placed on a table near the fireplace in the main room of the house for our enjoyment.

House was not the right word to describe this place. Compound might be a more accurate term. Several structures, some attached, some separate. All the buildings were built in close proximity to each other on top of a hill. They shared the same flat-roofed architecture and the same stucco colors, common features giving the structures a uniform look, an obvious influence of what I called Persian décor, which dominated the houses in the valley. However, this compound was distinguished by ornate carvings which set it apart from houses in the village. A few of the buildings on the hill looked to be relatively new, while others appeared to be very old, but well maintained.

The building we occupied was very clean and well-kept. A wood fire burned in the large stone fireplace, warming the room. Cushioned furniture placed in front of the fire made it a comfortable place to rest.

'How are you doing?' Mandy asked.

Dressed once again in typical western clothes, a sweater, and jeans, the lady looked good. Her light brown hair was neatly combed. Minimum makeup had been applied. The black and white scarf she wore in the car to cover her head was missing, along with the traditional loose-fitting coat, which made her appear to be a local.

We had rested from our travels in our suite before being summoned to the main area of the compound. She informed me that we were invited for pre-dinner drinks. Dinner would be served afterwards. Please be ready. I put on the only pair of clean jeans and clean shirt I found in my luggage, assuming I would be meeting Kamyar's family. However, contrary to what was envisioned, it was just the two of us for drinks. The man who greeted us at the door served us the special drinks along with the tasty pastry. I had the feeling many people occupied the buildings in the compound, but at that moment, Mandy and I were alone in a large room, which made it feel almost uncomfortable.

'Will anyone be joining us for dinner?' I finally asked.

'No,' Mandy replied. 'When we were in Kabul, I told Kamyar you would probably need a couple of days to get well. He went away for business and will not return until tomorrow. He apologizes for not being here to greet you.'

'I understand,' I said. 'How soon will I get to see the mine?'

She paused before asking. 'Did you enjoy your journey?'

'Yes, except for a mild case of dysentery.'

'That wasn't my fault,' she replied.

'No, that was not your fault.'

'I tried to make it up to you.'

'I'm not complaining,' I replied, remembering last night.

'Good. Please tell Kamyar I did a good job as your tour guide.'

'I can do that.'

She was silent for a moment.

'Look,' I interrupted. 'I understand his reasons for taking me through India to get here. But it took a long time, and now I would like to get on with my work.'

'Are you in a hurry to leave?' she smiled.

Now that was a loaded question. She had been very kind to me, and I was grateful; Lord knows I was very grateful. But I was under the impression that what happened was not meant to be anything more than a welcome reprieve during a long and arduous journey. Okay, so if that was true, then why was she now asking why I was in a hurry? Was she really asking why I didn't want to stay longer to be with her? I didn't know, and she was very difficult to read. I literally had no idea why she asked her question, and more importantly… I didn't want to answer her in a way that could be misinterpreted, especially if I was wrong about why she asked. Because if she really wanted me to stay, to spend more time learning more about the mystery that was this woman, I was truly tempted.

Truth was, I had no answers for the questions that were roaming freely through my brain.

Finally, I said, 'No, I'm not in a hurry.'

AKRON, OHIO, FRIDAY, NOVEMBER 11, 7:35 AM, FRED

'Yes,' Fred Smith answered his phone.

'Got some good news for you. We know where he is,' the caller explained.

'Where?'

Fred's phone had rung when he was home. After looking at the caller ID, the number was a Washington, DC number, a pass-through number he knew was used by troops in Afghanistan.

'I could tell you the name of the village,' the caller explained. 'But it wouldn't mean anything to you. Let's just say it's a village in the mountains in the north close to the Pakistan border.'

'Okay.'

'So, what do you want me to do about him?'

'I want my problem eliminated,' Fred answered succinctly.

'You sure?'

'Yes, I'm sure,' Fred's voice exhibiting a high degree of exasperation.

'You don't care how?'

'No, I don't care.'

'Okay. I'll handle it from here once your money shows up in my bank account.'

'This can never lead back to me.' Fred needed to be certain.

'I promise, the money is untraceable. Wire it by bank draft to my account in the Caymans as we discussed.'

'Are you absolutely sure?' Fred asked again. 'How about this phone call? Is the Pentagon monitoring these calls?'

'No, it's not an official call. It's private and it's encrypted. Even the CIA can't break our codes.'

'No recording is being made.'

'No, you have my word,' Colonel Jack Raymond answered.

mark

AFGHANISTAN, SATURDAY, NOVEMBER 12, 3:35 AM, JOHN

One thing I have noticed from traveling to many places on the globe is that night sounds are different everywhere you go.

This place, this house on a hill, where I was staying, was no exception. It was out in the country, where it was very quiet, unlike the constant background buzz of busy city streets which discourage the natural calls and cries of nature. As I lay awake, I could hear the plaintive cries of animals, like a coyote's long, solitary cries echoing from one end of the valley to the other.

She lay quietly next to me, apparently sleeping soundly, undisturbed by the animal sounds.

I had been pleasantly surprised when she crawled into my bed. The house was large. I assumed it contained many bedrooms. The pretense of being my wife, the manufactured lie which had accompanied us on our journey, I could think of no reason to continue in this charade. Now that we had arrived at our destination, our contrived drama should not have been necessary. She could have slept anywhere she wanted. She was an intelligent woman, and yet she had chosen to sleep with me in my bed.

I did not object.

We dined earlier, the two of us, no one else. Our meal was brought to us by the only person we had met in the compound, the man who had greeted us at the door. The food was good, a local dish consisting of lamb and rice with a green bean vegetable, served with wine. Although unusual in flavor, it was very good. Fortunately, my stomach disturbances were behind me. I was hungry. The dinner was enjoyable except for one item, an uncomfortable silence hovering over our meal like an undesirable guest.

Mandy was unusually quiet, said nothing unless spoken to. When I ventured to ask her a question, she would reply with a succinct answer delivered in one or two lines before falling silent again, eating her meal slowly, contemplatively, almost delicately.

My habit has always been to eat quickly. I was finished long before her. And when I was done, I had nothing to do except watch her.

'Do you want another portion?' Mandy looked up, noticing my plate was empty. 'I can have another plate brought for you.'

'No, I'm full. Thank you.'

'Do you want anything else?'

'No, I'm happy to sip my wine and watch you eat.'

She thought about this for only a second, 'Please don't do that. I don't like it when men stare at me.'

'You know you are very beautiful. You've probably had this problem before.'

'Yes, and I don't like it. I prefer to be appreciated for other things than the way my face looks.'

'Like what?'

'Like what I have done with my life.'

'Like to share?' I asked.

She looked at me inquisitively. 'Do you really want to know?'

'I do.'

'Okay, I was a very good student and I can speak several languages.'

'That's a good start. What else?'

'That's enough for now.'

'And it's none of my business,'

'Yes, none of your business, Steve.'

'You do know my name is John,' I countered.

'I know, but for this trip, you are Steve.

'Okay, I'll be Steve if that's the way you want it,' I said with a smile. 'Does this mean you are still my wife?'

'As long as it's necessary.'

For some reason, the night was long. After getting into bed, I couldn't sleep. I was restless, turning over often. Perhaps it was being in a strange place, not of my choosing. I didn't know where I was. All I knew was that I was somewhere in the mountains in a strange country. I began to wonder if getting out of here would be as much of a problem as it was to come here. I couldn't think of another time in my life when I was in a place where I couldn't conveniently get to an airport and leave any time if I chose.

Well… that wasn't exactly true. A flood had once swept me down an isolated river valley in Thailand. I had to hike out on foot, which took days. Perhaps this memory was what made me uneasy, being in the mountains again with no obvious escape route, none within my control. Perhaps this was what made my current experience feel difficult. It brought back too many unpleasant memories. I didn't like the thought of being dependent on others for my survival. I didn't like being in this situation. It weighed on me, a source of uneasy concern which had no immediate reason for worry. At least none that I knew of. Nevertheless, it bothered me and it reminded me I owed Charlie a call.

He had been on my mind, but an opportunity to call him had not been available. I knew I owed him a call, but she had been with me constantly, except when I was getting cleaned up for dinner in the bathroom, and I didn't want to risk a call then. She could have overheard me. The walls were not thick. I couldn't take that chance. As a result, Charlie didn't know where I was, and even if I called him, I didn't know what I could tell him. I couldn't tell him where I was because I didn't know, just somewhere in Afghanistan in the mountains. And that wasn't much information, not enough for him to get me out in an emergency.

I was on my own.

I turned over in bed as my mind strayed from one overanxious, worrisome thought to another without a break in the action. My constant restless agitation must have disturbed her. Sliding over, she rested against my side for warmth. We lay together in silence for long minutes as the night whispered to me through the mournful calls of the animals I heard in the darkness, love songs from outside our walls, evidence of life and longing which are a common thread for all of us who live on this small planet.

I was drawn to her, ached to make love to her again.

Perhaps anticipating my need, she whispered, 'John, I'm alone too many nights when I wish I had someone who would hold me, just hold me quietly so I can go to sleep without fear.'

I did as she asked, held her, and rested, feeling her warm, round, luscious body while wanting her in the worst way. But I did as she asked, I held her, nothing more, resting in the night with her body in my arms, strangely comforted by this mystery of a woman.

In time… the night closed in and I fell into an unconscious dark place where I finally slept without dreaming.

8:10 AM, JOHN

The light of a new day arrived late that morning after rising slowly over a mountain peak in the distance, casting a broad, steady stream of warm sunlight through the windows of the bedroom.

I was alone.

She must have slipped quietly out of bed before I woke up, dressed, and left the room for me to occupy in peace. I showered, shaved, and dressed in jeans and warm clothes, wearing a long-sleeved shirt under a sweater, unsure of what the day would require.

Wandering down the hall, I followed the smell of cooking food. Breakfast hopefully, I was hungry.

He was sitting with her when I came into the room, talking quietly at the table by the window where we ate last night.

Outside the window, long fields of rolling grasslands were interrupted by a range of steep rocky mountains, riding high into a clear blue sky to greet a few lazy clouds that lingered near their summits.

He rose when he saw me, Kamyar extended his hand.

Remembering instantly what I liked about this man, it was his smile, his greeting card.

'Professor Johnson,' he grinned. Mandy tells me your first name is Steve.'

'Yes, that's also what she tells me.' I returned his smile and shook his hand.

'Welcome to my village, Steve,' he said. 'Or should I call you Mr. Van Laan?'

'John, would be fine.'

'Of course, John. Please sit.'

'This is a beautiful place,' I took a seat at the table.

'It is very special in the summer. The fruit from the trees is sweet, and flowers are in bloom.'

'Sounds wonderful,' I replied.

'Good, next summer, you will have my invitation.'

'Thank you.'

'Now, let me ask you. Is there anything you would wish? It is very important to me that you are comfortable. Hospitality to strangers is important in my culture.'

'Not at this time.'

'Was Mandy helpful in your travels?'

I grinned. 'Yes, she has been very kind to me.'

'Good. I am very pleased to have you here as my guest.'

'It is good to be here.'

When he paused, I asked, 'When will we see the mine?'

'All in good time, John. First, it is important that I show you my valley. We will go to the mine in the afternoon.'

'I'm anxious to see your mine,' I replied. 'That's why I came.'

'I know, and your journey has been long.'

'Yes, it was.'

'It was necessary,' he offered as an explanation.

'I understand.'

'Good, now you must eat some food so we can get started. You will find the clothes you need in the closet in your room. Put them on, including the soft cloth hat. It is important no one knows I have an American with me today.'

'Okay.'

'And please, wear sunglasses. The color of your eyes may give you away.'

'Okay.'

'Do you have sunglasses?'

'Yes.'

9:45 AM, JOHN

Two armed men walked ahead of us, two others behind, carrying automatic weapons.

They made me very uncomfortable.

Kamyar was dressed no different than other men, in clothes similar to what he had given me to wear. With the exception of a turban wrapped around his head covering his short, dark black hair, he wore the same loose-fitting blousy shirt under a jacket and equally baggy pants made of off white cotton material, traditional clothing of the area. Seemingly unconcerned by the presence of any threat to his life, he stopped often to talk in his native tongue to villagers who greeted him, joking sometimes, smiling. Other times, he looked concerned, his eyebrows narrowed, his lips tightened, he spoke slowly with compassion, taking his time to explain what was obviously important to people who sought his attention. Not all of his conversations appeared to be congenial. Sometimes the tone of the discussions sounded more like an argument than a meeting of like minds. His body language gave him away. Sometimes stern, his back remained straight and tall; he never wavered in his demeanor, never backed down, never walked away from anyone who was talking to him. Everyone except one man, a long-bearded, dirty-clothed man who spoke softly, said something sounding more like a slogan than a greeting. Kamyar looked him in the eye, wished him a Muslin greeting, said something very straightforward before walking away from the man without further comment.

We traveled on foot; our SUVs were parked after they dropped us off at the village.

Ahmed had been our driver down the hill to the village from Kamyar's home. However, he did not walk with us. Occasionally, I saw him during the day, never near, but close enough to keep an eye on his boss from a distance. I wondered how many men Kamyar had in the town looking after his welfare.

As we walked, Kamyar explained that he was the head of his clan, responsible to the people who had occupied this village and several others in the valley for many generations. He said his position was not official. It was more ceremonial and traditional, rooted in ancient customs and the traditions of ancient tribes, for which he was the rightful ruler, a position that granted him vast tracts of land and wealth. However, his position was not recognized in Kabul, but this mattered not to him since he did not require the support of dishonest politicians to justify his rights. That was what he said. He needed only the trust of his people, and he earned their trust by judging them with compassion and intelligence. Only then did he deserve his position. He said he had worked hard to gain their approval.

I listened without comment. I was not here to judge the man. I was here as a buyer, a businessman wishing to do business. His position in this village was his affair, not mine.

He admitted that not everyone accepted him. Along with politicians in Kabul, there were other men who wished to control these valleys. The Taliban in the area had for many years attempted to gain a foothold. So far, he had been able to keep them out. He said he had accomplished this by sharing his wealth with his people. He was Muslin. He ruled in the name of his God. He said he ruled with the Koran as his guide. The Koran instructed him to be generous. However, not all religious leaders in the area liked him. Some favored the Taliban, wanted him removed, dead, even. His job had been extremely difficult in recent years, but he had diligently resisted. He did not want his valley to suffer as others had suffered under the rule of the Taliban. Fortunately, his remote region of the country had been an exception. To date, his people had chosen him over the Taliban.

The American military seemed to have a different opinion. Apparently, they did not understand how he had been able to keep the Taliban out. They feared he had joined forces with the enemy. He knew they didn't trust him, considered him a potential enemy, but without evidence to justify their opinion, they had left him mostly alone, however, not without warning him of the consequences if he were found to have collaborated with the Taliban. They made this very clear.

I had no way of knowing if he was telling the truth, none except to witness how he acted when he was with villagers, and what I saw was encouraging. They appeared to like and respect him. All except the dirty man with a long beard who had accosted him verbally.

We visited a school in the village. Students were active in their classrooms, even on a Saturday. A young girl, perhaps seven or eight years old, greeted him with a smile. He patted her head gently, said something to her in his native language. Her big, dark eyes glistened with pride as he talked to her. She turned and headed into a schoolroom.

I asked him what he said to her.

He told her to do well, study hard. It was important that she learn to read and write.

He explained, both boys and girls were educated in this school. That made the Taliban angry. They did not think girls should be educated. They considered women subservient to men. Kamyar said they were ignorant fools. He had insisted that his school teach girls as well as boys. Even though some of the elders in the village had disagreed with him, he had prevailed.

God wanted all his children to excel. This is what he said to people who disagreed with him. It was his opinion that if the village was to grow, it needed women doctors and engineers. The valley could not prosper unless all of God's children contributed to its future when they were grown.

Ignorance breeds distrust and hate, he told me. It was very important that all of his people were educated. The best students were sent to schools of higher education in other lands, but not many, because it was very expensive. He paid for their education.

A small hospital in the village served the needs of the people. It was staffed with one doctor and several nurses. It was not adequate to help all the people in the village, but it was a start. He said he wanted to build a bigger hospital as soon as possible. Some of the money from gem sales would be put to this task. This was the reason his work with me was important.

I asked him where he received his education.

He had been very fortunate. His grandfather had sent him to a university in England. He had returned to his village because of his love for his valley. However, not all the students who went away to school returned. Some remained in the country where they received their education. His brother was one of those. He now lived in the USA, near Detroit, Michigan.

Kamyar had been staying with his brother the day he visited me in Grand Haven.

2:05 PM, JOHN

After lunch in the village, we drove into the mountains in a caravan of three vehicles, traveling long and twisting two-rut trails, sometimes perched perilously close to the edge of rock walls where the mountain fell several hundred yards to deep, stone-cluttered gorges.

The last miles were accomplished on foot. It took time and effort. The trail was steep in places, a stone-marked trek up a high mountain. If you didn't know the area, it would have been easy to become lost forever. Fortunately, I was with men who seemed to know where they were going. We stopped often and I began to think Kamyar did this for my sake. He knew the air was thin, and he was concerned that I was unaccustomed to the altitude. The truth was I was grateful, although I was anxious to see the mine. I rested when I could, sipping water from bottles his men carried in backpacks.

From time to time, Kamyar would scan the skies as if he were afraid someone was tracking him in a plane. Fortunately, we saw no one; only hard rock walls, a few short trees, and very little vegetation. Below us was a valley surrounded by mountains which rose into a blue sky. I was happy the weather was cooperating. Although the air was cool, the sun was warm as we made our way up the mountain.

Several times, Kamyar mentioned we were getting close. It is not far now, he tried to be encouraging. Then we walk again for another half hour, climbing ever higher. I began to wonder if we would ever reach the mine. At one point, I thought I might have to ask Kamyar for another rest. My leg muscles were rebelling, strained, and cramping. Breathing heavily with each step, I inhaled deep breathes of the thin air, working hard to keep up with these men who were accustomed to walking at this altitude. But I said nothing, didn't want to appear soft. My body slowly deteriorated with each step more difficult than the last.

When I feared I could go no farther, when I was almost ready to give in and tell Kamyar I was done, couldn't take another step…

a cave, an insignificant dark hole in the side of the mountain, appeared about fifty feet up the trail from us. Nothing appeared to be unusual, nothing indicating this was the place, nothing which held promise we were finally at our destination and I could rest. A man, his clothes dirty, came out of the hole in the mountain, appeared in the sun, and waved at Kamyar, who returned his greeting.

'How are you doing, my friend?' Kamyar turned to me.

'Fine,' I lied.

'The mine is in that cave,' Kamyar explained. 'I hope you are not afraid of going inside the mountain.'

'No,' I lied again.

'Good.'

3:25PM, JOHN

In the artificial light, the green gemstones sparkled from quartz-ankerite-pyrite veins in the walls of the cave.

A series of lights powered by a rumbling outside diesel generator lit the cave. In the light, the gems were easy to see, numerous in quantity, and of good size. It was simply a matter of chipping the stones out of the walls of the cave, taking wealth from the mountain, careful not to damage the stones.

Emeralds are delicate gemstones. Fissures, small imperfections in the stones, make them vulnerable to breaking if a miner is not careful. About ten or more men worked the mine with hand tools. They used no dynamite, no big axes, took their time to release the valuable stones, one at a time, from a place where they had been held captive for thousands of years, ever since their formation in the bowels of the earth. Driven up towards the surface when the mountain rose high into the sky, they had remained in this dark place where no light could show their elegance. Not until now, when miners found them and cut them free.

Kamyar said nothing during this part of the journey. He simply let me look around, watch the work, fascinated by what I saw.

'Do you have any questions?' he finally asked.

'How did you discover the mine?'

'While walking the trail, a villager sought shelter from a coming storm,' he explained. 'The man was driven inside this cave when a bolt of lightning struck close to the opening, lighting the walls in a million green flashes of light. He knew what the green stones were. Every Afghan in this area is aware of these green stones.'

'And how did you get involved?' I asked.

'He was a poor man. He knew he needed help. He came to me with his discovery because he trusted I would not cheat him.'

'I see.'

'That is him,' Kamyar pointed to one of the men who seemed to be directing the other miners.'

'He must be a very rich man,' I observed. 'Why is he working?'

'Work is important to every Afghan. He finds fulfillment in his work. He enjoys coming here every day. Plus, he does not want to be cheated,' Kamyar smiled.

'And what is your part?'

'I am his partner. We work together. We have an understanding.'

I looked around again, watching the work continue. It was hard work, the men were dirty, the air was polluted with dust, even though a large fan turned constantly, pushing the dirty air out of the mouth of the cave. I was satisfied. I didn't need to see any more. Everything verified what Kamyar told me. The mine was real, the stones genuine. I was ready to return, knowing I had a long walk ahead of me, retracing my steps down the mountain, perhaps a more difficult task than climbing.

A man approached Kamyar and whispered to him. Kamyar immediately headed towards the entrance to the cave. I stayed behind, fascinated with the work. One of the men handed me a particularly large stone, which he had cut from the face of the rock wall. It was beautiful. I knew someday it would be cut into a gemstone that could be worth thousands of dollars. I was very impressed. I returned the stone to him.

Kamyar came back, his face ashen in the stark bright lights. 'Come outside,' he directed me. 'I have something I need to tell you in private.'

In silence, we made our way carefully out the rock-walled cave toward sunlight.

Once outside, he spoke quickly, concern in his voice, 'I'm sorry, but I must go. I cannot stay here with you. I must return to the village. There has been a tragedy. I must return immediately to help.' He seemed very upset, not like his usual calm, businesslike composure.

'My men will help you return. I will see you at my house tonight,' he turned, heading down the trail at a rapid pace with several of his guards in pursuit.

6:45 PM, JOHN

Hiking down the mountain seemed to take far longer to navigate than going up.

Perhaps because I was already dead tired from climbing. Or maybe because going down a mountain trail is often more difficult than going up. I had to constantly look down, stepping carefully to avoid turning an ankle on a loose stone. The walls of the mountain steepened as we descended, becoming more perilous.

My guides did not speak English. They didn't complain when I had to stop along the trail to catch my breath and drink some water. They simply waited patiently, continuing when I could find the strength to go again, showing me the way, one man in front and one behind. The journey became torturous at times, taking too long and requiring excessive caution, as I felt my legs weaken, knowing I would sleep well that night.

As we continued, I wondered what had drawn Kamyar to leave in a hurry. He said something about a tragedy, but he did not explain. It could be anything. It did no good to speculate. I assumed he didn't tell me because it didn't concern me. Still, I wondered.

Finally, our SUV appeared at the bottom of the walking trail. I took the front seat, breathing a sigh of relief. Ahmed started the car. He had waited for us. As he drove, the curving mountain roads receded in the distance. Ahmed made good time driving the dusty, rutted roads through low rolling countryside paralleling a stream leading to the village. Traffic was unusually light as we approached the lights from the village in the evening. Very few people were on the road. Arriving in town, it was not immediately apparent what had occurred. Not until I saw a wall, which I thought I remembered was attached to a building. A broken wall, standing alone as a monument to what had been. The identity of the building did not come to me at first, not until I saw school books scattered across the road. That's when I knew.

Dried blood marred the surface of the wall, staining its sides as if someone had thrown the life-giving liquid at the wall as a sign of what happened here. Bricks and glass lay scattered across the ground, books and desks, and the remains of a window frame littered the main road of the village.

It was almost dark.

The sun had guiltily retreated from the anguish it witnessed, hid behind a mountain as if it did not wish to look down at the tragedy we saw as we drove slowly past the school.

The memory of this day will never leave me.

More than anything, I am haunted by the sound of wailing riding the wind. The pitiful agony from mothers crying over the remains of their dead children. Men, their clothes stained with blood and dirt, wearily worked, searching for signs of life in the debris. By the time we returned to the village, the little bodies of the school children, those who had survived the blast, had been taken to a hospital. The less fortunate had been carried to a makeshift morgue.

'Can I do anything to help?' I asked Ahmed.

'No,' he replied. 'Kamyar said to take you to the house.'

This was one of the few times he had ever talked to me. I didn't reply, just looked out my window as we slowly drove past the scene.

'He wanted you to see this,' Ahmed informed me.

'Where is he now?'

'He is at the hospital helping with the injured children.'

'I want to help.'

'No,' Ahmed said. 'When they see you are a foreigner, they may think you brought this destruction.'

'Why would they think that?'

'Because your country has brought much destruction to us,' he said without explanation.

'Stop the car,' I demanded. 'I don't care what they think. I'm going to help.'

'No,' Ahmed stated emphatically.

'No one will know who I am,' I protested. 'It's getting dark. They can't see my eyes.'

At Kamyar's request, I had dressed in the traditional clothes of the area. I was reasonably confident that apart from my face and eyes, nothing indicated who I was or where I came from.

'No,' Ahmed said again. 'Kamyar told me to take you to the house.' He continued driving, ignoring me.

Debris, bricks, and rocks blown into the road from the force of the blast lay strewn across the road, forcing him to slow down and turn. I took the opportunity to open the door and jump <u>out of the vehicle</u>, returning to the place where I had seen men working.

The area was a mess. Among the rocks and bricks from the school building, body parts, little hands and legs; a torn and twisted face with half the skin missing. Watching other men for direction, I followed their lead without saying a word, did what they were doing, placed the human remains on bloody sheets. The rubbish was tossed into piles behind the stone wall. As we worked to clean the debris from in and around the school, tears fell from my eyes as I labored in silence.

Lights arrived to facilitate the work as darkness fell over the gruesome scene. Everyone continued, mostly in silence. No one in the village wanted the dawn to awaken to this disastrous scene, making it even more difficult for the parents of children who had been injured and killed in the blast. No one wanted this memory to linger in their minds forever.

Ahmed came to help, whispering to me in English so no one could hear us talk. When I was addressed by another Afghan, I simply nodded and kept working, too broken to speak. Everyone understood. We worked in silence. We worked until dawn. Even though I was dead tired when I arrived in town, despite the hike into the mountains having drained my strength, I found a reserve of energy to keep going, to keep working. My back ached, my legs felt like stone, and my mind was unable to comprehend the depth of this tragedy.

When dawn finally appeared over the mountains, Ahmed shook my arm as if he were trying to wake me from a trance.

'It is time we go,' he demanded. 'Soon they will be able to see your eyes.'

I didn't want to leave. I wanted to stay, to find some peace with the men who had been my companions through the night, brought together by a tragedy of unimaginable horror. I wanted to tell them I shared their despair. But I knew I could not. This was not my village. These were not my children. They would not understand. I followed Ahmed to the car, feeling nothing but despair.

When we returned to the house, I took a shower, washed my hands, washed them again and again, trying to somehow wipe the tragic stains of dirt and blood from my mind.

· SUNDAY, NOVEMBER 13, 5:10 PM, JOHN

Once again, I entered a river in Thailand.

Once again, as I had done so many times in tortured dreams, I relived the memory from my past, swimming in a madly flowing river down a mountain. Once again, I saw dead and dying villagers floating beside me in a raging river which had overflowed its banks after a dam collapsed, draining the river, destroying a village, flowing down through rocky ravines in a savage desperate desire to empty its watery burden into the sea where the bodies could slowly disintegrate; evolving into the life of the sea to again become a function of life, not death.

Unfortunately, this symbolic act of cleansing was not possible at the school.

Nothing like when a river was available to sweep away the evidence of a great tragedy. It was up to us to clean, to hide the evidence of tragedy from sight as much as possible. We had worked through the night, doing what we could. But we could not do enough. It was impossible to accomplish our task, not completely, not ever completely. It would take months of rebuilding to bring back the school building. And the children who had died, no one could ever return these children to their community, to their parents. Nothing could take away their loss, obliterate their memory except time. And it would be a long, long time, if ever… maybe never… before the people of this village would forget what happened.

Waking from my nightmare, the events of the previous day painfully greeted a new day, or what was left of it. It was afternoon before I finally woke up. Straining to get up out of bed, my body rebelled with every attempt to test my capabilities. I moved slowly, aching and dull. I showered again, shaved, and dressed, attempting as much as possible to look presentable before heading down the hall leading to the main room of the house, looking for Mandy and Kamyar.

They were seated by the window, talking softly to each other.

Kamyar stood when he saw me. 'Ahmed told me what you did,' he said. 'I want to thank you.'

'No need, I had to do something,' I replied, reliving the night in my mind. 'I hope I didn't cause you a problem.'

He looked at me carefully as if he was seeing me for the first time. 'No. I don't think anyone knew who you were.'

'Good.'

'Sit down, John. Can I get you something to drink?' he asked.

'Yes.' I was suddenly very thirsty.

The man who had previously served dinner appeared on cue, brought a soft drink. I sipped it slowly.

'Are you okay, John?' Mandy asked, using my real name.

'No, I'm not okay,' I replied, finding some reserve of energy to express my anger. 'I don't understand what happened?'

'The Taliban, a suicide bomber did this,' Kamyar said with disgust. 'They don't like our school. They have been threatening to blow it up for months.'

'But why? Why children? Why kill children?'

'I think I told you they don't think we should be teaching girls, and the boys should not be taught anything but the Koran.'

'You defied them by operating the school.'

'Yes,' Kamyar said. 'But I believe God wants all his children to excel, all of them, including girls.'

'They disagree.'

'Yes, they disagree.'

'And they expressed their disagreement by blowing up your school, including the children.'

'Yes.'

'Unimaginable,' I replied.

'This is a different world,' Mandy tried to explain.

'Is it that much different?' I asked.

No one spoke. I sipped my soft drink, feeling the ache in my shoulders and a pain in my head.

'Will you go after them?' I asked.

'The men who bombed the school?' he questioned.

'Yes.'

'Who are they, John? Who are the men who did this? Who is responsible? The men who planned this crime or the men who spread lies that motivate men to do this crime? And what would I do if I found them?'

'I don't know; have every one of them hanged for killing your children.' I was angry. The images of the children's torn bodies ran through my mind, all the dripping blood, the body parts, the dusty destruction. I wanted some resolution for what I had witnessed.

'You are not listening to me, John,' Kamyar explained patiently. There are many men who spread lies and violence. Do I kill them all? Do I kill every cleric who spreads lies which lead to violence? And what would happen if I did? Wouldn't this lead to an escalation of the violence, cause other men to seek revenge for what I did. No John, I have no solution to this problem. Except, I will fight to defend my people when attacked. But I will do nothing more. I will do nothing to escalate this conflict. I will let God judge these people. This is his work, not mine.'

'So, you plan to do nothing.'

'No, John. I will do something very important. I will reopen the school. I will defy them by doing what I believe God would wish me to do.

There is only one path to peace, and it is not through violence.'

7:05 PM, JOHN

Dinner was good, served again by the man who first met us at the door.

Our silent friend never spoke; he simply went about his duties with quiet efficiency. We ate in peace, lost in our own thoughts. After dinner, Mandy and I moved to comfortable chairs by a window after she raided Kamyar's hidden liquor cabinet.

Our host had departed before dinner, explaining he had a meeting in town. Before leaving, he asked if I could wait until tomorrow afternoon to drive to Kabul. He had a few tasks that could not wait. He explained that his schedule had been interrupted by the bombing at the school. He said he was sorry for the delay. It could not be avoided.

I agreed even though I was anxious to leave. I wanted to go… now… not wait until tomorrow afternoon.

He said he would be traveling with us this time. He had business in Kabul. A flight had been arranged for us. He would be traveling with us after he concluded his business with the government. He said we did not need to return through India. He didn't care if someone tracked us from the airport as we left the country. The location of the mine was not in jeopardy.

I didn't complain about the delay because I didn't have much choice in the matter. It would have done no good, except to create ill will. I was dependent on Kamyar until we were out of Afghanistan.

Mandy poured some of the golden elixir into a glass and gave it to me. I took a deep sip and settled into a big, cushioned armchair, temporarily lost in thought. By this time in the evening the sun had hidden away, casting a red glow behind a silhouette of black mountains in the distance. The tragedy that struck yesterday, felt completely out of place in this green valley adorned by colored trees of fall in various hues of blending red and yellow.

'I'm sorry you had to see the bombing, John,' Mandy said.

'Yes, me too.'

She quietly sipped her drink, looking into the distance.

'You still haven't told me what you are doing here,' I changed the subject. 'Why did you move to India?'

'It's not a pretty story.'

'Want to talk about it?'

'I would rather not.'

The wind quickened, shaking the leaves in trees outside our windows. Sheltered behind the glass, I sipped my drink, temporarily mesmerized by the wind. I had been nervous during our trip from India, but not now. Now I was past nervous. My nerves were raw from grotesque images constantly flashing through my brain. I could not stop seeing the small, bloody hands and feet of the children I had reverently placed on a white sheet. It all seemed unreal, impossible, except for one thing. I had been there. I had seen the devastation. I had helped clean up the mess. It was all too real, too ugly. I needed to focus on something else, something that might clear my mind of these images. I needed relief.

'You and Kamyar seem to be friendly,' I stated. 'Is your relationship more than simply business?'

She answered decisively, 'That's no concern of yours.'

'Sorry.'

'No need to apologize.'

'Okay.'

I took another sip and let my mind wander before asking, because I needed answers. I couldn't go on without answers to questions that continued to spin like a broken record through my maddening brain. 'How could they do it?' I asked. 'How could anyone kill and mangle those children?'

She looked at me. 'You're angry.'

'Yes, I'm very angry.'

She didn't answer immediately. 'Life is not as precious here as in your world,' she finally said.

'Why? Don't the mothers in this village cry just as deeply as in our country when a child dies?' I said to her. 'So, tell me, what's the difference?'

'Perhaps you are right. Maybe there is no difference.'

'Okay, then, how could this have happened?'

'I don't know, John. I don't think like these people. But if anything is different, it is that religion plays a predominant role in their culture.'

I thought about what she said for a moment. 'Mandy, I consider myself a religious person. But I would never do anything like this, not ever. And certainly not in the name of my religion.'

'I believe you. You would not, but you are not them.'

'No, I'm not.'

'You're a very complicated man,' she said after a moment. 'Far more complicated than I originally thought.'

'What does that mean?'

'I don't know. We shall just have to find out.'

11:45 PM, JOHN

The night whispered to me as I lay in bed, a lonely whispering carried on the cries of mothers who had lost children in the blast.

I could not hear their crying, but I sensed their despair. I knew it was real. I knew it was close. The burden of their sorrow was too close, too real, too deeply felt to be ignored. It rode on a lonely wind. It devoured the night, took away my ability to sleep. I lay in bed listening, hearing their wailing cries from my memory, sensing their sorrow, a sorrow which would never be lost.

She had made love to me.

Mandy had tried to fill the void of my grief. I was grateful to her, grateful for all the moments of pleasure that allowed me to forget the tragedy for a brief time. She filled my senses with her body, with her long, loving, curved body, her naked thighs, her luscious, bountiful breasts, soft and wonderful. She presented her body for my pleasure alone, for me to touch, to hold, to kiss a taut nipple of her desire with my tongue. She had cared for my soul, opened her body to me, and I had accepted her gift, returned her favor, loved her as hard as she had loved me in long, gracious moments rocking to a tribal rhythm which came from deep within my soul.

When we were done, when she had finished offering her sacrificial gift, she lay naked beside me in our bed under sheets. Her body slept close to me, unashamed of the gift she had offered me that night.

Was she good, was she beautiful, did I enjoy our time together in this bed in a strange house, lost in a distant valley surrounded by a culture I could never understand? Yes, she was good, very good, and I was very grateful. But it was not enough. I could not shake a dire depression that had taken over my being, plunging me into a madness I could not escape. The images of the tragic night would not leave my brain, would not allow me to forget, to sleep in contentment, not for long, not for longer than an occasional drifting anxious dream, nightmares which woke me again in more pain than before. The pain of the tragedy was too close, too intense, drifting on a wind which made no sound.

She slept quietly in the night. I touched her shoulder beneath the sheets to be certain she was real, wanting desperately to know that some beauty existed in life other than the evil that seemed to be everywhere.

MONDAY, NOVEMBER 14, 9:10 AM, JOHN

I called Charlie early in the morning when she was out of the room, told him where I was, as much as I knew.

I also gave him a short version of what had happened since I last talked to him; mostly told him about the bombing of a village school.

He didn't sound too concerned.

I asked him why not.

He said he knew where I was and what had happened at the school.

'How do you know?'

'I have my ways,' he commented without explaining.

'Am I in any danger here?'

'I don't know.'

'Why not?'

'I didn't say I knew everything.'

'So, what good are you?'

'Not much good. But if you get into real trouble, I may be able to get you out. But not if I don't know where you are. Do you understand now why it's important to keep me informed?'

'I guess.'

'John, just keep your nose clean. Call me if you need help, okay? I'll see what I can do.'

'Okay.'

After hanging up, I wasn't sure how I felt about my buddy Charlie. Did I like the fact that he had been secretly tracking my movement? And what good was he really if I needed help? I was a long way from Kabul over dirt roads. I hadn't seen a US soldier in days.

But then, I would be leaving soon. None of this would matter in a few days.

After packing my bag with all the dirty clothes that badly needed to be washed, I sat down with a book to read, to pass the time, almost falling asleep in a chair after a few minutes, unable to keep my eyes open. I was exhausted. I must have dozed off.

The stark reality of a single loud gunshot woke me in a hurry, adrenaline instantly flowing through my raw-nerved body. Several more shots followed quickly, automatic weapons in sharp retorts of anger. A bullet broke the glass window in my bedroom, glass shattering across the stone floor in sharp-edged fragments, opening the room up to the outside, hearing shouts of distress coming from everywhere. Another bullet hit closer, burying into the wall not far from my head. I instinctively ducked, down on my hands and knees, when Mandy ran into the room.

'We need to get out of here,' she screamed.

I grabbed my suitcase.

'Forget the suitcase,' she demanded.

Ahmed entered the room, a gleaming metal gun in his hand.

'Follow me,' he said calmly with authority.

We ran down a hall following Ahmed, who ran with a noticeable limp.

'Where's your gun?' Mandy asked me with a weapon in her hand.

'Back in the bedroom.'

She gave me a look.

'This way.' Ahmed turned down a narrow windowless hall somewhere deep within the compound, down some stairs leading to more halls and a sparsely lit tunnel which went for a long distance ending in a garage. He hit a button on the wall, a metal door opened, large enough for a car to exit. Walking slowly outside, he scanned the area for enemy gunmen. Shouts and shooting could be heard some distance away, not close to us.

'Get in,' he ordered. Opening the door of a black SUV parked in the garage, he slid into the seat behind the wheel; hit the gas before I had a chance to close my door.

We headed for hills in the distance going as fast as a two-track, dirt road allowed through rolling dusty terrain. Mandy looked unconcerned, sitting up front with Ahmed.

I was again relegated to a back seat, like before when we were driving from India.

KABUL, AFGHANISTAN, 9:55 PM, JOHN

Our SUV drove up to the front door of the Hotel Serena in Kabul, as it had before.

To me, it seemed as if a lifetime had passed since we were last there. Like we had taken a journey into a foreign land, a journey which had taken years and covered vast distances only to return to this place of opulent luxury.

In truth, the only journey we took that day was a long and arduous drive down unpaved roads in the back country, which only a native knew existed. At times, the roads split into two tracks, winding up through hills that overlooked the valley. I didn't ask Ahmed if he knew where he was going, just assumed he was avoiding the main roads in case someone was looking for us, like someone who wanted to kill me. I couldn't get it out of my head that the attack was aimed at me. But the truth was, I had no real reason to think this, nothing to justify my feelings, just foolish, self-centered suspicions, probably brought on by panic. I tried to put the thought out of my head, but I couldn't.

'Mandy,' I leaned forward and tapped her on the shoulder. 'What was that all about?'

'I don't know.'

'Does Ahmed know?'

She said something to him in his native language. He simply shook his head from side to side without answering.

I settled back, closed my eyes, tried to get some rest as night descended over the land.

The lights of the city of Kabul eventually became visible in the distance. Ahmed took to the main roads when we were closer to town, blending into a civilization that knew nothing of the horror we had experienced only hours before.

'I don't have any luggage,' I whispered to Mandy as we walked inside the expansive lobby of the Serena Hotel.

'Don't worry about it,' she replied. 'I'll take care of everything. Money solves all problems in this city.'

'Do you mind if I go for a walk,' I asked. 'I need to stretch my legs and clear my mind.'

'Don't go far.'

'I'll be in the courtyard.' I wandered off as she approached the desk.

As I turned towards the front door, ornate golden ladles caught my attention, displayed behind glass in a wall of the hotel lobby. Outside, a sculpted garden under lights held rose bushes, green ferns, and pines, fountains with water rising out of tranquil pools. The garden seemed unreal, and maybe in some respects it was. In this place where most of the country was impoverished and uncultivated, this hotel presented a different world, one which was a sharp contrast to how the general population of Afghanistan lived. It was a picture of luxury, a place that was totally incompatible with the violence and fear which seemed to permeate every living moment. I assumed it catered to upper-class visitors, dignitaries, and politicians who came here requiring some assurance that it was a civilized country.

11:05 PM, JOHN

It was late.

I wasn't hungry when I stepped into our hotel room; too wound up to even think about food. I only wanted oblivious sleep to try to forget the events of the last few days.

Mandy opted for the liquor cabinet in the room. 'Want something to drink?' she asked.

'Any whiskey in there?'

'Yes, do you care what kind?'

'Not as long as it contains alcohol.'

She found glasses, poured herself a wine, and me a whiskey.

'Do you want some ice?' she asked.

'No.'

She fell into a large cushioned chair, took a sip of wine, and looked exhausted.

'Are you as tired as I am?' I asked.

'More.'

'You were pretty cool under fire today.'

'I was terrified, John.'

'You didn't look at it.'

'I may not have looked it, but I was. I didn't bargain for this. I need to get back to Mumbai where I understand the rules. This place doesn't seem to have any rules.'

I sipped my drink, thinking about what she said. 'It makes going back home look good, don't you think?'

'America has its own special brand of terror,' she took a sip of wine.

I didn't know what she meant and didn't think it was my place to ask.

But she answered anyway, without any prompting, explaining with a faraway look in her eye. 'He was a different man than the boy I fell in love with.' She said the words as if she were in a trance, as if she needed to tell someone. It came from deep inside her, where she had buried her hurt for a long time. The wine and the terror of the day must have broken through her mental barriers. She couldn't hold it in any longer. 'I married him when I was too young, when I didn't know anything,' she said. 'My life became a living hell.'

She continued after a pause, staring out a hotel window as if she could see him there. 'He beat me. When he got drunk, he beat me. I never knew why. I never knew when. It just happened. I think he liked to hit me. I was his rag doll. He thought he could do whatever he wanted to me. He thought he owned me.'

'I'm sorry,' I responded.

'No need to be sorry. You weren't responsible. I was. I married the goon.'

I took a sip of whiskey, letting the strong drink slide down my throat, warm my body, offering some peace after a day of high drama. I wasn't sure I wanted to hear her sad story, not after all the violence we had just witnessed, but I sensed she needed to tell me.

'Is that why you are in India?' I asked. 'To get away from him?'

'Yes.'

'Why didn't you just divorce him?'

'He was rich. I was a poor girl. Everyone thought I had hit the jackpot, married a good-looking, rich kid who would make my life a dream come true. He made it a dream alright, an awful nightmare.'

'You couldn't get away from him?'

'No, I couldn't. He would never let me go. He made that clear. He said if I tried to divorce him, he would kill me.'

'Could he do that?'

'I believed he could. He had enough money to do anything he wanted. His father was rich, owned a business that made millions. My husband was his only son. He was spoiled from birth.'

'So, you ran away.'

'Yes, as far as I could go.'

'Did you change your name?'

'Yes.'

'Your real name is not Mandy?'

'No.'

'I'm sorry,' I said again, because I didn't know what else to say.

'It's not your fault, John.'

'I know.'

'Thanks anyway.'

We sat for a time, drinking our wine and whiskey. Minutes passed, lost in thought. We came from different worlds, meeting by chance in this strange foreign land. We shared this time together for who knew what reason. It seemed incomprehensible in a way and yet perhaps it was meant to be. It was what needed to happen even though it made no sense.

'I think I should stop running,' she said. 'It's doing me no good. I'm still scared all the time, just like before. I thought if I could get away from him, my life would be better.'

'It's not better?'

'No, John, it's not better. Just different.'

The day had left both of us mentally and physically harmed. I had no words for her, no words of comfort, no words that could take away her pain. She was right. Pain and problems existed everywhere on this small planet. No place can totally escape sorrow. Running away seldom solves anything.

A restless silence filled our room.

She stood up finally, went into the bathroom after turning down all the lights except for one lamp next to my chair. When she came out, she slowly got undressed until her naked body glowed in the dim lights of my mind. She was a very beautiful woman, carefully proportioned in all the ways that a woman is lovely, big, bright eyes, her hair hand-combed back from her forehead, her breasts young and firm, her waist trim, her legs long and strong. I couldn't take my eyes off her. Even though I knew it was improper to stare, I couldn't help myself.

'Are you going to join me?' she asked, standing next to the bed. Pulling back the covers, she slid under the sheets, resting her head on a pillow with her eyes beckoning.

After getting ready for bed, I turned off the lamp, slid under the sheets, and curled up next to her body.

'Just hold me, John,' she whispered with her back to me.

I again did as she asked, holding her in the dark night until she turned over to face me, kissing me slowly on the lips.

'You are a good man,' she said, pausing. 'Would you like to make love to me?'

I touched her breast, ran my hand through her hair.

'Yes.'

When I reached down to touch her between her legs, she was waiting for me in anticipation.

TUESDAY, NOVEMBER 15, 6:55 PM, JOHN

Security at our hotel was handled with precision.

Men in uniforms with guns on their hips made timely patrols of the grounds. Their orderly maneuvers were an important element of the hotel's reputation as a safe haven in this city of intermittent violence. The hotel guests took little notice of their guards. Most of the inhabitants of this fine establishment went about their business, smiling and gesturing as if the probability of a serious incident didn't exist, expressing very little concern for the dangerous horrors which occurred not far from the cultivated grounds of this luxury hotel.

No expense had been spared in making this place a visual art-form extraordinaire, from the classical Islamic architecture to its cultivated gardens overlooking a famous park. An embassy, I think Australia, was housed within its structure. I spent most of my morning touring the facility. On one of my tours, I discovered the hotel had an Olympic-sized swimming pool. Ahmed suggested we not stray outside the grounds of the hotel. I went for a walk anyway. He followed, always within view, never far away.

Mandy spent her time on the telephone in our room. I didn't know what she was doing, and I didn't ask. It was not my business. She met me for lunch, told me Kamyar had arrived in Kabul. He was busy with a meeting and we would see him at dinner.

He showed up as promised in the evening, came to our table in the restaurant. 'We need to talk, John,' he said without sitting down.

'Okay.'

'Not here,' he suggested. 'Follow me.'

He led me outside into the courtyard to a secluded spot behind some trees. Ahmed followed at a distance. The evening light was fading; the sun hiding behind mountains in the west. Kamyar sat on a low cement wall surrounding a pool of calm water.

'Please sit,' he directed me. 'I'm afraid we have a problem, you and I.'

'What?' I asked.

'An American soldier was killed yesterday morning in the raid on my house. I am so sorry,' he apologized.

'What for? You don't need to be sorry, do you?' I replied. 'You didn't attack anyone. They attacked you.'

'Yes, that is true.'

'Tell me what you know.'

'A body was left behind by the attackers,' he explained. 'Dog tags identified him as an American soldier. He is a big man with blond hair. He does not look like an Afghan. There is no confusion in this matter.'

I said nothing for a moment, trying to analyze the information. Finally, I asked the obvious question, 'Are you saying that some Americans were involved in the raid your compound?'

'Yes.'

'Why?'

'Why did they attack me?'

'Yes, why would they do that?'

'I don't know.'

'Did you do something to make them angry?'

'I know of no reason. I do know they don't like me because I don't always cooperate with them. But I have never attacked them and I can think of no reason for them to attack me.'

'When you say you do not always cooperate with them, what is it they want from you?'

'They see a terrorist behind every wall. They want me to accuse men whom they suspect of being insurgents. I can have them put in prison. But I won't do this because I know these men. I know they are not terrorists. The Americans sometimes disagreed. They became angry with me when I would not help them. But I will not back down. I do not think they like me.'

'Yes, but did they ever threaten to attack you?'

'No, I have never felt threatened. Not until now.'

'It makes no sense.'

'There is one other possible explanation.' Kamyar looked at me.

'What is that?'

'They were after you.'

'That's preposterous.'

'My men tell me they were attempting to enter the area of the house where you were. They shot into your room. They did not shoot into any other room.'

'How would they even know I was there?'

'I understand, but I thought you should know.'

'Okay, thanks, but I don't think they were after me.'

Kamyar said nothing.

"What are you going to do with the dead American?' I asked him.

'I will bury him in the desert.'

'You can't do that.'

'Why?'

'His family deserves to know what happened to him,' I demanded.

'He attacked me,' Kamyar said, expressing anger for the first time in our conversation.

'Yes, but he was probably following some idiotic order. He's a kid. He's not responsible.'

Kamyar thought about what I said. 'If I return him to the Americans, they will know he was killed by people in my village. They will want revenge.'

'Doesn't matter. You must do this. Do it for me if for no other reason. His family must know what happened to him.'

'This is a hard decision, John. I do not want to offend you, but you must understand this puts me in a difficult place.'

'I know, Kamyar, but it's the honorable thing to do.'

I knew saying this would be a problem for him. Honor is important in his culture. In some respects, it is everything to an Afghan.

Kamyar looked away for a moment before saying, 'I will do this for you, John. I will do as you ask. But you must help me with this thing. I have done nothing to bring this tragedy to my village. I have enough problems with the Taliban, as you have personally witnessed. I do not need to make an enemy of the Americans.'

'I will do what I can to help you,' I said, thinking that I could call Charlie.

'Good, now we must eat dinner. We are leaving tonight.'

'Tonight?'

'Yes, I want you out of here before anything bad happens to you.'

'You really think it's possible that I'm responsible for what happened at your house?'

'I don't know what to believe. I am sorry, John. But the evidence suggests you may have been the target.'

'I still don't believe it.'

He said nothing in response except to suggest we return to dinner.

8:25 PM, JOHN

Silence was the main feature of our dinner; the atmosphere was spoiled and poisoned by the events of the last few days.

Conversation was sparse. No one spoke more than a few sentences before silence set in again. It wasn't because the meal was bad. The food was great, prepared to perfection. The dining staff attended to our every need. Under different circumstances, I would have enjoyed the meal very much, but I wasn't hungry. The disagreement I had with Kamyar in the courtyard was twisting in my gut.

I had come on this trip to solidify my relationship with him. I wanted to be friends, to have a good business relationship. His emerald mine was a valuable source of product for my company. He was my client. My job was to establish the foundation of a long-term relationship, which could mean millions of dollars of profit for a company where I was a major stockholder. I didn't want anything to go wrong. And yet, everything had gone wrong. The horrendous bombing of his village school had been the first in a downward spiral of events that soured the atmosphere. The assault on Kamyar's compound had followed close behind, and the possibility that I may have been responsible made the situation even worse. To add to the list, the issue of the dead American soldier complicated things further. It had been a basis for disagreement with him. I was afraid it alone may have ruined our relationship.

Reality was, I was leaving Afghanistan on an ugly note with no time to turn the tide. As Kamyar ate in silence, I could think of nothing to say to him, nothing which might rescue the situation. He was a proud man. I had learned this during my trip. He worked hard. He had more than enough enemies and problems. He didn't need one more. He didn't need me to be a complication. He needed me to be someone he could trust, and I wasn't sure I had proved this to him.

His silence, more than anything else, seemed to indicate he didn't wish to continue our relationship.

Like her boss, Mandy ate in silence. And her silence was another warning sign that I had a problem. I had to assume that he had suggested that she forget about me. It was time to move on. They would find someone else to buy their emeralds.

The waiter brought coffee. Our dirty dishes were taken from the table by the staff.

'What time is my flight?' I asked Kamyar.

He had informed me at dinner that he had booked a flight for me. I knew I was leaving Afghanistan, but I hadn't thought to ask him exactly when. Too many other issues had been running through my head. One was my luggage. Fortunately, it had been returned to me from the compound. Kamyar had it brought with him when he drove to town. The other issue, which had been resolved, was the return of my real passport. He assured me it was in my luggage. Without my passport, I would have trouble with customs when I arrived on US soil. Then there was the matter of Charlie's phone. I didn't want to lose it. It was government property. It was in my luggage, and I owed Charlie a call. Now that I had my luggage back, I planned to call him when I was out of the country. I had questions to ask Charlie, but they would have to wait until I was sure our conversation could not be overheard.

'Ten thirty.' Kamyar surprised me. 'You need to leave soon to go to the airport,' he explained.

I looked at Mandy, expecting some response, like it's been fun. I'm sorry to see you go, but she said nothing.

'Okay.' I wiped my hands with a cloth napkin; put it on the table, accepting my fate was sealed. They were happy to see me go.

'You okay?' I asked Mandy, I guess because I couldn't believe she could be so cold, to turn it off as quickly as she had turned it on. 'You have been very quiet.'

'I'm fine,' she responded curtly.

'Where will you go after today?' I asked her as an afterthought.

'I will return to doing my job,' she said simply.

'Has she told you what she does for me?' Kamyar asked.

'No.'

I had never asked her what she did besides work as a travel guide. The truth was, I didn't want to know. I wanted her to be exactly what she said she was, nothing more. But despite my not wanting to believe it, I had concluded that she was probably nothing more than a high-priced call girl on a mission, and nothing I observed challenged my conclusion. All of which made me think I was right about her.

'She works for me at my company,' Kamyar said. She is very good at her job. She helps me with my customers.'

'What customers?' I asked, now more than ever convinced I was right. I was just another satisfied customer of an escort service.

'I manufacture electronic equipment for automobiles in Mumbai,' Kamyar surprised me. 'My company sells parts to US and European automobile companies. Mandy works in sales. She spends her time making sure our products meet the technical specifications of our customers.'

'You never told me,' I said to her.

'You never asked,' she countered.

She probably knew what I had been thinking, and she had gone along with my misconception, played the game, played me in a way.

'She's very good at her job,' Kamyar expressed. 'Her language skills are excellent, and her understanding of our product line and electronics is excellent.'

'Where did you learn about electronics?' I asked her.

'School, I graduated from the University of Wisconsin with a degree in electrical engineering.'

'Is that where you met your husband?'

'Yes.'

'I thought you met him in high school.'

'I never said that.'

'No, I guess you never did. You just said that you were too young when you got married.'

'I was. I was twenty-one. I was naive.'

'And you, Kamyar, you never told me you owned a company that manufactures car parts.'

'I guess we have much to learn from each other,' Kamyar suggested.

'I guess we do.'

'One question.'

'Yes.'

'Why is your factory in Mumbai? Why not in Afghanistan, in your village?'

'The answer to your question is complex, and I'm not sure I have enough time tonight to answer your question properly. Let me simply explain that it is much easier to do business in Mumbai, India, than in Afghanistan. The people in my village are content with their lives. I do not think they would like to work in a factory.'

'One more question.'

'Okay, John, then you must go to the airport.'

'Why did you send Mandy to escort me?'

'You are a very important person,' he explained. 'When I told Mandy about you, she volunteered for the job.'

'I see,' I replied, beginning to question my previous conclusions. Perhaps I was being too pessimistic. There was only one way to find out if I was right and so I asked. 'Is that still true?'

'Of course,' he answered decisively. 'Nothing has changed. We must do good business together.'

KABUL INTERNATIONAL AIRPORT, 9:55 PM, JOHN

They were gone, and I felt utterly alone in the large airport lounge, sitting in a room with strangers —mostly Afghans and other Arabs—waiting for a redeye flight.

A sense of lingering doubt still worried my thoughts as I waited to board the plane. Even though I had been successful in what I had hoped to accomplish on this trip. And yet, the tragedies I witnessed cast a cloud of lingering doubt over what had been accomplished. I had been a witness to too much death. The death of the school children weighed especially heavily on my mind. I couldn't get the images of their dismembered bodies out of my head.

And then there was Mandy. She was the other haunting question mark.

She returned to our hotel by taxi after dropping me at the airport. We talked only briefly on the road to the airport as Ahmed drove us. He stayed behind with me at the airport. I assumed this was at Kamyar's request to be certain I boarded my plane safely. Ahmed was somewhere in the airport; I didn't know where. I only knew he was keeping an eye on me.

Mandy had sat in the back seat with me. She told me she would be flying to Mumbai in the morning. Her office was in India. From there, she flew all over the world as part of her job.

I asked her if I could do anything for her. She said no. She was well paid for her job. She had everything she needed in Mumbai. She asked me if I now understood why she had volunteered to accompany me to Kabul. Did I have any lingering misconceptions about the nature of her duties?

Of course, I knew what she was asking. She was telling me she was not a call girl, a paid escort. She had travelled with me as a favor to her boss.

'So, it was just business?' I replied.

'Just business, John.'

'Nothing more?'

She paused before answering, 'Not at first, but maybe later,' she said with a smile.

'Okay.'

'And for you, Mr. John Van Laan, was it okay for you?'

'Yes, Mandy. It was more than okay for me.'

'Good.' She smiled.

I kissed her goodbye at the Airport while Ahmed was parking and asked her if I would ever see her again. She said she didn't know. Life was full of surprises. I thanked her for everything. I didn't know what else to say. I hugged her, said that if she ever was in the US, I would love to see her again.

She smiled, turned, and hailed a taxi, got in without looking back.

I showed my Canadian passport at the airline counter as Kamyar instructed me. A clerk gave me a boarding pass for the flight. It said Steve Taylor was flying to Dubai with connections to Amsterdam in the Netherlands. Kamyar instructed me to destroy the fake passport once I was in Europe. I was on my own from there. I would need to make my own flight arrangements from Holland. I assumed that meant I would probably have to stay overnight first before I could book a flight to somewhere in the US, connecting to Grand Rapids, MI, and home.

I had shaken hands and said goodbye to Kamyar at the hotel After thanking him for his hospitality. I said I was sorry if I was the cause of the attack at his compound.

He had told me he lost two good men, and several more were injured. That and the bomb at the school had created a nightmare for him. He had much work to do when he returned to his home. One item was to return a dead American soldier to his base. He had not yet decided how to accomplish this, but he assured me he would do as I asked.

Almost as an afterthought, I suggested I would like to make a substantial contribution towards the rebuilding of his school. I told him my company had a foundation that financed projects such as this. I would introduce the subject to the foundation board as soon as I returned. I didn't think I would have any problem convincing them to help.

An awkward moment of silence followed. I needed to know. I wanted to confirm what I assumed was true, so I just asked one more time to be sure. 'You know I never would have come here if I thought I would be responsible for what happened to your people, to the children, and the men who died?' Then I paused before saying, 'And I hope this does not spoil our friendship.'

He smiled. 'You don't have to apologize. We are friends now. And what you did to help at the school, I will not forget that… my friend.'

AKRON, OHIO, WEDNESDAY, NOVEMBER 16, 10:30 AM, FRED

Fred Smith received the call he had been waiting for.

He was told that the mission had been conducted as planned. And the team that accompanied the Taliban militia were Army Rangers, highly trained and well equipped. They should have been successful, but as his friend, the Colonel, explained, the opposition had more defenders at the compound than anticipated. Worse yet, they were heavily armed, and apparently, an underground escape route was available. None of this was anticipated when the mission was planned. It should have been an easy task, in and out quickly. Very little risk was contemplated. But as it turned out, the mission was very risky. Several American soldiers had been wounded. One was missing, either captured or dead. Either way, it was a disaster.

'I paid them,' the Colonel said with finality.

'Why pay them?' Fred asked. 'They accomplished nothing. Fact is, they made a mess of everything.'

Colonel Jack Raymond paused before answering, holding his anger. 'Mr. Smith,' he said as calmly as he could. 'I know this was our deal. Pay them after the target has been eliminated. But you must understand, these men risked their lives in this mission. Some of them are wounded, and one of their buddies is MIA. They did their job. It just wasn't in the cards.'

'The compound is a nest of insurgents,' Fred countered. 'Didn't you say that?'

'Yes, I said that.'

'Well, why not go in and bomb the hell out of the place?' Fred demanded. 'Send a drone.'

'Mr. Smith, please try to understand. I did not have authorization to attack the village or any dwelling in it. The place is suspected, sure, but nothing has been proven conclusively against the man who owns it. The mission was conducted as an exploratory exercise, which got out of control.'

'Well, the guy who owns it is more than just suspected now,' Fred said. 'He is responsible for wounded American soldiers.'

'Yes,' Jack said. 'He's a problem now. I will make sure this is understood.'

'Okay,' Fred said. 'I guess I get it. I'm sorry if I seem angry. I just wanted it done.'

'I understand,' Jack answered.

'So, are you going to take care of it? Get the job done now?'

'I'm not sure I can.'

'Why not?' Fred was completely exasperated. A hundred thousand American dollars had been paid to the Colonel and his men.'

'I'm sorry. Information I have received indicates the target has left the country.'

AMSTERDAM, NETHERLANDS, 10:15 PM, JOHN

To say that I was exhausted by the time I arrived at my hotel room in the Netherlands would have been an understatement.

I was so tired I could barely stand. The layover in Dubai had taken too long, an exasperating two and a half hours of trying to stay awake while waiting for my connecting flight to Amsterdam, Schiphol Airport. I got some rest on the plane, but not enough. I felt like I needed a week of sleep to catch up after everything that happened. I chose a hotel that looked modern but was not expensive, not the kind of place John Van Laan would normally select. The Van der Valk Hotel near the airport seemed a good choice for what I needed, a place where Steve Taylor could disappear and John Van Laan would reenter the world of the living. I used my fake passport when checking in at the hotel, but used my real name when making a reservation for a flight to New York in the morning. A computer in the lobby was a convenient method to book a flight.

My hotel room was comfortable, not overly large, and not anywhere nearly as grand as the accommodations I experienced in the Middle East. In a way, this seemed odd. Holland was a modern country compared to India, Pakistan, and Afghanistan, which were considered third-world countries. And yet the level of opulence which existed in their sheltered alcoves devoted to the rich and powerful was beyond expectation. I had enjoyed this aspect of my travels. However, the rest of my trip bordered between interesting and horrible.

After taking a shower, cleaning up from hours of sweaty travel, I had one item to do before I could sleep. I dreaded the call, but I dialed Charlie's his number anyway.

'I was wondering when you would call. I was beginning to think you were dead,' Charlie said before I could say a word.

'I'm not dead.'

'Good, I'm glad we have that established. Now you want to tell me why you have taken so long to check in,' Charlie demanded. 'I thought I asked you to call me every day.'

I explained in as few words as possible what had happened since I last talked to him, trying to justify why couldn't I call him? He listened with comment.

'So, Charlie. Who attacked the compound where I was staying? There are two schools of thought about who the target was, me or my host. Which one do you think it was?'

'How should I know?'

'I thought you said you had a friend in the military who was keeping an eye out for me.'

'Yes, I did, but I have not heard anything from him.'

'Perhaps you would like to call him and find out why American soldiers were involved in an attack on the house where I was staying. In my book, I don't consider that looking out for my welfare.'

'You sure about this?' Charlie asked. 'I don't want to bother him if it isn't true.'

'Yes, I'm sure about it. Kamyar told me one of the attackers was killed. He was blond-haired, had dog tags around his neck, and was dressed in army fatigues with full battle gear. And by the way, the reason his body will be returned to his base is because I requested it.'

'That was decent of you.'

'You're welcome. It wasn't what my host wanted. He suggested burying the intruder in a desert. I don't blame him. Some of the soldiers who shot up his place, killing and wounding some of his men, were Americans.'

Charlie didn't say anything immediately. 'I'll look into it,' he finally agreed. 'But I'm not promising anything.'

'Why not?'

'Because the matter may be classified.'

'Don't you have security clearance?'

'Yes, but this is the army we are talking about. They don't always cooperate with the CIA.'

'You know, Charlie, that's just wrong. You guys are supposed to be on the same side,' I said in frustration. I was tired. I had been shot at. I wanted answers.

'I know, but that's just the way it is.'

'Well, find out anyway. Because I'm pissed and I want to know what happened.'

'I'll do my best,' Charlie said.

I slumped off to bed after hanging up, totally frustrated with my conversation with Charlie. I knew I shouldn't have gotten mad at him, but I had almost been killed.

I figured I was owed.

GRAND HAVEN, MICHIGAN, SATURDAY, NOVEMBER 19, 7:15 PM, JOHN

It was already a quarter after seven.

The lady was late to the restaurant, and she was on my mind. I couldn't help it.

She had been on my mind ever since I got home. Her parting words before my trip had been less than amicable. Rachel didn't want me to go to Afghanistan. She made this perfectly clear. In fact, she made it more than perfectly clear. She said our relationship was over if I went. She had been adamant. And yet I wasn't sure if she really meant it. And now that I was home, now she was again on my mind.

So, I called her in the morning, caught her before she headed for the gym. She said she couldn't talk. Her coat was on, and she was halfway out the door when she heard the phone.

I told her I was back in town. Would she like to have dinner with me?

She didn't answer right away as I hoped. She took her time and I began to think she was going to say no.

'Are you still mad at me for going to Afghanistan?' I asked.

'I'll see you at Jelly's at seven,' she answered unenthusiastically.

I took a sip of beer while waiting for her to show at the restaurant, watching the evening sky over the channel slip into gray darkness. November on the lakeshore is often cloudy. This November night was no exception. The air was cool and damp as I drove my Ferrari to the restaurant.

I didn't have a good feeling about tonight's activities. For one, she did not suggest I pick her up, just agreed to meet me at the restaurant, meaning I didn't have an automatic invitation to drive her home, to crawl into bed with her, to make love to her luscious body. This would have to be negotiated later, and I didn't like my chances. Memories of my last discussion with her ran through my head as I waited. Nothing in our previous conversation indicated we had a future. I was grateful she had agreed to have dinner with me, but I was not overly optimistic about the future.

When she finally arrived, she arrived in a rush, swept into the room like she was on a tight schedule, threw her coat on an empty chair, and sat down.

The restaurant was busy, not filled, but busy. It was November, and the summer crowd was absent. A wall of mirrors behind the bar reflected images of several patrons seated at the marble countertop, sipping drinks and talking loudly. The tables next to windows overlooking the channel were occupied by customers. The place was not large, with dark wood walls and dark furniture complemented by gleaming silverware and glasses. An open menu in front of me on a table had been ignored. I had been busy contemplating what to tell her about my trip. Or more importantly, what I should not tell her.

A hostess had kindly seated me at a corner table off to one side of the room. I hoped this would give us an opportunity to talk in private. The crowd provided an overwhelming din of noise, enough to drown out our conversation.

Lights from the pier into the big lake were visible from where I sat, a line of lights reflecting off rolling mounds of water driving up the channel. It was a windy evening, not untypical for fall, a blustery time on the large inland lake. Winter was coming. The water was restless. Below my window, waves washed over the concrete walls of the channel. It was not an evening to go for a walk.

Still, it was very pleasant, warm inside the restaurant.

'Sorry, John,' Rachel said as she sat down across from me. 'Medical emergency with one of my patients. I got here as soon as I could.'

She looked good. The lady looked great. Her dark brown curls had been combed by the wind, freely falling around her face. She was wearing her contacts, not the white-rimmed doctor glasses. I hoped that was a good sign. Her white cashmere sweater showed off her feminine wares. Makeup outlined big, beautiful, brown eyes. She was a very pretty lady.

'Not a problem, Rachel,' I said. 'I'm glad you came.'

'Were you worried I wouldn't come?'

'Yes,' I answered honestly

She smiled at me. 'Well, here I am. How was your trip?'

'It was interesting.'

I couldn't tell her everything, certainly not the part about Mandy or whatever her name was. And then there was the incident at Kamyar's house when I was almost killed. I wasn't sure I wanted to tell her about that. She had said my trip was too dangerous. She didn't want me to go. She had agreed with Charlie in this regard. I didn't want to have to admit she was right.

'You survived?' she noted dryly.

'Yes, as you can see. I survived.'

'Good. Did you accomplish your objectives?'

'Yes, I saw the mine. It's real. The emeralds are genuine.'

'Where is it?' she asked.

'I don't really know exactly, somewhere in the northwest part of Afghanistan.'

'Did you see any of the country?'

'Yes,' I replied, remembering vividly the devastation at the school, the torn and bloody body parts I had carried to a white sheet discolored with red, under spotlights in the night. And of course, I had seen far more of the country than only this one disastrous scene, but this was what came to mind immediately. It would be the one thing I would always remember from my trip. But again, I didn't want to tell her.

'The country is beautiful,' I said instead. 'The valley below the mine is a lush green paradise full of fruit trees.'

'Did you go up into the mountains?'

'Yes, I hiked up to the mine. It took several hours after a long ride up two-track roads in a truck.'

11:55 PM, JOHN

The wind was howling outside my bedroom window, a constant, low, unpleasant sound blowing through the trees, branches waving in a breeze.

My wind speed indicator recorded at a steady forty miles per hour, gusting to fifty. But inside my cottage, I was warm in my bed, comfortable and sheltered from a storm rushing against the beach with the furious elegance of a wild animal, beating against the shoreline as if the beach was its prey to be devoured. One after another, the big rollers wound up high before crashing over in angry, disturbing fury on the beach, rushing up the shore before retreating in frustration, returning to their home, the big lake.

I was alone.

I was comfortable and warm, but I was not happy to be alone. She had not offered to go home with me, nor had she invited me to her place. In fact, it was far worse. Our relationship was over. She had told me we were done.

Oh, she said she still loved me. She said she would always love me. She had thanked me for awaking the sensual side of her brain, for making her aware of the fact that she was a woman, a woman capable of loving a man.

'So why?' I asked. 'Why can't we be together? If you love me, then why can't you be with me?' It seemed an honest question. I thought it deserved an answer.

She looked at me long and hard before answering. 'I thought about you often when you were gone, John… Did you think about me?'

'I was very busy, Rachel,' I answered honestly. I wanted to be truthful with her. She told me we were done before I left. I took her at her word. I had tried not to think about her.

'You could have called.'

'I didn't think you wanted me to call. After our last conversation, I wasn't sure you wanted anything to do with me.'

'I didn't.'

'Then why would you want me to call?'

'Because I was worried about you.'

'Rachel, that makes no sense.'

'What… that I was worried about you?'

'Yes. Why would you worry about someone you don't want to be with?'

'John, did you really think I wouldn't worry about you?'

I didn't know how to respond, so I said nothing.

'Why didn't you call?' she asked again.

'I told you why.'

'Well, I wish you had called. I worried about you every day. Finally, I just pictured you dead and tried to forget about you.'

'Rachel.'

'You don't get it, do you, John?'

'No, Rachel. I don't get it.'

I could see tears in her eyes. 'I tried not to worry about you, John, ' she explained. 'I thought after we talked, I could forget you. And I tried, but it didn't work. I couldn't stop thinking about you.'

'I'm sorry. I wish I had known.'

'It wasn't your fault, John. It was mine.'

'Why do you say that?'

'Because I should be stronger. I should be able to handle a situation like this, but I'm not.'

I took a sip of wine because the glass was in my hand. 'Do you want some wine?'

'No.'

'Can I get you anything?'

'No, I came to tell you I have taken steps to deal with my problem,' she explained in her analytical, medical tone of voice, a tone I had often heard in the past when she was doctoring. I never liked it when she talked to me in this tone. It never meant anything good.

'I have decided I need to move on,' she continued with determination. 'I have started dating again. I'm seeing a man. He's a doctor. He's busy like me. We share a similar lifestyle. I think I like him, and I know he likes me. So, you see, John. I'm doing fine. I'm moving on with my life. You don't have to be concerned about me anymore. You don't need to call me anymore.' She rattled on like this was a speech she had prepared before coming to dinner, memorized it, and spoke the words verbatim as she had rehearsed.

'What about me?' I asked.

'What about you, John?'

'Do I really need to answer that question?'

'John, please!!! We both know you will do fine. You have your business, your money. You don't need me.' She paused. 'Besides, we both know you came to me to help you get over the pain of Sandy's death. Oh, don't get me wrong, I was happy to have been there for you, but you are better now. I can see you have healed. I'm a doctor, remember. I understand these things. You don't need me anymore.'

We didn't have dinner together. In fact, she didn't even have a drink with me. She stood up and walked out. As soon as she had delivered her prepared speech, she was gone. I paid the waitress for my drink and drove home.

As I lay in bed listening to the wind howl outside my cottage window, I missed her. I missed her and wanted her in the worst way, but I was happy for her at the same time. She was doing what she needed to do. And perhaps she was right. Maybe it was always about Sandy, about getting on with my life after her death. Sandy had said something like this before she died, said Rachel could help me. And apparently I had helped Rachel as well. So, now it was time for both of us to move on with our lives.

Rachel had her life to live, and I was no longer included in her plans.

MONDAY, NOVEMBER 21, 10:25 AM, JOHN

He was a quick man who did not smile often.

Seeming to be constantly in a hurry. Jahwed Abdul, Kamyar's brother, was a tall, thin man who didn't look very much like his brother, taller with the same dark black hair cut short. His face seemed oddly pinched; narrow with a thin mustache distorting his upper lip and deeply set eyes which were constantly surveying you as if he still didn't know who you were. He was not an unattractive man, but not handsome like Kamyar. But it was not his appearance that made you wary of him, it was the way he acted, almost like a wild beast who didn't trust you any more than you trusted him.

This was my first impression, but I have been wrong about people before. First impressions are not always accurate. It is much better to get to know a person before passing judgment.

He called on Sunday, asked if he could visit, said he would drive to my home Monday morning from Dearborn, Michigan, if I was free. He said he wished to discuss my arrangement with his brother. Talk about emeralds from Afghanistan. Of course, I agreed.

Charlie was on the phone when he knocked on my back door. We were arguing.

'Someone's at the door,' I said, thankful for a brief reprieve. 'Hold that thought. I'll be right back.'

I shook Jahwed's hand after opening the door. 'Thanks for coming... Jaah-wed,' I tried to pronounce his name. 'Is that right?'

'Call me Joey,' he said, speaking English very well with only a hint of an accent.

'I'm on the phone. Please, take a seat in the living room. I'll be right with you.'

He quickly turned his back on me.

'Forgive my hospitality,' I stopped him when he was halfway down the hall. 'Do you need anything, a bathroom, something to drink?'

'I'm fine,' he replied. 'Do not be concerned about me, Mr. Van Laan. Take care of your phone call. I will be here waiting when you are finished.'

'Thanks,' I stepped into my office and closed the door for privacy.

'Now, where were we?' I asked Charlie.

'You were telling me I don't know what I'm talking about,' Charlie replied sarcastically.

'Right, you don't. The soldier wasn't killed in the mountains above the valley. He was killed in a valley when he was attacking a house where I was staying.'

'And you know this because you saw it happen,' Charlie asked. 'You saw the soldier get shot.'

'No, Charlie, I did not. I was running for my life at the time, trying to stay alive. So no, I didn't see him die.'

'But someone told you this is what happened. Is that right?'

'Yes, that's right. Someone I trust told me.'

'And this guy who told you, he is an Afghan from the region where the soldier was killed.'

'Yes, he owns the house that was being attacked. For all I know, he was the target.'

'And you want me to believe him, an Afghan, not an American general who told me a different story. My general said the soldier was killed while on a peaceful mission in the hills above the town.'

'Charlie, I was there. Listen to me. I was in a house built in a valley, not in the hills. I saw bullets fly. I was almost hit by two of them. Kamyar thinks I could have been the target, and I'm not so sure he isn't right.'

'Really, John. Tell me… just why would American soldiers be targeting you in Afghanistan?'

'I don't know.'

'Right, and I don't know either, because it doesn't make sense.'

I had nothing to say. Charlie was right, of course. He was always maddening, right? He studied the facts, drew his conclusions from solid evidence, and nothing else. I had no way of arguing with my buddy Charlie.

'Okay,' I finally said. 'I know it sounds preposterous. But I don't know what else to tell you.'

'Okay, then think about this. Maybe this friend of yours is a Taliban or an al-Qaeda. He could be using you and your company to finance acts of terror against this country. Do you think this is a possibility, John?'

'No, I don't believe it is, Charlie.'

'Why not?'

'Because I know this man. I don't believe he is a bad character.'

'How long have you known him, John?'

'Not very long.'

'I rest my case.' Charlie was done arguing with me, and I knew it would do no good to continue.

'I have to go, Charlie. Let's talk later.'

'Later.' He hung up, obviously not happy with me.

Jahwed, or Joey as he wished to be known, was waiting when I entered the living room.

'Can I get you anything to drink?' I asked.

'No,' he replied curtly. 'I see you are a busy man. I do not wish to take any more of your time than is necessary.'

'Take all the time you wish.'

He explained he had come to talk about his brother's emeralds. Now that the validity of the mine was established, he wished to discuss our arrangement, prices, delivery, payment, etc. He said he would be the main contact for his brother in the US. He gave me his telephone number in Dearborn. He said he ran a business there connected with his brother's factories in India. His factory in Dearborn modified parts shipped from India. It was also the local sales office for the Big Three automakers in Detroit.

As we worked through the details of our arrangement, I was impressed with his professionalism. It was obvious he was very smart. At one point in our conversation, I got Jason on a conference phone so he was up to date on our negotiations. Everything was recorded. The basic elements of our agreement were this: emeralds would first be sent to a trusted associate in Sri Lanka for sorting. After being analyzed for quality and quantity, payment for the stones would be made from my Charlottesville office to a bank account in Switzerland. I gave him the address in Sri Lanka and the name of my associate for shipping. It was a simple arrangement. When he seemed satisfied, he thanked me before quickly standing up to leave.

'Can I buy you lunch?' I asked, thinking he had driven from the other side of the state —a two-and-a-half-hour drive — for a meeting that lasted no more than fifteen minutes. 'We could drive into town,' I suggested.

He looked at me for a second as if he was considering my offer. 'No,' he finally replied. 'I do not wish to drive into your town.' He turned to leave.

The door to my cottage closed, and he was gone.

6:35 PM, JOHN

My work was done by late afternoon.

After returning phone calls and writing a report detailing my trip to Afghanistan for the Board of Directors, I called it a day.

A draft of my report had been emailed to Helen, my secretary in Charlottesville, Virginia, the home office with instructions to clean it up, fix the punctuation, and spelling. Once that was accomplished, she would send it to the board members. The report only told part of the story, the part that specifically concerned the company. The rest of the story was personal. However, I did write a cursory note about a bombing at a school. I didn't want to alarm the members unduly, but I felt like I needed to tell them. I wasn't worried that they would be overly concerned. Mines in other countries that supplied our company with gemstones existed in zones of political instability. Risk is an element in every business.

It was cocktail time by the time I finished.

When Sandy was alive, we would have a drink at cocktail time and discuss the issues of the day. But Sandy had died of cancer, and Rachel would not be coming here anymore. Rachel was now living a life that did not involve me.

I was alone.

Mandy briefly came to mind, but she lived thousands of miles away, and I wasn't certain we had connected on much more than a physical level. It had been fun and it had been frightening. The trip had created many emotions. She was one of them, just a memory now.

I sat alone with a glass of bourbon. My thoughts were my only company. I missed the women in my life. I missed them all. I thought about Ilana, my island beauty, and then there was Monica, who had died in a hail of bullets in a New York hotel room. I wondered what it was about women that makes men need them so much. Was it because we are raised by our mothers, and even when we are older, when we are all grown, do we still long for a mother's love? Do we need a woman in our lives as a substitute for our mothers?

Some of us are fortunate to have a mother who loved us. Some are not. If not, well… it seemed to me the less fortunate sons may need a woman even more than the others. We need what had been denied us; the love only a woman can give.

I had been one of those unloved sons. My mother never cared much for me, not when I was young, not when it was important. She was too concerned with other issues during my formative years. I was something she wished to showcase to her friends. And in this regard, I was not much good for her. I got into too much trouble, didn't pay attention in school, didn't always obey her rules; the usual bad boy complex. However, now that she is older, she tells me she loves me, and I believe her and I am grateful, but it is too late for us. She was not there for me when I needed her most.

The bourbon in my glass was almost gone. It was time to find something to eat. But I poured another glass of bourbon instead, put on a Ray LaMontagne CD, and mellowed out.

Times spent with the women in my life ran through my alcohol dampened brain in no apparent order, a collage of tattered memories… most good, some not.

GRAND HAVEN, MICHIGAN, SATURDAY, JANUARY 28, 2012, 5:50 PM, JOHN

The dead of winter, cold and forbidding, temperatures in the low single digits.

As the light of another day receded, a blanket of icy white fell from the sky over a gray, frozen lake that looked like an arctic desert. Wind blew steadily, twenty to thirty miles an hour. It had been snowing off and on, all day, sometimes so hard I couldn't see anything outside my windows except a blank gray, indefinite nothing.

Too cold for a walk, even for a short time, I had been holed up inside.

After she called, I checked my stash of food items and found my refrigerator and pantry sadly lacking. There was plenty of cold beer, enough milk for cereal, as well as a few other food groups, such as salad stuff, bread, sandwich meat, and cheese. But eggs and toast for breakfast in case she stayed overnight were sadly missing. A quick trip to the grocery store was required.

She had promised nothing when she called, only said she was in the neighborhood and would I mind if she stopped over later in the afternoon, wondering hesitantly if she would be interrupting anything important or causing a problem, such as a girlfriend who might be visiting.

I told her I didn't have a girlfriend.

And 'why is that?' she had asked.

'None of your business' was my reply.

'Okay, good,' she said. Then she would come.

Great. Did she know where I lived?

'I'll find it,' she answered and hung up.

Up until the time of her call, my day could have been described as dismal at best. The fact was that the weather had been terrible for weeks, with drifting snow and bitter cold winds. Her phone call was the best thing that happened to me in a long time. I had been working from my home office at my cottage; I found I could accomplish whatever was required through the internet almost as well as from my office in Charlottesville. But that meant I had nothing to alleviate a growing cabin fever. Too many days of being inside were starting to wear on my mind. I went to the gym a few times and swam for exercise at the Y, despite finding it really tough to get up for swimming when it was so bloody cold outside. I did it anyway, wanting to maintain a minimum level of physical well-being.

The holidays had come and gone. I had survived them both, but not without difficulty. It was not much fun being home alone. I wasn't in the mood to hang out with my family. Most of my visits were cut short, as I found excuses to head home early and read a book, watch some TV, or do anything to make it through another day.

A board meeting was planned for early next month in New York. From New York, I had a flight booked to Belize for a few weeks to spend some time with Ilana and her husband, sailing and swimming, anything to get out of the north country for a while, knowing sunshine and warm temperatures would be good for my mental health.

After she called, I adjusted my daily schedule, deciding to wait until she arrived to have a drink. But she was late, and when it began to look like she was not coming, I became convinced, she had stood me up. I poured a whiskey to appease my disappointment and settled on a couch with some nuts, turned on my stereo, and listened to a Brandy Carlile CD.

The view of the lake outside was disdainfully abysmal. The sky had darkened, the sun disappearing into an obscure, graying horizon, indistinguishable in the receding light. From what I could observe, the lake looked to be frozen into the sky, creating an icy highway into infinite space. Allowing my mind to wander up the highway to distances too far to imagine, I grew sleepy, leaned back on my couch, and allowed my eyes to close briefly as night took possession of day.

A knock on my door awakened me to a different reality. I wondered briefly if I was dreaming. Was I so badly wanting to see her that I had created an illusion of reality in my overactive imagination to appease my desires? I had given up on her, assumed she was not coming. The weather was too bad, and the roads were impossible. She had wisely stayed away. It took a second knock to revive me fully.

After opening the door, she stepped inside, covered with snow. Her full-length, dark burgundy cashmere coat was dusted with white crystals, which immediately began to melt once inside my warm cottage.

Running a gloved hand over her hair to wipe off some snow, she frowned, 'I thought you were going to make me stand at the door all night.'

'Sorry,' I apologized. 'I think I dozed off.'

'What, not sufficiently excited to see me?'

'No, it's just, I had given up on you. I didn't think you were coming.'

'Why not?'

'The weather is terrible.'

'Yes, it is.'

'You came anyway.'

'Did you forget, John? I told you I'm a Wisconsin girl? A little snow is not going to stop me. I know how to drive in the stuff.'

'I'm glad you made it.'

'Yes, me too. It took a lot longer than I thought.'

I smiled.

'What do you have to drink in this place. I need to do something to warm up.' Mandy was still wearing her warm coat.

'Want some hot tea?'

'No, I want a glass of wine.'

7:10 PM, JOHN

Fire crackled and sizzled in the open stone fireplace in my living room.

Remnants of snow frozen on the kindling melted as the twigs began to burn over a pile of flaming, crumpled newspaper.

She sat on the floor as I stoked the fire, tossing an occasional broken branch into the burning refuse. I had collected the fallen branches last fall from a forest behind my cottage, cut the larger wood into fire-size logs, and stacked it near my back door. The pile was covered in snow when I went to retrieve the wood for a fire and it took only a few minutes working outside for my hands to get cold, even though I wore heavy gloves. After clearing the snow off the wood, I brought some inside.

When the fire was finally burning hot, she began to relax, never straying far from the glowing ember's warm reach.

'I think I have been living in India too long,' she commented. 'I'm not used to the cold anymore.'

'How's your drink?'

'The wine is good.'

'So, what brings you here?'

'You did, silly,' she answered. 'I wanted to see you again.'

'You traveled all the way from India to see me?' I questioned her mental health.

'No. I'm came to help Joey in Detroit. I've been in this country for several weeks.'

'So, you didn't make a special trip just to see me?'

'No, silly. Does that disappoint you?' she smiled.

'Kind of.' It was my turn to smile.

'Well, get over it… Aren't you happy to see me? Because I can leave.'

'No, please don't. I'm very happy to see you. I'm just trying to understand the ground rules.'

'There are no rules.'

'I see.'

'Are you okay with that?'

'I am.'

'Good. Then get me another drink.'

When I returned with a glass of wine, her cashmere coat was lying on my couch. Dressed in jeans and a tight white wool sweater, which did nothing to hide her ample curves, the nights I had previously spent with her came back to me with a yearning I had not experienced for the last few lonely months.

'You finally warm?' I asked.

'Yes, the fire is great.'

I sat down beside her on the floor with a glass of Scotch and took a sip. It had been decided not to go to dinner at a restaurant as I had planned. She said she had been driving in the cold long enough for one day. She wanted to stay here, where it was warm, and drink some wine. I served up a meager offering of cheese and crackers, placing the food next to where she warmed herself by the fire. In time, the flames grew steady and hot, warming my large living room.

'What is that noise?' she asked.

The wind was howling outside in the dark night. With nothing to slow its determined progress across a flat, icy expanse of water known as Lake Michigan, it rebelled loudly as it came ashore, roaring through barren tree branches, rushing inland filled with falling snow, whitewashing the land.

'Wind,' I answered.

She said nothing, sipped her wine as the fire glowed. A few more logs thrown on the burning coals ignited quickly, flames rising in the fireplace, heating the room to a comfortable temperature. I turned down the lights, relying on the fire to see her. She moved beside me and kissed me on the cheek. Removing her sweater, but not her bra, she then began to unbutton her jeans.

'Can I help you?' I offered.

'No,' she replied as she took off her jeans and socks without my assistance, dressed only in a bra and panties.

I did as she asked, said nothing more, and simply watched the flames cover her luscious body with a golden glow.

'We have all night, John,' Mandy stated. 'I want to make it last. Now get comfortable and come over and hold me. Do you think you can do that, John, just like we did in Pakistan? Do you remember the night when you first held me?'

'Yes, I remember.'

'I want that again, John. That's why I came to see you.'

'Okay.'

SUNDAY, JANUARY 29, 7:20 AM, JOHN

Eggs were lined up on the kitchen counter next to the stove to be done over easy as requested by her ladyship, who was resting comfortably in bed. A couple of slices of bread sat on a plate by a toaster next to jam and butter, all ready to go.

'Would you like breakfast in bed?' I shouted from the kitchen. Dressed in a bathrobe and slippers.

'No, I'll be right in,' she replied.

Coffee was brewing. I poured orange juice into glasses, set plates and silverware on the table in the living room, which had a view of the lake. The wind was still blowing hard. Snow is coming down intermittently. There wasn't much to see outside, just a gray blur of snow and ice. I had restarted the fire. It was a cold day. The fire's warmth was welcome.

I smiled and went to work, cracking eggs over a pan, turning them over when they were half done, and placing bread in a toaster just as she emerged from the bathroom. An old pink bathrobe she found in a closet covered her nicely. She had washed her face, brushed her hair, and looked great as far as I was concerned. She didn't need any makeup. Her smile was enough.

'Do you always keep a woman's bathrobe in your closet just in case you get lucky?' she asked.

'No, it belonged to my girlfriend.'

'Girlfriend as in past girlfriend?'

'Yes, she died.'

'I'm sorry.'

'No need to be sorry. It's a long story. I can tell you sometime if you wish.'

Our night had been long and luxurious. For hours, we talked, got caught up as the fire burned hot, covering our heated bodies with its luxurious warmth. I asked her if she worried about being found by her former husband when she was in the States. She said no. She was traveling under the same passport she had used in

Afghanistan, the passport of Mrs. Steve Taylor, a Canadian national.

I asked her if this meant she was still married to me.

If you like, was her answer.

So… what was she doing in the US?

She said Kamyar had developed a new product, and the US employees needed to be educated about how it worked. She was working with the sales force, demonstrating its attributes, as well as accompanying them on sales calls.

I asked her about the new product.

She said it was a computer that monitored engine functions, producing a ten percent decrease in fuel consumption. Apparently, Kamyar was the principal driving force behind the company, a computer genius. He had designed it. The product was manufactured in Mumbai before being sent to Detroit, where it was modified to fit the engines of the Big Three automobile companies. In most cases, this meant nothing more than applying it to a plastic case with the automobile company's logo on the outside.

'Is Kamyar that important to the success of his company?' I asked.

'Yes, he's the man.'

'Everything going well in Dearborn?' I asked.

'Everything except Joey. He's not like his brother, not as motivated as Kamyar. I have to hold his hand to get some things done.'

'That's why you are here?'

'Yes,' she said. 'And because I wanted to see you again.'

'You didn't give me any reason to think that when I left Afghanistan.'

'Did you need me to tell you?'

'No, I guess not.'

She smiled. 'Perhaps we should go to bed again so I can offer you more reassurance.'

'Why not right here by the fire?' I suggested.

'Sure, why not?'

APRIL 18, 4:55 PM, JOHN

Signs of spring appeared, however reluctantly.

Tulips rose as if by miracle, their green sprouts driving through black earth into warm air and sunshine from a bulb which had hibernated underground for long months of winter storms and snow. Buds appeared on trees, the first signs of summer growth, hints of green which would soon fill the forest behind my cottage.

The rebirth of spring happens much more slowly along the lakeshore. The large body of cold, fresh water known as Lake Michigan decelerates the process, depressing air temperatures by as much as ten to fifteen degrees cooler than a few miles inland. It is necessary to be more patient when living by the lake, and the mental discipline required can be difficult after long months of cold and snow.

I had been relatively busy during the winter months, traveling between my home on the lake and my office in Charlottesville, Virginia. Board meetings had taken up some of my time, one in New York City, a place filled with unwelcome memories. Still, I enjoyed being in the Big Apple while attempting to suppress my worst memories, which came to visit me occasionally without warning, especially the memory of the night when my girlfriend, Monica, had died at the Plaza Hotel.

A recent meeting of my company's foundation set the wheels in motion that I had promised Kamyar. Financial aid was sent to Afghanistan, money for a school in his village, replacing the one that a bomb had destroyed. According to Kamyar, the work had already begun. He was grateful for my financial assistance. He asked if I would like to return someday to view the progress. I said I appreciated the invitation and would make a conscious effort to visit in the future. And I thanked him again for his business. His gemstones were flowing through my company. It was a considerable piece of business. He reminded me again of my promise to keep his secret, not to reveal where the stones originated.

A few weeks were spent in Belize, visiting Ilana and her husband, sailing and free diving in the warm seas off the island of Ambergris. It was pleasant. It was great to see Ilana again. The couple appeared to be content in their marriage. I was happy for them.

Most of my winter days and weeks at the cottage were spent reading and attempting to adjust to being alone. All the women in my life were either dead or had deserted me for one reason or another. It was difficult, but I was determined. I needed to move on in my life.

Speaking of women, Mandy didn't stay long, two nights, one day only. Said she had to return to Detroit for work before flying to India. No promises were made. When I asked if she would be returning any time soon, she simply said she had enjoyed our time together. She hoped I did as well. Was that enough? she asked. Because if it wasn't, then she wouldn't bother me in the future. She didn't want to be a problem.

I said she was not a problem. Stop in anytime.

The phone rang while I was thinking about her. I had been reading, but the words were not responding in my brain, sentences without meaning. I wasn't concentrating. The lake was riled up outside my windows, waves driving towards shore, topped with whitecaps, crashing on a helpless beach, shifting ever-evolving sands. A gray spring sky was uninviting, the weather promising little relief; another dull spring day waiting for summer. I wondered, thought, hoped perhaps Mandy was on the phone. I wasn't expecting a call from anyone else.

'Hello,' I answered tentatively.

'John,' a male caller, returned my greeting, immediately dismantling my hopes. I recognized the voice. 'Hey, Charlie.'

'John, I have some news I feel obligated to pass on.'

'What is it?' I asked, now on alert. The tone of his voice sounded concerned. He was not his usual jovial self.

'This is totally confidential,' he warned me. 'You can't tell anyone.'

'I understand. Now just tell me because you are starting to get on my nerves. You aren't calling to give me good news, are you?'

'No, I'm afraid not.'

'Okay, out with it.'

He paused, seemed reluctant to continue.

'You called me, Charlie. I didn't call you. You said you wanted to tell me something when you called?'

'It's about Kamyar Abdul.'

'What about Kamyar?'

Charlie hesitated, 'Not over the phone. Would it be okay if I fly in for a visit this weekend?'

'I suppose,' I responded. I had nothing planned, thinking it wouldn't be so bad to spend time with Charlie again, even if he was the bearer of bad news.

'Good, that will give us more time to talk.'

'How serious is this?' I asked. 'Because I'm doing considerable business with Kamyar.'

'It's serious. You may have to end your relationship.'

'You had better have a good reason, because there's no way I want to do that, Charlie.'

'You may not have a choice.'

'Charlie, what the hell are you talking about?'

'I'll see you Saturday. My secretary will email my flight details. Plan to pick me up at the airport in Grand Rapids?'

'I can't wait to see your smiling face.'

'Right,' Charlie said. 'Just be there.'

'I'll think about it.'

CHARLOTTE, NORTH CAROLINA, FRIDAY, APRIL 20, 3:05 PM, MANDY

She had seen it all before, too many times to be a coincidence.

Mandy watched sadly as security guards took Joey out of line at the airport, marched him past the other waiting passengers, and walked him towards a door marked Airport Security. She wished she could do something to help, but there was nothing she could do for him.

Already behind schedule due to their flight from Charlotte, North Carolina, to Detroit, Michigan, they had arrived at the airport anxious to move on. Having driven from a BMW plant in Spartanburg, North Carolina, to Charlotte for a direct flight to Detroit, they rushed to drop off their rented car and made a mad dash through the airport to the security check-in. That's where Joey was detained.

Her week had been difficult. She had done her best to keep Joey under control, but it wasn't easy. He was an exceptionally intelligent man, a graduate of MIT with a degree in nuclear physics. He had little patience for stupidity in others, a character trait that did nothing to assist her in their sales efforts.

They had spent a week touring automobile plants in the South, assisting engineers in manufacturing facilities, helping them understand the newest innovations offered by Kamyar's company. Most of the initial sales work had been accomplished at the company headquarters, the international offices for BMW in Munich, Germany. Mandy had headed up this effort. Kamyar had supported her. He was the driving force in the company. It was his innovative designs that had built the business. The products were manufactured in India using inexpensive labor before being shipped to Europe or the United States for adaptation to individual cars. Price is what initially got the business off the ground. But it was Kamyar's innovations that really made it hum.

She was very familiar with the product, and her technological knowledge assisted her when traveling with Joey who enjoyed being with a beautiful woman. But for her, he was a problem. Although he was very intelligent and completely understood the product, he lacked certain qualities normally associated with common sense. He didn't know how to relate to people. And it took all of Mandy's considerable talent to keep him in line. Most of the time, she would have been happier to make calls without him. But he always insisted on tagging along. Nothing would change his mind. This was his company, after all. He told her he had a right to go with her.

She had discussed Joey's problems with Kamyar many times. He said he understood. Joey was his brother. He knew him well. He knew Joey's weaknesses. But Kamyar said he couldn't do anything to help. He thought all Joey lacked was experience, and traveling with her would help him learn. Kamyar hoped his brother would eventually modify his behavior and become a better representative of the company. In the meantime, Mandy would simply have to hold his hand.

Airport security did not help. They did nothing to improve Joey's attitude. They only made it worse. She sighed as she watched them take him away. Escorted by two uniformed airport security guards, he disappeared behind a closed door. Although he always dressed well, in American suits with a tie, his features were Middle Eastern. Security profiled him. His passport indicated he was from Afghanistan. This was all they needed to detain him.

She knew what would happen next. He had told her about his previous experiences, how he was questioned at length, sometimes strip-searched, and made to wait for hours. In all probability, he would be late for their flight. It was Friday. She knew he was looking forward to returning to Michigan, to his wife and two sons. He had told her how exhausted he was. These visits were a drain on him. He was not a people person.

Security never bothered her. Her Canadian passport was never questioned. After going through security, she checked her flight. It was on schedule and would take off in twenty-five minutes. She had two choices. She could wait for Joey, but in doing so, she would probably miss her flight. Or she could just go. He would have to get home on his own.

Tomorrow was Saturday. She had been in the United States for approximately two weeks. Monday was a return flight to India. She had a couple of free days. She thought about John. Maybe drive up to see him.

Making up her mind quickly, she headed for her gate.

GRAND RAPIDS, MICHIGAN, SATURDAY, APRIL 21, 9:10 AM, JOHN

She called when I was driving to Grand Rapids, near the airport, to pick up Charlie.

To say I was surprised to hear from her voice would have been an understatement. Mandy had not been on my mind recently, but Charlie had. His news was my main concern. I did not want anything to interfere with my business with Kamyar. I had been preparing for him, drafting speeches in my mind, hoping to change Charlie's mind. Whatever he had to say couldn't be that bad, not worth losing a multimillion-dollar contract. I had to find a way to convince Charlie.

'Hi, John,' she said in a cheery voice over my cell phone.

'Mandy?' I questioned.

'Were you expecting another woman?'

'No, I just didn't expect to hear from you this morning.'

'Are you disappointed?'

'No, of course not.'

'Good, because I would like to see you.'

'When?' My brain went into serious alert, please not this weekend, I silently begged.

'Today.'

'Can it wait?'

'Sure, see you in a couple of months. I'm headed to India Monday.'

Now I had a problem, a big problem.

I was fifteen minutes from the airport to pick up Charlie. He had already said he wanted to stay overnight at my cottage, mentioning we had a lot to talk about. He planned to return to Washington, D.C., on Sunday morning.

GRAND HAVEN, 3:10 PM, JOHN

'Damn it, Charlie, there has to be another way.'

The sliders in the great room at the cottage were partially open to a gentle, warm breeze. A partly cloudy day with warm spring temperatures was being wasted. I had spent most of the day inside arguing with Charlie.

'I'm sorry, John. You can do as you wish,' Charlie stated. 'You are an American citizen. This is not a police state. I can't tell you what to do. I can only suggest what I would do in a similar situation.'

'Yeah, right, since when did the CIA begin to indulge in suggestions? To my knowledge, your tactics are normally much more heavy-handed.'

'Well, you're wrong, John,' Charlie stated. 'Do as you please, but I don't think it would do your reputation any good if it was discovered you were aiding and abetting the enemy.'

He was talking about my deal with Kamyar. Seems the CIA was concerned about someone bringing a bomb into this country. They had decided Kamyar might be involved. He had been labeled an insurgent by the CIA, whatever that meant. I was never quite sure what the word 'insurgent' meant when the media used it, and I sure as hell didn't understand its meaning now, especially when it was being used by an organization as abstruse as the CIA. Regardless, according to Charlie, Kamyar was an insurgent. And anyone doing business with him could be considered to be aiding and abetting the enemy. That was Charlie's logic, and Charlie was never one to be faulted by his logic.

'Why don't we ask Mandy about him? She knows him better than I do.' I stated without thinking. I was mad. I had run out of arguments. Charlie was not listening.

Now... I hadn't planned on telling Charlie about Mandy. I had decided to simply tell him I made a reservation for him at the hotel in Grand Rapids. Sorry, buddy, but something came up since I talked to you last. You can't stay with me at my cottage tonight.

But I hadn't told him, not yet. And the reason I hadn't told him was because I didn't think we would still be talking. I had hoped to conclude my business with Charlie hours earlier, drive him to GR long before Mandy was scheduled to arrive at my cottage.

I glanced at my watch. Hours had slipped away arguing with Charlie. She was due to arrive any minute. I was in trouble.

'Who is Mandy?' Charlie demanded.

'She's the reason you can't stay here tonight. I have a date with her.'

'What are you talking about? Are you kicking me out?'

'I am.'

'For a woman?'

'Yes, are you surprised?'

'No.'

'Good, I didn't think you would be. I made a reservation for you at the Marriott in Grand Rapids, paid for your dinner, and got you all set up. I hope you don't mind.'

'Thanks, John. You really didn't have to do that.'

'No, but I did. Now you have to go. Take my car, leave it at the airport. I'll get it later.'

He paused. 'Okay, but first, who is Mandy?'

Charlie was a detail guy. I should never have brought up her name. It became immediately clear that he wouldn't leave until I told him all about her.

6:20 PM, JOHN

The sun set in relative obscurity, disappearing behind a gray cloud horizon that had formed in late afternoon after a blue-sky day.

I was disappointed. No sunset tonight. But somehow the dismal scenery seemed in a way as a fitting end to a day which had begun with much anticipation, but did not deliver as promised.

Charlie had been gone for a few hours, but only after I verbally shoved him out the door, handed him the keys to my car, and told him to go to Grand Rapids, where I had reserved a hotel room for him.

He didn't go easy. He first demanded I tell him everything about the woman I expected to arrive at any minute, the reason I wanted him out of my house. He delayed his exit, continued asking questions, and only went away after he was convinced, she was not coming. I'm sure he wanted to meet her, see for himself what she was like. Charlie was a spook after all, and a good one. Whenever possible, he wanted to know everything there was to know about any person of interest in a case he was working.

It was fortunate she was late. I'm not sure what would have happened if Charlie had been here when she came. He probably would have asked her a bunch of questions about Kamyar, all of which would have made her wonder why he was so interested. And that would have led to her asking me about him after he left, and that would have been a problem. Because I, of course, could not tell her the real reason Charlie had been here. So, I was more than happy she came late.

When she finally came, I was glad to see her, but I don't think I showed it because it didn't take long for us to have a disagreement. I don't know why, really. The issue was so trivial. I guess it was because Charlie was on my nerves, and I didn't like the fact that she was late. I had been worried about her. I didn't tell her that, but I did ask her why. She explained that a client had called with a technical problem related to the new product. She had to talk him through it, and it took time, a couple of hours.

I wondered why Joey couldn't do it. Why did she need to talk to the client?

She sighed and said Joey would only have made it worse.

I didn't totally understand that. And if I had known the time of her arrival, I could have driven Charlie to Grand Rapids and returned with my car. Instead, I would have to beg a ride into town in the future and drive it back. Plus, during the time I spent waiting impatiently for her, I had been beating myself up for mentioning her name to Charlie. My friendly spook wanted to know everything about her, every detail of her relationship with Kamyar and me. I told him most of what he wanted to know, except what was private. Which was okay with him since he said he could guess that part.

And as it turned out, I didn't know enough. Charlie's innate curiosity was not satisfied. For instance, he wanted to know her real name, but I didn't know it or exactly where she was from. I only knew she came from Wisconsin, went to college there, and got a degree in engineering. I told him she was traveling under a false passport; Mandy Taylor was the name on a Canadian passport. I said she did this to avoid being found by her ex-husband, who was a violent nutcase.

Charlie found this part of her story particularly suspicious. He said he would look into it. I begged him not to expose her. I told him her husband had threatened to kill her. But I wasn't sure my buddy Charlie believed me. Before driving away, he asked me to get her real name and where she was born. He said he would check her out and get back to me. Then he added as a suggestion: don't do anything stupid until he could check her out. And he demanded I not tell her about our conversation, about Kamyar being on the radar screen of the CIA.

All this made me very unhappy. I don't like keeping secrets, especially from someone with whom I was interested in having a relationship. I didn't think that would lead to anything good.

As a result, I wasn't in a good mood, and it didn't take long for my sour mood to manifest itself in a disagreement, a minor disagreement, but a disagreement nevertheless.

6:30 PM, MANDY

Mandy took another sip of her wine and tried to relax, to think, to decide what to do.

The broad expanse of the lake drew her in and gave her some comfort in a difficult situation. Waves lapped calmly on an unseen shore below where she rested on a couch in John's cottage, wondering briefly if all men turn violent eventually. Did it only take time for them to show their true colors? Perhaps she had been wrong all along about John. Was he like her husband? Were all males like him? She didn't think so, but she had collected very little evidence over time to back up her theory. John was only the second man she had let into her life. After her first terrible experience, she had stayed away from men, turned them back whenever they attempted to gain a tiny entrance into her life.

Kamyar had been good for her in this respect. He had never approached her for anything besides a business relationship. He recognized her talents and respected her desire to do her job simply, nothing more. Eventually, she told him her story, why she had run away to India. Not because he asked, but because she needed to tell someone.

He had helped her when she needed help most. He got her a new identity, a fake passport, and a visa so she could live in India and travel if she desired. Some of this was for his benefit. He needed her talents when selling his product in foreign markets, and she had responded to his kindness by doing all she could to help advance his company. In return, he paid her well and helped her settle in Mumbai.

When he initially had told her about a John, explaining that he who was coming for a visit, Kamyar had explained it was a very delicate situation. He didn't know who to trust with the assignment. He had asked for her advice, which is something he had come to do often in recent months, relying on her for her wisdom. He told her about the reason for the visit, about the emerald mine, something he had previously kept from her. He explained the value of the gemstones and their potential impact on the people in his villages, particularly in supporting schools and hospitals. He said he planned to use some of the money for these projects.

She believed him, and after he explained the situation to her in detail, she knew she had to help.

He asked her if she really wanted to. He told her she only needed to be a guide; nothing else was required.

She said she understood. She said she would do it. She would be a tour guide for an American businessman. She would pretend to be his wife because a husband and wife traveling together was less suspicious.

Now she wondered if this had been a good decision.

'Are you okay?' John asked her.

She realized she had been silent for several minutes. Neither of them had spoken since he expressed his frustration with her for being late. She had apologized, but he seemed upset. It wasn't the words he said that worried her; it was how he was acting. It was his body language. Clearly, he was upset, agitated. She worried that this was the beginning of trouble. She had seen it before in her husband. First, he became upset. Then he became violent.

'I'm fine,' she paused before adding, 'Perhaps I should go.'

'Why?'

'I don't know. You don't seem happy to see me.'

'I am. It's just, I'm sorry. It has been a long day.'

'I think I'll go.' She stood.

He began to approach her.

She stepped back, fear in her eyes, flashbacks of when her husband beat her rushed through her mind.

John stopped; saw the look in her eyes. 'Mandy,' he said. 'You have nothing to fear from me. I will never hurt you.'

She wasn't easily convinced. She had stayed away from men for a reason. The last few years of her life were spent avoiding situations like this.

'Let me order something to eat,' he said. 'I know a good Chinese restaurant.'

'I don't know,' she replied. 'I think I should go.'

The fear was real, the memories of those black nights and dark days when her husband beat her; those blood-spattered memories were not dead. They were still alive, and it didn't take much for them to rear their ugly head again. Panic attacks drawn from these memories were never far from the surface of her mind. She had hoped they were a thing of the past. Now she knew this was not true. Perhaps it would never be true. Perhaps she would live forever with fear.

When traveling with John, he seemed to be a kind man, thoughtful, and accepting of her help and guidance, never dominating in their conversation. She thought he was different. She knew she needed a man. Even though she had buried her desires deep in her soul, so deep she hoped they would never resurface again, she knew someday she would desire a man again. And this was the man she desired. She had given to him, and he gave to her without demanding anything in return. But now he was showing a different side to his personality, a weaker side. It scared her, brought back the black memories.

Kathrine, Kate, Kate Talsma was scared. She wanted to go, needed to be gone.

She found her coat and headed for the door as fear grabbed her heart and twisted until it hurt to breathe.

GRAND RAPIDS, MICHIGAN, 7:10 PM, CHARLIE

The steak was tasty; the beer was thirst-quenching and cold; everything was paid for by John as he promised.

This was the best part and the only part that gave Charlie any satisfaction. His hotel room in the JW Marriott on the Grand River was first class, the restaurant modern, and the service great. He had stayed in far worse places when traveling at government expense. Charlie knew he should be happy, but he was anything but happy.

For one, this was the first time John had ever kicked him out. John had always been very kind and considerate. Charlie liked this in him. After years of being discriminated against because of his race, Charlie was not a very accepting guy. He was cautioned to avoid being hurt. He had few friends, mostly because he didn't easily let many people into his life. John was an exception, especially since he was a white guy. Their friendship had developed slowly and only after a considerable amount of time and experience, only after John had thoroughly proved his loyalty. Only then did Charlie fully trust him.

He guessed John assumed he wouldn't be too mad if he kicked him out, not just this once. They had been friends for several years. John had explained: he could not have anticipated the problem. It just happened, not in his control. It was because of a woman. John's relationship with this woman was in the formative stages. John asked Charlie if he would please go to a hotel in GR. He said he was sorry. She had called him in the morning and asked if she could come over. John did not want to say no to her.

Charlie understood the part about it being a woman. Charlie could have anticipated this. If John had a weakness, it was women. So, it made sense. But still, it didn't sit well with him. He didn't like eating alone. He had anticipated having a pleasant evening with John, some beer, and some laughter. Charlie had been looking forward to spending some time with his old friend. Truth was, he was disappointed.

But that wasn't the worst part. The business about his lady friend being a companion to a man Charlie considered a potential terrorist; this was bad. But what to do? He didn't know. It was complicated. What was obvious to Charlie as he thought about it was that he would now have to get John involved, work again as his field agent. But after their last debacle, the last time he had asked John to do him a favor, after how badly that turned out, he wasn't sure he wanted to involve John again if he could help it. But he couldn't figure out any other way out of this mess.

Charlie cut off another chunk of juicy steak and stuffed it absentmindedly into his mouth, savoring its delicious flavor. He was disgusted with the whole situation. It should have been easy. He had come to tell John to back off, walk away from this Afghan guy and his emeralds. And John should have agreed. But now a woman was involved. And women only make complicated situations more complicated. In John's case, this was always true. It was now not likely that John would walk away.

It was a complicated mess, and Charlie did not like messes.

GRAND HAVEN, 7:15 PM, KATE

The sign at a road intersection in the town of Grand Haven indicated directions to a state park.

Kate turned and drove down the road through a residential neighborhood, passing a kid peddling a bike on the sidewalk. After going up and down several small hills where houses lined both sides of the street with green lawns and old trees, a big lake appeared over a hilltop, an awe-inspiring expanse of water stretching from one side of the horizon to the other for as far as she could see. The road turned parallel to a beach of rolling sandy dunes. She drove slowly, trying to calm down, taking deep breaths, regaining a grip on reality.

People were walking on the beach near the shore. It was still light, an hour before sunset. A pleasant evening, warm and calm; her car window was open as she drove. A city parking lot off the road overlooked the lake. Kate turned into the lot and parked her car in a spot where she could view the lake.

Waves washed on shore in monotonous regularity as she rested in her car, attempting to cleanse her mind of fears, the memories of all those bad times. She remembered telling her husband she wanted a divorce. He had bought a gun the next day and showed it to her in the evening, telling her he would never let her leave him. That's when she knew she had no choice. She needed to run if she wanted to live. She packed a small suitcase of clothes and a few credit cards when he was at work the next day and walked out of her house of horrors, never looking back. Her credit cards bought an airplane ticket to India. She didn't know why she chose this destination; just something drew her to its temples. Something she had read about the wisdom and serenity of its religions. She landed in New Delhi, took a bus to Mumbai, where it was easy to become lost in the vast multitude of its inhabitants. A job waiting tables in an international hotel restaurant sustained her for several months before seeing an ad for a job in Kamyar's company. That was her lucky break.

The expansive body of water beyond her windshield beckoned. Opening the door of her car on a whim, she took off her shoes. The warm sand flowed through her toes as she walked slowly to the water's edge; her eyes searching a gray evening sky for a solution to her problems.

This was silly, she concluded after a short stroll along the shoreline. John had done nothing wrong. Not really. It was her; her fears were the problem. She needed to get over her fears. If she was ever going to love again, she needed to be brave.

She dialed his number on her cell phone as she stood on the shore.

'John… It's Mandy. May I come back?'

10:55 PM, JOHN

A gentle breeze carrying sounds of waves lapping on shore entered through an open window in the bedroom.

It was a warm night for early spring. Only a sheet and blanket were needed to be comfortable. I wasn't sure she was sleeping. I only knew her body felt good in my arms as we lay in bed. She had asked me to hold her again, nothing else, hold her like I did when we were traveling through India. Could I do that? she asked, just hold her again, nothing else, no sex. That was what she desired.

I did as she asked, happy to feel her soft, round body close to me.

When she returned after calling to ask if she could come back, I didn't ask her why she left or why she came back. Nothing was said. I just let her enter my cottage as if nothing had happened. She smiled shyly and hung up her coat. Her suitcase was in the car. She asked if I would get it for her.

A couple of chicken potpies were in the freezer. This was as good as I could do on short notice. I didn't dare go into town for takeout. I didn't want to leave her alone in the cottage. I was afraid she would walk out again. The pies were easy to prepare, standard fare for my bachelor lifestyle. I put them in the oven and set the timer while she sat in the great room sipping wine. While the aroma from the cooking pies began to float through the cottage, we went out on the front deck with our cocktails.

There was not much to see; a calm evening sky had slowly evolved to black through shades of gray clouds over the rolling waters of the lake. She was quiet, resting, lost in her thoughts. I let her be. I had been insensitive when she arrived in the afternoon, concerned only with my problems. I didn't consider her needs. What happened was my fault. I needed to make amends. I did everything I could to make her feel comfortable.

She smiled often. I think she knew I was trying. Without complaint, she ate my simple meal offering. Halfway through, she asked, 'Do you, by any chance, have some applesauce?'

'Actually, I do.'

She smiled again.

I found a half-used jar in the refrigerator. 'Want it in a bowl?' I asked to be proper.

'No, just give me the jar.' She twisted off the top and poured it on top of her chicken potpie.

I followed her lead, savoring the concoction.

'Where did you learn that?' I asked.

'What, putting applesauce on a potpie?'

'Yes.'

'At home when I was a kid.'

'Yeah, me too,' I noted.

She didn't say anything at first, just continued to eat in silence. But eventually, she asked the question which was on my mind, 'You're wondering if I'm Dutch like you?'

'I was.'

'I am.'

'Are you kidding?'

'No, do you want to know my real name?' she said, attempting to hold down her fears.

'Only if you want to tell me.'

It didn't come out immediately. She held back for a moment, didn't say anything... 'Kathrine Talsma. That's my maiden name.'

'It's nice to meet you, Kathrine,' I acknowledged her admission as if it were no big deal. However, I sensed it was a big deal for her, but I didn't say anything more.

'You can call me Kate or Kate,' she volunteered with a weak smile.

'I like Kate.'

'And John?'

'Yes, Kate.'

'You can only call me by my real name when we are together in private. But in public, I'm Mandy.'

'You're still afraid of your husband?'

'Yes,' she answered with a faraway look in her eyes.

MONDAY, APRIL 23, 9:45 AM, JOHN

'Well?' Charlie barked into his phone as soon as I answered.

'Well, what?' I answered.

'You know what. Tell me what you found out about the girl.'

'What, no niceties this morning, no thanks, John, for a great room at the Marriott. I assume you had a good meal. I haven't received the bill yet, but I'm guessing you didn't spare expenses.'

'Why should I?' he asked. 'You dumped me, sent me to a hotel to get rid of me. Do you really think I should be grateful?'

'I guess not. Sorry about that.'

'Well, was it worth it?' he demanded.

'You mean did I get laid?'

'Yea, well did you?'

'None of your business.'

'It's my business if you are sleeping with a terrorist.'

'She's no terrorist.'

'And you know that because?'

'Because I know.' Charlie was starting to get on my nerves.

My buddy had nothing to say for a moment.

'So, does your silence mean you accept my opinion?' I asked.

'No, it does not… John. Let's get serious for a moment. Things have just gone from bad to worse.'

'What are you talking about?'

Charlie explained. His morning briefing included a story about a nuclear bomb that was missing. The Russian counterpart to the CIA, the KGB, had finally acknowledged it was missing after spending a month trying to find it. They put out a confidential worldwide alert and sent it to all cooperating intelligence services. Every avenue was being explored. When Charlie looked through his notes on Kamyar, he noticed Kamyar's brother, Jahwed Abdul, had a minor degree in nuclear physics. And this caused an alarm to ring in Charlie's head. When he told his superior about Joey, Charlie was promptly instructed to do whatever he could to run down the lead.

'Is this why you are calling me this morning, Charlie? Because you're worried Kamyar is bringing a nuclear bomb into the country?'

'It's a possibility,' Charlie answered.

'Everything is a possibility. But what is the probability of such a preposterous proposition?' I was pissed. This thing with Charlie was getting out of control. Now he was talking nuclear bombs.

'I did some checking,' Charlie said, ignoring me. 'Kamyar's company is importing a large container from Russia this month. Do you think that's coincidental or should it be checked out?'

'He imports large containers almost every week. It's part of his business.'

'You don't think it's worth checking out?'

'No.'

'I'm going to look into it anyway,' Charlie affirmed.

'Sure, check it out if you wish. But I don't think you will find a nuclear bomb in the container.'

'Why not?'

'Because I told you, I have met this man and he does not strike me as a mass murderer.'

'I'm sorry,' Charlie said. 'But I didn't notice a framed degree in criminal psychology on your office wall. Exactly how is it you know this?'

I said nothing in reply.

'We can't allow a nuclear bomb to enter this country.' Charlie continued, ignoring me.

'Why not? There are plenty of nuclear bombs in this country already.' Charlie had gotten under my skin. I didn't know why, but I was in the mood to argue with him.

'You know what I mean,' he countered.

'No, I don't.'

'I mean not in the wrong hands.'

'And who has the right hands, Charlie?' I demanded. 'Who has the right to have a nuclear bomb, any nuclear bomb? Why does the US have the right and not anyone else?'

'Do I really have to answer your question?' Charlie demanded.

'Yes, answer it.'

'Because we are responsible for the use of our weapons.'

'Really, Charlie?' Have we always been responsible when it comes to war? How many wars have we conducted in the last fifty years that we never should have been involved in? And what makes you so certain we will be responsible in the future?'

Charlie had nothing to say.

'If we were really interested in acting responsibly, we would destroy all our nuclear weapons and never build another one,' I argued.

'That would make us vulnerable to any nation that has a bomb.'

'Really, do you really think exchanging nuclear bombs is like trading bullets in a Western gun fight? We will all be dead if a nuclear war breaks out, Charlie. We should take the lead, destroy our bombs, and demand everyone else do the same. That is the only way the human race will be safe. Because if we don't, someday, someone is going to blow up one of those things and the consequences will be like going to hell… Can we afford to take that chance? What do you think, Charlie?'

'Okay, okay, John. I get your point. In the meantime, I have a job to do and I need you to help me do it. Now tell me, what did you find out about the girl?'

'I found out she is a great lady who has seen a world of troubles. She needs our help, Charlie.'

'Okay, okay. You know how this works,' Charlie replied. 'I'll help you… but only if you agree to help me in return.'

AMSTERDAM, THE NETHERLANDS, TUESDAY, MAY 15, 10:05 AM, JOHN

Traditional architecture, five stories high, the exterior of the imposing block-long hotel was tan brick with white wood trim around the windows.

The Intercontinental Amstel Amsterdam Hotel was conveniently located in the center of the city on a large canal. She had chosen it, not me. I told Kate she could stay wherever she wanted. I would pick up the tab.

The hotel wouldn't have been my choice, too ornate, but she looked happy as she showed me around the lobby, pointing to a gold chandelier which hung under a vaulted ceiling supported by sculpted white pillars, reminding me of a palace, luxury wherever you turned.

Everything had been arranged for several weeks. Kamyar didn't want anything left to chance. After my last trip which included a gun battle at his home, he wanted to avoid a repeat disaster. The plan was for me to get in and get out quickly. A trip to the mine was not on the itinerary this time, only a visit to the village school to see construction progress. I agreed to come because it would impolite to refuse Kamyar when he personally called to invite me.

Before leaving, I had to find the passport from my last trip when I was Steve Taylor. I was instructed to use it again for this trip into Afghanistan. This time, Steve Taylor was to be an emissary of a charity that funded the school. The charity in my case was my foundation which had given money to a charitable organization devoted to funding schools in poor, developing nations. The money was earmarked for one village, Kamyar's village. This was a condition of the gift and it was from an anonymous donor. No one knew the money came from a company that specialized in colored gemstones.

It had been weeks since I had seen Kate, not since late in April. She had been busy helping Kamyar with his new product. We had talked a few times. This was the extent of our relationship, nothing too exciting. She had sounded good when I talked to her, busy with her work. When I told her I was traveling to Afghanistan, she agreed to meet me in Amsterdam, fly with me, and pretend once again to be my wife again.

I didn't object.

However, Charlie did. He objected and heavily told me in no uncertain terms not to go. He said it was too dangerous. However, he was wasting his time, and he knew it. He only wanted to make his point so I couldn't blame him if events went badly.

Charlie had been helping me. A background check on Katherine Talsma was run through his agency at his request. Everything she told me was correct, about her degree, about where she went to school, about her marriage. Her husband's name was Kevin Bradford. His dad practically owned a small farming town in Iowa, including the local Chevy dealership, the John Deere farm equipment dealership, a grocery store, and a gas station. Charlie said the name Bradford was on almost every building in town.

Charlie, being my good friend, then reminded me I was screwing a married woman. He asked me what I was going to do about this.

'It's a special circumstance,' I replied. 'She isn't really married anymore, hasn't been with the guy for a long time.'

'She's still legally married,' he noted.

'Yea, I get that.'

'So, what are you going to do about her?'

'I don't know, Charlie. I'll think about it.'

'You need to do more than that.'

'I will.'

'Good.'

'Look, Charlie. Are you more interested in the fact I'm screwing a married woman or a terrorist?'

'Both.'

'Fine, I'm dating a married terrorist. Anything else you want to know.'

Charlie didn't seem too happy, but he did agree to have someone keep an eye on me when I was in Afghanistan. He said he would call his general friend again. He suggested I try to avoid areas of the country where terrorists were known to be active. Specifically, he said to stay out of the hills around Kamyar's village.

I told him I wasn't in any hills the last time I was attacked.

'That's not what I was told,' he replied.

'Well, whoever you talked to was lying. And by the way, the last time you asked your friend the general to help, it didn't work out so well. I almost got killed.'

Charlie was still not convinced that Kamyar wasn't involved in a terrorist organization. He demanded that I let him know if I observed anything even slightly suspicious while I was with the man.

I reluctantly agreed.

Kate arrived in Amsterdam before me. I phoned her at the airport after exiting my plane. She said she would meet me in the hotel lobby which where I found her after taking a taxi from the airport. She directed me to an elevator. The door opened. I followed her inside the enclosed compartment, dragging my carry-on suitcase, listening to the elevator rise several stories. A long hall led to the door to our room. She slid her keycard into a lock and opened the door. Floor length, dark blue curtains matching a bedspread, and assorted furniture greeted my view. It was a pleasant room with white walls. A Delft China blue lamp on a table reminded me of my mother's collection of similar designs.

'Do you like it?' Kate grinned. 'Doesn't it remind you of home?'

'It's fine.'

'I thought you would be pleased. It's perfect for a couple of Dutch kids like us, don't you think?' She smiled.

'It's great,' I tried to look happy. And I was. I was just tired from a long night of air travel.

'Well, maybe this will make you a little happier.' She turned down the bedspread before coming over to give me a kiss. 'Want to make love?' she asked. 'We didn't get to do it the last time I saw you. I'm sorry about that. I want to make it up to you.'

'Sure,' I picked her up and carried her to the bed, where I unceremoniously dumped her on the mattress.

I was no longer tired.

11:10 PM, JOHN

A leisurely boat ride down canals crisscrossing the city of Amsterdam was the first item on her agenda. Lunch was served on the vessel while we leisurely viewed the sights.

I had to be literally dragged out of the hotel after we made love, told we needed to see the city. Personally, I would have preferred to stay in bed with her, take a catnap to relieve jet lag, but it seemed she had other plans.

The Van Gogh Museum took up most of our afternoon, which we found while riding bikes. Dinner was served at our hotel. The restaurant was ornate, highlighted by a window view of a canal glittering under street lights after sundown. The meal was expensive. The food was good. I don't remember too much else. I was dead tired.

Mostly, I tried to stay awake and keep going. I was worn out and fading fast. She, on the other hand, seemed to be having a great time, energized by what she saw. All of which was in total contrast to the last time I saw her when she came to my cottage. That time, she had been very pensive, introverted, and self-absorbed; like she were fighting some personal demon. This time, she was a completely different person. Kate smiled often, laughed, and talked nonstop. I had trouble keeping up with her pace. When walking, she was in high gear. On a bike, she was driven to see as much of the city as she could. I was wearing down completely towards late afternoon. I hadn't slept much on the flight over the Atlantic, but I kept going somehow; after finding some reserves of energy I didn't know I had. I think because it was great to be with her again.

After dinner, she notified me that we would be visiting a nightclub she had heard about.

I did my best to tell her in every way I could think of, without begging, that I would rather get some sleep. However, nothing worked. Apparently, she didn't know how to take a hint.

The Mansion was the name of the club she had selected for our evening entertainment. Located in a magnificent townhouse, which was said to have once been owned by the royal family, the decor was glorious. A nightclub downstairs featured darkly lit walls, contrasting granite floors, chrome, and black leather modern furniture in stark emphasis. The music was loud, the beat absorbing. It was hard to resist the overpowering sound waves, which seemed to penetrate every sinew of my body. The driving cords dominated my senses, kept me awake. She loved the place. Kate dragged me onto the dance floor despite my reluctance. Dancing with flowing abandonment, her body efficiently mimicked the spirit of every crescendoing chorus of notes. I moved to the music with far less artistic flair than her, totally engrossed in the sweet motion of her body.

The memory of making love to her in the morning came back to me while we were on the dance floor. The sweet images of this time flowed in concert with the music, stimulating my brain waves as I relived the joy of reveling in her naked, feminine body. Making love to her was more than just erotic joy; it was the way she moved in unison with me. The way her body seemed to fit with my body, the symmetry we shared together under luxurious hotel sheets. I enjoyed every exquisite minute of being with her. And now as she danced, these memories seemed to be explicitly highlighted in the pulsating strobe lights over the dance floor, in every note of pounding music.

She was at that moment as close as I could imagine to perfection.

LANGLEY, VIRGINIA, 11:10 PM, CHARLIE

He had waited until late that evening to make the call, and by the time he called, it was morning where he was calling.

One more job to complete, then Charlie's day would be over… finally.

It had been a long day for Charlie, a long day and a long evening of hassling with superiors, managing assets, writing reports, and attempting to balance his budget. Along with a couple of emergencies, which were standard daily routine for a case worker in his capacity, he had a hundred mundane, mind-numbing tasks to complete, all dictated by some efficiency expert who was high up in the chain of command. It may have seemed like efficiency to someone else, but to Charlie, the dictates from above only slowed down his important work of keeping the United States of America safe from outside threats.

The number he dialed used a special line, an encrypted transcontinental telephone line, and was answered at US Army Headquarters in Kabul, Afghanistan.

The sergeant who answered the call put it through to his commanding officer.

'Absolutely,' the general agreed after identifying the caller from the States. 'We'll keep an eye on your boy. When is he due in Kabul?'

'Thursday sometime,' Charlie answered. 'He's flying to Kabul, traveling under a false passport again, you remember. Steve Taylor is the name on the document.'

'Yes, I remember. He's the guy who claimed our soldiers shot at him.'

'That's him.'

'I'll assign one of my best men to him this time.'

'I appreciate it,' Charlie answered.

'He's a friend of yours?' the general inquired.

'In a way.'

'Why's he traveling under an assumed name?'

'It's a long story.'

'It's always a long story with you CIA guys,' the general remarked.

'Sorry.'

'No need to be sorry. Nothing bad is going to happen to your boy this time. I'm making darn sure.'

'Thanks, general.'

'No problem, Charlie. Have a good day.'

AFGHANISTAN, FRIDAY, MAY 18, 9:20 AM, JOHN

It wasn't until late Thursday night that we arrived at Kamyar's compound.

If I thought I was tired before, I didn't know what the word tired meant. By Thursday evening, I was not only tired, I was exhausted, famished, thirsty, and needed to pee. What I wanted more than anything else in the world was a bed to lie down and close my eyes for a month.

Our trip had consisted of a whirlwind of constantly moving images. Beginning in Amsterdam with the drumbeat of nightclub music still reverberating through my skull as I tried to sleep in our hotel, but managed only a few restless dreams before getting up early and taking a taxi to Schiphol Airport outside of the city. A redeye flight had been booked, with eleven hours of flying and one stopover somewhere, I don't remember which airport. I sleepwalked through the transition, boarding another plane for Kabul, Afghanistan.

Ahmed picked us up at the airport in the morning. No time to rest, no Hotel in Kabul this time. After retrieving our baggage, we were on the road. He drove. Kate sat in the front seat, same place as last time. I again was relegated to the back seat, where I tried to rest, which was almost impossible. Roads were uneven, filled with potholes. Our SUV bounced and bumped, Ahmed driving as fast as the road allowed. He did not speak, which was normal for him. Kate seemed preoccupied. I was dead tired. So tired, I remember almost nothing of the trip except that we arrived at Kamyar's compound in the dark, making it impossible to see anything for the last few hours of our trip.

A light meal greeted us, served again by the same man who had helped us before. He spoke as many words as Ahmed. Kate answered the questions he asked in his native language. I ate very little. My stomach was pretty messed up from lack of sleep and stress. Mostly, I wanted to go to bed, which I was finally permitted.

'Same bedroom as the last time?' I asked Kate.

She nodded affirmatively.

I stood up at the table without finishing my meal or saying another word and headed down the hall, dragging my suitcase behind me. In only a matter of minutes, I was in bed, my head on a pillow, instantly sleeping.

After what felt like only a few minutes, she rolled over and gently nudged me awake. 'Time to wake up, sleepyhead,' Kate whispered in my ear.

'I just went to sleep,' I replied, half in a daze, yearning to be allowed to turn over and return to sleep.

'It's morning, silly,' Kate announced. 'We have a lot to do today.'

I reached for her, wondering if I was dreaming, finding a naked thigh in the process, wanting to discover more about who belonged to this wonderful apparition, this ghost from my dreams. I took her in my arms.

'No, no,' she protested. 'I let you sleep as long as I could. We need to get up.'

'This won't take long,' I held her tightly around her waist, burying my face in her soft round breasts, feeling every curve, every muscle in her body tighten as she resisted, tried to get away until finally… her body relaxed, moved closer, submitted to my dreams of her, dreams that had roamed through my mind as I slept, dreams that now became a reality better than anything I had imagined.

FRIDAY, MAY 18, 11:05 AM, JOHN

Construction workers and students shared newly constructed halls of the school together, seemingly unconcerned that their individual duties might interfere in any way with the others. Nothing could be allowed to deter the education of the children.

Kamyar smiled often, spoke words of encouragement to both groups, urging them to do well. Kate translated his words for me as we followed him. He seemed particularly happy that day, a man in control of his destiny. He said he was very satisfied with the progress of the rebuilding.

As I watched him converse with the children and the workers, it was clear he was a natural leader, comfortable in his environment, both encouraging and instructive. He stopped often to offer advice. The children smiled when he took time to talk to them. The workers listened carefully to his words. He stood almost a full foot taller than most of his countrymen, a handsome man with a quick smile; his physical presence and casual demeanor lent authority to his words.

He had explained to us at breakfast, work began within days of the bombing. Men and women worked side by side whenever they had free time. Everyone in the village, almost everyone that is, valued the school. Only one conservative cleric and a few of his miserly followers were opposed to girls attending the school for religious reasons. And the cleric would have been happier if the boys spent their days studying and memorizing the Koran, no math and science for them. According to him, everything else was a waste of time.

Kamyar said, 'This cleric has been a problem for some time now.' After trying to reason with the man but finding this impossible, Kamyar had simply imposed his will on the village. As the traditional ruler of the area, his word was law. Although… rumors recently indicated some inhabitants in the village were talking behind his back, siding with the cleric. Fortunately, Kamyar had prevailed to date, mostly because of what he was able to contribute to the welfare of the villagers. His money gave him an advantage over the cleric. But he said he didn't know how long he would be able to exert influence. His country was becoming politically unstable. It was changing. He was determined to do what he could for as long as he was able. For this reason, the emerald mine was important. It gave him the resources to maintain control.

It was spring when I arrived. I couldn't believe the transition from my previous trip. The valley had turned a verdant shade of green, trees blooming in the sunshine. Some of the trees yielded figs, others grew pomegranates; a few nourished plums which were particularly delicious. Vineyards lined roads in places. Distant mountains created a gray background against the vibrant colors of spring in the lush valley.

'I never knew a beautiful area such as this existed in Afghanistan,' I had said to Kate while we were driving the road to the village from Kamyar's compound. 'All we see back home is videos of dirt and rocks.'

'Do you think you are Afghanistan?' she asked.

'Where am I?'

'You are on one side of a line on a map made by foreigners who never lived in this area for very long. The local people who have lived here for generations do not care about these lines. Maps made by foreigners mean nothing to them. These people have different lines in their minds, lines made hundreds of years before a European ever set foot in this place. The old lines are the only lines which matter to the people in these valleys.'

'So, I'm not in Afghanistan?' I questioned her.

'Do you know where you are?'

'No, I guess I don't.'

'Does it matter to you?'

'I suppose it doesn't.'

The children smiled as we toured the school. One young girl took my breath away. Long dark hair, big eyes, and a smile that never left her face. She looked to be about twelve years old.

Coming up to Kamyar, she boldly put out her hand. He graciously took her hand as she personally thanked him for rebuilding her school.

He smiled. 'You are welcome,' he said in the child's native language.

'I can't believe the progress. I didn't think the building would be this far along,' I said to Kate.

'We could not afford to lose a day of school,' Kamyar overheard my comment. 'These children, they are our future, and the future waits for no one.'

2:55 PM, JOHN

After a delicious lunch at a café in the village, Kamyar suggested. 'It is a beautiful spring day. A perfect day for a drive into the hills.'

Kate frowned. She had been acted nervously, but she had said nothing to indicate what was bothering her and I had not questioned her, assuming she was simply tired. When she asked him a question in his native language, which I did not understand, he simply turned his head from side to side, indicating he disagreed.

We were loaded into the convoy, which had driven us from his compound in the morning, three vehicles, SUVs. Kamyar rode with us in the last of these. Ahmed, as usual, drove. This time Kate sat in the back with me, and Kamyar was up front chatting with Ahmed, who was talking more than I had ever heard him.

'Where are we going?' I asked Kate.

'We are visiting a waterfall flowing from a high mountain stream,' she said.

'Have you been there before?'

'Yes.'

'Is it beautiful?'

'Very.'

'What did you say to Kamyar?' I was curious.

'It's not important,' she brushed me off.

After a short drive through the valley, our convoy turned onto a side road, heading into the hills. Rutted and bumpy, the road twisted and turned through a series of canyons rising ever higher into the foothills of the mountains. It was a scenic area. I spent my time looking out the window enjoying the view. Kate was unusually quiet. The road climbed ever higher into the mountains, narrowing before turning sharply where a walled canyon lined the road on both sides.

An unexpected dust storm erupted ahead, followed instantly by a heart-stopping shock wave from a loud explosion, which hit the leading SUV, sending it into the air, bouncing off the side of a canyon wall before turning on its side, sliding to a halt, and blocking the road. A second explosion hit not far behind us, sending sharp metal fragments, shrapnel, shattering our rear window in an explosion of glass. Kate and I instinctively ducked. I grabbed her arm, opening the rear door. We were easy targets in the SUV. Dragging her behind me, we ran for a large boulder that had fallen from the canyon walls high above us. Bullets spat dust at our feet as we sprinted in panic. Ahmed and Kamyar followed close behind as a pathetic wailing followed in our ears, screams of men torn apart by the bomb that hit the leading SUV, radiating from settling dust. Accented by a barrage of exploding mortars raining down from above, our SUVs were destroyed in seconds, disintegrating into metal rubble as we hid behind boulders. Acrid smoke from burning tires and gasoline reeked in foul air, making it difficult to breathe without coughing. Kamyar's guards, who had been riding in the second vehicle, were returning fire. Having been able to get out of their vehicle before it was destroyed, they were well-equipped with automatic weapons.

The canyon was a trap. Our attackers had a major strategic advantage. We could hold them off from positions behind large boulders, but not for long, not forever. Eventually, their mortars would find our hiding places. We had a few options, nowhere to run.

Charlie's phone was in my jacket pocket. He had again insisted I bring it for the trip. I almost forgot the thing when I was packing, but at the last minute, I grabbed it on the way out the door. It was time to make a call I had hoped to avoid.

'What are you doing?' Kate asked when I took the phone from my jacket pocket.

'Calling in the US Calvary?'

'You are not going to get a cell phone connection here.'

'This is a satellite phone.'

A mortar hit nearby. For a moment, I thought I had lost my hearing.

Thankfully, Charlie answered almost immediately. 'What's up, buddy?'

Sounds of mortars and gunfire made it almost impossible to hear. 'I'm in some trouble,' I yelled into the phone.

'Yea, I can hear your problem. Tell me what's going on?'

'We are trapped in a canyon in the mountains somewhere in northern Afghanistan.' I hoped he could hear me over the noise. The wailing screams of the wounded men from the lead SUV had slowly eased; they were probably dead or dying, bleeding out from their wounds.

'I got you,' he said after finding my position from the phone. 'I'll call my general, send some help. Can you hold out until they arrive?'

'I don't know. The situation is critical.'

'Got it, John. I'll call back as soon as I have help coming your way.'

'Don't take long.'

Kate had a gun in her hand. 'Who were you talking to?'

'I'll tell you later.'

3:40 PM, JOHN

I was no help.

My gun was in my luggage in the compound.

Mortars hit ever closer, louder, as we cowered behind a boulder. We were outnumbered and outgunned. Seconds evolved into minutes, the noise of battle constant, so loud it became disorientating, difficult to think. Minutes blended into hours of fear, mortars, and nonstop gunfire. No help was coming, not soon enough.

Kate shot off a couple of helpless rounds from her pistol in desperation. She couldn't see her targets, just shot randomly, hoping to hold off what was inevitable. I knew what she knew. We had almost no chance of making it out of this alive. We were going to die.

The sound of automatic weapons rang in my ears nonstop. Our bodyguards were trying urgently to defend us, but they were not much help against a better-equipped enemy. Mortars blasted rocks and dirt a few feet from where we hid, their explosive, death-dealing aggression ever closer.

Some larger, more substantial boulders could be seen nearer the canyon wall, only a few yards from where we hid. 'Mortars are getting too close,' I screamed at Kate. 'We need to try for those rocks.'

She looked in the direction I indicated; but saw only an open area of dirt between us and the rocks, a death zone where we had no cover.

'They are going to get us if we don't move,' I yelled.

It was only a few yards to the larger boulders. If we ran, we were easy targets, but if we stayed, we were dead.

'Let's make a run for it,' I screamed.

She hesitated. I saw the fear in her eyes. She nodded, finally.

'I'll go first,' I volunteered, hoping to draw fire.

When she didn't say anything, I took off running without waiting for her, going hard and low. The first couple of yards, nothing, then bullets sliced through the air, ricocheting off a canyon wall as I slid behind a boulder. Kate followed close behind, ahead of an explosion destroying the area where we had been hiding. A lone bullet cut her arm above the elbow, bleeding into her shirt as she slid in dirt at my feet.

'You're hit?' I knelt down to help her.

'My arm,' she winced.

'Give me your gun. Wrap your shirt over the wound to stop the bleeding,' I suggested.

She did as I instructed, held her arm tightly, her eyes crying in pain.

I stared into the void above us, into open air between our boulder and canyon walls, seeing nothing of our attackers, hearing only their anger, their reign of terrible cutting, wounding, killing machines of modern technology spreading an ever-tightening grip of destruction everywhere. The ground around us seemed to literally stir, rattle, erupt constantly as if it were an animal skin, alive with constant, twitching explosions.

Finally, I closed my eyes and held Kate, waiting for what I assumed was inevitable, waiting for the angry animal around me to take me in its mouth of hard, lead teeth, crush my body until I was nothing more than a mass of running, oozing biological material without purpose or soul.

4:10 PM, JOHN

An eerie silence, an abrupt and unanticipated cessation of the conflict, drifted uncomfortably through the canyon.

Dust settled softly, taken on a gentle spring breeze to another place, a place where it was peaceful, where screaming and explosions were not a way of life. We did not trust the peace. We stayed hidden behind our rock shelters, which had been our only salvation for what seemed like an hour but was in truth a very short time exaggerated by the ferocity of the assault. As we waited, we listened for new sounds of aggression which would signal the next assault we knew was inevitable, the final assault which would end in our deaths.

Distant clapping of helicopter rotors shook the air, disturbing our quiet... Barely perceived at first, the penetrating sound of their whirling blades closed fast on our position. The helicopters brought us new fear. We had endured too much earth-shaking mayhem in too short a time. We were drunk on the adrenaline of anticipated death. Our brains were unable to comprehend the meaning of their sounds, scrambled by a mad, unyielding clamor of war. We did not wish to hear anything but the sounds of silence, of nothing, of peace.

Kate put her hand in mine, gripped it tightly.

'Could they be your friends?' she asked hopefully, looking up in the direction of the helicopters.

'I don't know,' I responded honestly.

Two of the mechanical birds hovered above us, looking for trouble. When the pilots saw nothing in the canyons above us, a third helicopter swooped down, landed not far away in an open area a few hundred yards from rock walls that had encapsulated us, held us captive while an enemy pulverized almost everything around us from a secure position.

Several men in uniform, US Army uniforms, jumped from a metal compartment carried on wings of wide, still twirling rotors. Guns at their sides, dressed in full battle gear, including helmets and armor shielding vests, the soldiers ran towards where we hid. Others followed, carrying supplies, medical equipment.

'John Van Laan,' one of them yelled. 'We are here to help you. Show yourself.'

I got up slowly, emerged from behind the boulder where I had been hiding. Kate stood behind me.

'Are you okay, sir?' a lieutenant asked when he spotted me.

'Yes,' I said weakly.

Kamyar, Ahmed, and three of his guards came out from behind the rocks.

'Hands high,' the lieutenant yelled when he saw the Afghans.

'They are friends,' I instructed him.

The lieutenant looked at me, questioning my words.

'They are my friends,' I said again, this time with more emphasis. 'They are not the enemy.

The lieutenant stood his ground, seemingly reluctant to believe me.

'Put your hands down,' I instructed Kamyar.

He did as I requested.

The Lieutenant relaxed his stance.

'There may be wounded men up ahead,' I said to the Lieutenant. 'You need to help them. And this woman needs a bandage.' Kate was holding her arm, blood dripping from the red cloth of her shirt.

A medic instructed Kate to put out her arm so he could examine her wound. Another medic went with Kamyar, walking towards where the lead SUV was still burning in the road. I followed. All three men who had been riding in this vehicle were dead. Their SUV was a mess of torn metal, lying on its side. The undercarriage had been blown open by a blast, exposing the passenger compartment. The driver was still inside, unrecognizable, nothing more than red meat and bones. He never had a chance. One of the other men lay on the road. He had dragged his torn body from the wreckage. His leg above the knee was missing. He could not have lived long. The third man was not as badly wounded, but he was dead, bled out. He may have lived if help had arrived sooner.

Kamyar examined each body carefully.

'I will have to tell their families they are dead,' he said solemnly. 'They were my friends.'

'I'm sorry,' I said to him.

'This had been a good day, John,' he replied, his voice low. 'Full of hope… Now it is a sad day.'

4:25 PM, KATE

Kate sat on a rock as the medic worked on her arm.

Her knees were weak, and her ears were still ringing with the sounds of explosions.

After giving her a shot to numb the pain in her arm, the medic cleaned the wound with antibiotics and placed a bandage over the cut. It was not deep, he told her. It should heal just fine, with only a small scar. If she was concerned about how her arm might look after it healed, he advised her to see a plastic surgeon.

Suddenly feeling cold, she thanked him, put on a jacket, careful not to disturb the bandage. The medic had given her some pills for pain. She didn't need the pills. It didn't hurt too badly, probably later. It was more the trauma of the event that concerned her; her stomach was upset, and her head hurt from loud noises. She was trying to be calm but it was difficult.

'Are you okay?' the young medic asked her. He could see she was upset.

'I'm fine,' she replied bravely.

'Something like this is not easy to absorb, miss,' he cautioned her. 'I have seen strong men cry after going through an experience like this. It's okay to be upset.'

'Thank you, soldier. I'll make it.'

He looked at her. She was very attractive. 'If I may ask, what are you doing here?'

'No, you may not.'

'Sorry, I didn't mean to pry,' he apologized.

'That's okay. I appreciate your concern, but I will be fine.' She took a deep breath and stood when John returned from the carnage up the road.

The soldier turned and walked away.

'You okay?' John asked.

'Everyone seems to want to ask that question,' Kate replied, now getting angry. 'I'm fine.'

He looked at her, still concerned.

'I guess I owe you my life,' she said after calming down. 'How did you manage to bring in the Army?'

'I know someone whose friend is a US Army General in Kabul,' John replied.

'And all you had to do was to call him.'

'Yes,' he answered simply, without further explanation.

'I guess it is good to have friends in high places.'

'It is.'

Kamyar arrived and again asked her if she was okay.

'Yes, boss, it's just a scratch,' she replied with a smile.

'Good.'

'Kate,' John said. 'I'm leaving on the helicopter, going directly to the airport for a flight home. Do you want to come with me?'

'What?' She was having trouble thinking clearly. Everything in her brain was confused, flashbacks of the attack still echoing through her anxiety.

'I have been told I need to leave immediately with the Lieutenant. I don't have a choice,' John told her. 'He is also going to arrange transportation out of here for Kamyar. You can go with me now, or you can stay with your boss and leave later. It's up to you.'

She could tell by the way he said it that he wanted her to go with him. She tried to think, but her mind just continued to rotate through a series of confusing overlapping impressions that made no coherent sense. She knew she was falling for John. She wanted to go with him. But she had fallen for a man before, and it had ended in disaster. Kamyar had helped her then. She had a responsibility to him. Her boss was first on her agenda.

'No, I will stay with Kamyar,' she replied.

'Will I see you again?' John asked, obviously disappointed.

'When I come to the States, I'll look you up.'

'Okay.' He gave her a gentle hug.

Everyone was watching. She couldn't do what she really wanted. She wanted to hold him tightly, kiss him, go with him. Instead, she pressed his hand and stepped back.

He turned and followed the Lieutenant to the waiting helicopter.

SATURDAY, MAY 19, 6:45 PM, KAMYAR

Kamyar slumped into a chair.

The area of his compound where he was sitting was reserved for family only. No one else was allowed; no visitors, no relatives, no one who wanted a favor or money or influence. This was where his family could live in peace, resting from the pressures of his world.

His only child, his daughter was playing with toys in a corner of the room when he sat down. She smiled when she saw him, and ran to him. 'Papa, Papa,' she held him tight, knowing what all children instinctively know. She knew when her father needed her love and attention.

With his daughter's arms around his neck, everything in the universe was good again for Kamyar. All the death, all the terrible atrocity of the attack was relegated to another room, to another place in his mind where he did not have to think about what he had seen that day.

'Would you like something to eat?' she asked him in Pashto.

'No, I would like to only sit for a moment,' he answered in her native tongue.

His wife smiled and turned to walk away.

'Want me to read you a story?' Kamyar asked his daughter.

English was spoken in his home. He wanted his daughter to understand the language that had become the unofficial language in the world. Some day she would inherit his assets and his responsibilities. If she was to do his work, she would need to know English. So, although it pained his wife, he spoke to his daughter only in a foreign tongue. And although his child was only seven years old and did not yet understand the significance of his instruction, she spoke to him in this language as he instructed. In truth, she found it exciting. She was learning to read in two languages, and this meant she had many books to enjoy.

'Oh, Papa, let me read you a book instead,' she said proudly.

'Can you read?' he asked, even though he knew the answer. She was a fast learner, and he was very proud of her.

'Of course, I can. I am a very smart woman.'

'Yes, you are.'

Her mother returned, frowned when she heard her daughter speaking English. Although her mother was proud of her child, she knew her daughter would face many obstacles when she grew up. Life for a woman was difficult in Afghanistan. It would be even more difficult for a woman who was raised to take over the responsibilities of a man, especially a man such as her father. Her mother had wished with all her heart that she could have had a son. She had prayed to Allah on bended knees for hours. Her prayers had not been answered initially. For years, she thought that she would have no children. When she finally became pregnant, she thought her prayers had been answered. However, when her child was born a girl, she was heartbroken.

Kamyar did not share his wife's grief. He accepted his child, loved her, and groomed her for the work he knew would one day come to her.

As his daughter read to him, his mind wandered over the events of the day. He had personally visited the home of each of the men who had been killed in the attack. He had offered sympathy. And in addition, he had made a promise to help each family financially. He told the wives that their children would not starve. He would make sure they were cared for. He said their husband was a brave man who had sacrificed his life to protect him. In turn, he would take care of their families. A monthly stipend would be delivered to them without fail.

The visits had been difficult despite his promises. Wives and mothers had cried in his arms. Children with sad faces had sat and listened to him, not understanding why their father had not returned home, still unaware of the full consequences of living in a house without a father. He had felt their grief and wished he could do more. But he could do no more. Allah would have to console them now.

Before his daughter finished reading the story, his wife returned with a cell phone in her hand.

'It's your brother in America,' she said in her native language.

She had steadfastly refused to learn English. This did not make Kamyar happy, but he could do nothing to change her mind. She was not interested in the outside world. She did not like to travel. She was happy only when she was at home and could visit with her sisters and her neighbors, shop at the town market, and pray at the local Mosque. She was a very religious woman and did not like to stray too far from her roots. She did not understand her husband and his need to travel. She had told him he had everything he needed in his village. Why, she had asked, did he need to go away?

Kamyar reluctantly took the phone. He was tired and in no mood to talk to his brother.

'Yes,' he answered.

'Are you okay?' Joey asked. 'I heard what happened.'

'I am fine. I was not injured.'

'That is good, brother. But this thing that happened to you is not a good thing. It is a very bad thing.'

'Yes, I agree.'

'Who did this thing?'

'I assume, Taliban. They are not happy I am rebuilding the school.'

Joey paused before replying. 'I don't think so.'

'What do you know?' Kamyar demanded.

'I made some calls,' Joey explained. 'I was told the Taliban had nothing to do with the attack.'

'How can you know this?' Kamyar demanded.

'I have friends,' Joey said simply.

'Joey, you know I have warned you about these friends.'

'You are my brother. I respect you. But you cannot choose my friends.'

Kamyar said nothing, fuming inside. His brother's friends were conservative Muslims. He had had this discussion with his brother in the past, but his brother would not listen. Kamyar had hoped that his brother would eventually get over his association with these men. Kamyar hoped wealth and responsibility would change Joey, move him away from these men. But this had not happened, not yet. And although Kamyar was concerned, for now, there was nothing he could do.

'I don't believe your friends,' Kamyar said. 'I think they tried to kill me.'

'You are wrong, brother,' Joey challenged his brother.

'Who else would do this thing?' Kamyar tried to reason with him.

'I don't know,' Joey said with no humor in his voice. 'Perhaps you should ask your American friend.'

GRAND HAVEN, MICHIGAN, SUNDAY, MAY 20, 6:15 PM, JOHN

Charlie waited until late Sunday afternoon to call me.

The weather that day was unusually warm with a gentle east wind. A golf course was my chosen reprieve that morning. I badly needed something to take my mind off the events of the last few days.

I arrived home late Saturday afternoon after flying all night and the next day. Charlie didn't offer me the courtesy of waiting for a commercial flight to get out of Afghanistan. He insisted I take an arranged flight accompanying a brigade of troops on their way home after months of duty; a transcontinental flight courtesy of the United States Air Force. Needless to say, most of the soldiers were a happy, boisterous group of guys and women, delighted to be traveling home after months of tedium punctuated by minutes of hell and damnation in violent, deadly confrontations that seemingly came out of nowhere. One minute, peace… the next minute, all hell would break loose.

But as I looked around the troop carrier, I spotted a few exceptions; unhappy faces not unlike the face I saw in a mirror at the airport washroom before I boarded the plane. Those faces, like mine, looked wasted, staring into the distance, unable to comprehend what they could not understand: the death and destruction they had witnessed. These soldiers were wounded, some mentally, some physically, traveling with a medical team who were looking after them. A few were missing limbs, bandages covering what was left of their broken bodies. Some slept in an induced coma, their eyes temporarily closed to a horror which was their past and would be their future.

I looked away, cried inside when I saw them. It was painful. They would never be the same. They were alive, but a part of them had died in a foreign country. They were a terrible contrast to the others, to the happy soldiers who had survived intact to return home to loved ones. Those soldiers were excited, relieved of a duty they should never have been asked to assume.

Sleep was absent without leave as I flew across the oceans. The soldiers were a constant reminder of what I had just witnessed. I would rather have been on a commercial flight in the company of travelers who didn't remind me of death and destruction. But Charlie was not to be deterred. He arranged everything. His friend, the general, was told I was a valuable asset of the CIA. The Army was instructed to get me out of the country before something bad happened again. I had no choice in the matter.

After I returned home, I slept fitfully, waking up more tired than when I went to bed. I needed a change of scenery, and the long green grass of a golf course supplied that need. Although I hit more bad shots than good, the camaraderie was enjoyable. My buddies knew nothing of my experience in Afghanistan, and I did not tell them; I simply laughed and played under blue skies and sunshine while trying to forget.

'How are you doing?' Charlie asked after I greeted him on the phone.

'How do you think I am doing?'

When I returned home from golf, I turned on my TV and poured a stiff drink.

'Not good,' Charlie answered.

The other item on my mind all afternoon, or should I say the other person who was messing with my mental well-being, was Kate. Leaving her as I did in Afghanistan was not very satisfying. It had happened too fast. I don't think that either of us was completely coherent at the time, our brains scrambled, the sounds of explosions still echoing across our skulls. I had hoped to spend more time with her, but my sudden forced departure had spoiled those plans. And I had to assume that the attack did nothing to improve our situation. Instead left a dirty stain on our relationship, one which I was not given an opportunity to appease. What had seemed promising before I traveled to Afghanistan had turned sour. Truth was, she was the main reason I made the trip. Although Kamyar had asked me to visit, I accepted his invitation mostly because I hoped to see her again. And before Charlie called, I had been daydreaming in a slightly alcoholic daze; fantasizing about calling her, hoping for, I didn't know what… just something better than our last conversation, something which perhaps promised the possibility of a future. Wisely, I decided against this course of action. I was under no illusions concerning our relationship. We had met and had some good days, but no commitments had been made by either one of us, nothing had been promised, nothing had been said, nothing had been anticipated. She lived thousands of miles away. This was a major obstacle. This geographical gap would be difficult to overcome. I tried to put her out of my head.

'What was your first clue?' I answered Charlie.

He hesitated before saying, 'Something like what you saw in Afghanistan is difficult to stomach.'

'You talking about the bloody, dead bodies lying in a road, missing their arms and legs.'

'I'm sorry, John. I know it had to be tough.'

'I thought you had a guy in Afghanistan who was supposed to be looking out for me.'

Charlie said nothing.

'Sorry, I guess I should be thanking you.' I tried to apologize.

'For saving your ass one more time.'

'Yea, for saving my sorry ass.'

'I advised you not to go. You do remember?' Charlie made his point.

'Vaguely.'

'Think a little harder. Then try to remember this the next time I offer you advice.'

'I'll try.'

'Good.'

'Charlie, I've been thinking about what happened, and one thing bothers me.'

'What's that?'

'The guys who were trying to kill us; they had us dead to rights. We were going to die if the army had not come to our rescue.'

'Yes.' Charlie was listening.

'Well, just before the Army helicopters arrived, the bad guys disappeared?'

'Maybe they heard the helicopters coming.'

'No, they stopped firing several minutes before we heard the birds.'

'I don't know,' Charlie said honestly. 'Maybe they thought they had done enough damage for one day. What's your explanation?'

'I don't have one. That's what bothers me.'

'Are you wondering if someone warned them that the army was coming?' Charlie was a smart guy.

'Yes, that's exactly what I'm wondering.'

'Well, stop thinking, because it isn't possible. The army's communications system can't be compromised.'

SATURDAY, JUNE 30, 4:30 PM, JOHN

When my phone rang, I didn't move fast enough.

The caller hung up before I could drag my weary body off the couch to look for my cell phone. Never could remember where I put that darn thing; I had to follow the sound of it ringing, which took some time, too much time.

Summer had not yet arrived on the shores of Lake Michigan, not as early as I wished. It can remain cool well into the month of June. The expansive body of fresh water just below my deck was the culprit. The big lake was cold, too cold for a swim unless you were highly motivated, and I wasn't that motivated.

I played golf in the morning with buddies, walked the course, all eighteen holes with a caddy. It was an enjoyable round. Extra money, pocket change only, was exchanged after the round; some of it came my way. We never bet big stakes. The few dollars exchanged were simply a tangible token of pride. I played well, and my partner contributed. We 'hammed and egged' our way to a win, as they say. I wasn't too tired by the time I returned home. I assumed this was good. I had nothing planned for the afternoon other than spring cleaning, which was badly needed; trimming, blowing, sweeping, etc., enough to wear me out for another day. After working for a few hours, I was dog tired and lay down on my couch for a nap.

And that, unfortunately, was when my cell phone rang.

Time had been a drag for the last few weeks. Not much going on. Rachel had called, just once, just to be nice; to bring me up to date on her life. She said she was dating a great guy, a doctor who was funny, nice, and good-looking. She sounded very happy, and I was happy for her. I thanked her for calling. Said, call anytime. But the truth was, I didn't honestly expect to hear from her again any time soon, and that was okay with me. Although… that wasn't completely true. I had an empty feeling in my gut after she hung up. I missed her. I missed being with a woman. But at the same time, I was happy for her. I assumed the guy she was dating would give her the stability and security I never could.

Life can be such a tangled mess sometimes. It's almost best not to think about it. Just let it happen. But that's sometimes easier said than done. I was alone most of the time, and it bothered me. I didn't like it. But I was trying to make the best of it, filling my time with work.

Travel to Charlottesville for a few days of meetings in my company's office was required. That kept me occupied for one week. In addition, I spent time preparing for my next board meeting. And it was also important for me to stay in touch with the people in my company who were dealing with Kamyar and Joey. However, I had not talked to either Afghan after the last incident, the fiasco when Kamyar's guards had been blown up in a roadside bomb. But that didn't stop Kamyar's emeralds from flowing through my company. The gemstones were very popular, and they were generating substantial profits. Kamyar's bank account in Switzerland must have been swelling from all the money we were sending him to buy his stones. All this was good, and it kept me busy. But I wasn't busy in the way I liked to be busy. I needed something else in my life, someone else in my life.

The area code of the missed caller was from somewhere on the eastern side of the state. I didn't recognize the number. Thought it could have been a wrong number or a solicitation for money.

I headed for the couch to rest when my cell phone buzzed, indicating a voicemail had been sent.

AKRON, OHIO, 4:35 PM, FRED

Fred Smith had been expecting a call.

He didn't know when it was coming, and when it finally did come, it didn't take long for him to express his frustration.

He wanted to know why it took so long for the Colonel to call. And what was the holdup? Why wasn't it done?

The Colonel tried to be patient. He reminded Mr. Smith of all the favors he had done for him in the past. He told him he would take care of the matter. It would just take time and planning. The target was no longer in Afghanistan, making it more difficult and expensive to complete his mission. And that was why he was calling, to inform Mr. Smith that another money installment was required.

This did not make Fred any happier. He could not have been more frustrated. He told the Colonel he had already paid good money for completion of the job. He reminded the Colonel, told him he didn't need to kill the target, only teach him a lesson he would never forget. Rough him up, break a few bones. Was that so hard? Why had it not been accomplished? Why had the Colonel's men failed? Fred said he didn't think he should have to pay any more money, not under the circumstances.

The Colonel patiently explained: his men had made every effort to accomplish their mission. They had fulfilled their duty. Although the target had survived, this was not their fault. In addition, his men were now back home in the USA. Many of them had expenses resulting from a change in status. Families needed to be relocated. There were bills to be paid. Life in the army was not an easy affair. The Colonel asked Mr. Smith to think of it as his patriotic duty to help his men. He reminded Fred of the millions of dollars in military contracts he had helped funnel through Fred's company. He assumed Fred would be willing to help now in a time of need.

Fred fumed, but he kept his cool. How much did the Colonel want, and could the Colonel guarantee the job would get done this time?

Yes, the Colonel guaranteed the mission would be accomplished. In addition, he promised to call Fred with weekly progress reports.

NOVI, MICHIGAN, 4:40 PM, KATE

Work was done. She could finally relax.

Her week had been difficult. Joey, her boss, had been demanding. He made appointments for her, appointments which she was expected to complete on her own. She had been traveling throughout the Southwest, seeing clients in a dozen American cities.

Apparently, sometime after her last trip to the States, it had finally dawned on Joey that Kate was better suited to handle sales than he was. And she couldn't disagree. Despite his genius mentality, his brain had not been supplied with a normal or even adequate portion of common sense.

Or perhaps, the problem was that he thought he was too smart to waste his time on issues relating to human behavior. In his opinion, this was the work of fools. Most humans were too stupid to be of any interest to Joey. It was not worth his time to determine what made them tick. His mind was created to solve far more important questions, questions that related to areas of study such as physics, mathematics, and chemistry. This was where Joey excelled.

As a result, he had decided to turn over the marketing of his brother's products to his American employee. Kate was smart and she was beautiful. It didn't take a genius to understand why clients liked her, why they would prefer to deal with her rather than with him. Besides, he had more important work to do. Having passed off the sales work to her, he was free to pursue those things in life that interested him.

Kate knew what he was doing. She knew all along he was too smart for his own good. She had warned her brother about him. But Kamyar was not willing to listen. Joey was his brother. He did not want to listen to anything negative concerning him, especially not from her, not from a woman. Although he tolerated many things from her, he would not tolerate her criticism of his sibling. He told her to never talk of these things again if she wished to retain her job.

A written report to Kamyar was her last task of the day. He had requested that she send him a weekly report whenever she was in the States: details including the clients she had visited, their comments, both good and bad, and what they had purchased or were thinking of purchasing. He explained why this was necessary. The information helped him design his products. He had originally asked Joey to do this, but Joey said he was too busy with more important work. Kamyar didn't have to say it, but essentially this meant Kate was being asked to make up for his brother's failings.

After Kate completed her report and it was emailed to Kamyar, she felt suddenly tired and lonely. She called John on impulse. She hadn't planned to call him, but she did because she needed someone to talk to, someone not involved in her work, someone she could call for fun. She had no one else, not in the States. She had many friends in India, but not here, not any she dared to call. She was afraid to talk to her old friends; afraid they would give her away to her husband. She decided it would be better to stay dead. Except for a few trusted family members, her brother in particular, no one knew she was alive. When she returned to the United States, she worked, nothing else, always going back to India as soon as she was done. Driven to leave as soon as possible to escape that awful place in her mind, the place where she had been beaten. The stains of those horrific times still colored her thinking with deep shades of sadness. She did not like revisiting those memories. She did not like returning to the States. She did it only because her work required her to go.

The call she made to John had gone unanswered, and against her better judgment, she left him a voicemail, short and sweet. Call back if he wished, if he had time.

As she sat by a phone wondering if John would return her call, she thought again about an incident that had been bothering her ever since it happened. The occurrence had been brief and nothing had come from it, but it worried her. A man had called her name, her real name, from across a lobby, 'Kate.'

She was walking through a large office building with several floors, many employees, and dozens of open cubicles filled with workers. A client who was in charge of the engineering department for a manufacturing plant had a corner office.

Kate had instinctively turned her head when she heard her name. She knew she should not have, but once it was done, it was done; she couldn't take it back. And for one brief moment, she had looked at the man who had said her name. She thought she recognized him, a college friend of her husband. She wasn't sure. She had only a second to recognize him. Immediately turning away, ignoring the man, she had walked into the office of her client and shut the door.

She wasn't certain, but it was possible that he had called her name a second time, 'Kate, is that you?' as the door closed. It was possible, but she was distracted at the time, shaking hands with her client, smiling, and thanking him for seeing her.

The meeting had taken over an hour. The client had asked her many questions. Some were repetitive, as if he didn't want her to leave, culminating in asking her out for dinner. She had politely declined, saying she had a previous engagement, which wasn't true. It was her established policy never to mix business with pleasure. But she didn't tell him, just said she was sorry, perhaps some other time.

Thankfully, the man who had called her name was nowhere in sight when she exited her client's office. As quickly as possible, she left the building without seeing that man again.

4:45 PM, JOHN

Hearing her voicemail, although very brief, her few words lifted my spirits.

Her voice was soft, her message simple; call back if I wished, if I had time. Well, I had the time. I had nothing but time. I called her.

'Hi John,' she replied softly, sounding tired.

'You called?'

'Yes.'

'Where are you?'

'I'm in Detroit.'

I looked at my watch, almost five in the afternoon. Detroit was three hours by car across the state of Michigan. I could be there by eight if I hustled.

'Can I come?' I asked.

She didn't reply immediately. 'It's too late. I just called to talk.'

'Okay,' I replied, somewhat disappointed, 'What would you like to talk about?'

'I don't know, how have you been? I haven't seen you for, I don't know, how long has it been?'

'Over a month.'

'Did you think you would ever hear from me again?'

'I didn't know. We didn't exactly separate under the best of circumstances.'

'Yes, it was not a good time.'

'I wanted to say more, but you know, everyone was standing around and I had to go.'

'Yes, I wish we had more time.'

'What would you have said?' I asked her. 'I mean, if we had time.'

The phone was silent. Finally, she said, 'I don't know. I wasn't thinking very well at the time. I was just glad we weren't killed.'

'Yes.'

'What did you want to say?' she asked, putting me on the spot.

'I wanted to tell you I hoped I could see you again.'

Again, the phone was silent.

'You sound tired,' I commented. 'Are you okay?'

'I am,' she sighed, adding, 'It has been a long week.' And again, for some unknown reason, she remembered the time when a man called her name, accompanied by an uncomfortable, deep-seated fear which rose silently out of her gut. She tried to put it out of her mind, but it wouldn't go away.

'I'll be okay,' she added, but she didn't sound too convincing.

'Kate, I can be there in about three hours. Where are you staying?'

'John, you don't have to do that.'

'I want to. I want to see you.'

Pause.

'Okay, I guess.'

NOVI, MICHIGAN, 11:45 PM, JOHN

The sweet naked body of a woman lay next to me, her soft breathing in the darkness telling me she was sleeping soundly.

I knew she was comfortable, content. I had given her what I had to give; the simple luxury of another human being who cared for her, who would never harm her ever, who would protect her as much as possible from whatever was bothering her.

The Staybridge Suites in Novi, Michigan, was nothing fancy, not like some of the luxury hotels in India and Pakistan we had shared. She said it suited her needs. It was a small efficiency with a kitchen and a sitting area. A desk was covered with work. She was not here often. Most of the time, she was on the road at Joey's request.

The aroma of a simple meal prepared in her kitchen greeted me at her door when I arrived.

'Dinner is served,' she smiled. 'You must be hungry.'

She gave in when I kissed her hard on the lips, held her close, and felt her irresistible body fold into mine. Instinctively, without malice of forethought, I took her slim body around the waist, picked her up, and carried her to her in the direction of a bedroom.

'May I turn down the stove first?' she asked.

'I guess.' I put her down.

After turning down the stove, she took my hand and led me to her bedroom.

Lifting her blouse over her head, I carefully undressed her, pants, underwear, and shoes, everything until she was naked. While I kissed her soft breasts, she held my head. Turning her around so her back was to me, my hands explored and caressed every curve of her lovely body. Bending her over onto the bed, I released my belt buckle, unzipped my zipper, and allowed my jeans to fall to the floor, not wanting to wait.

She sighed before twisting away. Laughing at me, she said, 'Now that is not fair.' I was taking advantage of her. It was her turn to undress me, which she did with relish, taking her time, too much time as far as I was concerned. She instructed me to stop fidgeting and stand still so she could do her job properly.

Pulling the comforter off her bed onto the floor with one motion, she pushed me backwards until I fell on the bed, where she jumped on me, kissed me on the lips, on the neck, on the chest, kissed me until I gasped.

We ate her simple meal after making love. A bottle of good red wine disappeared as we laughed and talked. A chicken something was the main course, along with some green beans. She said she was sorry, but when traveling, she didn't buy many groceries. She preferred to eat at restaurants or leftovers she took to her motel.

I told her a meal had never tasted as good. I meant it. Wine went down easily.

We didn't talk long. At her request, a pay-per-view movie was put on her TV. I don't remember which one. I was nodding off before the intro was finished, and she fell asleep before I did. Without complaining, I picked her up, turned off the TV, and carried her to bed again, this time more gently.

She was sleeping before I covered her with a blanket.

ON A ROAD TO GRAND HAVEN, SUNDAY, JUNE 31, 6:55 PM, JOHN

Traffic was light, the expressway tediously straight with uninteresting curves offering no challenge.

I had driven this highway many times. It held no surprises, and I was in no hurry. Yet, my silver Ferrari was making good time, held in check only by the threat of being ticketed for speeding. Thankfully, a radar detector on my dashboard registered no police interference on the road ahead. I slowed only for traffic, opened it up when the road was clear, and let the engine breathe.

As I got closer to my cottage, traveling the last few miles before turning off the expressway, the three-hour trip from Detroit seemed to have taken twice as long as the trip in the opposite direction yesterday. I was excited to see her yesterday. I had something to look forward to. Now, I knew I wouldn't see her for weeks, maybe more than a month.

She had asked me to leave midafternoon, saying she needed time to pack. Her flight out of Detroit Metro Airport was early in the morning; a layover in New York was scheduled before the first leg of several long flights arriving finally in her hometown of Mumbai, India. She seemed anxious to go home. I didn't argue with her, although I sensed something was bothering her. I didn't know what. When I asked her, she said she would be fine once she arrived home.

Home, it seemed all wrong for home to be a place as foreign and different as Mumbai. I wasn't sure I could ever get used to that city. But not her. The city's exuberant and abundant human activity offered her a sanctuary. She was more comfortable there than in the States. That's what she said.

Scrambled eggs and toast were breakfast, which she made in her tiny kitchen. Not much in the way of conversation accompanied our meal. But it was good to be with her, to see her smile often. While she was cleaning the kitchen, I mentioned something about the future, about how I would like to see more of her if possible.

She said nothing, looking out a window before finishing in the kitchen. Could we go for a walk? she finally suggested.

Morning air was cool and clear. A slight breeze out of the northwest played with the surface water in the Detroit River. It was a typical spring morning full of summer promise, not yet too warm, but the sun made it very tolerable if you wore a sweater. It was her suggestion that we drive downtown to walk along a river. The city was quiet on a Sunday morning.

A bench along the Riverwalk looked inviting. The view across the River to Windsor, Ontario, was pleasant. She started hesitantly, unsure if she should complain, as Joey, her boss, was bothering her. She wondered if she could talk to me about him. Perhaps I could offer her some advice.

'What's he doing?' I replied, thinking it might be something inappropriate. 'You know there are laws against that sort of thing in this country.'

'It's nothing like that.' She read my mind. 'He has never approached me for sex.'

'So, what's the problem?'

'I don't know, just seems like he has changed in the last few months. More and more, he relies on me to do his job. I haven't told Kamyar yet because every time I bring up Joey to him, he doesn't want to hear what I have to say. I'm not allowed to criticize his brother. I can't talk to Kamyar about him.'

'How has Joey changed?'

'Well, for one thing, he's more religious, leaving work several times every week. He won't tell anyone where he goes, but I think he goes to the local mosque. He prays three times a day, shuts the door, and kneels in his office on a rug. He never did that before.'

'That's not a crime.'

'I know, but it's affecting his work. He's not paying attention, and I'm beginning to hear complaints from my customers. My problem is that there's nothing I can do to fix the problem. Joey won't let me get involved in operations at our plant. He has told me to stay out of that area. That's his responsibility.'

'So, your hands are tied.'

'Yes, and it's frustrating because I have become the public face of the company. And I'm the one who hears all the complaints. Joey doesn't.'

'I don't know what to tell you.'

'I want the company to succeed, for Kamyar as well as for me. My future is tied up in the company.'

I was silent.

'Let's walk. I'm sorry I bothered you with this.'

'No, it's okay. I just wish I could help you.'

We continued along the river.

'Do you want me to talk to Kamyar?' I suggested.

'No, that will only make things worse. He would immediately suspect I was using you. He wouldn't like it.'

'And you can't talk to Kamyar?'

'No, I've tried. I have put some customer complaints in my reports. But he is unwilling to blame his brother for the problems.'

As the sun warmed the air, city dwellers joined us, strolling along a river that flowed by a teeming population filled with so many problems, only a short distance from this beautiful place.

'You still haven't answered the question I asked you this morning.'

She stopped, turned to me. 'I would like to see more of you, too, John. But we live on different continents. I cannot live here. And I don't suppose you would be willing to move to Mumbai.'

'You could spend more time here,' I suggested.

'I like it in Mumbai, John. You may find that hard to believe. But I like the city, the energy, the people, the cosmopolitan atmosphere. People from all over the world live in my city. It has much to offer. I have friends there. I have made a life for myself there. I'm sorry that doesn't fit into your plans, but it's my life and I'm unwilling to change it.'

As I drove, getting closer to my cottage, a sign for an exit to Spring Lake came into view. I hit the paddle shifter for the transmission, listened as the high-pitched engine revved. The Ferrari slowed, swept through an exit ramp at speed, merging into a two-lane road where I immediately encountered local traffic.

She had offered me no real hope; only promised to call again when she was in the USA. I told her I would send a plane if that would help. Just ask.

She had smiled and said to give her a call the next time I was in India.

She would love to show me her city.

EDEN, IOWA, MONDAY, JULY 2, 3:00 PM, KEVIN

Kevin got the call late in the afternoon.

A muscular, handsome man with straight black hair, cut short, Kevin's restless, deeply set blue eyes were the only clue to a violent history. His day had been nothing exceptional, working at his father's plant. Eden Fertilizer Company supplied chemicals to the area farmers, making their corn and wheat grow strong, sustaining an agricultural economy that dominated the small conservative farming communities in the state.

The company was located on the Iowa River. Manufacturing fertilizer was a dangerous business. Fire was a constant threat. Kevin was careful, respectful of his profession. His father had taught him well. He was good at his job. In addition, Kevin did nothing in public to give away the instability that lay deep in his brain. Only an occasional flare-up, a temper tantrum, revealed his mental volatility. But he had been careful to hide this characteristic from everyone. Ever since Kate left him, ever since the rumors started, he did nothing to prove to anyone he was responsible for her disappearance. His version of the story was she had stolen a large amount of money and disappeared, probably living the good life on a Caribbean Island somewhere. He said he was heartbroken. He played the part of a victim. And if it wasn't for that damn brother of Kate, no one would have suspected the real problem.

Kate's brother had openly confronted Kevin shortly after she disappeared. Everyone in the small town had heard the story. Dan Talsma had come to Kevin's office, barged in unannounced, and loudly demanded that Kevin stay away from his sister. If he didn't, Dan threatened to file charges for domestic violence.

Dan's parents had two children, just him and his sister Kate. He owned the family farm outside of town, which he had inherited from his father, who died early of lung cancer. Their mother was in a retirement home with Alzheimer's. The farm covered hundreds of acres, produced dairy, corn, and wheat products. Dan was one of the few people in the community who could say he was not beholden to the Bradford family. But he was too smart to think the charges would stand. Nothing had been documented; no evidence of beatings had ever been reported to the police. And even if they were, the cops would not file charges. The Bradford family literally owned the town, having the sheriff in their back pocket through their financial support of his election.

When asked by the police, Dan told them Kate was alive and well. She had decided to leave the country. Kate had later verified this with a call from Europe. Kevin was never in any legal trouble. Even though rumors had spread through the small town of Eden; eventually after months had passed, everyone forgot about Kate Bradford.

In addition to the fertilizer plant, the Bradford family dominated the town by holding title to most of the other important franchises. The fertilizer plant was the key. It supplied a never-ending source of funds, which Kevin's father had used to purchase several businesses in town; the ones he didn't already own. The owners were intimidated into either selling out or shutting down. Mr. Heyward Bradford was also the town's major benefactor, giving large sums of money to local charities. Most of the townspeople worked directly for him. Only a few people in town were in a position to go against his will.

Kevin had been trained by his father to take over management of the fertilizer plant. He was recently named president of the company. All this was good in the eyes of his father. Everything except the disappearance of Kevin's wife. That was a thorn in his father's side. Heywood Bradford badly wanted a grandson to continue his legacy, but that wasn't happening. His son Kevin had stubbornly refused to divorce Kate. He told his father that someday he would get her back.

Mr. Heywood Bradford had other grandkids, children of his daughters. But the problem with these grandkids was that their last name was not Bradford. Heywood wanted a Bradford to continue his legacy, and he had no other sons. He was counting on Kevin, hoping he would remarry.

The call was put through to Kevin's office by his secretary. Normally, she would not have done this. Unsolicited callers were discouraged. But the caller, named Adam Wendell, told her he was a friend of Kevin from college. He was calling from Spartanburg, South Carolina.

'Do you want to take the call?' she asked Kevin on his intercom.

'Sure, put him through,' Kevin answered, bored at the time. His job was not demanding. The plant ran itself for the most part. Competent managers had been hired who knew the business. Kevin only needed to make sure nothing went wrong and the profits flowed monthly into a local bank owned by his father.

'Adam,' Kevin said. 'How are you hanging?'

'Just fine and you?' Adam replied.

'What can I do for you?' Kevin asked, assuming Adam had called to ask a favor. People were always calling, asking for contributions, loans, and jobs. It was well documented that the Bradford family had millions, some of which had been given to his old alma mater in Wisconsin in the Bradford name.

'I saw Kate last week,' Adam said.

'What?' Kevin was taken by surprise at the mention of her name.

'I said, I saw Kate last week. Made me think of you. Just thought I would call and see how my old drinking buddy is doing.'

'Where are you calling from?'

'Where I work, here in Spartanburg, South Carolina, at the Volkswagen Plant.'

'Are you sure it was Kate?'

'Yes, of course, I'm sure. She's just as beautiful as ever. Say, how are you two doing?'

'Oh, we split up.' Kevin still felt the pain of her walking out on him.

'Sorry to hear that.'

'It happens.'

'Don't I know it,' Adam answered.

They chatted for a few minutes until Kevin could think of a way to casually ask what he needed to know. 'Say, what was Kate doing at your plant?'

'She represents a company in Detroit, Michigan, which sells us car parts,' Adam said.

'How do you know that?'

'I checked with my boss. I became curious after seeing her. He gave me her business card. And this is the odd thing. She has changed her name. Did you know that?'

'Yea,' Kevin lied. 'She got it into her head to do that after we split up.'

'I see,' Adam said, sensing that something in all this was not quite right, but ignoring his instincts.

'Yes,' Kevin said. 'What name does she use now? Truth is, I have lost track of her.'

'Mandy Taylor,' Adam said.

'Oh, that's right. What's the name of the company she works for?'

LANGLEY, VIRGINIA, TUESDAY, JULY 3, 5:55 PM, CHARLIE

Charlie listened to a phone call ring somewhere in Michigan.

Finally, before he could leave a voicemail, John answered.

'Hey Charlie,'

'It's me, your buddy Charlie.'

'Don't you ever go home, Charlie?' John asked after looking at this caller ID.

'I'm a public servant. I'm completely devoted to doing my duty for my country.'

'Well, you're probably the only one. Most public servants have more vacation days a year than Santa Claus.'

'Very funny. Now, can we get down to business so I can go home?' Charlie asked.

'Really, you have a home?'

'Yes, and I would like to go there before it gets dark.'

'What are you doing tomorrow? You taking a holiday?'

'Yes, if you must know. My girlfriend and I are headed to the beach for the day.

'You mean she hasn't left you yet?' John laughed.

'No, she actually likes me.'

'Can't understand that.'

'John, can we move on?'

'Sure, what's on your mind?'

Charlie took a breath before beginning. 'This thing I told you about several months ago, about the missing nuclear bomb. Do you remember?'

'Yes, it's pretty hard to forget about something like that.'

'Well, the situation has escalated,' Charlie explained. 'The bomb is still missing. The Russian authorities can't locate it, and my agency has been instructed to run down every possible lead in an effort to locate it. That's why I'm calling. Have you heard anything that would make you think your friends in Detroit and India are involved in a plot to set off a nuclear bomb in this country?'

John took a moment to reply using as few words as possible, explaining to Charlie that he had no evidence that could implicate the brothers Abdul in nefarious activities. However, he was reminded of a recent conversation with Kate. He told Charlie what Kate had told him, about her concerns for Joey, her boss, about Joey becoming more religious and paying less attention to his job.

Charlie didn't like the sound of this. He asked John to do some more poking around, see if the guy was interested in more than just being a better Muslin.

John agreed. He said he would call Kate and ask if she had noticed anything suspicious.

'Thanks,' Charlie said. 'I appreciate it.'

'Anything for an old buddy,' John replied. 'I'll call in a couple of days after I have talked to her. But truthfully, I don't expect to learn anything that might help you. These guys are making a lot of money. Why would they get involved in something like a nuclear bomb?'

Charlie replied. 'Nothing in something like this makes sense, but that doesn't stop shit from happening.'

John replied. 'Okay, I'll see what I can find out.'

'Thanks.'

GRAND HAVEN, MICHIGAN, JULY 4, 6:50 AM, JOHN

A cup of steaming hot coffee warmed my hand and tasted good while sitting on a cool morning deck overlooking the lake.

The water was calm. Streaks of rose-colored light crossed the lake from the rising sun in the east, highlighting some clouds hovering near the horizon, lasting for only a few minutes of quiet contemplation before disappearing forever.

I took another sip of coffee, allowing the abstract designs in the sky to take me away to another place. Mumbai, India, was nine and a half time zones separated from Michigan. My day had just begun. Her day was mostly over, and it was not a holiday where she lived. She inhabited a completely different place and time from me. I didn't like being so far away from her, but there was little I could do to change it.

I dialed her number.

'Kate'.

'Yes, John.'

'How are you?'

'Good and you.'

'I'm good.'

'You do know you are the only person who calls me by my real name besides my brother,' she said.

'Is it okay to call you that on the phone?' I asked. 'Because I call you Mandy if you want.'

'No, I rather like it when you call me Kate.'

The phone went awkwardly silent for a moment.

'Why are you calling, John?' she asked. 'I haven't been gone that long.'

'Just wanted to wish you a happy Fourth of July.'

'Thanks, I guess.'

Silence.

'John,'

'Yes.'

'What do you want, John?'

'Why do you think I want anything?'

'John.'

'Okay, sorry…' I apologized. 'It's just, I called because my friend at the CIA called me yesterday.' I began awkwardly. 'A nuclear bomb is missing in Russia. The agency is running down all possible leads. He wanted me to call you and ask if you have noticed anything suspicious, you know, about your bosses.'

'You're kidding,' Kate replied. 'Do you really think Kamyar would have anything to do with something like that?'

'No, Kate. I don't. But I'm not the one asking.'

'That's preposterous.'

'I agree, but what about Joey? You don't think he could be involved in a terrorist organization?'

'No, I don't,' Kate was adamant.

'Okay, good. I had to ask. I hope you won't hold it against me.'

'I won't, and actually, I'm glad you called. I was going to call you. I'm returning to the States next week.'

'Really, why? I thought you said you would be gone for a month or more.'

'I thought so too, but Joey is becoming more and more of a nuisance. He wants me back. In fact, he's lobbying his brother to have me transferred permanently to the US. I don't want to go. I told Kamyar. But Kamyar is considering it for the sake of the company. That's what he says, but I know it's because Joey wants me there to do his job and because Kamyar is reluctant to say 'no' to his brother.'

'You could live here in Grand Haven with me,' I suggested without thinking it through. 'I can arrange for a plane to fly you back and forth to Detroit.'

'Well, John,' Kate replied slowly. 'That's a very generous offer. But it's a bit premature, don't you think?'

'Sorry, just thinking out loud… It could save you some money.'

'Yea, I'll bet that's what you were thinking.'

I could see her smiling in my mind. 'Okay, guilty as charged. I'll just leave the offer on the table. You do as you wish.'

'Thanks, John. I'll keep it in mind. Why don't I call you when I have made my travel arrangements? We can talk more then.'

'Sure, great.'

'In the meantime, please tell your CIA buddy, he doesn't need to be concerned about the Abdul brothers.'

'I'll convey the message.'

'Thanks… Say, what are you doing today? Any Fourth of July plans? Any girlfriends lined up at the door for some holiday festivities?'

'No, no girlfriends, just dinner with friends, a couple of old schoolmates.'

'Enjoy.'

'I will. It was nice talking to you, Kate.'

'You too, I'll call, I promise. Give me a few days to make plans.'

'Okay.'

'Bye, John.'

'Goodbye, Kate.'

I wanted to say more, but it seemed inappropriate, the distance too far. I hung up.

Her voice just a memory, flying on zephyrs over miles of churning ocean waves.

AKRON, OHIO, FRIDAY, JULY 6, 2:10 PM, FRED

The Colonel called Fred Smith in Akron, Ohio, as promised, to give him progress report number one.

'Reconnaissance puts John Van Laan in Grand Haven, Michigan,' he said. 'He lives alone in a cottage on Lake Michigan. He's an easy target. Just exactly what would you like me to do to him?' the Colonel asked Fred.

'Just beat him up real good. Make it look like a robbery,' Fred replied. 'I can't afford to be involved in a murder investigation. Killing him off in Afghanistan is one thing. Committing murder on US soil is another. Do you understand?'

'Yes,' the Colonel replied. 'Mission parameters are now set. How long before you would like this mission completed?'

'As soon as possible, you moron,' Fred replied. 'Do I have to do all your thinking for you?'

'No, sir! Understood. I'll give you an update as soon as we have a timetable for the mission.'

'I don't need any goddam timetable. Just call me when it is done,' Fred was becoming more and more upset. It briefly occurred to him; he should never have gotten involved with this idiot in the first place.

'Understood,' the Colonel replied. 'I'll call as soon as the mission is completed.'

'You do that,' Fred slammed down his phone.

GRAND HAVEN, TUESDAY, JULY 10, 7:10 PM, JOHN

A warm summer day, hot actually, hot enough to go for a swim in the late afternoon to cool off.

The sun was high in the sky, reflecting off the lake, warming my front deck when she called. I had already consumed a couple of drinks while sitting under an umbrella to escape the sun. A dinner of leftovers had been adequate nourishment, but not much more. A stereo was blaring in the background, a Bocelli CD. I was relaxing after a day which had become all too common recently; work in the morning, golf in the afternoon, followed by a swim which made my body ache with exhaustion as I dragged my half-dead carcass out of the lake.

It was probably good that I had a couple of whiskeys before she called. It helped me avoid reacting negatively to her news. I didn't instinctively express how disappointed I was that she had failed to call as promised before coming to the States. I just listened without comment.

She explained it was easier this way. She needed to live in Detroit. Her new duties demanded that she spend most of her time in the office. Apparently, Joey had assigned her more responsibility than she anticipated. She was now in charge of the US operations for Kamyar's company. With the exception of the manufacturing plant, she was told to manage the affairs of the company. Along with her marketing duties, Joey had put her in charge of the office staff. She said her new duties required her to maintain a visible presence in the Dearborn office. Employees had been told by Joey to go to her if they had questions. And he said to call him if she was given a question she couldn't answer. Otherwise, use your good judgment, I know you will be good at this job, he assured her. I know I can trust you.

Trust was an important factor. Joey trusted Kate. Apparently, she was the only person he trusted. That's what Kate told me. That's why Joey had asked Kamyar to send her to the States.

All this was a major change for Kate.

The duties she had in Mumbai had to be turned over to someone new. She did not like that. She did not want to leave. When she told Kamyar what Joey wanted her to do in the US, he simply shrugged his shoulders and said to go. The only requirement she needed to do before she left India was to find a replacement, someone who could take over her work in Mumbai.

She ran Kamyar's office in Mumbai. Originally hired to be his secretary, but as time passed, she had gained his confidence. Her education in engineering gave her an advantage. She understood the basic workings of his products. It didn't take long for Kamyar to realize her abilities. She was a quick learner. Nothing was ever said. Nothing was ever put in writing. Over time, he tacitly increased her salary while assigning her more and more responsibility.

Joey knew this, of course. So, when he needed someone to help him with his work, he naturally asked Kamyar for her. He knew his brother would not deny him. Kamyar had always looked out for his younger sibling. Spoiled him from the beginning. Even when Joey was a small boy, it was obvious to Kamyar that Joey was someone who would require supervision throughout his life. Despite his brilliant mind, he needed assistance in navigating common elements of life, and Kamyar always provided this service for his brother. Joey tagged along behind his older brother from the moment he could walk. And so, it was only natural for Kamyar to agree to allow Kate to assist him now.

She arrived in the USA on Monday. She didn't call me before coming. She just settled into a long-term efficiency apartment at the Staybridge Suites in Novi, Michigan. She told me her work was full-time during the week, but she would be free this weekend. She called to ask if I would like her to visit.

I said I could send a plane for her.

She said this would not be necessary. She was happy to drive.

'See you late Friday evening'

KABUL, AFGHANISTAN, WEDNESDAY, JULY 11, 3:30 PM

Joey helped his friends load the crate, making certain everything was properly secured.

He had flown to Afghanistan to supervise. Exact specifications were required for shipment of the material. This was not a lesser-grade warehouse product, made in a third-world country by men who didn't understand physics. This was the stuff of genius, HEU, or as it was better known, highly enriched uranium. It was a substance intricately understood by Joey, who had attended one of the finest engineering schools in the world, MIT.

He was especially proud of his work. Customs officials could scrutinize the container to their heart's content as it traveled through borders to its final destination. He was confident it would survive their inspection as well as the physical rigors of its journey. The preparation had taken considerable time and effort, time that he was away from his job.

It was for this reason that he brought Mandy to the US. That's what he called her. He didn't know her real name. All he knew was that she was capable of managing his operation, which allowed him to travel.

However, the truth was far more complex.

Even though he would never admit it, she was more capable of running the US subsidiary of his brother's company than he was. She knew the product. She knew the clients. She could handle the day-to-day work that was required. He was very fortunate to have her in the US, working at the Detroit plant.

He had specifically asked her to keep his absence from the office confidential, especially from his brother. If Kamyar called, Joey told Mandy to tell Kamyar he was busy at that time and he would call his brother back shortly. Kate was then to call his cell phone and leave a one-word message, just say Kamyar. He would call his brother within half an hour of receiving her message.

'Careful now,' he instructed the men who were helping him load the crate. 'I don't want anything damaged.'

Obtaining fuel for the device had been the hard part. He did not require a large amount of the explosive material. The amount was small, approximately the size of an apple, but more than sufficient to do serious damage.

The explosive material would be shipped in a crate that contained new products from Kamyar's company, a new dashboard console that included a navigation screen, a CD player, and other high-tech features. The new console was designed by his brother to be lighter and better than the current models. But more importantly, from Joey's perspective, the outside dimensions of the product was large enough, perfect for enclosing the small amount of the material Joey had purchased. And for this purpose, he had replica made in his laboratory in Michigan and shipped to a warehouse in Kabul.

After the HEU was placed inside the fabricated product, it looked similar to other consoles made by his brother's company. The only difference being that it was heavier than the others because the material inside it was tightly sealed in lead. Nothing inside it could be allowed to escape into the atmosphere, nothing which might give away the true nature of the crate's contents. The only way to determine the deadly nature of the contents in the case was to break the seal and disassemble the console. Everything had been built to perfection. Joey had financed the cost of the project with his money. He did not want to leave anything to chance.

The crate would be shipped to Mumbai first, where Joey would attach stickers on the outside indicating it was a product of his brother's company. From Mumbai, it would fly to Dearborn, Michigan, marked special delivery which was normal for certain rush orders.

He took a moment, stood back to proudly observe his work. Once the material was in the States, it would be placed in his masterpiece, his gift to his people, his reason for being born.

A ROAD BETWEEN DETROIT AND GRAND HAVEN, FRIDAY, JULY 13, 9:40 PM, KATE

At that moment in time, Kate wasn't so sure she should have accepted John's offer to send a plane.

Although it had seemed a major waste of money when he suggested it, flying would have been significantly easier than driving four hours at the end of a long week of work. Getting out of Detroit on a summer weekend had been a nightmare for her, with traffic backed up for miles, going slowly. It had taken an hour to clear the city traffic heading northwest to the other side of the state.

Her eyelids were heavy. By her calculation, she still had an hour to go. Shaking her head to clear cobwebs, she stared ahead. She had passed Grand Rapids, navigated its busy traffic, taking a bypass around the growing city.

Lately, her work had been particularly difficult. Along with the duties of running a subsidiary of Kamyar's company, Kate discovered that navigating the office politics in Joey's company was a major challenge. It became apparent from almost her first hour in her new job that Joey might just have been the worst manager in history. She encountered nothing but problems from the moment she stepped into the office. It seemed every employee wanted to talk to her, and every conversation demanded considerable time and energy. It was like floodgates had opened. Employees finally had someone they could talk to. They told her, Joey would not listen. He was a terrible boss. They played into her ego; they said they were happy an American had finally been assigned to the company.

There were many problems, and they all needed immediate attention. She had anticipated none of this. She had assumed she would simply have to answer a few questions, deal with a few customers, and make certain work progressed as required. She thought it would be simple. But her new job was anything but simple. It was a mess, and the worst part was that she couldn't bring any of it to Kamyar. He wouldn't want to hear about the mess his brother had created.

Kate wondered how the company functioned at all. It was so badly managed that it should have crumbled under the weight of the problems she encountered. It became quickly apparent the only reason for its limited success was the product produced in India. It was clearly superior to anything competitors offered in everything including cost. But she already knew this.

She had worked tirelessly from the time she arrived in the office on Monday morning, and the pressure did not let up all week. One after another, the employees filed unsummoned into her office to complain. The word had gone out like wildfire. The new boss, you can talk to the new boss, not like the old boss, not like that foreigner who didn't want to talk to anyone, who wouldn't listen to suggestions that could make it better. Kate wondered why any of the employees had stayed. She guessed that if the economy wasn't so terrible in the Detroit area, if jobs weren't scarce, most of the employees would have resigned long ago. As it was, she soon learned many good employees had left for better opportunities.

Her first job was to reassure everyone that she would listen to them. If they had a legitimate complaint or suggestion for how to make things better, she would listen and make the appropriate changes. She asked only that they continue to work, give her an opportunity to deal with the problems. It would take time, but she assured them they were being heard.

Of all the countless conversations that ran rampant through her head as she attempted to keep her attention focused on her driving, one stood out. This conversation had taken precedence over all the other complaints. An attractive female employee had come to her late in the afternoon, just before five. This was the reason Kate was late. After talking to this employee, Kate had to return to her motel to pack. She had hoped to be out of her office early, but this had not happened.

The employee's name was Laura. Actually, this was not her real name. Her real name was Laila, the name she received from her Pakistani parents. She had Americanized her name, decided she would be Laura. It was a name far easier for people in her adopted country to pronounce. She wanted to blend in. She didn't want to stand out. Her wardrobe revealed this; she dressed like other modern young American girls. It was fun, she told Kate, she loved being here, the music, the freedom. It was all so different from her country.

Then something happened. Joey had lured her into the plant by suggesting he was considering giving her a promotion. He wanted to show her something, he said. In a back room which was empty except for equipment that was not being used, he forced her to have sex with him. Laura said he did this with no sense of shame. He had simply told her she deserved it. The way she dressed, the clothes she wore, were an abomination. He said she was Muslin; she needed to be taught a lesson. He said he would teach her. He would administer the proper judgment on her. He forced her to undress. He beat her and raped her. She had complied because she could not fight him. He was stronger, and he was her boss. She needed her job. She begged him to leave her alone, but he would not listen.

Laura had cried when she told Kate her story. Kate held her, said she understood. Kate told her something would be done. But now, as Kate drove, she didn't know what to do. Laura had not reported the incident to the police. There was no evidence to back up her story because Laura did not want anyone to know what had happened. She did not want the incident to stain her reputation. She was not married, she told Kate. She was afraid no man, especially a Muslin man, would want her if he knew what happened to her.

Kate was powerless to help Laura, except to complain to Kamyar. But she doubted Kamyar would listen. Kate's hands were tied. She could do nothing except confront Joey directly. But she doubted Joey would admit to his crime.

Over and over her problem ran through Kate's head as the road ahead took less and less of her attention. Lines weaved into subtle curves intertwined with her troubled thoughts, blending into a drowsy twilight scene resembling reality, but not real.

Her eyes closed momentarily. Her head slumped towards the wheel.

GRAND HAVEN, 10:55 PM, JOHN

I finally turned off the TV when I couldn't stand watching it anymore.

Although the truth was that I really hadn't been watching it with any sense of recognition; I was just sitting in front of flashing pictures crossing the screen, hoping the mesmerizing images would help pass the time.

It was not working.

Time was not passing, frozen… minutes dragging as I waited.

Stars covered a dark night sky when I went out onto my front deck overlooking the lake for some fresh air, hoping to clear my head. I had been anxiously looking forward to Kate's arrival all day, and she should have been here by now.

She was not. She was overdue.

But then, I didn't know when to expect her. I had not exactly asked her when she was coming. And she had just said she would pack after work and drive across the state to spend the weekend with me. Don't wait to have dinner. She doubted she would arrive in time. This was all I knew because it was all she had told me, and I had not pressed her for more information. She would come when she could.

I had to be patient.

But now, as I waited, every scenario I envisioned had her arriving at my place no later than nine thirty, ten at the latest. Four hours maximum to drive, perhaps some time to pack after work before coming, depending on when she left her office, probably around five. Everything indicated she should have been here by now. Even if she was delayed, she should have been here by now.

I was worried.

I wanted to call her cell phone badly, but I delayed. I didn't want to appear to be a nervous, anxious, overbearing male. She was an independent woman. She had lived alone for years, traveled to a foreign country, and set up a new life all on her own.

She didn't need me looking over her shoulder. That, I felt, would get me thrown out the proverbial door.

Pacing the deck anxiously, I absentmindedly took another sip of whiskey to calm my fragile nerves. I waited and I worried and I paced. And when I finally couldn't stand it anymore, I called her.

Her ringing cell phone sounded empty in my ear, distant, hollow as if she would never answer. Standing in the dark, holding my phone to my ear, a recorded voice finally answered. 'This is Mandy, leave me a message.'

It was a warm night with a southeastern land breeze, very comfortable. I was dressed in jeans and a short-sleeved shirt. The lake was calm. A quarter moon cast a trail of light drifting slowly across the water.

I took another sip of whiskey.

The sound of footsteps on the deck behind me caught me by surprise.

'You called,' Kate announced calmly.

'I did,' I admitted, turning to see her smiling at me in the moonlight. 'I was worried about you.'

'Sorry, I'm late. I should have called,' she apologized.

The memory of how close she had come to going off the road briefly crossed her mind. She had almost not made it. Opening her eyes at the last second before her rented Chevrolet sedan hit the noise strip on the shoulder of the expressway, she jerked the wheel back onto the road. The car slid sideways across two lanes before grabbing adhesion and straightening out. Fortunately, no one was near her at the time. Badly shaken, adrenaline rushed through her veins, and she was wide awake for the last few miles of the trip.

'I almost didn't make it,' she admitted.

'What happened?' I asked.

'I'll tell you later. Right now, I need a bathroom and a place to put my luggage. And if you don't mind, I could use a drink and then maybe some food.

Do you think you can manage?'

SATURDAY, JULY 14, 9:55 AM, JOHN

The sun rose warm and strong.

It was forecast to be a beautiful summer day. I had plans in mind for the two of us, including a road trip to a nearby artist community for lunch. Maybe some beach time in the afternoon, then dinner at one of my favorite restaurants. But my sleepy-headed lady friend was still in bed, and the morning was already half over. My plans were in a waiting pattern.

Getting up early, I made coffee in anticipation of her waking up, took Danish rolls out of my refrigerator, and sat on the front deck drinking coffee as the sun rose overhead, beating down on my back, making it uncomfortably hot. Going inside to escape the heat, I grabbed a Danish without waiting for her.

Last night didn't go as I had anticipated. Kate had asked politely if she could go to bed as soon as she finished a sandwich and a glass of wine which washed down my meager food offering. We talked while she ate. Or I should say, she talked and I listened. She told me first about her near accident on the highway, said she almost fell asleep at the wheel, said her week had been from hell, totally exhausted her. She launched into a monologue that was as confusing as it was disturbing. It seems she had walked into a bee's nest of managerial problems in Detroit. Joey had left her a mess which would take weeks to repair. She asked me if I would help her, offer her some advice. She said she needed help. She felt she was in way over her head. This was not what she had bargained for when she agreed to come here as Joey's backup.

But first, she needed to sleep. She said she was dead tired. Would I mind if she just went to bed? She promised to make it up to me in the morning.

When I slid under the covers into bed after locking doors and turning out lights, she was already sleeping, blankets pulled up over her shoulders. Her face looked beautiful, eyes closed, hair tossed across a pillow in the dim shadows of the night. I slept off and on, wishing for more, but content that this lovely lady was here beside me.

'Well,' she said, appearing suddenly on my deck dressed only in a sheer pajama top and panties which left little to my imagination. 'What are you waiting for?'

'It's almost ten o'clock,' I replied, smiling. 'I didn't think you were ever going to get up.'

'I'm awake now and I remember promising I would take care of you in the morning.'

A momentary breeze blew the flimsy cloth of her pajamas against the outlines of her full, round breasts, brushing her curls from her face as she grinned at me.

'Okay, I'm coming.' I put my coffee cup on a table. Taking her in my arms, I carried her to my bedroom, where all my carefully concocted plans for the day were ignored. What remained of our morning was spent in bed. After making love, I fed her hot coffee and a Danish while listening to her launch in again about what was bothering her. One story was very disturbing.

She told me Joey had raped one of his employees. She said that she didn't know if there was anything she could do about it and she felt very sorry for the young woman.

9:05 PM, KATE

Sun sank low over the water, reflecting in a hot glare off the lake.

Lowering a baseball cap John had given her to shield her eyes from the afternoon sun, she sipped a glass of wine while lounging in a deck recliner next to him. It had taken all day, but at last she felt as if she was finally relaxing.

He had done everything she asked of him. They had gone nowhere, stayed at his cottage. After he told her his plans, she begged him, told him she had a difficult week. Could they just stay here and relax? Could they do that? she asked. He agreed.

Still in her bikini from an afternoon of lying in the sun, she put a sweater over her shoulders as the air cooled. Her skin felt hot. She suspected a mild sunburn.

The sun dipped slowly towards the horizon as she reflected on her day.

She had stayed too long in the sun, lying on the deck, going for a walk and a swim, even though the water was cool. This was John's doing. He convinced her. He said it would be great fun to go for a swim. Come on, he challenged her while strolling into a gently waving lake. You are going to love it.

She didn't love it at first. She hated it. The water was cool. She slowly tiptoed into a low surf, taking her time to get wet, feeling every inch of cool water climbing her thighs. The farther she walked into the lake, the deeper the water.

'Just dive in,' he said. 'It's torture to go slow.'

Finding some courage, she dove. Holding her breath, a rush of cool water caressed her sun-heated skin. Her body adjusted quickly. It felt great, refreshing. After a short swim, he waited for her on the beach with a big towel he wrapped around her shoulders.

Steaks he found in his refrigerator were grilled for dinner. Store-bought potato salad and good red wine complemented a simple meal. As they ate, she thanked him again for accommodating her wishes. He said he didn't mind.

· A walk on the beach after dinner was suggested. He found her hand and held it as they strolled slowly over still warm sands. She thought his gesture, holding her hand, was cute, almost as if this was their first taste of love. In a way, this was how it felt to her as if he was her first real love. She had married too early, and her marriage had turned into a disaster. This was her first opportunity at love as an adult, and she was enjoying the experience completely. He was so attentive, nothing like Kevin, her moron husband.

As quickly as the thought of Kevin entered her mind, she immediately attempted to dismiss him as if he were simply an illusion out of the past who did not matter anymore. But then the incident in South Carolina briefly passed through her brain, reminding her he was all too real.

'You getting cold?' John interrupted her troubled thoughts.

'A little,' she admitted.

'Let me get you a jacket.'

'I think I will go in and change.'

'Hurry up, the sun will be going down soon.'

'I need a shower,' she answered.

He didn't say anything, didn't argue with her, just watched her get up slowly and walk inside.

The shower was hot, rushing water over her naked shoulders and breasts. She enjoyed its cleansing action, washing off greasy suntan lotion and gritty beach sand. The shower door behind her opened. Putting his arm around her waist, John brushed her hair from her forehead and kissed her moist lips.

Outside his cottage, the sun slid unseen below the horizon, casting a flood of soft reds, deep purples, and long gray shadows into the sky in an ever-evolving abstract painting across a vast panorama.

She did not see the sunset that evening, even though it was spectacular.

She was far more content to exist in the delights his loving attention offered her.

MINNEAPOLIS, MINNESOTA, MONDAY, JULY 16, 2:20 PM, KEVIN

His office lobby was as old and tired-looking as the brick building it occupied in a suburb of the city of Minneapolis, Minnesota.

A stench of stale cigarette smoke blended with a sweet scent of air refresher failed to overpower the tobacco odor permeating the stained carpet and pathetic-looking, pale green, cloth furniture. The dust covered receptionist desk and chair situated in the middle of the room, appeared to have been unused for a long time. As Kevin waited, a man with a cell phone to his ear briefly poked his head out of his office long enough to tell Kevin he would be with him shortly. Take a chair, there's coffee on the table, help yourself to a cup. The office door closed. Kevin could hear the man talk, but he could not understand the conversation.

The coffee looked dark black with syrup-like consistency, and probably tasted like it. Kevin decided to forgo the brew. Instead, he briefly paged through a couple of months old magazines before placing a dated copy of Time magazine back on a table in disgust. He didn't like waiting.

It had been almost two weeks since he learned where Kate was working. He had taken his time. He was in no hurry. Now that he knew where she worked, he assumed he didn't need to be in a hurry. He didn't want to mess it up this time. If he didn't do it right this time, he knew she would never return to him, and he badly wanted her back.

He would tell her he had waited for her and he was a changed, better man now. Wouldn't she please come back? She had nothing to fear from him. This was his premeditated message.

But first he needed to find a way to approach her properly without scaring her. And to accomplish this, he was determined to learn as much as he could first: like where she was living, what her circumstances were, how she was making a living, things like that. Once he knew all the facts, he would decide what to do.

He didn't want to spook her.

That would not be wise.

And he didn't want her to see him until he was ready. So, he decided to hire someone to discover the information he required.

His father's company was represented by a big city law firm in Minneapolis where his personal lawyer worked. Kevin had called the man and asked for the name of a reliable detective who could be trusted to do a job for him, someone who would do it confidentially. The name of the man, his lawyer recommended, was Pete Mansell. Mr. Mansell's office was in Minneapolis.

'Come on in,' Pete startled Kevin. 'Sorry to keep you waiting.'

The old wooden desk in the man's office was large, covered with files. The place looked like it had not been cleaned for months.

'Have a seat,' Pete said. 'Now, what can I do for you?'

'I need some information,' Kevin stated.

'What kind of information?'

'Well, it's about my wife.'

'Okay,' Pete had heard this story before. Sounded like a routine case.

Kevin hesitated. 'This needs to stay confidential. My lawyer said I could trust you.'

'Once I take your case, I'm not obligated to tell anyone.'

'So, what I tell you will stay between you and me only?'

'Absolutely, client confidentiality,' Pete was becoming more interested. There was something about this young man that was different. Plus, Kevin's lawyer had called him, gave him a heads up. Money is not a problem. The kid is filthy rich.

'Just tell me what you want.' Pete attempted to put his client at ease.

Kevin hesitated. Now that he was here, he wondered if this was wise. Perhaps he should simply confront Kate on his own. This was going to take time.

'Look, Kevin,' Pete said. 'I'm very good at what I do. I can give you references if you want them. Trust me. I will be absolutely discreet.'

Kevin eyed the man. Pete was a middle-aged, large man, not overweight, but big, with thinning, graying, curly brown hair that needed combing. Wearing a laundered white shirt, which was wrinkled and appeared to have been worn for several days, his tie was undone at the neck. A black leather sport jacket had been thrown over a couch against a wall. Nothing in Pete's appearance gave Kevin any confidence. Except for the way he talked, he sounded like he knew his business. Kevin wanted to trust him. This was the first step to getting Kate back. He put his misgivings aside and told Pete his story.

'She's been gone for more than a year,' Kevin began. 'She ran away from home. I completely lost track of her until recently, when I discovered where she is working. Mr. Mansell. I want my wife back.'

'Okay,' Pete said, thinking something about this case was different than most. He just couldn't put his finger on what it was. 'Tell me everything you know,' he said. 'Don't leave anything out. If you want me to help you, I need to know it all, including why she left you, and don't lie.'

'She took my money,' Kevin replied. 'A lot of money and left the country.'

'Did you report her to the police?' Pete asked.

'No, she's my wife, Mr. Mansell. I just want her back.'

Pete leaned back in his chair. 'Are you rich?'

Yes, sir. I guess you could say that.'

'So, this is just about money?'

'Yes,' Kevin lied.

NOVI, MICHIGAN, TUES, JULY 17, 5:10 PM, KATE

Kate worked at her desk, finishing a few last-minute details.

Across from her a pretty young female employee with dark black hair, sat looking less than comfortable in a conservative skirt and a white blouse buttoned at her neck. Ever since being raped, her choice of clothes had changed dramatically. Her skirts were longer, below the knees. Blouses revealed no skin below her neck.

'Maybe I should just go home.' Laura suddenly expressed a desire to leave. Although the office was air-conditioned, sweat formed on her forehead as she thought about what she had told her new American boss; worried that it was going to get her fired.

'Just a few more minutes,' Kate replied without looking up as she worked. 'We need to wait until the other workers have gone home.'

'I'm sorry, Miss Taylor,' Laura said. 'I'm thinking this is a bad idea.'

'No,' Kate replied. 'We cannot let Mr. Kahn get away with what he did to you, Laura. I will talk to him and make him understand he cannot do this again. If he does, I'll take him to the police if I have to do it myself.'

'He will fire me. He told me he would do this if I told anyone about him.'

'No, he will not. I won't let him.' Kate suddenly became angry. 'I'll appeal to his brother in Afghanistan if he tries.'

'What good will that do? These men, they are all alike,' Laura spat out the words. 'His brother will not care about me.'

'I'll make sure he does. And if Joey tries to fire you, I'll quit, and I don't think he wants that.'

'I don't know.' Laura was confused. What had seemed so certain when she first told Kate about the incident now seemed unclear.

'Would you want him to do to your sister what he did to you?' Kate asked her.

'My sister does not work here.'

'Yes, but you must think of all women as your sisters. I am your sister in this,' Kate said. 'That's why I'm helping you.'

Laura said nothing. This American woman seemed so confident. Laura wondered where she got the guts to stand up to a man who was her boss. It was not like this in her country. A woman did not have the status to talk back to her boss or any man.

'Do you understand why we must do this?' Kate asked Laura.

'I don't know, Miss Taylor. It is very hard for me.'

'I know, but it's important.'

Laura looked down.

When Joey returned to work sometime late next week, Kate was determined to confront him. But first she needed the facts. It would be too easy for Joey to dismiss it if she couldn't justify her accusation. He could just say the young woman was lying. To accomplish what she needed, Kate needed Laura to show her where the rape took place.

'Let's go,' Kate put down her pen, deciding her work could wait. This was more important.

Approximately fifty thousand square feet of warehouse and manufacturing space were located in a metal-roofed building, which housed the US subsidiary of Kamyar's company. Off I-96 on the outskirts of Detroit in Novi, Michigan, a brick structure attached to the warehouse building was where Kate and Joey had an office. The warehouse housed the manufacturing arm of the operation. It was where units were modified to fit the specifications of each automobile company.

Walking through the partially lit, deserted plant took time, avoiding the shadows of equipment and supplies. Laura slowly directed Kate, finding her way to an unmarked door in a back corner of the building. Only a few lights were on at the time, making it difficult to see. When she got near the door, she suddenly stopped and pointed, standing back, afraid to take another step. Her memory of this place made it hard for her to move.

'It's okay,' Kate tried to reassure her. 'No one is going to harm you'

Kate tried the door handle. It was locked. But after inserting her master key, hoping it would work, it opened.

The room was dark and she was forced to search an inside wall for a light switch. Feeling several, she methodically switched them on one by one until the room was bright with overhead lights. What she expected to see and what she actually saw were completely different. Instead of a dusty, unused room with a few discarded tools, the room looked like an ultra-clean laboratory, with benches and tools arranged neatly. Spread throughout the room was some very sophisticated looking equipment designed for highly specific purposes. Kate did not know what each of the instruments and equipment was, but she did know that nothing in this room was cheap. Especially interesting was several white suits which resembled something designed for a spacewalk, hung next to an interior room made from walls of thick Plexiglas.

Radiation symbols decorated the windows.

Kate's concerns for Laura instantaneously vanished in a disturbing cobweb of questions. Taking out her Apple phone, she started taking pictures as Laura stood in the doorway, watching, afraid to take one more step inside.

GRAND HAVEN, THURSDAY, JULY 19, 9:10 PM, COLONEL JACK RAYMOND

Mission aborted.

It was time to head back to their motel for the night. Their target was safely holed up in his house, unlikely to come out at this time.

'Okay, boys,' the Colonel spoke into his phone. 'Let's pack it in. See you back at the operations center.'

He was grateful for work. After returning to the States, he had spent a considerable amount of time looking for a job. His furlough was just about up. He was getting towards the end of his military gig. It was time to find a civilian job, but after years of serving his country in dangerous places like Afghanistan, he was not well-trained for civilian duty. Recently, he had begun to contemplate establishing a private security company, providing bodyguards and offering other special services. He knew many returning servicemen were qualified for this work and would love to have a high-paying job after years of duty. And why not? They had served their country and risked their life for the freedom of others. It was time for society to pay its debt.

But that was for later. Now he had a contract which needed to be serviced. If successful, he could use his present employer as a reference to future clients. Mr. Fred Smith would make an impressive reference. But first, the Colonel needed to complete his mission. This contract was the first step in beginning a new career.

On paper, the job was not contemplated to be overly difficult, but it had proven to be far more problematic than anticipated. The house where the target lived was isolated, located off the main road, through a quarter of a mile of forest land. This should have made approaching the target easy, but when team discovered a number of security cameras placed in the woods near the back entrance to the house. This was unexpected and it made it difficult to get near the house without being detected.

The only other entrance to the house was on a deck overlooking a beach. But the area between the deck and the shore was down a steep sand dune and completely open. With neighbors close on both sides, it would be impossible to go in this way without someone seeing his guys. And more than anything, they did not want to be arrested. To be successful, their mission had to be completed with a minimum of risk. As a result, the target's home was ruled out.

Plans needed to be modified.

It was decided to watch and wait for an optimum time when their target was vulnerable and the chances of being arrested were extremely small.

FRIDAY, JULY 20, 7:20 PM, JOHN

I was thankful Kate arrived on time.

She left work early on Friday, avoiding weekend traffic, and drove across the state without incident. But as soon as she arrived, I knew something was wrong. It was written all over her face. The worry lines between her eyes were pinched tight. When I asked her what was bothering her, she said she didn't want to talk about it, begging instead for glass of wine.

'Want to go for a swim first?' I suggested. 'You look like you could use some cooling off.'

It was a hot day. The water in the lake was warm, above seventy degrees.

She paused, thought about it before saying, 'Sure, why not. Give me a minute to get into my bathing suit.'

As she headed to my bedroom, dragging her luggage, I retrieved a couple of beach towels from a closet.

Charlie had called earlier in the week, saying the missing nuclear bombs had been located inside Russia. The CIA was instructed to stand down. The crisis was over. He said this was good news for me. It proved my client was not involved in a plot to bomb the US.

I didn't disagree with my buddy Charlie. Not that I didn't want to. I wanted to tell him there never was a crisis, not with my client anyway. Don't jump to conclusions next time, Charlie, not unless you have concrete evidence. Otherwise, leave me alone. But I didn't say anything. Just thanked him for letting me know.

I assumed it was also good news for Kate, and she sure looked like she could use some good news. It was one item on her to-do list, she could cross off.

'Let's go,' she smiled, heading for my deck dressed only in a white bikini.

I followed her down the steps to the beach, watched in amusement as she bravely tiptoed into the water, hesitated for a second before diving in and swimming a few yards, standing in waist-deep water. The sun glistened off her irresistibly gorgeous body, reflecting in watery drops sliding down the luscious curves of her torso as she brushed her hair from her forehead. Momentarily mesmerized by an image of absolute beauty, I stood on the shore.

'Come on in, chicken,' she smiled at me, breaking my reverie.

Following her lead, I took a few running steps before diving into the cool water. I swam underwater until I spotted her beautiful legs standing on a sandbar. Rising up in a rush, I kissed her hard on the lips. Laughing, she kissed me back. Wiggling out of my arms, she swam out where the water was deeper. I chased after her again, caught up to where she stood with her head and shoulders above the water. I held her around the waist with one arm and slid my hand inside her bikini bottom.

She twisted away again, laughing at me. 'No, no, that's for later,' she smiled.

'Oh, come on,' I teased her. 'It would be fun in the water.'

'Anticipation is half the fun,' she chastised me before swimming towards shore.

I smiled and took off after her. I had to admit it; she was a good swimmer. She had a lead on me, and it wasn't easy to catch her. She arrived on shore before me, grabbed a towel, and headed up the stairs on the run. Defeated, I followed.

A cold beer from the fridge was my choice. She had a glass of wine after drying off. Lying on a lounge chair, her eyes temporarily closed as she soaked up the last retreating rays from a setting sun which was still hot even as it slowly slid towards the horizon.

'Feel better now?' I asked her.

'Yes,' she sighed.

'You hungry yet?'

'I have something I would like to show you,' she announced without responding to my suggestion.

A couple of steaks were cooling in my fridge. It was late and I was famished.

'Can it wait until after dinner? I'm hungry.' I asked.

'Sure.'

8:15 PM, JOHN

Steaks, thick juicy T-bones, sizzled on a grill as my saliva juices kicked into full gear while tending to the cooking meat.

'Take a look at these,' she walked up behind me on the back deck, where I had placed a small grill. 'I'll tend to the steaks while you look at the pictures on my phone,' she suggested, handing me her instrument.

'Sure, the steaks are just about done. Give them a couple of more minutes, then take them off the grill,' I said, observing that apparently, Kate didn't want to wait until after dinner to show me her news. As she sipped her wine, occasionally poking the steaks with a spatula, I viewed the first picture on her phone. What I saw was a large room filled with tables and instruments where no one was working in the room at the time.

'What am I looking at?' I asked her.

'You are looking at a highly sophisticated laboratory.'

'What's it for?'

'That's the sixty-four-thousand-dollar question. I've been doing some research since taking these pictures. I can't be certain, but there are some really deadly possibilities.'

'Such as?' I asked, remembering that her education at the University of Wisconsin was for a degree in engineering.

'Such as a bomb factory,' she declared. 'Maybe even a nuclear bomb factory.' Taking her phone from me, she scrolled through several pictures until she found the one she wanted me to see; a picture of a glass room.

'See these labels on the windows of that room,' she stated before again taking her phone from me to find the next picture she wanted me to see. That picture showed a close-up of one of the labels.

'The label indicates the presence of radiation danger,' she explained.

'Okay.'

'Turn to the next picture.'

'What are those white suits?' I asked, becoming more and more concerned.

'Those are designed to shield workers from radiation.'

The steaks started to burn, fire and smoke billowing from the grill.

'Damn it, Kate,' I said, turning to the steaks. Taking a spatula from her hand, I removed the now well-done beef, no longer cooked to my taste, which was medium rare.

Not that that really mattered any more. My appetite was long gone.

10:20 PM, JOHN

Salvaging some nourishment from the well-done steaks, our dinner was dismal by any standards, highlighted only by a couple of glasses of wine each.

Neither of us had much to say. A mystery laboratory located in a manufacturing plant in Dearborn, Michigan, had cast a shadow of dread over what should have been a relaxing Friday evening meal. Picking up the dirty dishes, I headed to the kitchen. Kate followed with leftovers, which she placed into containers before refrigerating. I'm not much good when it comes to culinary arts, but I have learned how to clean up after eating: rinsing the dirty dishes and putting them into the dishwasher. It's not a very exciting skill, but it's necessary for life as a bachelor.

'I'm not sure what to do about Laura,' Kate said more to herself than to me as she watched me work.

'What do you mean?'

Kate had mentioned the young lady's name at dinner, saying she was the reason she had discovered the laboratory. Kate never would have found it if it hadn't been for Laura.

Without answering my question, she refilled her wine glass and headed for the living room. I followed as soon as I was done with the dishes, but not before filling a glass with Scotch and a few ice cubes.

'I wanted to confront Joey about what he did to her,' she replied after I sat down. 'That's why I went to that room, to gather evidence so he couldn't deny what he did. But now, after seeing what is in that room, I'm not so sure I should talk to him.'

'Why not?'

'Because then he may begin to wonder if I know about the room where he raped her.'

'So what? Someone has to stand up to him.'

'I understand, John. Believe me, I do. But what if he doesn't want anyone to know about that room? He just might kill me to prevent me from talking. So, what do I do… Do I risk being killed?'

'Do you think he's capable of doing something like that?'

'That's the problem. I don't know what he is capable of,' she replied. 'That's what scares me.'

I said nothing for a minute.

'Do you really think he could be building a bomb back there?'

'I don't know.'

'But it's possible.'

'Yes. It's possible. He has a degree in physics from MIT.'

'I need to take this to Charlie,' I concluded. 'This is way out of our league. Give me your phone so I can send him the pictures.'

As predicted, Charlie called about a half hour after I sent Kate's pictures in an email. He promised to look into the matter in the morning. He cautioned us; it could all be very innocent. Don't jump to conclusions, Charlie warned us. Only facts count in the game of espionage. A good spy doesn't make judgments based on assumptions.

That got me mad and although I tried to hold back, I just couldn't, 'That's bullshit, Charlie.' I finally told him what I wanted to say to him before. I said he was the one who had jumped to conclusions about Kamyar when a nuclear bomb went missing in Russia. He started it.

He argued that the inquiry into Kamyar was not his doing. If I was offended at the time, I should have said so. He was just doing his job.

Okay… we both calmed down. He promised to get back to me as soon as he had something and I thanked him and hung up, feeling more distressed than before I called him. Knowing that getting mad at Charlie accomplished nothing.

Kate sensed my foul mood and decided we had had enough fun for one day. Said she was tired. Our evening was ruined. Like an old married couple, we went to bed to sleep, nothing else, no extracurricular activities; just boring, meaningless, mind-numbing sleep.

Hoping Charlie would call in the morning with good news.

11:05 PM, PRIVATE DETECTIVE, PETE MANSEL

Lights were extinguished in the cottage as he watched from a safe distance.

It was a warm summer evening, and if it wasn't for the bugs, Pete would have been perfectly comfortable standing against a large oak tree in a forest behind the cottage, hoping for an opportunity to observe the occupants of the lakeshore house. But after assuming they must have turned in for the night, he carefully made his way back through the woods using a flashlight to see, heading for the street. A bike path was on the other side of the street, running parallel to Lakeshore Avenue led to a side street where he had parked his car about a mile away.

After writing notes in a book using his car's interior lights, Pete Mansell turned the key in his car's ignition. It was time to drive to his hotel room for the night. Another day, another dollar; his work was done. His report to his client would indicate the woman was involved with another man. She was a married woman, according to Kevin. No divorce had been issued. She was having an affair.

Messy business, this work of his, but typical of what he had discovered about the human race. Although… in a way he could not define with any certainty, this case appeared to be more problematic than most. The wife had apparently run away. Pete wondered what drove her to such a desperate measure. Her husband was obviously a very rich young man. He was good-looking, tall, with short blond hair and an easy smile. On the outside, Kevin seemed to be good husband material. But in Pete's experience, looks could be deceiving. What lurked behind the surface of a smile and a quick joke was not always what it appeared to be. Something about his client bothered Pete. He was beginning to wonder if finding this woman for her husband was a good idea.

Driving dark roads at night was a lonely business; only a few cars shared the road. His motel room for the night was located in the town of Grand Haven on Highway 31. It wasn't a great place, but it was cheap, and he didn't intend to stay for more than a few days. He assumed the woman would return to Detroit on Monday for work.

Oh, well, he thought to himself. If he didn't take this job, someone else would. He needed the money. He had bills to pay. The work was good work, easy. And the client had given him a healthy retainer which meant he had a responsibility to fulfill his contract. The consequences of what he reported to his client were not his doing.

He didn't notice another car that was following his car into town, remaining at a reasonable distance behind. The occupant of this car was using his cell phone as he drove, telling a Colonel they had company.

Some guy had spent the evening in the woods behind the cottage of their intended target.

SATURDAY, JULY 21, 2:20 PM, KATE

Not a cloud in sight.

Nothing to offer relief from a hot summer sun beating down relentlessly out of a clear blue sky, overheating her tender skin. Sweat dripped from her forehead as she lay on a lounge chair on the deck overlooking a gently rolling lake. Every once in a while, a reluctant waif of a breeze flowed over her licentious curves; the grace of which was broken only by a thin, pale yellow cloth covering her most private parts with a minimum sense of propriety. The sun's heat felt good, warming and relaxing her aching muscles, which had been strung taut from another high-tension week of work that had tested every ounce of patience she had in her body.

Nothing had prepared her for the job that bastard Joey had laid in her lap. She had no idea how hard it would be. She badly wanted out. She wanted to call Kamyar, appeal to him, tell him she just couldn't, wouldn't do this job anymore, not for one more day.

But she knew Kamyar wouldn't want to listen. After agreeing to Joey's request to send Kate, Kamyar had taken her aside and given her a pep talk. He told her he had faith in her. This was her chance. He said he knew she could do it.

At the time, she wondered why, why the pep talk. Now, she knew. He knew the situation in his US subsidiary was not good. Secretly, he was probably happy Joey had asked for her. Kamyar couldn't replace his brother without creating a problem in his family. Not without having an excuse to send her.

Nothing else had made sense at the time. She didn't understand why had he been so eager to send her? She had thought it was odd. She assumed she was doing a good job for him in India. She wondered why he sent her while knowing that she didn't want to return to the US, not permanently.

But he sent her anyway.

She was not happy.

But then, she remembered how good he had been to her. This was her chance to repay Kamyar for helping her rebuild her life. She did not want to fail him. But this job was stressful from the minute she walked in the door in the morning, to the time when she could finally go home late in the evening. So much needed to be done. Perhaps one day it would be better. Once she had better personnel in place, people she could rely on to do their job. Then her job would be easier. However, that required replacing employees, and firing was no fun; it was not what she had bargained for. She had hoped to simply babysit the company while Joey was away. Now she knew that Joey must agree to step aside. She wondered if she could find a way to move Joey out without offending him. That would be difficult... unless... he actually wanted to step aside. She sensed he was uncomfortable with the responsibilities of running a company. He was not a people person. He liked the money and the prestige that went with his position, but he didn't like managing people. His MO was to sit in his office and issue directives. Sometimes these directives were followed, and sometimes they were not. Joey never really knew.

Kate briefly considered the idea of letting Joey remain the titular head of the company, the president in name only. She could become the Chief Operating Officer, the COO. Perhaps Joey would accept the idea if she presented it tactfully.

But then, Kate remembered she had one other problem; the one obstacle she didn't know how to handle. The locked room in the back of the building was the unwieldy elephant in her plans, the one major complication that could render everything else insignificant. She didn't know what to do about this room. Just the thought of the equipment in this room made her restless.

Why is life always so complicated, she wondered? Why can't it ever be simple? Isn't peace what most people simply desire, just to live in peace? Why is a small minority of the human race always ruining it for everyone else; creating chaos out of peace, destruction rather than construction? And why are the rest of us forced to live in fear caused by these few unruly members of our fraternity?

She took a sip of cool lemonade from an ice-filled glass John had brought her earlier. The cool, sweet liquid tasted good, refreshing her momentarily.

Her skin was burning, hot. It was time to get out from under the sun. Picking up a towel, she headed down wooden steps to the beach for a swim. Scorching sand uncomfortably heated the bottom of her feet when she reached the beach, forcing her to run quickly across the sand to the cool water of the lake for relief. Diving into the lake, a sense of release rushed over her body, cooling her overheated skin. She swam leisurely, enjoying the clear lake water.

A few boats cruising a couple of hundred yards away, gave her no immediate cause her concern. She turned towards shore, refreshed, and determined to put her troubles out of her mind for the rest of the weekend.

2:35 PM, JOHN

She had gone down to the beach, probably for a swim.

I could see her from the window in my office. Thinking it would be fun to join her, I went to my bedroom to change into a swimsuit when my telephone rang. Charlie, as usual, was a master of bad timing.

'What do you want?' I asked. 'I'm in a hurry.'

'Really, what's so important you don't have time to talk to your buddy?'

I didn't respond.

'For a semi-retired guy,' he continued. 'You seem to always be in a hurry.'

'Life's short, Charlie. I have things to do.'

'Like what?'

'Do you really want to know?'

'Yes, what's it like to live a life of leisure?' he asked. 'I'm not sure I'll ever get a chance to experience it myself.'

'I'd feel sorry for you, Charlie, but the last time I checked, I think you said being a spook was what you always wanted to do with your life.'

'It has its moments.'

'Okay, good. Now we have that settled, can you tell me what you want so I can go for a swim?'

'Thought so.'

'Thought what?'

'Thought you had nothing important to do.'

'Charlie, why did you call?'

'Sure. I called to tell you I'm sending Bill to help her.'

'Help her with what?' I asked impatiently.

'Let me explain,' Charlie answered with a sigh.

I sat down on the side of my bed, resigned to the fact that this was going to take time.

Charlie's news was mixed. His research discovered Joey had applied for and received a license to experiment with uranium for medical purposes. A proposal had been written outlining a new method of radiation treatment for cancer patients. Charlie said Joey was experimenting with a new process to better target cancer cells. It was hoped to be far less dangerous than the current radiation. All this meant his laboratory was strictly within the law. His equipment was legal. There was nothing on the surface that would justify any suspicion.

However, Charlie was never a man who was easily deterred. He wanted to be absolutely certain that Joey wasn't involved in any nefarious activities, such as building a bomb. As a precaution, he said he was sending Bill to install cameras in the laboratory. Recordings could covertly monitor Joey's work. If anything, suspicious was discovered from surveillance, Charlie would deal with it. But for now, our concerns were temporarily null and void. Charlie said we could go on with our lives without being concerned. This was Charlie's problem now.

I thanked Charlie and hung up. It was time for a swim. After putting on my suit, I headed out the bedroom door. Through the living room sliders, I saw Kate come up onto the deck from the beach with a towel over her shoulders and her hair was wet.

I was too late.

WEDNESDAY, JULY 25, 4:15 PM, JOHN

A small ceramic statue of an Irish setter sat on my desk and stared up at me.

I had purchased the statue because it reminded me of my dog when I was a boy. He had been my best buddy when I was growing up, my only friend some days. Blue was his name. I raised him from a puppy. He was loyal, always there for me when I needed someone to understand. He was sad when I was sad, and he was happy when I was happy. We would go for long walks in the woods. And he loved chasing an old tennis ball which he would bring me, drop it at my feet, and beg me to throw it one more time. When he got old, he would get tired quickly and walk away from the ball after he had enough, just drop it and lie down.

When he couldn't run anymore because his hips were bad and his lungs were filled with fluid, they had him put down. That is what my parents called it, but I knew what it was. It was his death, and I have missed him ever since the day he died. I will never forget the look on his face when I left him at the vet. He wanted to come with me to run and play, but he couldn't get up. He was too old, too old to run anymore. Joy had gone out of his life. Yet, there was no giving up in him. He begged me with his eyes to take him home.

I have often wondered if I should have taken him home to die. But I didn't want him to die in pain. It was better to let the vet give him a shot to put him out of his misery.

When my time comes, I hope someone will do this for me. When the joy is gone, just put me down, even if I say I don't want to die. I don't want to be a burden to others.

I looked away from the small ceramic dog on my desk. I was not delusional, not yet. I still had some life in me. I was not ready to die.

Cameras had been installed in the laboratory in Novi. Kate had called to say they were in place. Joey was due to return tomorrow. His work in the lab would be monitored. Bill had installed the cameras with her help. She made certain no one would interfere with Bill when he was in the lab. The surveillance instruments were small, impossible to find unless you knew where they were. Feeds from the cameras could be monitored at CIA Headquarters in Langley, Virginia. Experts in the field of nuclear physics would be able to determine if something beyond medical research was being concocted.

That was good news. The matter was out of our hands.

The other good news was that she was coming for the weekend. Late Friday, Kate said she would drive up, spend Saturday and most of Sunday with me before returning to Detroit. She told me she wasn't sure Joey would want her to stay after he returned. She said she was going to discuss her situation with him on Friday. She wanted to ask him if her position in the company was permanent. And if it was, then she was going to demand some changes. But she didn't know how he would react. He might just send her back to India.

And that was not good news. But it was still good to hear her voice on the phone.

My life had begun to revolve around our weekends together. Weekdays were different. They dragged. I tried to stay busy with work, telephone calls, and reports, but it was the middle of summer. Work normally slows in the summer, not much to do. I did some landscaping around the cottage to keep busy, but my heart wasn't really into it. I just couldn't get motivated. And she was the reason. It was her, all her, her doing. Her presence added meaning to my life. Meaning which was missing when she was gone. Her laughter, her sense of joy, of life, the good times we had together. The weekends with her were too good and too fleeting, only two days in seven. Not enough, not what I wanted, but it was better than the alternative, which was nothing. Just the mention of her returning to India put a strain on our telephone conversation. But I said nothing, nothing by the tone of my voice, nothing which would give away how I felt about her returning to India. I hoped she could not see through my façade, but I wasn't sure. Most of the time, I am too transparent. I know this. My emotions are too near the surface, worn on my sleeve as my mother used to say.

She could always see right through me. I could never lie to her and get away with it.

The clock on my computer indicated it was almost five, enough for today. I could finish my work tomorrow. It was time for a swim. The afternoon sun was hot. Thunderstorms were forecast for the evening. Dark clouds could be seen on the horizon, far out over the lake.

If I hurried, I could get in a swim before the storm hit.

NOVI, MICHIGAN, FRIDAY, JULY 26, 11:20 AM, KATE

Kate's phone rang.

'His taxi just pulled into the parking lot,' the receptionist said.

'Thanks.' Kate hung up her phone to go into the lobby to approach Joey.

She had been waiting for him all week. She wanted answers. Mostly, she was interested in knowing if Joey expected her to stay or return to India. Every day she was in this country, every additional hour added to her growing unease. She worried her husband, Kevin, would find her. And then it would all begin again: the pain, the fear.

Although she wondered if this was true, she was a grown woman now, no longer dependent on him. She had a life that didn't include him. She didn't need his money anymore. He couldn't boss her around. He couldn't tell her what to do. He couldn't hit her, torture her, or threaten her.

She could refuse him now.

And yet... she feared him. The memory of those days and months of terrible tension was still too recent, fear not forgotten. Being anywhere in this country was too close to him. She knew her anxiety was irrational, but it didn't stop her from being a little afraid all the time. She needed an ocean, several oceans in fact, and a few continents between herself and that man. She felt much better when she was in India.

Her only complication was John. Despite her sworn vow to avoid becoming attached to a man, it was happening. She was falling for him. It was time to leave before it got too serious. The fact was it was past time. Once she had returned to India, her old life could resume. Her feelings for John would ease. This is what she told herself. This is what she hoped for. It was time to go. She needed to talk to Joey.

Joey was dragging his suitcase through the front door when she spotted him.

'Hi, Mandy,' he said, without looking her in the eye.

'Hi, Joey. I would like to talk to you as soon as you get settled.' She smiled at him reassuringly.

'Yes… sure… just give me a minute.'

'Okay.'

'Say, has the latest shipment of parts arrived from India?' he asked as if it were an afterthought.

'Yes, it came in this morning.'

'Really, I assumed it wouldn't get in until the first part of next week.'

'You put a rush on it,' Kate answered from her memory of seeing the shipping orders.

'Yes, yes, I did. Where is it?'

'In the back, on the dock.'

'Has it been opened yet?'

'No, not to my knowledge.'

'Good.' Joey turned to hurry away.

'Don't forget I want to talk to you,' Kate said, as he headed for the hall leading to his office.

'Yes, of course.' Joey stopped suddenly, changed directions, and walked towards a door to the manufacturing area.

Opening the door, he disappeared, leaving his suitcase behind in the lobby.

HOLLAND, MICHIGAN, SATURDAY, JULY 28, 8:05 PM, JOHN

'Something is bothering you.'

Our weekend together had progressed without incident. The weather was good, mid-summer weather, hot and cloudless skies. The lake was warm, good for swimming and sailing my beach catamaran in the afternoon. Dinner at a restaurant, the Irish Pub, had been good. We had driven into Holland, Michigan. The main downtown area of the city is located close to Lake Macatawa, only about fifteen miles from my cottage. Our table was outside in the fresh air. It was a nice evening, warm with a slight cooling breeze. Kate was dressed in pale yellow shorts and a white sleeveless top, which looked great against her tan skin. A couple of sweaters had been brought in case it got cool, which it did not.

I had beer and a New York strip steak for dinner. She had a glass of wine with seared scallops. My hope was that the wine and dinner would relax her. She had acted uptight ever since arriving late Friday. She wasn't her usual high-spirited self, no jokes, only a few smiles, absentmindedly acting as if she wished she were somewhere else. I assumed it was her work, which I knew was difficult. I decided to say nothing, try to treat her with kindness, and hope she would recover. But her mood had not improved. If anything, it seemed to be getting worse as our weekend progressed.

'I'm fine, John,' she replied.

'No, you're not fine,' I countered. 'You haven't been your normal exuberant self all weekend.

'Okay, I'm not fine. I didn't have a good week,' she countered spitefully. 'Is that a crime?'

'Anything you want to talk about?' Obviously, I had touched a nerve. Probably should have kept my mouth shut.

'No,' she answered with grim determination.

Dessert had been ordered. It came while we were talking. The waitress simply put the plates on our table without comment.

Perhaps our young female server sensed that everything was not perfect between the occupants of her table. She had decided it was best to stay out of our way.

Kate had ordered some ice cream, but only after I insisted. Originally, she had said no to my suggestion for dessert. However, I didn't want our dinner to end. I wanted to talk to her. Apple pie was my choice. I picked up my fork to partake in its delicious flavors.

'Can we just go?' Kate said suddenly for no apparent reason.

'You don't want your ice cream?'

'No, I want to go.'

'Okay,' I motioned to the waitress.

When the waitress came to our table, I asked for our bill.

10:10 PM, KATE

A strong man reached around her before she could react, put his arm over her neck, and held her, covering her mouth with his hand so she couldn't scream.

The back of her head hit a wall hard, and she was jarred badly when he shoved her, his body heavy, leaning against her smaller body, holding her against the wall. She was having trouble breathing. The bricks of the building pressed into her back, hurting her. Helpless against the larger man, there was nothing she could do except stand and watch what happened next.

The alley off the main street of town was narrow between two buildings. They had been walking, not talking at the time; just proceeding in silence. heading to an isolated parking lot to retrieve their car, when they were assaulted.

She was in a sullen mood, just wishing she were somewhere else. It was late in the evening after shops had been closed for hours. Not many locals roamed the area, just a few souls who, like John and Kate, had been to a restaurant. This should not have been a problem, according to John. He told her the town of Holland, Michigan, was a small lakeshore community that prided itself on being friendly with a low crime rate. However, the reputation of the town apparently did not exempt the empty alley from being a perfect place to complete his mission. The Colonel and his men had been patient, following, waiting, looking for the right place and time.

It had finally come.

Between Kate and John stood two strong men who prevented John from coming to her rescue.

'Let her go,' John demanded angrily.

'Really, what are you going to do about it?' the Colonel asked John.

John charged the Colonel, temporarily knocking him backwards from a blow to the face with his forearm. The Colonel's companion hit John in the back of the neck when John attempted to push past the Colonel to where Kate was being held against the wall. Falling hard on the pavement, semiconscious, John was picked up and held under his shoulders by one of the Colonel's men. He twisted in the man's grasp, shaking his head as if he was trying to get his senses back. The Colonel swung; hit John hard in the face before he could fully recover.

Head down, blood ran from his nose as Kate winced. A second blow jarred his head again, opening a cut in his forehead which bled into his eye, making it difficult to see. Swinging again, the Colonel went this time for his gut. John doubled over in pain. The Colonel's companion held his arms, keeping him from falling. Another vicious blow to his forehead was hard for Kate to watch. She turned away while still being pinned against the side of the building, closing her eyes to the absolute brutality. But this could not prevent her from hearing dull thuds, blows hitting John's body over and over again. As if she was reliving the beatings she had taken from her husband, Kate felt every blow to John's body as if it were her own, the hurt, the defenseless humiliation which comes from knowing you are vulnerable, you are weak and can do nothing to stop the hurt except to cry and scream and hope the pain will end soon.

'That's enough,' a man said when she didn't think it would ever end.

She opened her eyes. A man she had not seen before was standing in the alley.

'Stay out of this,' the Colonel said to Pete Mansell. 'Just turn around and mind your own business, buddy.'

'This man you are killing, he is my business,' Pete replied calmly, holding his hand behind his back under his shirt. He had been following John and Kate all evening, gathering information, taking pictures for a report he was preparing for Kevin. He had not wanted to intervene when he witnessed the mugging. But when the beating became too brutal to watch, Pete stepped in.

'Take care of him,' the Colonel ordered his subordinate.

The man released John, who fell semiconscious to the pavement. The Colonel's companion took one step towards Pete.

'That's far enough,' Pete said. Taking a gun from behind his back, he pointed it at the man who was advancing towards him.

No one moved.

Pete's gun altered the atmosphere, charged it with an electrical energy which only comes when death is near. Every person, except the semi-conscious victim, was recalculating their position, their strengths, and vulnerabilities, which now existed in this too-real drama.

'What is your intention?' the Colonel asked Pete.

'My intention is to escort all of you to a police station. You have committed a crime.'

'I can't let you do that,' the Colonel replied.

'I don't think you are in a position to dictate anything,' Pete said. 'Case you haven't noticed, I'm the only person holding a gun.'

'In combat, sir, a gun is a limited weapon; it does not dictate victory unless it is used properly,' the Colonel spoke his words as if he were an authority.

'Is that so?' Pete said.

'Yes,' the Colonel motioned for his men to spread out. The man who had been holding Kate against the wall released her and did as his companions were ordered, slowly taking steps to the left and right of Pete, creating a circle that began to close in around him.

Pete fired at the Colonel before his two companions could advance. The Colonel screamed an obscenity in frustration; fell to the ground in pain with a bullet in his leg. His men took off, running in different directions. Pete raised his gun, took aim, and quickly decided against firing his weapon. A shot, if the bullet missed its intended target, could easily injure or kill an innocent bystander.

The Colonel's men disappeared around a corner.

11:05 PM, GRAND HAVEN, MICHIGAN, KATE

After lifting his shirt over his head, she threw the blood-stained garment on a chair in the bedroom.

Kate then unbuckled his belt and pulled down the zipper on his pants, letting it fall to the floor as he stood unsteady beside his bed, holding his rib cage, which he admitted hurt every time he took a breath.

'Okay, sit down,' she suggested.

John did as she asked without complaining. She knelt down in front of him and began to untie his shoes, removing each one carefully along with his socks.

His forehead was covered with a large white bandage over stitches. Emergency doctors had cleaned up his wounds, stitched a few of his cuts, taken an X-ray, and generally checked him out, suggesting that an overnight stay in the hospital for observation would be a good idea. John had declined, saying he wanted to go home. He was okay.

Kate wasn't so sure this was a wise decision, but she didn't argue with him, followed along behind as he was wheelchaired to the entrance door of the emergency center, where he waited for her to retrieve his Ferrari. A male medical attendant helped him enter the low-slung car, which was not easy even when he was healthy. He groaned, but did not complain, settled into the passenger car seat for the drive to the cottage.

It was late by the time they arrived. The cops had asked too many questions at the scene of the crime. John had few answers for them, saying he didn't know the men who beat him. Didn't know why they did what they did. It was a mystery to him. He wasn't much help.

The other mystery was the man who had come to their rescue. Neither John nor Kate knew a Pete Mansell, the name their rescuer had given to the police. Mr. Mansell had explained he just happened to be in the area and was happy to be able to help.

The man who had been shot identified himself as a Colonel in the United States Army, said it like he was proud of it, just returned from Afghanistan. He offered no explanation for his behavior, steadfastly refused to answer any and all questions. The police put him in the back of a cruiser. He was taken to the hospital along with John, who was transported in an ambulance. Kate followed in John's car.

'Okay, let me help you lie down,' Kate said. She put her hand under his back to assist him in slowly lowering his bruised, black, and blue body into bed, swinging his legs up on the mattress. When he was lying down, she adjusted two pillows under his head. The doctor wanted his head elevated during the night. He didn't look too comfortable.

'You going to be okay?' she asked.

'No, but I'll make it,' John replied.

'Can I get you anything?'

'Just a glass of water.'

As she went to the kitchen for a cold glass of water, she struggled with her thoughts, what to do. He obviously was going to need help for a few days. He was badly hurt. Should she offer to stay? Would he want her to? She knew how he must feel. She had been badly hurt by her husband, Kevin. No one had been there to help her on those occasions. She had wanted help. She had needed help after he beat her, but he wouldn't allow it. He didn't want anyone to know. He had made excuses for her absence, kept everyone away from her until she was healed. No one knew her situation, no one except a few close friends who could be trusted to keep a secret. She was afraid of what Kevin would do if he found out she had reported what he had done. Even her mother didn't know. Her relationship with her mother was complicated. His mother adored Kevin, thought he was a grand prize, caught in her web of matrimony. If only her mother knew.

Kate got some ice cubes from the refrigerator. Making up her mind quickly, she knew instinctively she couldn't abandon John. She had to stay. He was like her now, a victim. She knew how lonely it was to be hurt and helpless.

Returning to his bedroom, she placed the glass of water with ice on a table beside his bed.

'Anything else you need?' she asked.

'Just you in my bed,' John replied.

'I'm not sure that's a good idea. I wouldn't want to accidentally turn over and hurt you. Why don't I sleep in the bedroom down the hall? I'll keep my door open. If you need anything during the night, just call. I'm a light sleeper. I'll hear you.'

He looked up at her with hurt eyes. 'Sorry, I wanted our evening to be relaxing and fun.'

'This wasn't your fault. You don't have to apologize. Now get some sleep. I'll be here in the morning to help you get up.'

'Thanks,' he closed his eyes.

She shut off the light in his bedroom, turned at the door, and looked inside. Illuminated only by light from the hall, she could see him as he rested in shadows. She knew he would sleep most of the night. The doctor had given him something for his pain. It would be different in the morning. That's when it would be the worst. She knew this from experience; from all the beating she had taken. The next morning was always the worst. They had something in common now. She and John had both been badly beaten. There was a bond now between them, a thread of experience which closed around their relationship and made it different from what it was only a few hours ago.

Before, she may have been able to leave him, return to India, and resume her former life. But that didn't mean it wouldn't have been without some difficulty. She liked him. She was happy she had an opportunity to get to know him. But she needed her life in India.

Everything was different, now.

Now she felt a connection to him which was stronger than before, not something she could easily ignore.

GRAND HAVEN, SUNDAY, JULY 29, 6:10 AM, JOHN

I had been awake for hours, feeling hurt in places on my body I didn't even know were damaged.

Although I was tempted to take some pain medicine during the night, I had decided against it. The pain wasn't that bad. I could manage without the pills. I didn't want to be groggy when she woke up. I knew Kate would be leaving in the afternoon to return to Detroit for work. I wanted to spend the day with her. I could sleep later.

After getting up to go to the bathroom in the early morning, I decided against returning to bed. I had spent enough uncomfortable time in that bed. I went to my living room instead, sat on a couch, put my head back, and let my brain wander as the sky outside my windows came alive with the light of a new day.

Nothing made sense.

I didn't know the guy who beat me. He had identified himself as some colonel in the army and said he had just returned from Afghanistan. He offered the police his rank and serial number, nothing more, and acted like a prisoner of war. What the heck was going on in his stupid head? And why had he singled me out for a beating? What had I ever done to him?

Maybe he had post-traumatic stress, and I just happened to be in the wrong place at the wrong time. I was a punching bag for his pent-up anger at the war. Okay, if that was true, I felt sorry for him. Afghanistan was a mess. I knew that firsthand. Fortunately, some guy had come along and rescued me. I could have been killed otherwise. I made a mental note to find out where this guy lived and send him a gift in appreciation of his kindness.

'John,' Kate said from the hall outside my bedroom, sounding worried.

'I'm in here,' I replied softly because I couldn't talk real loud.

'What are you doing out of bed?' she rushed in.

'Didn't like it in bed. I decided to sit out here where I could think.'

'You should be in bed.'

'I'm fine, Kate, just hurting, but nothing I can't stand.'

'Do you want me to get you a pill?' She stood in front of me, dressed in an open bathrobe that partially covered a skimpy pajama top and bottom.

'No, I want you to take off that bathrobe so we can make love.'

She closed the bathrobe around her lovely, round body and looked down at me in disdain. 'I don't think that's in your future for a few days.'

'Doesn't sound like any fun.'

'You don't need fun. You need to heal,' she declared.

'I guess you're right.' I grimaced while trying to adjust my position on the couch. It hurt to sit in one place for too long. 'Come sit down beside me.' I patted the couch.

'Why don't I make some coffee first?'

'Sure.'

'Then I want to talk to you.'

'Okay, I guess,' thinking that sounded ominous.

MUSKEGON, MICHIGAN, 6:15 AM, PETE

After parking his car in the lower levels of the ferry boat, Pete headed upstairs, out onto the deck of the ship. It was a beautiful morning, with light breezes and warm weather.

He had gotten up early, headed to Muskegon, where he caught the 6 A.M. ferry to Milwaukee. He hoped to be home in Minneapolis by afternoon to spend the rest of the day with his family before heading to his office in the morning to write his report for Kevin.

He had learned all he needed to know over the last week: where Mrs. Kate Talsma was working, what her job was, who she was spending her weekends with, and what alias she was using. He had taken pictures, made notes, and was confident his report contained all the information his client required.

Fortunately for Mrs. Bradford's boyfriend, Pete just happened to be trailing the couple last night. Although he didn't want to interfere, after watching for several minutes, he couldn't let the woman's boyfriend continue to take a beating. It was too gruesome to watch.

Pete had a gun. He had a license for it. The weapon had never been used, but last night seemed like a good time to break his self-prescribed rule, and that was a promise he had made to himself to never fire the thing, just use it for intimidation and only in self-defense from irate husbands or other scoundrels who were being investigated as part of his work. He had purchased the gun after being threatened in his office.

The lake ferry took several hours off his travel time. It was expensive, but it was a beautiful morning to be on a boat. He was anxious to return home to see his family. Pete decided the cost was worth it. Besides, he could include the expense in the bill he would give to the young Mr. Kevin. His client was rich. The lawyer who had recommended Pete for the job had given him a heads up. So, all in all, it was a good morning. His work had been completed successfully. In addition, he had saved a man's life in the process.

Pete allowed a warm breeze to blow through his hair as the ferry cleared the harbor at Muskegon. Four Detroit diesels, 4000s, droned to life, pulsating with 3000 horsepower each, elevating the catamaran ferry boat up on two pontoons, where it would reach speeds of over thirty miles per hour. The weather was cooperating; it looked like it would be an easy crossing, with relatively few waves and a morning breeze initially offshore.

Pete wondered about the man he had shot. The police didn't offer much help in this department. And the man was not being cooperative when Pete last saw him. He wasn't hurt badly, just shot in the leg. Pete was thankful he had taken classes on how to use his gun. He had aimed for the man's legs when the guy advanced towards him, didn't want to kill him, just slow him down. Pete had told the police it was self-defense. He was convinced the man planned to attack him. He said he was sorry, but he had no choice except to fire his weapon. The cops seemed to understand.

They didn't ask Pete to stick around; they just asked for an address where he could be reached if they had any more questions.

GRAND HAVEN, MICHIGAN, 7:25 AM

He was a tough guy.

That was Ottawa County Sheriff Deputy Josh Smith's opinion when he called me.

The Colonel initially acted like a real idiot; he wouldn't talk, just continued to repeat his name, rank, and serial number like he was a prisoner of war. But everyone has a breaking point, according to the deputy. In the end, the Colonel didn't last long. In the early hours of the morning, he finally broke down and agreed to talk.

Deputy Smith explained, 'The wound to his leg was mostly superficial, skin and muscle only. No bones or important arteries were hit. The doctors in the emergency room released him to the custody of the Ottawa County Sheriff Department after they were through stitching him up. He was taken to the County Headquarters, where he was held in an interrogation room. He turned down an offer for a lawyer, said he didn't need one, and he had done nothing wrong.

That seemed odd to the Deputy, but he didn't try to talk the Colonel into accepting a lawyer; he just gave him coffee to keep him awake and continued to question him throughout the night. After being told repeatedly that he would do serious time if he didn't come clean and help them understand why he had assaulted a local citizen, the Colonel finally confessed he had been hired by a man named Fred Smith. Seems this Mr. Smith has a personal grudge against me, and the Colonel was hired to teach me a lesson. The Colonel said it was nothing personal. He was just doing his job, just as he had when he was in the Army. He assumed the police would understand. Because didn't they do the same thing? Just do their duty, obey their superiors? This was how he rationalized his actions. According to the Colonel, Mr. Smith had told him the job needed to be done for the good of the country. Said I had betrayed my country. Said I was a traitor and the Colonel was a patriot, just doing his duty.

When the Deputy asked him what I had done to deserve this treatment, the Colonel said he didn't know. That information was held in confidence by Mr. Smith. His job was not to ask questions. His job was to follow orders.

I asked what was going to happen to the Colonel now. The Deputy told me if he cooperated with the prosecutor's office, his time in jail would be reduced. He would still have to serve some time, but not as long as he would have if he didn't cooperate. That's what finally got him to talk. He didn't want to do the time.

'So, do you know a Fred Smith?' the Deputy tentatively asked.

'I do.'

'Do you know why he would send someone like an army colonel to come after you?'

'I think I do,' I replied.

'Do you want to tell me what it is?'

'Sure, I did a service for the President of the United States.'

'I see,' the cop replied, sounding cocky, like he didn't believe me.

I asked him if he would like me to give him the name of a CIA agent who could verify what I told him was true.

'No, that will not be necessary.'

'Let me tell you anyway,' I replied. 'The name of the CIA agent who can vouch for me is Mr. Charles Steward. You can call him at Langley, Virginia, CIA Headquarters.' I knew I shouldn't be getting mad. But I didn't want this cop or anyone else, for that matter, doubting my word. I lived in the county where he worked. I wanted the cops on my side. After I gave him Charlie's telephone number, he said nothing. I don't think he knew what to say. And I did nothing to help him out of his predicament.

'Are we clear on this matter?' I finally asked him. 'I can call Mr. Stewart if you like and have him talk to you.'

'No, no, that won't be necessary.'

I remained silent.

The Deputy asked, 'Would it be okay to send someone out to your house to get a statement? Are you up to talking this morning, Mr. Van Laan?'

'I am.'

'Good, I'll send someone right over.'

'I'll be here. Say, what is going to happen to Fred Smith?'

'Well, if he's convicted of hiring someone to kill or assault you, that's the same as doing the deed himself. He could go to jail for a long time.'

'Thank you, officer,' I replied.

'You're welcome.'

I put down my phone and sighed.

It all made sense; mystery solved. Fred Smith had come after me. He didn't come in person. That was not his MO. He was too chicken to do something like that. He sent someone else to do his dirty work. I hoped the Feds would arrest him and make the case stick this time, put him in a federal penitentiary. That would be a relief. Until then, I had to be more diligent. Now that I knew he was after me again, I had to be smarter. And the other thing I had to do was to call Charlie. He would want to know what happened. And to be certain the cops believed me, I would ask him to call Deputy Josh Smith of the Ottawa County Sheriff's Department.

Although I was hurting and sore in so many places, I couldn't count them all, my mood improved greatly after talking to the deputy. I was having a good morning. The deputy had confirmed something I suspected for a long time but couldn't confirm. Fred Smith was the source of my problems and Mr. Smith was in a lot of trouble now. Hopefully, this would put an end to this affair.

That was great, and it alone made for a good morning, but it was not as important as the news Kate gave me. The mystery of her long-term intentions was revealed. She said she wasn't returning to Novi to work with Joey. More importantly, she wasn't returning to India, not anytime soon. She didn't care what Joey or his brother wanted; she was going to stay with me, take care of me, and help me get well. She said I needed someone now, and that someone was her.

I didn't know exactly what to say when she told me. Her news was a complete surprise and I could help but wonder what had brought on this change of heart? I had always assumed she would return to India. She didn't say it in so many words, but her message was conveyed through many subtle references, such as her fondness for her life in India. The people, the places she talked about, the culture, everything seemed to glow when she described her experiences. Even slums came to life in pleasant terms when she described the people, how they cooperated in their poverty, how they worked together to make their lives better; building flimsy communities tied together with bonds more important than bricks and wood, bonds made of trust and consideration. In many respects, I envied her for her love of her new country, and I had no doubt she would return when she could. And I had considered trying to stop her. India was where she belonged.

I suspected her change of heart had something to do with the beating I took. It altered the way she looked at me. I could see it in her eyes. There was compassion now where before there had been only affectionate indifference. We had shared good times together, but she left no doubt that these times could not last. We should enjoy every moment we were together, because someday that time would end.

She came out of my bathroom dressed only in a bathrobe. Her hair was wet, tied up in a towel after a shower. A smile was on her face.

'What was that phone call? Anything important?' she asked.

'Yes, come sit by me so I can tell you.'

'Let me get dressed first.'

'That's not necessary. Just come sit by me.'

'You sure?'

'Yes, bring your clean naked body over here. I have something important to tell you. Besides, I like you better without clothes.'

'Are we feeling better this morning?' Kate asked.

'We are, just don't ask me to move.'

'So, it's safe to sit by you.'

'You will be very safe. I'm not much danger to anyone this morning.'

NOVI, MICHIGAN, THURSDAY, AUGUST 2, 4:45 PM, JOEY

The wooden case stamped with international shipping labels was hidden under a table in a shadowed back corner of his laboratory.

Joey had personally delivered it to that location his lab. Ater waiting until everyone was gone for the weekend, a process which did not take long on a midsummer Friday afternoon. His employees were naturally anxious to leave. Weekend activities were planned with families and friends. The building was empty before five o'clock rolled around, lights turned down, halls empty, long lines of machinery silent, motionless equipment serving no purpose except to take up space in a large open building.

Still, he had waited another hour, worked at his desk until he was absolutely certain that the building was unoccupied and no one would return for an item they had forgotten. When he was completely satisfied, he called his wife so she would not worry, and told her he had work to finish. He would be home as soon as he completed a few important details.

Only he knew what to look for, a special identification mark cut into the wood side of the shipping case. Operating a high-low, he lifted the case from the floor of the dock where it had been delivered and wheeled it into his lab, where he placed it under a table in an area he had specifically chosen before going to Afghanistan.

It had not been moved since then, untouched by human hands for several days. He was in no hurry. He wanted no suspicions. He would be patient and careful. Everything depended on him now and he had no intention of failing.

It would all happen as it was intended when the time was right.

EDEN, IOWA, 4:10 PM, PETE

Pete breathed a sigh of relief as he exited Kevin's office.

He was done… finally.

He had given his report to Kevin in person, all the details which had been collected through his investigation. The report was as exact and detailed as any he had prepared in the past. Pete was proud of his work. Yet, something bothered him as he headed down a hall from the large office which Mr. Kevin Bradford occupied in the Eden Fertilizer Company facilities. His car was in the parking lot. He had a long drive ahead of him. He was anxious to get on the road. The meeting with Kevin had taken longer than Pete had hoped. Three hours was his anticipated drive time. Not an unwieldy trip, just long enough that it made no sense to fly. Flying was costly and not always reliable.

Pete's meeting with Kevin had begun after lunch. Scheduled for two hours in his mind, it had lasted much longer, over four hours. Kevin wanted to know everything. He was not satisfied with the information in the report. He wanted all the details, especially the juicy ones, which concerned his wife Kate's affair with a guy she was seeing. What kind of person was her lover? Where did he work? Was he handsome? Was he a big guy? Did she stay at his house overnight? How often? Were they having sex? Kevin asked many questions.

Pete did his best to answer every question, but he couldn't answer every question because he wasn't under the impression that this was a divorce investigation. He thought Kevin had only asked him to find his wife was so he could get back together with her.

'Isn't that what you wanted?' Pete asked.

At this point in the conversation, Kevin got slightly upset, said he had told Pete to find out everything there was to know about what Kate was doing. Certainly, her love life was important. What did Pete not understand about his job?

Pete tried to answer his client's questions accurately, telling him everything he knew about Kate's boyfriend. He hoped the information would satisfy Kevin. And even though he had not planned to tell Kevin about the assault on Kate's boyfriend, it slipped out.

As a rule, Pete attempted to avoid getting involved in his clients or their wife's personal life. Pete liked being invisible; just an information-gathering machine who was not asked to judge the people he investigated. In Pete's opinion, they were simply occupants of the human race, prone to be weak and reckless because that was their nature, frail creatures whose improprieties kept him in business. Pete wanted no part of their twisted lives. He liked doing his work and going home, exorcising all the lurid details of his client's lives from his mind by the time he drove into his driveway. The incident in the alley was unfortunate. It had just happened, an uncontrolled event which Pete had found distasteful, not part of his job. He had hoped to keep it out of his report. But for some reason, which he regretted later, he had told Kevin about the beating Kate's boyfriend had taken because he hoped it would finally satisfy Kevin's curiosity. Pete was tired of answering questions. His mind was on his drive home at the time, thinking about how long it would take and what he would do when he arrived. He was getting tired. His meeting needed to come to an end. However, instead of bringing the meeting to a quick end, Kevin found the story of the beating especially interesting. He battered Pete with a whole new series of questions. How badly was Kate's boyfriend hurt? Where was he hit, and how did he react? Was he taken to the hospital? Kevin wanted to know everything and he seemed to relish the answers Pete gave him, as if they gave him pleasure.

When Kevin asked how Kate reacted to the beating, Pete said he didn't know. He was too busy breaking up a fight.

'You broke it up?' Kevin asked.

'Yes.'

'Why did you do that?' Kevin demanded.

'It needed to be done.'

'Why?' Kevin looked annoyed.

'Because the guy was getting killed,' Pete said simply.

'How did you break it up?'

'I shot the guy who was doing it.'

'You did?'

'I did.'

Kevin looked away, said nothing for a moment before asking, 'Was Kate hurt?'

'No, aside from being pushed up against a wall, she was not hurt.'

Kevin did not smile.

Pete waited for his client to ask another question. When he did not, Pete asked, 'Is there anything else I can do for you?'

'Where do you think she is now?' Kevin wanted to know.

'I don't know. I suppose she's in Dearborn at work.'

'This place where she goes every weekend to see her boyfriend, where is that again?'

'Grand Haven, Michigan, the address is in my report.'

'Okay, thanks.' Kevin stared out of his office window.

Pete waited, thinking Kevin would ask one more question. When he didn't, Pete asked, 'Can I go now?'

'Yea, go, I'll call you if I need anything else,' Kevin said without looking at Pete.

'My bill is in the folder.'

'You'll get paid. Now leave.'

The meeting left an empty feeling in Pete's gut as he walked down the hall. He was glad he was done with the case. If this Kevin guy wanted anything else, Pete decided to decline. Pete didn't like the guy. He didn't know why.

He just didn't like him.

GRAND HAVEN, SATURDAY, AUGUST 4, 4:10 PM, JOHN

A week of sunshine had altered the color of her skin. Now, her body literally glistened in the late afternoon sun with a deep, rosy red tan,

She looked beautiful, healthy and content, lying on a lounge chair, soaking up the last retreating rays of warmth. No longer directly overhead, the sun reflected off the large expanse of glassy, tranquil water that lay beyond the beach, stretching to a horizon lost under a halo of humid grey mist. It was difficult to determine where the water ended and the sky began, almost as if you could make the transition effortlessly in a boat driven far out into the lake, riding high into the sky to the stars beyond.

Her hair had bleached during the summer, becoming a blend of natural brown and blonde curls tightened from humidity and time spent swimming in the lake.

Looking very healthy in her bikini, Kate opened her eyes to see me staring at her. 'Anything I can do for you, Mr. Van Laan?' she asked.

'No, just admiring the scenery.'

'Like what you see?'

'I like it very much,' I smiled.

'Are we feeling better today?'

'Much better, thanks for asking.'

We had driven into town to see my doctor in the morning, and had my stitches removed. He said everything was healing fine. He asked if I had experienced any problems during the week, such as loss of memory or fainting spells. I answered no. My head was normal, whatever that meant in my case.

My internal injuries, bruises, and other pains were slowly healing. Just having Kate at the cottage all week had improved my disposition immensely. As much as anything, I think she contributed to my physical well-being. I was getting around fine.

I went for a swim in the afternoon. The doctor said I could as soon as my stitches were removed; just take it easy for a few more weeks. It would take time before the cuts on my forehead were healed well enough to be presentable in public. In the meantime, we decided to hang out at the cottage and enjoy what remained of the summer.

'Are we feeling a little frisky today?' Kate looked at me.

'Did you mean horny?' I asked.

'I guess you could say that.'

'Well, your bikini doesn't exactly support the discipline of abstinence.'

'I apologize,' she sat up to take a sip of cool lemonade.

Beads of sweat gleaming on her chest fell in gentle streams down the soft, round contours of her breasts before being absorbed into a thin layer of covering cloth. I couldn't see her eyes behind her sunglasses, but I knew she was eyeing me warily; knowledgeable about what was going on in my male head. It had been a week since we last made love. My body had been broken and hurting, incapable of being with her in the biblical sense.

'I don't believe the doctor said anything about not indulging in sex,' I commented.

'Yes, I don't remember hearing him say anything like that.' The corners of her full red lips turned up in a smile.

'So, what are we waiting for?'

'You sure you are ready?'

'I'm sure, just be kind to me.'

She smiled, loosened the strings of her bikini top around her neck, let fall the eloquently cut cloth that was not designed to fully disguise the wonder that existed beneath it completely, destined more to enhance the imagination of those wishing to be nourished by a gift which had been given to women to suckle young children and fill the minds of men with longing. The bikini top fell into her hand, allowing her bountiful breasts to experience the heat of the sun, her nipples taunt in an afternoon breeze.

She headed for the cottage. Pausing at the sliding glass door, she turned to see if I was following.

Of course, I was.

TUESDAY, AUGUST 7, 2:20 PM, JOHN

'So, what's happening with him?' I asked Charlie.

Kate had gone for a walk on the beach. It was a nice summer day, hot but with a light cooling breeze. I wanted to go with her, but I wasn't sufficiently healed to walk, not very far, ribs still complained when asked to exercise, although they were getting better every day.

Charlie had called to give me an update on Fred Smith. An investigation revealed the Colonel was in Afghanistan during the period when I was attacked. At the advice of counsel, he had declined to accept responsibility for those attacks, but Charlie said it was possible the Colonel was involved. If this could be proved, he was in big trouble. Using the resources of the United States Army to assault a US citizen in a foreign land was a big-time crime. The Army frowned on anything that even smelled of this kind of behavior. The Colonel's career in the armed forces was at an end. A dishonorable discharge was the least of his worries.

The other two guys who had helped him assault me had been arrested. They were identified from photos sent to me and Mr. Pete Mansell. The trio was currently in a federal prison awaiting formal charges. Charlie said they weren't going anywhere soon.

'Are you asking about Fred Smith?' Charlie said.

'Yes, where's he?'

'He's in jail in Ohio without bail. The judge was informed he has the resources to run if given the opportunity. Until the Army and the FBI clean up this mess, he's a prime suspect. They won't release him.'

'What do you think will happen now?'

'Someone in the group is going to talk. It's just a matter of time. We will get to the bottom of this. Don't you worry.'

'Thanks, Charlie.'

'Just doing my job.'

'I know, but still, I'm glad you're involved.'

'You can thank me later. So, how are you doing?'

'I'm healing.'

'Good.'

'Anything going on in Dearborn?' I asked.

'No, the cameras in the lab have so far recorded nothing suspicious. Could be a dead end.'

'How long will you keep an eye on Joey?'

'Not long. If nothing shows up, we'll suspend the operation in a few weeks.'

Our conversation continued for a few minutes. Nothing important was discussed, just the usual small talk. I invited him to visit my cottage when he had time, bring his girlfriend, and spend a few days. I told him Kate was staying with me. We could have a good time.

'I'm not sure I want to expose my girlfriend to you.' He commented.

'And why would that be?'

'Do I have to explain it to you?' he answered with a laugh.

'What, you're worried I'll take her away from you?'

'No, quite the contrary. I'm worried she won't have anything to do with me after she discovers you are my friend.'

'Very nice, thanks for the compliment, Charlie.'

'No problem.'

'Bye, Charlie.'

'See you, John.'

I put down the phone, feeling a sense of satisfaction. Just knowing Fred Smith was in jail was a relief. However, everything changed in a heartbeat when Kate walked into the cottage with her cell phone in her hand and a frown on her face.

'I have to go to Novi. Some unfinished business needs my attention,' she said with a determined look in her eye.

'What's the problem?'

'Laura called. Joey is after her again. She's afraid of him.'

'Do you want me to go with you?' I volunteered, knowing the situation could get messy.

'No. This is something I need to do myself. I don't want it to ruin your relationship with his brother. You stay out of it.'

'Okay, I guess.'

'I'm leaving in the morning. I should be back by afternoon if everything goes well.'

'Will Laura be okay in the meantime?'

'Yes. I told her to go home and stay there until I talked to Joey.'

NOVI, WEDNESDAY, AUGUST 8, 11:25 AM, KATE

Traffic slowed her journey considerably, backed up by an accident on I-96 near the Ann Arbor ramp, a location that was a normally hazardous area.

Frustrated, progress slow, sitting still on the expressway for impatient periods, Kate did not arrive at the Novi office in a good mood.

During the drive from Grand Haven, she had rehearsed in her mind what she would say to Joey. Deciding it would be best to be patient, she planned to explain to Joey exactly why he couldn't treat women badly, not in this country. It is against the law; she would tell him. He needed to be more careful. He could go to jail. All Laura had to do was report him, and the police could arrest him. She would remind him how Muslins were treated by the police. She would tell him it was not worth the risk. Besides, the Qur'an states that men and women are equal in the eyes of God. No man has the right to rule over a woman. Punishment for sins is in the hands of God, not man. Therefore, what Joey did was a sin.

This was her plan, but it wasn't what she really wanted to say to him. She wanted to tell the little bastard he was a despicable person, a disgrace to his race and his religion. This was not how Muslins should act. In fact, the more she thought about Joey, the madder she became… And the slow, delayed trip on the road did nothing to calm her anger. When she finally arrived, she was very upset. She told herself to calm down. There was a right way to handle this and a wrong way. The wrong way was to get mad. The right way was to make Joey understand he could not rape another woman for any reason.

'Is he in his office?' she asked the receptionist when she arrived inside the lobby. She had called ahead in the morning before leaving John's cottage, talked to his secretary, who told her Joey was in. He had nothing in his datebook. As far as his secretary knew, he would be in his office all day.

'He is,' the receptionist said. 'Shall I tell him you want to see him?'

'No, don't bother, I'll just go in.'

'I wouldn't do that if I were you,' the receptionist warned. 'His door had been closed all morning. He has been on the phone. He asked not to be disturbed.'

'Okay, call him and tell him I want to talk to him,' Kate said.

The receptionist nodded, picked up her phone, and dialed Joey's office. Kate listened as the young lady explained to Joey that Kate was in the lobby and wanted to talk to him. The receptionist nodded silently several times before hanging up.

'He told me to tell you that he has a few calls to make first. He will be ready for you shortly.'

Kate slumped down in a seat in the lobby to wait. She could have gone to her office, but this might set a bad precedent; Joey might think she had come back to work. She didn't want him to assume that. However, after about an hour of waiting patiently, Kate decided it would be less of a distraction for her to wait in her office than in the lobby.

Walking down a hall, she heard noise in her office, a man's voice on a phone. Apparently, someone now occupied her previous workspace. It hadn't taken Joey long to replace her.

She turned and retreated to the lobby to wait.

GRAND HAVEN, 6:05 PM, JOHN

A glass of whiskey was keeping my cell phone company as it sat on my desk silently waiting for Kate to call.

I could have called her, but I didn't, even though I was worried. She had lived on her own for years. She didn't need me worrying about her. Still, I was concerned.

Another sip of whiskey helped. My mind wandered. It was a calm evening on the lake with only a few clouds near the horizon.

Cell phone rang. I hoped it was Kate, and thankfully, her number showed on the caller ID.

'Hey, where are you?' I asked.

'I'm still in Novi. I just got done talking to Joey.'

'I thought you would be back here by now. I started to worry,' I admitted.

'I know, but I didn't get to talk to Joey until after five. He put me off.'

'How'd it go?'

'Not good. I'll tell you later. Right now, I'm sitting in my car in the company parking lot. Just thought I would call.' She paused. 'John, I think I will stay in Novi tonight. I'm really tired. It's been a long day.'

When I didn't say anything, she asked, 'Is that okay? Do you really need me to come back? I'd rather drive back in the morning.'

'Sure, if that's what you want.'

'I do. It'll give me a chance to pack my stuff and check out of my room. It's costing me money and I don't need it anymore.'

'Okay.'

'I'll call you later after I get something to eat.' She sounded exhausted.

NOVI, 6:08 PM, KEVIN

Kevin watched her rental car pull out of the company lot.

He had been in town since Monday morning, flew in from Iowa, rented a car, and found a hotel room. A parking place across the street from the company where she worked had a good view of the entrance to the building. When she did not show by Monday afternoon, he was disappointed, but determined to wait it out, assuming the information he had received from Pete Mansell was accurate.

He had decided that approaching her when she was with her boyfriend might prove to be a problem. Kevin badly wanted to talk to Kate when she was alone and he had decided that her hotel room would be the best place. Private at the end of the day, after she had finished working and was alone.

Tuesday again proved to be a disappointment, sitting alone in his rented car, watching and waiting. It wasn't until Wednesday afternoon that he was finally rewarded. He saw her walking to the front door of the building from his car the parking lot.

Waiting became more difficult now that he finally seen her again. But he was prepared, ate sandwiches in his car, drank water, listened to the radio, and waited patiently. It was after five o'clock when he again saw her trim figure walk down to her car and spent a few minutes talking on her phone.

Although he could not see her clearly in his binoculars, he knew it was her. Kate was still very beautiful, just as he remembered, just like the pictures he viewed sometimes at night when he was lonely. An ache, a pain in his side formed, a longing for her, just like before when he first met her. He felt the same emotions. It was exciting, the prospect of seeing her again, being with her, having sex. He remembered how it was. He wanted this again. He wanted it more than he could imagine.

He was determined to get her back. He would be kind this time. He would ask to be forgiven. He would tell her he had changed.

She would understand. She would take him back. He was very excited. He was convinced she would take him back.

Afternoon traffic was intense as he followed her car, never close, never so she would see someone following her. He almost lost sight of her car several times. He had to fight his way through traffic, cutting off a few big-city drivers who honked their horns in annoyance.

Tough, he thought. He was on a mission.

7:05 PM, KATE

The shower was on, and she was half undressed when she heard someone knocking at the door of her motel room.

Grabbing a bathrobe, she put it over her underwear and went to the door.

'Who is it?' Kate asked through the door.

'It's Kevin.'

A shot of instantly administered adrenaline ran rampant through her veins at the mention of his name and the unmistakable sound of his voice.

'What do you want?' she asked, as fear took control of her mind.

Always knowing this day might come, she had tried to mentally prepare. She knew she had to be ready. Every day since her return to the United States, she had thought about what to do if she saw him, but now that the time had finally come, she felt woefully unprepared.

'I just want to talk. Please let me in,' he asked.

'No, just go away, Kevin. I never want to see you again.'

'Kate, I'll go. I promise. Just let me see you one more time. Please let me say what I have come to say. Then if you want a divorce, I'll grant it.'

That was the one complication she knew needed to be resolved. While living in India, a divorce wasn't necessary. But now, in the States, things were different. Her legal status was unsettled. She wondered if she could trust him. Every instinct told her, no.

'Come on, Kate,' he said penitently through the door. 'I've changed. It has been a long time. Let's just talk like two adults. Then we can move on with our lives.'

It made sense. She knew they needed to resolve their situation. Maybe he had changed.

'Okay, but just for a few minutes.'

'I promise.'

She opened her door.

GRAND HAVEN, 11:40 PM, JOHN

Darkness lay heavy, like a stone sitting on my gut as I rested in bed, driving a deep pit into my spirit, making it difficult to sleep.

I had waited all evening for her to call, watching TV to pass the time. Kate had promised. She said she would call from her motel room and tell me what happened when she talked to Joey. She said it didn't go well. I was not surprised. I couldn't imagine that Joey would like a woman telling him what he could and could not do. His culture was male-dominated. I wondered what he said to her. But more importantly, I wanted to know that Kate was alright.

She had sounded exhausted when I last talked to her. I wondered if perhaps after packing, she was so tired she went straight to bed and forgot to call.

Ever since my run-in with the Colonel, Kate had been great to me. I didn't want to return the favor by disturbing her. I finally gave up around eleven and went to bed. It was too late to call.

I would have to wait until morning.

NOVI, THURSDAY, AUGUST 9, 12:10 AM, JOEY

Joey carefully opened the top of the wooden shipping case.

He had been moved it into the glass-enclosed room under bright lights. Dressed from head to toe in a white suit which looked as if it could be used in outer space, he was careful and deliberate in his work. Any wrong move now could prove to be a disaster to both him and anyone living within several miles of his company.

After speaking with Kate, he had not gone home as he had previously intended. Instead, he went directly to his lab. Because this was what he always did when life became confusing for him: he retreated to what he knew well, physics and electrical engineering, subjects that were difficult to understand for most people, but were child's play for Joey. He was a genius, and this was the one advantage his highly intelligent brain offered him: an opportunity to escape the real world by disappearing into a world of formulas and equations, a world that science made available. Vague moral standards did exist in this complex world. This was a simple world, a world of what worked and what did not.

Bombs were not judgmental in his mind.

They offered no verdicts concerning the guilt or the innocence of the people whose lives they affected. They simply destroyed what was within their reach at the time of ignition. Their purpose and their design were simply a matter of the material qualifications of their components. The logic of their actions had been predetermined light-years before when the world was formed. They simply required the right combination of elements brought together by imagination and intelligence.

For Joey, science was an island of logic in a sea of confusion. When properly understood, science was both brilliant and exciting. As the hours passed, Joey's mood lightened and his memory of a disturbing conversation with a woman faded into the past. She was no longer important except for one fact. Her accusations had spurred him to act.

She had made him mad. How could she talk to him as she did? She was a woman. He was a man. Back in his country, he could have had her whipped for being an arrogant, belligerent woman. She would have been put in her place. The whipping, the scars on her back, would forever be a reminder of her audacity. She would be made to understand; women were created to serve men.

But not in this country. In this country, women thought they could talk to men as she had talked to him. Women thought they had the right to accuse a man. Women thought they could say anything that came into their minds. She had sat in his office and accused him of doing something wrong, something she said was a crime. Rape was a crime. She said he was lucky she didn't report him to the police. If he ever did it again, she said she would have him arrested.

How could she do this? Did she not understand she worked for him; he was her boss? She had no right. Even though she had quit her job, he had told her she was fired. He no longer wanted her in his plant. He told her to get out. He was mad.

In his mind, he had done nothing wrong, nothing that deserved this treatment at the hands of a woman. When he had raped the female employee, he had done it for her good. She was becoming a loose woman, a disgrace to his people, to his religion, a tease and a slut. Her clothing had been too revealing. Her loose behavior had been the actions of a prostitute. He had saved her from an evil descent into hell. He had taught her a lesson she would never forget.

In this country, it was all backwards. Everything was backwards. The people in this country were arrogant. They thought they had the god-given right to invade any country they chose. They had gone into his country, Afghanistan. The United States Army had killed his brothers and sisters in villages where they lived. The United States had sent drones that delivered silent, fearful death, explosions that killed women and innocent children. They had no right. The United States should not be in his country.

He, Joey, would teach this country a lesson they would never forget. He would teach them that they could not indiscriminately kill and brutalize people in other countries without fear of retaliation.

Their press had called the people of Afghanistan who opposed their invasion, terrorists. But he considered himself a freedom fighter, fighting for the independence of his homeland. He wanted the hated Americans to leave his country. Never ever come back, or bad things will happen. That would be his message. Bomb us and we will bomb you. The bomb he was making was designed to kill people who had blindly supported the devastation Joey had witnessed in a village near where he lived. A drone had delivered a tangled, bloody scene across a previously peaceful village; a place filled with broken and torn bodies, pain, and crying mothers for their dead children.

Joey had been an unwilling eyewitness to this destruction. It had changed him forever. He had vowed revenge. The people of the United States would not be innocent victims of his bomb. They were collaborators in the destruction that he had witnessed firsthand. They deserved to die.

In a way, he was happy she had accused him. Her conversation made him act. He had been procrastinating for days, unwilling, unable to make up his mind that this was the right thing to do. Now he had no doubt.

He whistled as he worked his magic. Under intense lights in a glass-enclosed room he had built for this purpose alone, he carefully placed the highly enriched uranium into his invention, shutting a lead-filled cover over the excitable element of mass destruction. Connecting wires, tightening screws. Carefully with precision, the device slowly began to take shape, come into being; a machine only a genius could make.

Joey was in his element.

GRAND HAVEN, 1:55 AM, JOHN

It was like the night in India when she had carefully inched over in bed until she rested against my back without saying a word, her lovely, soft, round body caressing a thousand tense nerve ends in my skin, making me come alive with yearning.

Before I could open my mouth to speak, to beg for her attention, Kate instinctively covered my mouth with her hand.

'I'm really tired. I need to sleep,' she whispered. 'We can talk in the morning.'

I said nothing in response, simply rested, feeling the warm comfort a woman brings to a man's bed. She was safe. She was with me. I didn't need to worry about her anymore.

I had been sleeping and didn't hear her come in. It wasn't until I felt her enter my bed that I sensed someone was there. The scent of her sweet perfume aroused my senses, bringing me out of the world of dreams to a reality that held more promise than my anxious nightmares. The sound of her voice, her soft whispers, confirmed what I desired.

I rested.

The weight of a heavy rock lifted off my gut. I lay comfortably listening to her slow, low breathing in the night, knowing she was with me again.

Eventually, I fell into a sweet, dreamless sleep, which was refreshing.

8:35 AM, JOHN

The morning sun crept slyly in through our bedroom window, finding her still sleeping comfortably.

Gently, with almost childlike delight, the impish sun slowly caressed her beautiful face with the glow of a new day. She stirred without opening her eyes, stretched slowly under the bed sheets as if she was testing to see if it was okay to return to the land of the living.

Personally, I had been awake for an hour or more and out of bed; content that she was with me again. I didn't wish to disturb her, just let her sleep assuming she needed the rest. A hot cup of hot coffee tasted good as I watched TV news while waiting for her to wake up. Nothing out of the ordinary was reported, only the usual catastrophes, one after another. The news anchor was a gorgeous young woman who melted the screen with her smile. Having perfected the art of reading a teleprompter, she was very easy on my eyes. It was not difficult to understand why she had been hired.

'John.' Kate poked her head out of our bedroom door.

'Yes.' I turned to greet her.

'Just wanted to know where you were.'

'I'm here. Need anything?'

'A cup of coffee would be great. I'll be right out.'

I went into the kitchen to refill my coffee and pour her a cup, returning to the living room.

Her story was long and I should have been hungry for breakfast by the time she finally finished telling me, but I wasn't. Not after what she said.

'So, you drove back here, late last night to get away from your former husband, what's his name?' I asked, trying to comprehend the full extent of what she was telling me.

'Kevin.'

'Right, Kevin.'

'I didn't want to be in the same city with that man,' Kate said with revulsion.

'But why? You said that he didn't do anything to hurt you.'

'John, I know him. I could see his anger boiling just below the surface. He held it in, but he was getting frustrated with me. I was afraid. When he gets mad, his temper tantrums are vicious. I have seen it before. That man can change in a heartbeat. One second, he is talking like a rational person, the next he is a raving maniac.'

'I see.'

'No, you don't. It's almost impossible to understand until you have witnessed it personally.'

I didn't know what to say.

'I promised him I would think about getting back together with him,' she continued. 'I had to lie to him, John. I was afraid that if I didn't, he would go all crazy on me again. Just like before when he beat me.'

I looked at her, trying to comprehend how bad it must have been for her to live with a man like him.

'I waited until I was sure he had driven away,' she explained. 'Then I grabbed a few things and got into my car to come here.'

'He didn't follow you?' I questioned her.

'No. I was careful. I checked my rearview mirror constantly. No one followed me.'

'So, what now?'

'I don't know. I need a divorce. But that would mean seeing him again, and I don't want ever to see him again.'

'Do you think he knows about me?'

'I don't think he does, but I don't know.'

'How did he find you?'

'Probably an old class mate told him,' she said, replaying the story of how she had accidentally encountered a former college buddy of her husband while working on the road.

I contemplated the situation for a minute. 'I know a good lawyer,' I said. 'I'll call him. I'm not sure he handles divorce cases, but he can advise you, suggest someone who is good.'

'Thank you.'

'No problem.'

'Now about Joey, what are you going to do about him?' I asked.

'I don't know what to do about him.'

'He didn't want to listen to you?'

'No, he got mad and told me to get out. Never set foot in his company again.'

Kate said she tried to talk to Joey, explain to him why he couldn't indiscriminately rape women. He had no right. Women were not put on earth for his pleasure. They were not subservient to men. They were persons in their own right, equal in the eyes of God. What he had done was a crime and a sin. And the next time he did anything like this, Kate promised to report him to the police.

'Can Laura go back to work?' I asked her.

'I'm going to advise her to quit. But I don't know if she will listen to me. She needs her job. She doesn't speak English well. There are not many job opportunities for a woman like her, especially a Muslin woman.'

'That's tough.'

'It's reality, John. Life for a woman is not the same as it is for a man.'

'Will you report Joey if Laura tells you she has been raped again?'

'I will, but I'm not sure she will tell me. She doesn't want to get fired. Truth is, I'm not sure Joey will take her back now. Not after what I told him.'

I sipped my coffee, which had become cold as I listened. 'Want some more coffee?'

'I think I would like breakfast,' Kate replied.

'Okay.'

'Will you drive with me to Novi to get my things from the motel?' she asked. 'I don't want to go alone.'

'Sure, when do you want to go?'

'Today, after breakfast.'

'Sure.'

NOVI, MICHIGAN, 10:20 AM, KEVIN

Kevin wasn't discouraged, not yet.

Although Kate's car was not at her motel the next morning, he knew she had to return. After slipping the man at the desk a twenty, the manager of the Staybridge Suites assured Kevin his wife was still registered. Her clothes were still in a closet. She had to return some time to check out. In the meantime, her credit card was racking up daily charges.

He drove to her company several times, checked to see if her car was in the parking lot. When he didn't see it, he returned to the motel, waited in a distant parking lot, using binoculars to keep an eye on the location where he had seen her park her car the previous evening.

Sandwiches and bottled water had been purchased at a local convenience store early in the morning, preparing for a long wait, convinced he would have one more chance to win her over. If not; well, he took his handgun in case there was trouble from her boyfriend or someone else. He did not want any interference when it came time to talk to her and this was the rational he justified his possession of a weapon. It had not crossed his mind that he might be forced to use his gun to convince her to come with him. Not his conscious mind anyway; maybe his subconscious mind, but not anything he would admit to himself.

After all, hadn't she agreed to think about returning to Iowa with him? She had sounded convincing last night. He felt he had nothing to fear. He told himself over and over that he had nothing to fear. Be patient, she will show up soon.

Then they could move on with their lives.

ON THE ROAD TO NOVI NEAR LANSING, MICHIGAN 11:05 AM, JOHN

Traffic was relatively light on I-96, a four-lane divided highway that crossed the state from the western shores of Lake Michigan to the southeast side of Detroit.

Her rental car, a Ford Fusion, was in front of my silver Audi station wagon, cruising at a pedestrian seventy-two miles per hour, monotonously slow by my standards. Cars, semi-trailer trucks passed us in long lines. Still, she stubbornly maintained her speed in cruise, content it seemed to travel at what felt to me like snail speed to me, making it difficult to maintain my concentration.

We were on the expressway heading to her motel room to pack her clothes and check out. Our plan was to return her rental car and drive back to my cottage in my car. That's the reason we were driving separately. And it was why I had no one to talk to.

My cell phone beckoned.

'Call Charlie,' I said to the voice recognition system in the car. His phone rang.

He picked up. 'Hey, John.'

'What's going on, Charlie?'

'Not much, what's going on with you?'

'I'm bored, thought I would call you to brighten my day.'

'Hum, I didn't realize one of the services of the CIA was to entertain the electorate.'

'You are a public servant, aren't you?'

'In a way, I guess you could say that.'

'Well, then it's time to serve me.'

'What can I do for you, John? I'm kind of in the middle of something.'

'Anything on Joey?' I asked, half expecting to hear the CIA would soon be discontinuing their surveillance of his laboratory after discovering nothing of interest for several weeks.

'Funny you asked,' Charlie replied. 'I'm in Detroit setting up a command center on the other side of the state from you.'

'Really, why?'

'Mr. Joey Abdul was busy the other night. Looked to my guys like he was building something rather special. Tapes are being analyzed by experts as we speak, but initial evidence indicates it could be a bomb.'

'You're kidding.'

'No, not kidding, John. I have to go. Got a lot on my mind.'

'Charlie, I'm on my way to Detroit with Kate. Anything we can do to help.'

'Maybe, let me think about that. In the meantime, you might want to consider turning around and heading in the other direction. If what he's building is nuclear, the whole city could go up in a mushroom cloud.'

'That serious?'

'That's serious. And John, the information I just gave you is strictly confidential. If the public found out, the city could panic. I don't think I have to tell you what a mess that would be.'

'You have my word.'

'Good, now I have to go. Got a lot to do, things are moving fast.'

NOVI, 12:20 PM, JOHN

Kevin was nowhere in sight when we arrived at the Staybridge Suites Motel.

He was her main worry, the reason she asked me to come along. When Kate didn't see any sign of his car in the parking lot, she immediately went to her room and began to meticulously pack up her clothes and other belongings. I tried to help, but she interrupted my efforts to be of assistance, told me to stay out of the way, which I did because she was adamant, and told me in no uncertain terms to sit down, watch TV, or something. I would just mess up things. She would be done soon.

Her room was pleasant enough, nothing special, the usual long-term accommodations: a suite of rooms containing a desk, a small efficiency kitchen, a sitting area, a bed, and a bathroom. Interior decorating was in shades of brown, nothing particularly innocuous or inspiring. I turned on the TV, watched the news for a few minutes before becoming bored.

Charlie's telephone call was on my mind. If what he said was true, the situation was a potential disaster of immense size. A nuclear bomb, even a small one, could do considerable damage, destroy whole city blocks, kill hundreds, perhaps thousands of people.

Kate and I were in the danger zone. My first instinct was to run. I had not told Kate about the bomb because Charlie said the information was confidential. The CIA was handling it; tell no one.

And that's why I wanted her to hurry, but I didn't know how to make it happen.

My cell phone rang.

'John, are you in town?' Charlie asked. 'Or by some miracle of logic, did you actually take my advice and turn around?'

'I'm in town.'

'Never doubted it for a moment.'

'Did you expect anything else?'

'No, and as long as you are here, maybe you can help. We are trying figure out what Joey could be up to, any suggestions?'

'Can I ask Kate?'

'No. We can't involve her at this point. You have a security clearance. She doesn't. Plus, you know this guy as well as she does, right?'

'I suppose.'

'Where are you?'

'Staybridge Suites in Novi.'

'I'll come get you.' He hung before I could object.

'Kate, that was Charlie,' I explained. 'He needs my help with something important. He's coming to get me. Is that okay with you?'

'I should be fine here. You run along and help Charlie.'

12:40 PM, JOHN

CIA Headquarters in Langley, Virginia, had been thoroughly advised: the situation in Novi, Michigan, was deemed critical, awarded the highest level of national emergency. The operations arm of the CIA went into full alert. A CIA command vehicle as big as a motor home was flown in on an Air Force cargo plane early that morning.

Charlie opened the door of the command center allowing me to enter. The interior resembled a spaceship, containing every conceivable technological advantage that had been invented, as well as a few that were still in the experimental stage. A few fellow CIA operatives shook my hand as Charlie showed me around, but not for long. Within minutes, we were rushed into a room containing a large conference table surrounded by chairs. On Charlie's suggestion, I took a seat behind him.

After a short wait, an older gentleman in a suit stood up at the end of the table. Tall with long curly gray hair combed back neatly, he was a handsome man whose mannerisms dictated authority.

He introduced the situation: Last night, after building a device which was deemed to be a highly explosive bomb by experts, Joey placed the devise in a wood case, closed the case, and moved it out of the lab where it could not be viewed by installed cameras. The outside of his building was currently being monitored from several helicopters, which were presently in the air, aiming high-resolution cameras at every exit door and every dock in the building. Everyone and everything going in or out of the building was currently being viewed on a series of TV screens attached to a wall at the end of the table where we were sitting.

It was assumed that Joey and his bomb were still in the building. Triggering the devise inside the building was considered a low probability since he was still inside. And although the town of Novi, where the bomb was currently located, was not uninhabited, it was not a major population center. And it was assumed that Joey's bomb could do far more damage and make a much greater impact if detonated in another location, such as downtown Detroit or another major population center.

'Any ideas on why Mr. Abdul would build a bomb?' asked the gray-haired gentleman standing at the end of the table, looking specifically for suggestions about where the best place would be to detonate a device of this nature. The assembled agents circulated various ideas, all plausible, but nothing which stood out, Charlie took the opportunity to introduce me to the other agents, explaining my relationship to Mr. Abdul.

'Any ideas, John? You know this guy,' Charlie asked.

I paused before answering. 'From my observations, he is a very smart, but also very insecure. If I could put myself in his shoes, I would trigger it at a sporting event. Or some other large gathering where it would have the greatest effect.'

'Does religion play a part in his mind?' an agent asked.

'I don't know. Although I was told he had become more religious recently. So, yes, that's possible. But in my opinion, the current situation in the Middle East, our war with Iraq and Afghanistan, is probably what's motivating him.'

My comment didn't immediately trigger a response. The room remained silent until the gentleman in charge asked dismissively. 'Are there any sports events in Detroit today?'

The answer to his question was immediate. 'The Detroit Tigers are playing a matinée home game this afternoon.'

'That's a possibility,' the gentleman standing at the end of the table responded. 'But it's not what we need to know. We need to know where this bomb is now. The situation is critical.'

'If we knew how it will be transported, we could track it.' An agent suggested.

'At a minimum, a small truck is required,' a woman agent spoke up. 'Even though the bomb is small, it is far too heavy for a car to transport. A truck would be necessary.'

'Were any trucks seen leaving the building this morning?'

'No, sir, the docks have been quiet,' a young man in a suit replied.

'Good, from this time forward, all trucks leaving the docks should be stopped and searched.'

The young man stood up from the table. Talking into his cell phone as he walked away, he alerted a team on the ground. Stop and search all vehicles leaving the building, starting immediately.

'I'm just curious,' I interjected. 'But what are you waiting for?' I was getting frustrated with a discussion that seemed to be going nowhere and taking up precious time. 'If you are convinced a bomb is inside, why don't you go into the building and get the thing defused before it can do any damage?'

'We are preparing to go in,' Charlie replied. 'But you need to understand. An operation of this nature requires precision. We don't want Joey or anyone else blowing up the bomb before we can get to it. Our first objective is to have him and all other employees secured first. Teams are assembling as I speak. We should be ready to go in about a half hour.'

'Do you want to know how the building is laid out?' I volunteered, thinking Kate might be able to help.

'We know, a blueprint of the interior of the building has been obtained from the city.' Seems Charlie was way ahead of me.

My cell phone rang, embarrassingly. Kate's telephone number showed up in the caller ID. Everyone at the table turned in my direction. My first instinct was to ignore it.

'Take it, John,' Charlie said. 'You can go into the hall.'

I stood up, answering the call as soon as I was out of the room.

'I'm done,' Kate said. 'I would like to leave.'

'I'm kind of tied up,' I replied. 'Can you wait a few minutes?'

'John, I don't want to stay here any longer than I have to.'

'Okay, I'll see if Charlie can find someone to drive me,' I paused. 'Say, does Joey have any close friends?' I asked, thinking that if he was really considering setting off a bomb, he might need help.

'Not many,' Kate replied. 'Just a couple of guys that I know. One of his friends works in the laundry business and does our towels. Another friend owns vending machines, which he set up inside the building for our employees. Why do you ask?'

'Can't tell you.'

She didn't respond except to say, 'Okay, I'm waiting.'

'I'll call as soon as I can get away.'

'Please don't take long.'

'I won't.'

When I returned to the room, the agents were engaged in a heated discussion. I silently motioned to Charlie to get his attention. But before I could talk to him, my cell phone rang again. Kate was on the line. Annoyed, I returned to the hall, hit the accept button.

'John, he's here,' Kate screamed into the phone. 'He's trying to break down the door.'

'Who?'

'Kevin.'

'I'll be right there.'

1:05 PM, JOHN

Charlie's car rushed down Grand River Avenue, lights flashing on his dashboard, siren screaming.

The gray-haired, supervising CIA officer in charge demanded that Charlie go with me after I rushed into the conference room. Sorry to interrupt, I explained, but it's a personal matter and it can't wait. An abusive husband is assaulting a female friend. I need a car in a hurry... please.

I must have looked desperate. It all seemed surreal, in the middle of a national security crisis, a matter as common as spousal abuse seemed just as lethal as a bomb threat of the highest magnitude.

Charlie never hesitated, came with me. His car radio played the whole time we were driving. I heard it all. Preparations for an operation at Joey's building were almost complete. Swat teams were in place, and last-minute instructions were being handed down.

'Sorry,' I said to Charlie. 'I know you wish you were going in with them.'

'You should have told me about Kate,' he replied, eyes never leaving the road, weaving expertly around stationary cars.

'I thought you had enough problems without my introducing one more.'

'Yea, I do, but Kate's important.'

Traffic slowed or turned off the road to make way for our vehicle. Red lights were ignored, siren wailing. At speed, it took Charlie only a few minutes to drive to her motel. I was out of our car before Charlie came to a full stop, on the run. Inside the main entrance of the motel, I took the stairs two steps at a time. Her room was on the second floor down the hall.

The door frame was busted when I arrived. My heart rate jumped.

'Kate, you all right?' I stepped slowly inside

'Don't come in here,' a man said, standing with his back to me in the sitting area of Kate's room. A gun was in his hand, pointed directly at Kate, who was sitting on a couch, looking at me helplessly.

'This is between Kate and me,' Kevin said.

I continued inside.

'You the boyfriend?' he asked when he saw that I was not going to leave.

'Yes.'

'You need to stay out of this. It's none of your business. I'm her husband, not you.'

'I know who you are and what you have done.'

1:15 PM

Fifteen squad cars descended on the building simultaneously, no sirens, no flashing lights, nothing to warn anyone inside of their arrival.

Several vans followed. Helicopters hovered overhead surveying the scene. SWAT teams emptied out of the black cars, moving quickly on the run in a precise drill based on a plan memorized by each individual officer.

Wearing standard black uniforms with bullet-repelling vests, their heads were covered by helmets, and their hands held various weapons. In no less than four minutes, the building, the employees were all secure, including and most importantly, Mr. Joey Abdul, who was found and marched out of the building in handcuffs, taken in a car directly to a waiting van where he was questioned.

The bomb squad followed the officers inside, searching for the wooden case which had been seen on tape the previous night. Several specialists wearing white radiation suits and glass helmets waited impatiently outside, ready to defuse it once it was found.

When the case was not immediately discovered, experts with knowledge of nuclear weapons entered the building after it was fully evacuated. Using Geiger counters to track evidence of highly enriched uranium, their meters registered no radiation until they entered the laboratory in the back of the building. But only trace amounts were registered; nothing to indicate the presence of a lethal amount of uranium.

Inside the van, Joey was being less than cooperative. When questioned by the senior CIA officer in charge, he denied any knowledge of a bomb or the presence of explosive uranium.

'Why would I do such a thing?' Joey asked.

'We saw you build it,' the CIA Agent in charge replied.

'How could you do that?'

'We have cameras inside your lab. We saw you built a bomb last night.'

'If you know so much, why don't you show me the bomb?' Joey shot back arrogantly.

The senior officer sat back for a minute. 'Tell us where it is now, and you can avoid a lot of trouble.'

'What trouble?'

'There's a prison in Afghanistan which could have your initials on the outside of a metal door. I don't think you will like it there.'

'You can't do that. This is America. You have laws in this country.'

'I can and I will send you on a plane this afternoon to prison if you don't tell us immediately what we want to know. Do you understand? I'm not bluffing, Mr. Abdul. This is your last chance.'

Joey knew all about CIA prisons in Afghanistan. He had friends who had survived these places of despair. He did not want to go on a plane, but he was determined not to talk.

If he talked, his reason for being born would come to nothing.

2:05 PM, JOHN

'Kevin, please put down the gun,' Kate begged him.

'No, if I can't have you, then he can't either,' Kevin replied, looking grimly determined.

'Kevin, please.'

'Will you come with me?' he asked. 'Final chance.'

'You know I can't do that.'

'Then I have no choice.'

His gun fired, sounding like a cannon in the small room. A second shot rapidly followed the first, two shots in a row. Kevin fell over, hitting the floor, his eyes already blank and lifeless from a bullet in his brain.

Kate doubled over, blood erupting from a wound to her chest, soaking quickly into her blouse. Her eyes looked up at me, pleading, not wanting to acknowledge what she knew was true, before squeezing shut in obvious pain.

'Get a towel from the bathroom.' Charlie took over, bending over Kate, who was grimacing.

I did as he commanded, headed for the bathroom where I found a towel.

'Put it over the wound and press tightly,' Charlie said when I returned. 'Hold it on her chest while I pick her up. We need to get her to my car. We don't have time for an ambulance. She needs a hospital now. She's going to bleed out if we don't get her there in time.'

We headed down the hall, running in tandem, not an easy task, me with my hand holding the blood-soaked towel against her chest in a vain attempt to slow the bleeding. Charlie carried her in his arms, down the stairs, and out the front door, where his car waited with the flashers still rotating. He placed her in the back seat on my lap. I held the towel tightly against her chest, prayed, and watched for any signs of life in her body as he drove to the closest hospital, which showed on the navigation system in his car. She felt stiff in my arms; her eyes were tightly shut against the pain.

Henry Ford Medical Center in Novi was not far from her motel. At ninety miles per hour down the expressway, it didn't take long to arrive at the emergency care door. Charlie called ahead, alerted the staff, and a critically wounded woman from a gunshot to the chest was bleeding to death; get the trauma staff to the door. We are on our way to the hospital.

White coated medical attendants at the door placed her gently on a wheeled stretcher and pushed her directly to an operating room. I watched as a swinging metal door automatically shut, closing off my view of her being rushed rapidly down a hall, wondering if she would make it.

Charlie was on his phone when I went to find him.

'I'm kind of in a mess here.' Charlie interrupted his phone call to talk to me. 'You don't mind if I take off, do you? There's nothing more I can do here to help.'

'Go,' I replied. 'I'll stay with her.'

'Good.' He headed out the door to his car with his cell phone in his hand.

'Charlie, just a minute.' I remembered Kate's words. 'I don't know if you might need this information, but Kate mentioned to me that Joey has two close friends. One owns a dry-cleaning business, and the other owns a vending machine business. It's just possible they are working with him.'

'Thanks,' he turned and rushed away.

'Are you with the young lady who was just brought in?' A middle-aged female administrative assistant approached me.

'Yes, where has she been taken?'

'To an operating room.'

I said nothing.

'She's in good hands,' the woman said, seeing my obvious concern. 'Now if I can just get some information on the patient, please.'

'Sure, what do you need to know?'

'Let's start with name and address,' she asked, holding a clipboard.

I didn't know what to tell her.

'Her name is Kate.' I finally decided.

'Last name, please.'

'Talsma.'

'Does she have medical insurance?' the woman asked.

'I don't know.'

'I see.' The woman started to write something.

'I'll pay for everything,' I volunteered.

'What's your name?' she asked.

2:25 PM, CHARLIE

'Have you found the bomb yet?' Charlie asked as he sped down the expressway heading away from the hospital parking lot.

'No,' his supervisor answered.

'Is the suspect talking?'

'No, he's not cooperating.

'Okay,' Charlie replied. 'Do this for me. Check the morning helicopter tapes of the building for a vending machine truck or a laundry truck. I was told Mr. Abdul has friends in both businesses. Their vehicles could have been used to transport the bomb.'

'Okay,' his supervisor responded. 'I'll have the tapes checked. Say, where are you?'

'Heading downtown to the ballpark on a hunch,' Charlie replied.

'Okay, keep me informed.'

'Yes, sir.

2:55 PM, CHARLIE

Comerica Park, home of the Detroit Tigers, is a new ballpark replete with expensive boxes in the stands that favor the rich and nearly rich with all the food and booze one can possibly consume during a baseball game.

The stadium that day was filled with fans resting in green seats extending up from both sides of the infield and around the outfield, completely circling the contest arena. Inside this sea of seats was a flat area of grass so green and sand so perfect it looked unreal. No weeds would dare show their presence on these hallowed grounds where legends were made.

The game of baseball is a slow game by most standards, delayed by constant interruptions. Innings are forever ending and beginning. Just when the game gets exciting, when the bases are loaded and the possibility of something dramatic might happen, when the fans are on the edge of their seats cheering for the home team, a strike three pitch can end it all with a whimper.

Under the stadium are tunnels designed to feed the constant and seemingly insatiable appetites of an average baseball fan. More beer and hot dogs are consumed on an average afternoon in a baseball park than any other place on earth, mostly because there is so much leisure time between the action available to enjoy these summer culinary delights, especially on a hot afternoon like this August day when the sun was bright and the game was close. Batters were having a good day versus the pitching staffs of each team. Tied at eight runs apiece in the bottom of the sixth inning, the Tigers were up to bat. The Yankees brought in a long-range reliever after pulling their starting pitcher. With two men on base for the home team, one on first and another runner on third, it looked like the Tigers might be able to break the tie.

Charlie could hear the call of the game through the loudspeakers from below the stands as he searched the ballpark for a vending or a laundry truck that might hold a bomb capable of blowing up the stadium. It was a long shot, he knew. But the idea of bombing the stadium made sense from a logically tragic point of view. And the thought made Charlie shudder. A whole ballpark full of inebriated fans blown to heaven's door on the wings of a mushroom cloud; the world would never be the same.

'Send me a picture of the van,' Charlie said into his cell phone. 'Anything you have that might help.'

After reviewing tapes made from a circling helicopter in the sky, it was determined that a lowly van owned by a vending machine business had pulled up to one of the back docks of Joey's company early in the morning. The van had been ignored at the time, assuming it was just doing its job in the normal course of business, replenishing the vending machines inside the building. But after a closer inspection, it was noticed that something uncharacteristically large, some case which was difficult to see, had been loaded into the van before it drove slowly out of the parking lot. The CIA was currently reviewing tapes from highway surveillance cameras, attempting to trace the van. But this was difficult and labor-intensive work and not always successful. So far, they had only been able to trace the van as it traveled down I-96 before losing it in traffic as it headed towards downtown Detroit. The expressway was connected to a number of other highways, making it difficult to determine exactly where the van had gone and the city of Detroit is large in terms of geographic area, taking up almost twenty-two square miles of land, not including the sprawling suburbs. The van could have been going anywhere.

The pictures Charlie received on his phone from a helicopter showed the van from above, not ground level, making it difficult to visualize. Charlie had only a general idea of size and color.

Displaying his badge as he surveyed the large ballpark, it took time to walk around the stadium. Newly built not too many years before, Comerica Park was a state-of-the-art ballpark for a city that was mostly in shambles. From the perspective used to defend the excess amount of money spent to build the stadium, it was argued that giving the people of Detroit a new stadium would give them hope for the future. But from a thousand other perspectives, the millions of dollars lavished on the ballpark and exorbitant salaries of players could have been used more productively, spent to revive the city, restore basic public services, help return it to its glory days before it was devastated by wasteful and criminal decisions of its city council and international economic circumstances affecting the auto business which were beyond its control.

Making his way through the vast network of tunnels that serviced the ballpark, Charlie spotted a van parked in the shadows of the stadium.

The windows in the back door of the van were covered with black paint. He couldn't see inside. Charlie waited, thinking the driver might return, but when no one showed after a couple of minutes, he impatiently called his boss.

'What's the name of the vending machine business we are looking for?' he asked.

When told the name, Charlie froze for a second, clearly seeing letters spelling the name: 'Friendly Vending' crudely written by hand on the driver's door.

Even for a strong man like Charlie, a man accustomed to dealing with crisis, the thought of an A-bomb going off under a baseball park filled with fans, the imagined images of gross devastation, the potential carnage which a nuclear bomb could create… shot fear into his veins.

Charlie tried the door. It was locked.

'I found the truck,' he said soberly into his phone.

After listening to his supervisor's instructions to wait for the experts to arrive, he vocally disagreed. 'We don't have time. It's almost the beginning of the seventh inning. This thing could go off any minute. Hold on, I'm going to break in for a look.'

The back of his gun handle smashed through a window in the door of the van as a curious worker happened to be passing by, wondering why some guy was breaking into a stalled van. Charlie flashed his badge and told him to get back. Putting his hand through the broken window, he searched until he found a handle and opened the door. Stepping inside, he immediately spotted a wooden case, located on the floor behind the driver's seat.

'It's here,' Charlie said icily into his phone. 'I think you're going to have to talk me through this. Just tell me what to do.'

3:20 PM, JOHN

Magazines in the hospital waiting room were months old, tired, and worn from use.

The furniture was dusty. A TV on a wall was tuned to Fox News, which I never watch for fear of being brainwashed by the lovely young women with pretty smiles who are intent on spreading ultra-conservative opinions of world events. I wondered how in the world these young ladies knew anything at their age? But apparently it was now assumed in our brave new world of news, that sex appeal is an adequate substitute for experience and intelligence?

A few other poor souls waited silently with me through the tense minutes that seemed to drag for an eternity in the waiting room. With nothing else to do, my eyes were drawn to the TV screen. I couldn't help myself. It was better than thinking about her, about whether Kate was dying or dead. So much blood had emptied from her lovely body on the road to the hospital, too much blood. I wondered how she managed to survive without dying before arriving at the hospital. Charlie's cool head had got her there. If she lived, she would have had Charlie to thank.

When I looked down, I discovered my pants and shirt were soiled with her blood. I didn't care. At that moment, my appearance was the least of my concerns. Even so, I went into the bathroom to clean up, at a minimum, wash my face and hands while ignoring the blood stains on my clothes. They would have to wait.

Occasionally, an errant thought crossed my mind, like wondering what Charlie was doing. But the bomb was the least of my worries. The idea of being blown up was almost a relief, an escape from the jagged edges of worry that scraped against the hard walls in my skull. I didn't know if I would be able to handle the death of another lover in my life. If Kate died, she would be number three. First was Monica, who had died in New York City from a gunshot wound. The second was Sandy, who died a much more peaceful death in bed from cancer, using drugs to deny the dreaded disease its last painful grip on her body. I had somehow survived both of their deaths. But Kate, I didn't want to lose Kate, not when it should have been my responsibility to keep her safe from Kevin.

I should never have left her alone.

3:35 PM, CHARLIE

It took a couple of frantic minutes of running around, showing his badge to everyone in sight, until he found a maintenance worker at the ballpark who could furnish the tools he needed.

The late model van was cramped, dark, and dirty. First, Charlie had to locate a switch for the interior lights, which helped him find the handle for the back door which he then opened to let in some light. Using a crowbar, he pried the top off the wood case, but not before following instructions to carefully search for wires that might be attached to explosive material. Inside the case lay a long metal cylinder held securely in place by an intricate metal framework. Charlie warily eyed the bomb, searching for the screws that would allow him to open it.

Experts in the field office had previously viewed the taped recording from the night when Joey put the bomb together to determine how to take it apart. Each screw, wire, clamp, bolt, and nut had to be meticulously loosened and disconnected according to the instructions they gave Charlie. In the reverse order of the method Joey had used to make the bomb.

Painstakingly, he followed their meticulous instructions.

No announcement was made at the ballpark, and no evacuation order was given. If the bomb blew up, it would kill everyone within miles of the stadium. But there was not enough time to get all the fans far enough away to make a difference. And panic caused by such an announcement could potentially cause the death and injury of many, maybe hundreds of people. It was decided that defusing the bomb was the only way forward, hoping the task could be completed in time.

Charlie did the work as calmly as he could. Years of dealing with daily crises helped. He was a seasoned veteran of tense situations. His experience aided him; this, and the fact that he was a highly intelligent and disciplined individual.

The bomb was on a timer. Unfortunately, it was not known how much time was left, just that a digital instrument which resembled a timer could be observed inside the case once Charlie opened it. The other thing Charlie did not know was whether he was being exposed to lethal radiation. He did not have a Geiger counter. Not that it mattered. He had to open the case either way. It was his job to protect the people of the United States, and Charlie took his job seriously.

Working one task at a time, he had to wait after completing each operation before moving to the next set of instructions. And he attempted each task only after he was certain he understood exactly what he had to do. It was painstaking work, and it was taking a long time. But a mistake could spell disaster. He had no choice except to continue as he had been proceeding, working precisely through the complex puzzle that Mr. Joey Abdul had created.

It was the work of a genius, this bomb. This is what the experts were telling Charlie, but this didn't matter to him. He only wanted to get it defused and get out of the van before it blew up.

Hoping against hope that he was not sucking in enough radiation to die a slow death.

3:40 PM, JOHN

She walked into the waiting room as I held my breath.

A pretty, young doctor dressed in green scrubs came directly from the operating room. She had big, intelligent, dark eyes. Her hair was combed straight black, cut short. Her gown was soiled with red blood.

She was not the first doctor to come into the room; others had arrived as I waited and prayed. The doctors spoke to those friends and relatives who had been waiting like me to receive news of their loved ones. Mostly good news was given, speaking of successful operations delivered to the anxious inhabitants of this isolated room. Only one young man had not been so lucky. His wife had died on the operating table from injuries suffered in an automobile accident. Her parents had arrived in time to hear the news delivered by a young male doctor who could not have been much older than the husband who received the bad news. Her parents held the young man as he cried inconsolably.

'Mr. Van Laan.' The attractive female doctor looked around the room.

'Yes,' I got up on weak legs.

'Come with me,' she instructed.

She took me into the hall away from the prying eyes and ears of the others. I didn't take this as a good sign.

'The operation was successful,' the doctor told me with a half-smile. 'We were able to find the artery that a bullet had cut and stop the bleeding. She had some other injuries, but they were not life-threatening and we were able to deal with them as well.'

'That's good news.'

'Yes and no,' she replied. 'Your friend lost a lot of blood from her injury. Her brain may have been damaged from a lack of oxygen. We will not know until she wakes up from the operation. Even then, it may be some time before the full extent of the damage is known.'

I didn't say anything, didn't know what to say or ask.

'I'm sorry Mr. Van Laan. I wish I had better news. For now, she is alive. That's the good news. We will just have to wait and see how she does when she wakes up.'

'When will that be?' I asked.

'That's the hard part,' the doctor told me. 'We don't know. It is possible it will be a long time.'

'I see.'

'We are cleaning her up now. She will be moved to the ICU shortly. You can see her then. Just remember, you will need to be patient.'

3:45 PM, CHARLIE

Charlie clipped the last wire just before the white space suits marked with radiation logos arrived at the scene, emerging from a bus marked with a large red cross.

It was done.

He had done it. That's what the voice in his earphone told him. All connections to the batteries in the bomb had been severed. The timer could now be removed. As soon as he completed this final task, he was instructed in no uncertain terms to get out of the van and go with one of the arriving medical staff for an assessment.

After exiting the cramped interior of the van, Charlie stretched his back muscles, which had begun to tighten up during the extended time he was leaning over to work on the bomb. A young woman in one of the white space suits approached him. He could only see her face through the glass of her helmet. She told him to follow her. Charlie turned to see other space suits walking around the scene, mostly looking at handheld meters, checking for radiation.

He had to ask even though he was afraid of the answer. 'Are they getting a reading for radiation?'

'I'll check,' the woman in the helmet replied, understanding the importance of Charlie's question. 'Wait here.'

Charlie watched anxiously as she questioned one of the white suits. In response, a male head inside a glass helmet turned from side to side, indicating a negative response.

She returned to Charlie as she removed her helmet. Shaking her head, her blond hair waved in the breeze. 'It doesn't appear to be a problem,' she verified. 'But let's just get you into our bus and make sure,' she smiled. 'Come with me.'

Charlie dutifully followed her lead, stepping up into the bus marked by a red cross.

A young technician closed the door behind him.

MONDAY, AUGUST 13, 10:55 AM, JOHN

'I understand you're a hero. Saw it on the news,' I said to Charlie.

He slumped into a chair in Kate's antiseptic hospital room, looking really tired. 'Couldn't have done it without your help,' he said.

'You mean Kate's help,' I corrected him. 'She's the one who told me about Joey's friend in the vending machine business.'

'Right, without Kate's help,' Charlie acknowledged.

'Say, why didn't you mention her name in your TV interview?' I asked.

'I thought about it, but didn't think you two needed the publicity right now.'

'Yea, guess that's true... Thanks.'

'So, how are you doing?' he asked.

'I haven't gotten much sleep.'

'Me either. It's been a couple of long days,' he acknowledged. 'CIA doesn't treat their heroes very well. They demanded I fill out all the required reports and answer all their endless questions, like nothing out of the ordinary happened. Apparently, the possibility of a nuclear weapon going off in this country got the attention of some very important people and they wanted all the details.'

'Nothing was mentioned on the news about a nuclear bomb,' I noted. 'Just said it was a bomb threat which had been averted.'

'It was decided by the head office that the general public didn't need to know how close they came to being blown up into tiny atoms,' Charlie explained. 'The news release simply stated their government had once again done its job and protected them. According to our media experts, that's all the public really wants to know. They don't care about the grim details.'

I made no response to his comment. Asked instead about what happened to Joey.

'He's on a plane to a place you don't want to know about,' Charlie replied. Then he asked me after a pause, 'Do you think his brother was involved?'

'No, do you?'

'We have no evidence to indicate he was,' Charlie replied. 'I guess that's good news for you. Means you can continue to buy his gemstones.'

'I don't know. I haven't talked to him. After what happened to his brother, he may not want to have anything to do with me.'

'Let me know what he says when you talk to him,' Charlie requested.

'Okay.'

'So, how's she doing?' he asked.

Kate lay in a raised hospital bed covered with white sheets. Her eyes were closed; hair spread over her pillow. Long lines of plastic tubing dripped fluids into her from every angle. Every fifteen minutes or so, a nurse came into the room to check the levels of the bottles, look at a heart monitor which beeped confidently, take some notes, and silently exit the room.

'Nothing yet,' I replied. 'Still in a coma.'

'I'm so sorry,' he said.

'If she makes it, she has you to thank.'

'I did what I could.'

I turned to her. She looked so peaceful, like she was sleeping.

'What do her doctors say?' Charlie asked.

'They don't know. It's too early to tell. That's what they say, but I worry about what they are not saying, purposely delaying bad news.'

'Is there a chance she may never wake up?' Charlie asked the question, which lingered in acrid vapor that inhabited the hospital room, 'Sorry, I had to ask,' he apologized.

'I assume there is.'

Charlie looked away.

'The longer she remains unconscious, the more likely there's damage to her brain.'

'Has her family been notified?' he asked.

'Yes, they're flying in. Should be here in the morning.'

Minutes dragged; fluid dripped. I searched for a quiver in her eyelids, anything, any little movement in her hand, but saw nothing. Nothing to indicate a conscious mind.

'Sorry, I have to go,' Charlie broke the silence. 'Got to get back to Langley. Just thought I would stop in before I left town.'

I got up to shake his hand. 'Thanks, Charlie. You're a true friend.'

'I'll see you soon, John. Better times are ahead.' He gave me a hug.

'Hope so.'

GRAND HAVEN, MICHIGAN, SUNDAY, SEPTEMBER 2, 6:40 PM, JOHN

Labor Day weekend is the end of summer.

That's what I always think when this holiday rolls around each year. Summer is over. It's time to return to work, labor, do what we all have to do to make a living, feed our families, and take care of business. It's always the saddest holiday for me.

Despite my dour view of this holiday weekend, the sun was bright, still shining high and warm in the sky after six o'clock in the evening. Although it was not as high as in June when it is at its zenith, some good lazy days would still be available in the weeks to come before fall made its official appearance, dressed in low gray clouds, sending driving rain sweeping across the vast vistas of the lake.

The phone in my cottage rang. I got up from a lounge chair on the deck where I had been relaxing, took my drink with me, and went inside to answer it.

Kamyar had taken the news of his brother's crimes as well as could be expected. I suspected he always knew Joey was involved with the Taliban in Afghanistan. He had just hoped his younger brother would eventually grow up. See life for what it was, not a world full of hate, just people trying bravely to make it from one day to the next. The real battle of life is to maintain stability in a cruel world, hold your footing against the slope of the mountain we are all trying to climb, while helping our neighbors when they need a hand.

Bombs and wars are for the mentally unstable. Religion has nothing   to   do   with   it. But all religions have their fringe element, demented humans who walk the crust of this earth full of hate and spewing venom. The fact that these irresponsible people find enough support for their ill-conceived campaigns of murder and mayhem, enough support to cruelly involve the rest of us in their wars and their rampages, has always been a mystery to me. The amount of money spent on military hardware alone is a travesty in a world that needs every penny devoted to fighting hunger and disease.

Kamyar understands this and I am convinced he is one of the good guys. But his brother, a man who came from the same family, who was conceived in the same womb as he was, Joey was a completely different animal, driven mad perhaps by a mind so intelligent he never could seem to channel it into something productive. Kamyar and I talked about this, had a long conversation that leaped barriers that normally keep us humans from discussing the most important issues in life, boundaries formed by geographical and cultural differences.

Sometimes, it takes a crisis to communicate.

I told Charlie about my conversation with Kamyar. Charlie thanked me, but I don't think he was totally convinced. Charlie needs solid, concrete proof; proof that goes beyond words. Words are contracts that can be easily broken according to the philosophy of Charlie. He has heard too many lies. He is a man who needs irrefutable hard evidence.

I understand my buddy Charlie, and I don't argue with him.

Fred Smith has a trial date coming. He's waiting for his time in court. I'm sure he's confident that throwing money at his lawyers will get him a not-guilty verdict. I didn't know. I'm just happy that I don't have to worry about Mr. Fred Smith for a while.

Joey had disappeared. When I recently asked about him, Charlie said he knew no one by this name. I assume this meant my buddy Charlie does not want to talk about him anymore.

Kevin's family came to retrieve the body of their son. The police handled it. I had no contact with them.

The business in Novi, formerly run by Joey Abdul, was moved to another building and reconstituted under a different name. It is still a subsidiary of Kamyar's parent company in India. But all mention of its association with a former company has been deleted from the marketing material. It currently handles new products developed by Kamyar.

I returned to my deck overlooking the lake with my drink and sat down.

'Who was that on the phone?' Kate asked.

'A former girlfriend.'

'And what's the name of this former girlfriend?'

'Rachel.'

'And what did Rachel want?'

'She wanted to talk to me. I guess her last love affair didn't pan out.'

'So, does she want you back?'

'She didn't say that. She just asked if I was free for dinner sometime.'

'And what did you tell her?'

'I told her I was a little busy right now.'

'I see,' Kate took a sip of wine.

The sun slid below the horizon, spreading glorious streaking shades of luminescent light across the horizon, touching low flying clouds with tints of reds and pinks in iridescent shades too glorious to describe. Where wind flowed through the clouds, it spread abstract visions like dreams across our minds, entering our brains in places where our imagination roams, where music and color glide together on the wings of hope, yearning for a place where we can all rest in peace. After lost minutes of incomparable beauty, the sky slowly retreated to dark gray shades of night, as if the sky had been simply an apparition in our mind, a ghost which visits us each day, the evidence of which we long for during long dark nights when we cannot sleep, when we yearn for a new day, one more day, just one more day of light… Lord, we pray.

'I think you should have dinner with your former girlfriend Rachel.' Kate broke my mood.

It had taken her time to recover from the bullet that entered her chest. But as her doctor explained, miracles occur every day. We are simply not always aware of them. By all logic, Kate should have sustained brain damage from a lack of oxygen. Instead, after three long days and nights, she woke up and quickly resumed being her normal effervescent self.

When she was told that Kevin was dead, she exhibited no signs of happiness. Instead, she was sad, said she would talk to his family, tell them how sorry she was for their loss. I believed her. He was not a bad man, according to her, not always. It was just when he was consumed by his temper that he lost his way.

A lawyer had called. He told her Kevin never made a will. By law, his inheritance now belonged to his current wife, Kate. And this made her a very wealthy lady. In addition, Kamyar had called, begging her to return to India. He had new projects and ideas he wanted to discuss with her. He was the ultimate entrepreneur. He had companies to build. He needed her help. She had turned him down, saying she needed time to recover.

'And why would I want to have dinner with Rachel?' I asked Kate.

'Because I'm returning to India,' she announced.

My heart sank. I took a sip of whiskey. I always knew this was a possibility. I had just hoped she would stay.

'Kamyar needs me,' Kate explained. 'And John, I like it in India. The country suits me. The energy, the people, they are all so friendly. In this country, we are consumed with guns. Our TVs are filled with violence. The news broadcasters are always talking about war. It is not like that in India, not in the city where I live. I felt very comfortable there… I want to return.'

I didn't know what to say.

'Will you come visit me in India?' she asked.

'If you want… sure. I would like that.'

'Are you okay with my going?'

'If it's really what you want, then yes. I'm good.'

'Thank you, John. I will always love you.'

'I love you too, Kate.'

'Good, now come to bed with me so I can show you how much I love you.'

I stood up to follow her.

The sky had turned dark. It was a lovely evening with a million stars filling the heavens, offering some hope of life in the infinite distances that surround us.

'And John.' She turned to me at the door. 'I think you should call Rachel and go out for dinner with her.'

'I don't really want to think about Rachel right now.'

'Okay, but you must promise me you won't end up a lonely bachelor.' She was adamant, standing her ground and blocking the door. 'I wouldn't let you into my bed unless you promise.'

'Okay, I promise,' I said. It was getting cold, and I wanted to get her lovely body into my warm bed.

'Promise.'

'I said, I would.'

Once we were inside, the sliding glass door of the cottage closed to the outside deck with a hollow, locking click, sealing off the sound of beach grass gently rustling in a breeze.

Only faintly heard in the distance was the sound of waves which had traveled many miles and countless hours from a distant shore, rising up in revulsion to their death on a cruel beach, exercising their last rites in one final, valiant, life extinguishing complaint; crashing and washing up the sand… before silently, compliantly, sliding down the shore to return to the vast open waters of a lake which was the source of their existence…

THE END